A KILLER PLOT

A BOOKS BY THE BAY MYSTERY

A Killer Plot

Ellery Adams

WHEELER
CHIVERS

LIBRARY OF CONGRESS CATALOGING-IN-PUBLICATION DATA

Adams, Ellery.
  A killer plot : a books by the bay mystery / by Ellery Adams.
  — Large print ed.
    p. cm. — (Wheeler Publishing large print cozy mystery)
  Originally published: New York : Berkley Prime Crime, 2010.
  ISBN-13: 978-1-4104-3147-9 (pbk.)
  ISBN-10: 1-4104-3147-9 (pbk.)
  1. Authors—Fiction. 2. Murder—Investigation—Fiction.
  3. North Carolina—Fiction. 4. Large type books. I. Title.
  PS3601.D374K55 2010
  813'.6—dc22   2010034743

BRITISH LIBRARY CATALOGUING-IN-PUBLICATION DATA AVAILABLE
Published in 2010 in the U.S. by arrangement with The Berkley Publishing Group, a member of Penguin Group (USA) Inc.
Published in 2011 in the U.K. by arrangement with the author.

U.K. Hardcover: 978 1 408 49369 4 (Chivers Large Print)
U.K. Softcover: 978 1 408 49370 0 (Camden Large Print)

Printed in the United States of America
1 2 3 4 5 6 7 14 13 12 11 10

*For Mary Shirley Harrison,
dear friend and kindred spirit*

CHAPTER 1

Writers should be read, but neither seen nor heard.

— DAPHNE DU MAURIER

Two of Oyster Bay's lifelong citizens were in line at the Stop 'n' Shop, gossiping over carts stuffed with frozen entrées, potato chips, boxes of Krispy Kremes, and liters of soda when Olivia Limoges breezed through the market's automatic doors.

"Here she comes, Darlene. The grouchiest woman on the entire North Carolina coast," the first woman remarked, jerking her head toward the produce department.

"And the richest." Darlene watched as Olivia examined a pyramid of peaches, turning the fruit around and caressing the flushed, velvet skin of each golden orb before placing it in her cart. "She's good-lookin' enough. Doesn't have the curves most men wanna hold on to at night, but with all that money, you'd think she could net at least *one* fish."

"She might have more money than Oprah, but she ain't *exactly* a ray of sunshine," her companion pointed out. "Half the town's scared of her."

"That's because half the town works for her, Sue Ellen." Darlene pulled a sour face as her friend dumped a family-sized Stouffer's lasagna on the moving belt.

"She ever smile at you, Mandy?" the woman named Sue Ellen questioned the cashier.

Mandy cracked her gum and shrugged. "Ms. Olivia is nice enough, I reckon."

"Maybe she likes *younger* men. You know, one of those male models or somethin'. Or maybe she wants 'em to be rich and speak three languages and be as high and mighty as she is. She's too fussy if you ask me. That's why she doesn't have a man," Sue Ellen whispered, clearly impressed with her own insight as the cashier ran her friend's check through the register. "Who knows what's goin' on in that big ole house of hers?"

Darlene's dull brown eyes turned misty. "If *I* had all that money, I'd go on one of those cruises with them chocolate buffets. You ever heard of such an amazin' thing?

8

Whole fountains of chocolate! You can dunk strawberries or cookies or little bits of cake right in 'em. Lordy! I'd eat chocolate until I couldn't move."

Sue Ellen unloaded two jumbo-sized bags of potato chips and a bouquet of scentless carnations onto the belt. "She oughta *give back* to the community. After all, she grew up in Oyster Bay. Lots of folks kept an eye on her when her daddy was off on one of his trips."

"Which trips?" Darlene snorted cruelly. "The fishin' trips or the ones where he drifted along the coast with a net in the water and a case of whiskey by his side?"

"Either one. With her mama passin' on when she was still at such a tender age, that girl needed folks to look in on her. I recall *my* mama bringin' her a tuna casserole more than once. And how about that lighthouse cottage?" Sue Ellen was becoming flushed in righteous indignation. "The way she's lettin' it fall to pieces — it's a disgrace! She should fix it up and let the town use it. It's not *our* fault her daddy left her all alone out on that boat in the middle of a storm for —"

Bam! The woman's words stuck in her throat as a twenty-pound bag of Iams Premium dog food was slapped onto the belt, instantly flattening the potato chips and the tight cluster of carnations.

"Good morning, Mandy." The tall woman with white blond hair greeted the cashier as though the other customers did not exist. "Just the peaches and the dog food, please. And whatever you've already scanned from my neighbor's cart. You can charge me for the chips and flowers twice, seeing as they'll both have to be replaced."

Mandy nodded, biting back a smile. She rang up Olivia's fruit and kibble as well as the other woman's frozen dinners, rump roast, potato chips, flowers, cookie dough ice cream, and maxi pads. Olivia swiped a credit card through the reader, shouldered the dog food bag as though it was filled with helium, grabbed her peaches, and wished Mandy a pleasant day.

She walked out of the store, squinting as the sun bore down on her. She slid glasses over eyes that had been fiery with anger a moment ago but had now returned to a placid, lake-water blue.

Inside her Range Rover, Captain Haviland, her black-furred standard poodle, barked out a hello.

"You may find that a portion of your kibble's been pulverized into crumbs, Captain. I'm afraid my temper got the better of me." Olivia gunned the engine, drove seven blocks north, and swung into an available handicapped parking space. Haviland barked again and added an accusatory sniff.

"It's tourist season. There's no place else to park and if I *do* get ticketed, that'll just add more funds to the community treasure chest. Apparently, I don't give back enough," Olivia snidely informed her dog and together, they marched into Grumpy's Diner. Olivia established herself at the counter, ordered coffee, and perused the headlines of *The Washington Post*. However, her concentration was repeatedly broken by a group of people seated at the diner's largest booth. They were tossing out words like "dialogue," "point of view," and "setting," and since Olivia had been trying to write a book on and off for the past five years, her curiosity was aroused.

She kept the paper raised, as though an article on escalating interest rates was inordinately captivating, while she listened intently as a woman read aloud from what sounded like a work of romantic fiction.

"Maureen put her eye to the keyhole and gasped. There was her mistress, the duchess, in the arms of a strange man. His fingers were unlacing her gown, slowly, letting each

piece of delicate silk slide over his powerful fingers."

"What drivel," Olivia Limoges muttered to Haviland as the reader paused for breath. The poodle sneezed. Feeling that her canine companion hadn't been in clear agreement with her assessment, Olivia leaned to the right in order to eavesdrop further.

"He then turned her around, roughly, and pushed her frock to the floor. I could hear her gasp as he caressed the ribbons on her petticoat, his dark eyes never leaving the duchess's amber ones."

Olivia snorted. "Cats have amber eyes. *People* do not." She cast a glance at the author who had abruptly ceased speaking, seemingly reluctant to continue. She was a pretty woman — small-framed and smooth-skinned, with hair the color of sunlit wheat, but her face was discolored and puffy, indicating a consistent lack of sleep.

"Go on, Laurel, my dear. I sense we're nearing the *juicy* part," a middle-aged man with carefully gelled hair, a peach silk shirt, and finely manicured hands urged.

"Maureen knew she should back away from the door, but the stranger's movements were hypnotizing. His hand, which resembled the calloused palm of a man engaged in trade, not the smooth, pampered hands belonging to

12

a gentleman, eased apart my lady's bodice. His eyes lingered on the heaving swell of her breasts —"

Olivia couldn't contain herself. "Not heaving breasts!" she exclaimed with a wry laugh. "Anything but those!"

The woman named Laurel blushed furiously and dropped her paper onto the table in front of her.

"If you'd like to share your opinion, it'd be a mite easier if you joined their group instead of hollerin' across the counter. It's this kind of behavior that makes folks think you're an odd duck," a high-pitched voice emanating from Olivia's left scolded. "Good morning, Captain," the woman greeted the poodle warmly. "Your usual, sir?"

Haviland issued a polite bark and parted his mouth in order to smile at the familiar speaker.

"Good morning, Dixie." Olivia folded her paper in half and smoothed out the wrinkles. "And for your information, people think I'm odd because I'm rich and single and perfectly content. All three of those factors are a rarity here in Oyster Bay." Olivia lowered her empty coffee cup from the counter so the vertically challenged diner proprietor could fill it with her famously strong brew.

13

At a total height of four feet seven inches tall, including the two inches provided by a pair of roller skates and an inch of comb-teased, sun-streaked brown hair, Dixie Weaver had the body of a kindergartener. She was not as young or as well proportioned as a five-year-old however, being that she was a dwarf.

"Dwarf" was the term Dixie preferred, and the residents of their coastal town had learned long ago never to refer to her as a "little person."

"I'm of short stature," she had told Olivia soon after Olivia had moved back to town and had struck up an immediate friendship with the feisty, roller-skating diner owner. "I'm not *little*. 'Little' implies young or innocent. Like a cute puppy or a baby bird. I'm a middle-aged waitress with a litter of children and a permanent tan. I smoke and do shots of tequila and I'm *not* cute. 'Sides, I haven't been *innocent* since the eighth grade. And do you have any idea how much I hate havin' to wear clothes from Walmart's kid's department? I can't *exactly* pull off sexy wearin' Strawberry Shortcake, now can I?"

Today, Dixie was garbed in denim overalls, a green-and-white-striped T-shirt, and rainbow leg warmers. Her hair was meticu-

14

lously feathered as though she were a diminutive version of Farrah Fawcett and her large, ale brown eyes were amplified by a layer of frosty baby blue shadow that spanned the entire area of skin from upper lid to brow.

"Someone's in my booth," Olivia complained to Dixie, gesturing at the table in the corner of the room. Most of the Oyster Bay residents knew better than to plant their buttocks on the red vinyl cushions of that booth between eight and eight thirty A.M. That was when Olivia frequently showed up at Grumpy's to claim a booth. She'd then spend the better part of the morning there, eating, sipping coffee, and writing.

It was the only booth not surrounded by Andrew Lloyd Webber paraphernalia as it butted against the diner's front window. Dixie, who practically worshipped the king of musicals, had filled her establishment with posters, masks, and themed-decorations celebrating the composer's work. It was an adoration Olivia did not share with her closest friend, and she preferred the street view to being seated beneath a pair of Dixie's used roller skates and a poster of *Starlight Express* illuminated by strings of pink Christmas lights.

"You sound like one of the three bears."

Dixie lowered her voice to a squeaky growl. "Somebody's been eatin' in my booth and they're still *there!*"

The current occupants were not locals. They hadn't been seated for long either, as they had only been served beverages. Olivia was surprised to see four college-aged boys awake, dressed, and functioning so early in the day. Normally, they'd be slumbering with their mouths open on the floor of a six-bedroom vacation home surrounded by empty beer bottles, brimming ashtrays, and overturned bongs.

"You can eat here at the counter for once. It would do you good to rub elbows with your neighbors. Livin' out there on the Point, all alone with your ghosts, with only a dog to keep you company." She quickly stroked Haviland between the ears. "No offense to you, sweet darlin'." Dixie cocked a hip and rested her elbow on it, holding the steaming coffee carafe aloft. "It ain't good for you to be all work and no play. Why don't you take your highfalutin ass over to the *Song and Dance* booth and join that writer's club? They call themselves the Bayside Book Writers, and since you're tryin' to write, it seems to me like you all were destined to meet."

Olivia grunted. "What do you mean by

trying?" Still, she cast a quick glance at the document on her laptop screen and sighed. "I never realized it would be so hard to write a book. Do you know how many times I've started this novel? I've never consistently failed in achieving a personal goal before."

Before Dixie could reply, an elderly couple entered the diner and immediately looked befuddled. Dixie skated over, handed them menus, and pointed at the empty *Evita* booth. She then disappeared into the kitchen for several minutes, which Olivia suspected were spent smoking Parliaments out the fire door. When Dixie reemerged, she was carrying Olivia's breakfast on a decoupage tray. Pivoting onto the toes of her skates, she pushed the heavy china platter onto the counter.

"One spinach and feta omelet with half a grapefruit." She slid another plate in front of Haviland. "And scrambled eggs and sausage for you, my pet."

The poodle held out his paw. Dixie accepted it and then leaned against the empty stool next to Olivia. "So the book's not exactly writin' itself then?"

Olivia pushed her laptop aside in order to eat her breakfast. "I've reworked the first five chapters a dozen times. For some reason, I can't seem to move on to chapter six."

Dixie pretended not to notice a customer signaling for the check. "What's goin' on at the end of chapter five?"

"Kamila, my main character, has just been selected to join the harem of Ramses the Second. It's a huge honor, but she's determined to become his wife, not just a woman he couples with a few times a year. Once she separates from her family, however, and is inside the palace, she's terrified and insecure, despite her exceptional beauty. After all, she's only fourteen."

Dixie whistled. "That ain't too early to be a conniving slut. You walked into a high school lately?" Turning to nod at her impatient *Phantom* customer, Dixie said, "It seems to me that you'd describe the palace at this point in your story. How did folks treat this girl? Where is she sleepin'? Did she get a bunch of fancy clothes and jewelry when she moved in? Does everybody hate her 'cause she's the new girl? Are the other girls from foreign places? What does she eat? Folks love to read about food, ya know."

Olivia cut off a corner of her omelet. "I wish you'd read what I've written so far. I think you've got an editorial ear."

"No chance in hell, 'Livia. You're one of

the few people I call friend. I am not gonna mess with what we've got by pullin' apart your novel." Dixie turned away. "If you want to get someone's opinion, get off your rump and go talk to that writer's group. I'm tellin' you, *they* are what you need."

Haviland opened his eyes wide and made a sneezing noise — a signal to Olivia that his canine ears had picked up a solid recommendation.

"I don't know, Captain." Olivia concentrated on her omelet, trying to imagine reading page after page of grammatically incorrect, verbose claptrap, or florid romances such as the woman Laurel was penning. "I wonder what the rest of them are writing?" she asked her dining companion and stole a glance at the writer's group.

In addition to Laurel, there was a stunning young woman with glossy black hair tarnished by stripes of electric purple. She had large, sable-brown eyes and tea-hued skin, which she had pierced in multiple locations as though she'd deliberately set out to mar her exotic beauty. She wore a tight tank top embroidered with a pirate's flag, and her exposed arms were muscular and sinewy. Olivia had no difficulty picturing the girl creeping out at night in the form of a sleek black panther.

Sitting across from her was a young man in his mid to late twenties with a dramatic case of rosacea. His unfortunate skin condition precluded one from seeing that he was handsome, in a boyish way. With his elfin eyes, brilliant smile, and waves of reddish, unkempt hair, he reminded Olivia of Peter Pan.

The well-groomed, middle-aged man in the expensive peach silk shirt completed the assemblage of writers.

As Olivia blatantly stared at them, the man in peach caught her looking. He murmured something to his group and they quickly dispersed, their laughter trailing them out the door. He then settled onto the stool next to Olivia's and began to study her as she renewed her pretense of being fascinated by the day's news.

"I come in peace," the man said and held up his hands in a gesture of surrender. "*In fact,* Dixie advised me to speak to you, but to use extreme caution." He smiled, showing off a row of chemically whitened and perfectly straight teeth. "She spoke as though I'd be approaching a coiled cobra instead of the *vision* of feminine power and beauty that sits beside me."

Haviland whined and the man laughed. "Oh, you're right, friend. I'm laying it on too thick. But seriously." He focused on Olivia again. "Dixie says you might be able to solve our problem." He looked pained. "Our little critique group is looking for a new place to meet. I simply cannot concentrate within *miles* of that *Jesus Christ Superstar* poster."

Amused, Olivia struggled to keep her expression neutral as she openly assessed her neighbor. "What do you write?"

"I pen a celebrity gossip column. Under a female pseudonym, of course. Ever heard of Milano Cruise? That's me. But don't go shouting that from the rooftops or I'll be out of a job." He wiggled a pair of neatly curved brows. "Most of my stories find their way onto the Internet. Milano's MySpace page is one of the most popular in the world."

"You hardly need a critique group for that kind of work," Olivia said with a dismissive wave of her fork.

"No, indeed," the man agreed with a laugh. "I must confess that I'm *quite* good at my craft. However, I'm spending the summer in Oyster Bay in order to work on a top secret story. You see, it's my intention to create a fictionalized biography of sorts. Names and dates changed — that sort of thing." He lowered his voice. "Everyone would know who I was writing about, but I can't get sued this way, you see?" He cleared his throat and puffed his chest out. "There are just piles of money waiting to be made on my idea."

Olivia found herself warming toward the man. Firstly, Haviland seemed comfortable in his presence, and Olivia found him refreshingly candid. Most importantly, he was well mannered and clearly intelligent. "I have a banquet room in my restaurant, but it would be rather costly. How often do you meet, Mr. . . . ?"

"Camden Ford, at your service." He bowed his head in exaggerated gallantry. "We've only had two meetings, but we'd like to gather once a week. And costly isn't *really* the adjective to which I was aspiring."

"What about the library?"

"Those spectacled harpies won't let us partake of any alcohol." He smirked. "How can we be proper writers without booze? Coffee and eggs are not acceptable substitutes for old scotch or a fine cabernet. Also, two of my fellow writers have scheduling conflicts with morning meetings. One has to care for a pair of imps in diapers while the other sleeps until noon so she can work the night away sliding beer bottles across a dirty, sweating bar to equally dirty,

22

sweaty men."

A laugh escaped Olivia's throat. She felt inclined to introduce herself and Haviland to the entertaining newcomer.

"Limoges?" he asked in interest. "As in the fine porcelain?"

Pleased, Olivia nodded. "My family name comes from the French city where the porcelain was produced."

" 'Tis also the birthplace of my favorite comic hero, Astérix, *mais non?*" Camden stirred sugar into his coffee. "So are you a fabulously wealthy porcelain heiress?"

"Oak barrel heiress, actually." Olivia passed him the cream. "The kind specially produced for storing fine cognac."

Camden looked dutifully impressed. He then made a sweeping gesture with his arms. "Oyster Bay's not the type of town where I'd expect to meet someone like you. Unless you're hiding from a sordid past? An abusive lover? The IRS . . . ?"

Olivia disregarded his speculations. "We're hardly Beverly Hills gossip material either. There's neither a renowned plastic surgery center here nor an exclusive detox facility, so whose trail are you following?"

After taking a dainty sip of coffee, Camden winked. "Wouldn't *you* like to know?"

Indeed she would. Olivia liked to be

informed about the goings-on in her town, no matter how insignificant. "*Do* tell." She came close to pleading and then decided to come off as unconvinced. "There can hardly be any celebrity news to be gleaned in Oyster Bay."

"That is where you're mistaken, dear lady." He rose. "Come, let's move to a booth where I can gaze into your Adriatic blue eyes."

Olivia took her coffee and laptop and relocated to the vacated window booth. As soon as they were settled, Haviland ducked under the table, stretched out his front legs, and put his head on Camden's shoe. Olivia was surprised. It normally took the poodle quite a while before he felt comfortable with a stranger. The gossip writer seemed content to provide a pillow for the groggy canine. "Do you know the Talbot family?" he asked.

"Certainly. The Talbots are real estate developers."

"Not developers. Tycoons. Think big. As in Donald Trump big." Camden lowered his voice to a conspiratorial whisper. "*That's* just the parents. There are three kiddies too. The daughter designs haute couture and sleeps with NFL quarterbacks. The older son likes snorting coke and fondling beautiful young men, and the baby boy is the lead

24

singer of a hot punk band. He's nailed half the starlets on *E!*'s up-and-coming list, and *I* know for a fact that he's brought his latest paramour here, to the Talbot beach house. Oh, and did I mention that the gorgeous creature he's wooing is barely legal? *And* she's appearing in two big-budget films this summer after wrapping a third season as the star of a hit television show?" He crossed his arms smugly. "Manolo Cruise will dine off this story for years, thank you very much."

"Are the Talbots the family you plan to write about in your novel?"

Camden put a finger to his lips. "Absolutement. I wrote the first three chapters on the plane from LA to DC, but I require help choosing which of the so very, very juicy, dark, and scandalous events I should focus my poison pen upon." He stroked Haviland's soft ears, and both man and poodle sighed contentedly. "Madame Limoges, we need an alcoholic haven in which our creativity can flow. Dixie mentioned an unused cottage on your property. An isolated lighthouse keeper's house with the ambiance sure to encourage even the most reluctant of muses. Would you open it up to us for an hour or two each week?"

Olivia signaled Dixie angrily with her eyes.

"That place has been uninhabited for years. It's falling apart — utterly unsuitable for your purpose at this point in time."

"At *this* point in time," Camden repeated. "Dixie also relayed that your work in progress is historical fiction and that you've reached an impasse." He looked at Olivia warmly. "We need one another, my dear. Join the dark side. Sweep the dust out of that cottage, share your manuscript, and let's hit the bestseller list together." He reached over and gave her forearm a playful swat. "Don't pout, *ma chérie*. It'll be fun. I'll handle all the insipid, organizational stuff."

Olivia was silent for a long time. It was impossible to remain unaffected by Camden's charm. "I'll think about both offers," she promised sincerely.

"I have long since learned to take all I can get. Do call me if you're willing to take a chance, my dazzling, halo-haired Duchess of Oyster Bay." Camden placed a business card next to her water glass and then gently slid his foot out from beneath Haviland's snout. "Excuse me, my fine sir."

Olivia watched him walk away, strangely conflicted by the encounter. Camden was quite charismatic and she would enjoy spending more time in his company. But to commit to his group required some adjustments on her part. For one, such a change meant she'd have to walk into the home of her childhood. A structure haunted by loneliness and loss.

"Is Dixie right? Am I living with ghosts?" she murmured to the snoozing poodle. "Perhaps I am, or near enough anyway. Perhaps the time has come for an exorcism."

Olivia examined herself in the reflection of the mirror lining the back wall. She didn't see the handsome, confident woman her neighbors saw, but a skinny, frightened, and friendless child with white blond hair and eyes that spoke of the sea's secret depths.

Blinking, Olivia passed her hand across her face, as though she were wiping it away in the mirror. She nodded to her reflection and Haviland stirred as his mistress squared her shoulders and came to a decision.

Her purposeful feet might not have carried her so lightly through the door had she known that one of the diners she'd seen at Grumpy's that morning would soon be dead.

And it would be a death the likes of which the residents of Oyster Bay could never have imagined.

CHAPTER 2

Always do sober what you said you'd do
drunk. That will teach you to keep your
mouth shut.

— ERNEST HEMINGWAY

Olivia turned the skeleton key in the door
and paused. After so much time she wondered what sights awaited her within the
lighthouse keeper's cottage, the home of her
childhood. Thirty years had passed since
Grandmother Limoges had descended on
Oyster Bay, swooped up her only grand-
child, and installed her in one of the country's most elite, all-girl boarding schools.

Before then, she had been an unheeded
and unhindered ten-year-old girl named
Livie. A girl raised by her fisherman father.
Or the girl who raised herself, as some of
the townsfolk whispered.

Twisting the key farther, Olivia heard the
click of the lock releasing. As she eased the

door open, she half-expected a rush of whiskey-tinged air and lost dreams to burst out through the crack and knock her to the ground, but only a wisp of decay escaped from within.

"Come along, Haviland," Olivia whispered, irritated by the hush in her voice. "Run ahead and make sure there are no vermin waiting to scurry across my feet."

Pleased to obey, the poodle rushed into the house, barking a warning to any rodents or insects that would certainly have grown bold enough to claim proprietorship over the abandoned cottage.

Dust. Olivia walked over a solid film of the stuff, formed by layer upon layer of dirt, mold, spiderwebs, and time. Glad she had had the foresight to don her rubber boots before entering the house, she took several steps into the hall and turned right into the living room.

Olivia surveyed the room quickly, trying to keep the memories of moments spent in this space at bay. Her attempts were futile, of course, and the dark gloom seeped into her being and reduced her to the motherless child who spent her days in solitude, battling feelings of perpetual trepidation and oppressive isolation.

There was not enough natural light to

banish the shadows. It took the full measure of Olivia's arrested will to wrench the faded plaid curtains right off the rods. They pooled on the floor in clouds of dust, allowing the sun to illuminate the bloodred walls, the faded green fabric on the drooping sofa, the broken rung of the wooden ladder-back chair that had once been Olivia's assigned seat, and her father's prized collection of maritime art.

"How I hated these," she told Haviland, yet she couldn't refrain from reexamining the paintings. These were not scenes of pleasure cruises on flat, cerulean waters, but schooners with rent sails or shabby fishing trawlers being tossed about in angry oceans of black waves. An element of violence permeated each picture. Even in the few paintings depicting calm skies and still seas, the hint of a dorsal fin or a low bank of menacing thunderclouds implied imminent danger.

"I hate them still," she murmured.

Olivia returned to the central hallway, the floorboards groaning as she stepped on their warped wood. The door to the back bedroom was closed and Olivia paused with her hand on the knob. She'd buried her girlhood history beneath layers of travel, education, a razor-sharp business acumen, and by keeping her relationships casual. A few weeks of dinners in five-star restaurants, an opera or a play, perhaps an art gallery opening and then, eventually, sex. But as soon as the man indicated an interest in taking things to the next level by producing a family member for Olivia to meet or a request that they spend the night at her place instead of his, she'd break off the relationship with the swift definiteness of an executioner. Thus, unwounded and thoroughly in control, Olivia would retreat to familiar solitude.

That won't work in this town, she thought as she stared at the shut door. *They already know my secret, so I'm vulnerable here.* She sighed. *If I truly returned to exhume the past — scatter it like ashes — and get beyond chapter five once and for all, I must start with this room.*

Another breath of imprisoned air swirled around her knees as she entered her old room.

With one glance, it would have been obvious to the most witless bystander that this space belonged to a neglected child.

There was a cot pushed against the far wall — the kind of cot that folds in half and can be stored in a closet, that squeaks each time one shifts during sleep, and that has probing springs to dig into one's back and prevent sweet dreams from ever approaching too near. There was a comforter stained by mildew, a circle of black mold on the ceiling above the bed, and a lamp stalk filled by a cracked lightbulb positioned on top of an overturned wooden crate.

A three-tiered bookshelf near the door held an assortment of wrecked books. They were used to begin with, bought at library sales or from Goodwill, and reread so often that the pages were as supple as tissue paper. Below the single window, covered by an old crib sheet embellished by faded yellowed mermaids, was a dollhouse.

Olivia and her mother had built the dollhouse from a kit bought at the Five and Dime. During a rainy spring week, they'd glued, painted, and decorated the diminutive Victorian mansion. Now, its royal purple clapboard and ivory gingerbread had faded to a sickly lavender and brown.

Easing the front open, Olivia was unsurprised to find the interior riddled with spiderwebs and the carcasses of moths and beetles. The doll family had long since been removed from the house and all the furniture was gone, save for a four-poster bed and a claw-foot tub.

"Please. Be here," Olivia whispered hopefully and then stuck her fingers into the oversized fireplace located in the formal front parlor. She grasped a faux brass andiron and pulled — the motion as familiar to her as though she'd repeated it yesterday. The entire fireplace came away in her hand, revealing a small hidden cavity. Inside, there was a square of wax paper, which Olivia unfolded in hurried movements. Holding the treasure to the dust-filtered light, she sighed with relief.

Her eyes ran over the contours of the gold starfish pendant while her fingertips unclasped the fine gold chain. She bent her head, enjoying the feel of the cool gold against the back of her neck and the weight of the starfish as it nestled into the soft depression of flesh between her collarbones.

"Mother." She closed her eyes and cried silently for a little while. The dull ache in her heart throbbed to life and the image of her mother — tan, freckled, and laughing as she leapt through a fan of sprinkler water — appeared before Olivia's eyes. It was one of the last times they'd been together, and Olivia remembered the ghost of a rainbow shimmering in the water's mist, her mother's long legs severing the colors, only to discover they'd reformed instantaneously in her wake.

Olivia stood, thinking that her few precious memories of her mother were as ephemeral as that summer rainbow. Wiping her eyes, she brushed off the dirt clinging to her knees and pulled out her cell phone. "Enough!" she declared as she began to punch in numbers.

That woman in the food market was right, she thought. *The people of Oyster Bay saved my life. They found me on that boat and cared for me until Grandmother came. Revitalizing abandoned buildings, hiring the jobless, and opening the finest restaurant this place has ever seen has made me wealthier, but I've done nothing selfless to repay that debt.*

She listened to the cell phone ring. "Oyster Bay can have this house. As soon as I've expunged its history."

A man's voice burst a greeting through her phone's speaker and she walked out of her little girl bedroom without looking back, the only treasure left within its confines now safely hidden beneath her shirt. "Clive? It's Olivia. Listen, I'd like you to halt your work on the King Street building for the moment. Something more pressing has come up. Can you meet me at the lighthouse keeper's cottage right away?" She paused, listening to him ask what she had in mind.

"A total overhaul. New roof, siding, flooring, plumbing, you name it. And Clive" — she walked out of the house and didn't bother to shut the door — "I need it fast."

Several weeks later she called Camden Ford and offered the Bayside Book Writers the use of the banquet room of her restaurant, The Boot Top Bistro.

"Just this once," she informed him firmly. "By your next meeting, I'll have arranged for a more permanent gathering place."

"Splendid!" Camden gushed. "And will your supple slave girl be making her debut at our meeting? Kamila, Queen of the Harem! Ruler of Pharaoh's *ruler.*" He chuckled wickedly.

Olivia smiled at the other end of the phone. Ever since she'd put on her mother's necklace and awoke each morning to the sounds of hammering, nail guns, shouting, swearing, and salsa music coming from the crew working on the lighthouse keeper's cottage, she'd felt lighter in spirit than she had in years, but there were limits to how much change she could handle at once. "I think I'll stick to eavesdropping," she replied, though part of her longed to take a risk and open her work up to criticism. "I'm not quite ready to commit."

"I suspect you've said that phrase *many*

times in your life," Camden commented without judgment. "Darling, life is messy, but sometimes it's *fun* to get a little *dirty*. Spread your wings, jump off the diving board, make mud pies — I'll keep going with these clichés until you agree."

"Save them for your book," Olivia parried playfully and then changed the subject. "What about food?"

"Oh, whip us up some tapas-type tidbits," Camden ordered casually. "I'll treat this time, since we'll be celebrating our *freedom* from all things Andrew Lloyd Webber."

They discussed the meeting time and then said good-bye, but not before Camden threatened to call Fodor's and AAA and complain about cutting his tongue on a shard of shell found in The Boot Top's clam chowder if Olivia didn't agree to become a member of the Bayside Book Writers.

Olivia hissed, "You wouldn't!"

"I won't, because *you're* going to be at the meeting. I won't make you read *this* time, but consider it your only reprieve." Olivia heard the smile in Camden's voice. "I told you, my blond Amazon, we *need* one another."

Feeling momentarily expansive, Olivia answered, "As I'm being forced against my will, then I might as well see to the drinks. I can't sit through any more heaving bosoms without bourbon."

"Purely medicinal," Camden agreed readily and hung up.

A few evenings later, Olivia realized that the food she had chosen to serve the writers was completely wrong.

Michel, her chef, had outdone himself in producing a selection of succulent hors d'oeuvres. When a waiter had delivered the polished silver trays laden with black truffle canapés, smoked salmon roulades, prosciutto and gruyere pinwheels, shrimp wontons, and lamb meatballs in a pinot noir sauce, Olivia had been pleased with the artistic arrangement of the epicurean fare. But for a reason she could not fathom, the food had barely been touched by the author hopefuls gathered in the private banquet room.

Should I have served beer instead of wine? Olivia second-guessed her decision to decant two bottles of Meritage. Were the vintages too cigar box to the taste, too fruity, or overly hefty for her guests' palates? They had barely sipped from their Reidel tumblers.

Olivia's hands itched to be wrapped around a glass filled with half a finger's worth of twenty-five-year-old Chivas Regal, her customary evening intoxicant. Having become rather immune to the comfort or contentment of other people (unless they were patrons of The Boot Top), Olivia found her desire to gratify these strangers unsettling.

I should have ordered Dominos and served wine in the box, she thought, growing more irritated by the moment. The silence in the room was cloying and she distracted herself by fiddling with the floral centerpiece. That done, she checked her watch again. *Where the hell is Ford?*

"I suppose we should tell you who we are." The husky, melodious voice emanated from the exotic, part-Asian beauty whose black hair was now pink striped. Her dark brows were pierced with rows of silver hoops and she wore a diamond nose stud. She was attired in a short plaid skirt, a faded Hello Kitty shirt, and black leather boots. "Name's Millay Hallowell. Twenty-four years old, artist, and bartender. I'm writing a young adult fantasy novel. You know — the spicy kind where a bunch of sheltered virgins get raped by satyrs and stuff."

"Did I hear someone mention being ravished by goat boys?" Camden Ford inquired as he breezed into the room. "How delicious!"

A faint blush tinged Millay's cheeks as she crossed her arms over her chest and tried to look tough.

"Doing introductions, are we? Excellent! Who's next?" Camden gestured at the young man resembling Peter Pan.

"Um." He looked at Olivia as his fingers mangled a gruyere pinwheel. "I'm Harris Williams." He pushed a wave of soft hair from his forehead. "I'm into computers. I create graphics for fantasy games. I've got the best job in the world. Flexible hours, a good salary, and I have a lot in common with my coworkers. We're all pretty smart but we don't have the greatest people skills."

"Imagine that," Camden teased. "Go on, man, before the food gets cold."

"Sorry. Um, I'm a sci-fi guy. My book's about the imminent destruction of the Planet Zulton. A group of one hundred Zultons have been chosen to start a new colony on the planet Remus. Their leader is a warrior princess named Zenobia." Noticing the confused looks of his audience, Harris hurriedly concluded. "Anyway, a spacecraft carrying convicts destined for a life sentence of hard labor crash lands on Zulton and these guys kill a bunch of the Chosen Ones. Zenobia and one of the criminals —"

"Very *Flash Gordon,* isn't it!" Camden arched an eyebrow for Olivia's benefit and then directed his attention to a flustered woman in her early thirties. "And you've already had the pleasure of listening to some of Laurel's work. Give Olivia the 411 on your exciting life, my dear."

The woman giggled. "I don't know about *exciting,* but my name's Laurel Hobbs. I'm a stay-at-home mom with twin boys. Dallas and Dermot. They're twenty-seven months and a *real* handful. You've probably heard us in the grocery store." Even her laugh, high and melodious, was lovely. "I try to write when they're napping, but it's hard to find the time with laundry and making dinner and all the errands. The twins are at *such* a demanding age, but I think they're just naughty because they're so smart. Would you like to see a picture of them?" she asked Olivia and began fumbling beneath her chair. "I have a whole bunch in my purse."

Olivia stared at her in horror. Camden quickly intervened before Laurel could locate her purse. "Tell our hostess about your writing, darling."

Laurel blinked. "Oh, right!" she exclaimed with another nervous giggle. "My dream is to write romance novels. Like Nora Roberts or Danielle Steel. I've wanted to write books like theirs ever since I read my first romance in high school."

Camden smiled benevolently at Laurel and then gestured at Olivia. "You're at bat. Swing away."

Olivia smoothed the tablecloth. She'd never told anyone but Dixie about her novel and wondered what the others would think of her story line. Taking a deep breath, she tersely explained, "My manuscript in progress is a work of historical fiction. It's set in ancient Egypt and focuses on the struggles of a young concubine in the household of Ramses the Great."

"The little slut!" Camden poured himself a glass of wine. "Your Egyptian vixen would fit right in with my troupe of thinly veiled fictional celebrities. Yes, indeed. I know the real man my 'hero' is based on well enough to be certain he would simply *salivate* over a piece of tanned jail bait wearing a transparent linen shift."

Laurel gazed at the gossip writer in adoration. "I still can't believe you're friends with famous people!"

Camden flicked his wrist at her. "Puhlease! We are *not* friends. I know more big names than you could fit in this lovely, very feng shui room, but don't be impressed, my dear. Most celebrities are vain, vapid, and filled with vice." He plucked a shrimp wonton from the tray and placed it delicately in the center of a cocktail napkin. "Did you catch my alliteration there, my dears? Now Olivia, tell us about you."

"Please help yourselves." Olivia pointed a dictatorial finger at the food trays. She waited until the writers focused on refilling their plates and then said, "I'm Olivia Limoges. I live out on the point with my standard poodle, Captain Haviland. He's sleeping in my office at the moment," she added when Laurel peered under the table-cloth. "I'm unmarried and childless and plan to stay that way. Now that this place" — she gesticulated around the room — "and my rental properties are up and running, I'd like to proceed with my writing." She crossed her arms and looked at Ford. "Could you tell me more about the group's schedule and assignments?"

"Excellent canapés, my dear." Camden saluted her with his refreshed wineglass. "Thus far, we've congregated every other week, but we've all decided to meet weekly in order to make more progress. We each take turns having our work reviewed. Soon enough, it'll be your turn to bring us copies of your masterpiece, Olivia." He picked up a stack of papers from an end table. "Lucky for you, I've brought my pages tonight so you can take out all of your aggressions on my humble prose." He grinned at her. "This gives you an entire week to sharpen your pencil, my dear. Don't worry, I take criticism *very* well."

Olivia sniffed.

"Oh, but don't worry. We're not really mean to each other." Laurel had misinterpreted the noise as anxiety. "We say lots of nice things too!"

Millay rolled her eyes. "And *that's* a waste of time if you ask me! We'll never get better if we just sit around blowing smoke up each other's asses. When it's my turn, be as harsh as you want." She pointed a slim finger at Olivia. "Bring it, sister!"

Harris, who had been stealing glances at Millay all evening, dusted the crumbs from a prosciutto and gruyere pinwheel off his long-fingered hands and reached into a plastic bag resting next to his feet. "I had this cool English teacher in high school who never used a red pen. She said the color made students feel like they had written something *wrong* when her main intent was to give us helpful suggestions. She wrote comments using green ink, so I bought green pens for all of us. May we do no harm!"

He leapt out of his chair and promptly handed out packets containing two green ballpoint pens to his fellow writers.

"Thank you, Harris. You are *so* sweet." Laurel emitted a vibe of maternal approval. "I'd much rather be criticized in green than in red. I always dress my son Dermot in green. Dallas wears blue a lot. I'm afraid red would get them even more worked up than usual. It's such an energizing color. Why, we were practically banned from story time at the library after the day I dressed them both in red overalls!"

After accepting Harris's gift, Camden passed out copies of his chapter for review. "Now, I'm going to break protocol and refuse to read aloud tonight. Olivia here has an announcement to make and after she does, we're relocating to the bar to celebrate. No work this evening, my darlings! Tonight, we make merry!"

All eyes turned to Olivia. "Yes. Well. You all know where the lighthouse is, correct? Out on the point?" she added for Camden's sake. "The cottage is on my family's . . . I mean, *my* land, and it's currently being restored. It won't be totally ready for another week or so but we can hold our

44

future meetings there. At no charge, of course."

Camden led the group in a round of delighted surprise, and as the writers thanked Olivia, she waved them off. Warmed and slightly embarrassed by their gratitude, she suggested they follow her to the bar.

"See? You're not *quite* the Wicked Witch of the South," Camden whispered in her ear.

"Good evening, Gabe." Olivia ignored Camden and focused on The Boot Top's handsome bartender instead. "These folks are . . . my friends." *How odd to be calling them that,* she thought. "Please be certain to put their drinks on my tab."

The bartender, a young man in his late twenties with a deep tan and an attractive, all-American face, nodded in acquiescence. After serving Laurel a Manhattan, Gabe poured a generous amount of Chivas Regal over a few asymmetrical blocks of hand-chiseled ice and set the tumbler down in front of his employer.

Originally positioned at the far end of the bar, Millay slid away from Harris and jumped up onto the stool next to Olivia. "I didn't expect this place to be so hip," she commented, taking a slurp of beer.

Olivia bristled. "Why not? Because I'm so

advanced in years?"

"Huh?" Millay missed the note of sarcasm. "It's just that my parents love coming here. It's where they go for their *special* occasions, you know?" She gestured around the wood paneled bar. "They both teach at the community college and can only afford a place like this once in a while. After seeing what you charge for beer, I can see why. The year-rounders in Oyster Bay aren't exactly loaded. How do you stay in business?"

Pleased to note that the restaurant was nearly full, Olivia took Millay's question seriously. "There are quite a few tourists here tonight. We're always busy from May to October, especially since that famous article about Oyster Bay's appeal appeared in *Time.* In the winter, things will slow down, but as you said, people come here for birthdays and anniversaries and such. We also host Christmas parties for many local businesses. And we cater."

She looked around at the glazed ochre walls, which were covered by enormous paintings of wine bottles, at the pristine white cloths, and the terra-cotta hued napkin fans on the few unoccupied tables. Votive candles shone through cylinders of dark amber cut glass made in Indonesia.

The same shade of amber formed a thick stripe of paint on the walls and seemed to subtly box in the diners, creating an atmosphere of warm elegance with a hint of exclusivity.

"Interesting," Millay replied and Olivia couldn't tell whether she was sincere. "But don't you think you should consider some cooler music? This soft jazz stuff reminds me of the dentist. I *do* like the name though. Boot Top. I dig boots." She lifted both her ankles so that Olivia could admire her lace-up, stiletto-heeled, leather footwear, but Olivia was distracted by the arrival of an unfamiliar middle-aged man.

"Two fingers of Glenfiddich. No ice, please," he told Gabe in a pleasant baritone.

Millay noticed the newcomer in the mirror behind the bar and pivoted in her seat. "What about you?" She grinned flirtatiously. "Do you like my boot tops?"

The stranger smiled at her but didn't take his lead gray eyes from her face. "I believe the boot top in this case refers to the russet line on the walls."

Looking perplexed, Millay didn't respond, but Olivia locked eyes with the man and said, "Are you familiar with nautical terms Mr. . . . ?"

"McNulty. Flynn McNulty." Flynn stood

in order to shake hands with Olivia. "My knowledge of maritime matters is limited, but I believe that a boot top is the painted line just above the waterline on a seafaring vessel. Am I at least near the mark?"

"You're spot-on, Mr. McNulty." Olivia examined him over the lip of her tumbler.

Flynn assessed her simultaneously. "Another whiskey drinker?" He raised his glass in a salute. "I may actually be able to live in this town after all."

Millay snorted, a noise that seemed incongruent with her beauty. "It'll take more than booze to make Oyster Bay look good. Where did you live before?"

"Just outside of Raleigh in the Research Triangle Park area. I'm retiring from cubicle land in order to open a bookshop here. It's what I've always wanted to do and an aunt of mine was kind enough to leave me a small inheritance. I read about the town's building boom, and since the closest Barnes and Noble is over fifty miles away, I figured this was as fine a place as any to risk it all."

Olivia tried to ignore the quickening of her blood. A bookstore was her idea of paradise, but she'd preferred to browse in other people's shops in place of opening one of her own. She turned to tell Camden the news but saw that he was too engaged in flirting with the bartender to be diverted by anything she could say.

"Did you say something about books?" Harris inquired, seeking to join their conversation.

"Shelves of them. I'm out tonight to celebrate. My shop, Through the Wardrobe, will open its doors this Saturday. I was planning on a hugely publicized grand opening in about two weeks, but my stock arrived sooner than expected." He shrugged. "Now I'll just hang up some balloons and count on word-of-mouth advertising."

Millay pulled a face. "In this town, you'll get more word-of-mouth than you can stand, believe me."

"It's so awesome that you named your place after a C.S. Lewis novel!" Delighted, Harris finally tore his eyes from Millay's shapely legs and gave the newcomer his full attention. The two men launched into a discourse on the multifaceted subject matter tackled within *The Chronicles of Narnia.*

Clearly displeased over being ignored in favor of C.S. Lewis, Millay poked Flynn in the fleshy part of his thigh. "You might be stocking *our* books someday, you know. We're all writers."

"In that case, I'd better learn everyone's names," Flynn replied gallantly.

By the time the assembly had consumed three rounds of drinks, they were thoroughly convinced their fellow writers would completely devote themselves to their upcoming editorial responsibilities, giving each of them the forward push needed to complete a saleable novel. Even Olivia, who thus far had only warmed to Camden, found herself believing that joining the writer's group might be a step in the right direction toward becoming a social human being.

"I'm feeling so inspired by this meeting!" Laurel squealed excitedly as she bid everyone farewell. "But Steve will be waiting up for me. It's bad enough he had to babysit while I hung out at a posh restaurant drinking Manhattans." She hiccupped and quickly covered her mouth with her hand. "I hope he lets me come to our next meeting at Olivia's cottage," she said from behind her palm. "I'll have to detail his truck in exchange for being able to go out *four* nights in one month!"

"Don't forget to critique my chapter!" Camden called after her and then stroked his smooth chin thoughtfully. "Do you think she's serious about not being allowed to attend?"

"Or having to detail her husband's truck?" Olivia glanced at Laurel's vacant stool and frowned. "I'm greatly relieved to have no one telling *me* what to do."

Shortly following Laurel's departure, Flynn also left and the exuberant fellowship among the remaining writers seemed to deflate. Soon afterward, Harris and Millay drained the remains of their glasses and headed for home — or in Millay's case, the beginning of her nine to two o'clock shift at Fish Nets.

Camden kissed everyone on both cheeks, chiding them about being punctual and fulfilling their homework assignment by critiquing his chapter, and then turned back to Olivia.

"I think things went well, don't you?" And then, before she could answer, "Good God, it's Blake Talbot! And hanging onto his ropy arm is his latest conquest, Heidi St. Claire. Oh, am *I* ever at the right place at the right time!" He rubbed his hands together with relish. "Miss St. Claire is quite lovely in person, most unlike the freshly scrubbed, severely dressed character she plays on television."

"She's only a girl!" Olivia declared. "Really, Camden, she can't be more than sixteen."

"Just eighteen, but *this* girl, this rising star from Iowa, is about to burst onto the

Hollywood scene like a supernova! By this time next year, there'll be Heidi St. Claire dolls, a Heidi St. Claire clothing line, and a Heidi St. Claire fragrance. I am *clair*voyant about these things!" He wiggled his eyebrows. "I saw the trailers for her upcoming movie releases. She's going to win armloads of awards for her role opposite Russell Crowe. Remember this conversation come Oscar night!" Camden eyed the young woman discreetly using the mirror behind the bar. "Oh! Olivia, darling! They're here to have dinner. Can we please sit down at that little two-seater behind them? We can have coffee and dessert and I can eavesdrop to my heart's content? *Pul-lease!*"

"Don't they know who you are?" Olivia asked as she nodded at the maître d'. She gestured at the table behind the couple and allowed her suave employee to place a napkin on her lap with a flourish.

Camden perused the dessert menu. "Of course they don't know me," he whispered. "Blake Talbot, like everyone in Hollywood and across our little blue planet, believes that I am a *woman* named Milano Cruise, remember? Shall we partake of the chocolate crème brûlée?"

Olivia only needed to raise her eyes and a waiter instantly appeared. She ordered

Camden's dessert along with two decaffeinated cappuccinos.

"Now the trick," Camden whispered, "is for us to pretend to be engaged in an important and intimate conversation. We lean in like so, and we move our lips every now and again, and we nod. Nodding's good. And then, we listen to every word they say."

Although she was skeptical of Camden's plan, Olivia was too interested in discovering more about a member of the Talbot family to offer any dissent. As she concentrated on stirring cinnamon curls into her cappuccino, she overheard Heidi pleading with Blake.

"But I want this to be *official*." Her plaintive tone was distinctly juvenile. "If you come to my screening, then we'll be in all the magazines. It'll make a huge statement. My mom and stepdad will see that you're serious about *us,* and of course you'll sell a bunch of CDs just by being in *People.* Come on, Blakey. Do this for me."

"Heidi." Blake spoke her name with an undercurrent of scorn. "It's not like I haven't been in *People* before. Besides, I told you that I need to keep up the appearance of being single. Girls don't want to listen to the tunes of some whipped loser.

They like to dream, to hope that they'd have a chance with me. I've gotta stay a fantasy. Being your *boyfriend* doesn't fit with that whole picture. Don't you get that?"

Heidi's disappointed sigh seemed to blow across the room. She raised a flute filled with the restaurant's finest champagne to her lips but then placed it on the table again. "It's not *fair.*" Olivia could imagine her pursing her pretty lips. "But I can't keep lying to my parents. You know how close my mom and I are. What if she calls Lila's house? What if —"

"Look. I'm going to meet with some people late tonight and then, tomorrow morning, we're outta here. The Gulfstream is all gassed up. We'll climb aboard, pop a bottle of Moët, and . . ." Blake mercifully lowered his voice to an inaudible whisper, which was followed by a theatrical squeal from Heidi's side of the table. "After one night in Vegas, we'll be back in LA. You'll be home in time for dinner."

Olivia leaned toward Camden, whose gaze was fixated on the painting behind her shoulder. He waved a spoonful of crème brûlée in the air with his right hand. "Delicious!" he suddenly pronounced.

"He obviously doesn't care about her at all. Poor girl," Olivia murmured to Camden, shooting a sideways glance at the young man. She had to admit he was good-looking in a scruffy, rebellious sort of way. His black hair, dark eyes, and square jaw certainly lent him a masculine air, though he was far too reedy for Olivia's tastes. However, she could see that other women in The Boot Top were also casting covert looks in his direction, for there was a magnetism about Blake Talbot, a mixture of conceit and coarse beauty, that most women found destructively fascinating.

Camden was unsympathetic to Heidi's plight. "He never cares about any of them. Deep down, they all know it too, but we *all* deceive ourselves, do we not?"

"That we do," Olivia agreed. "And you've got foam on your lip."

Heidi continued her argument as Olivia and Camden fell silent again. "Why can't I meet your friends? I don't want to be in that beach house all by myself at night. I came out here to be with *you*." Her pout was as extreme as a toddler's.

"These men are not the kind of people you're used to," Blake answered flatly, grabbing the bottle of champagne from the silver ice bucket in the center of the table. He filled his glass to the brim and then jammed the bottle back into the chilled bucket without offering to replenish his date's empty flute. "You wouldn't fit in."

"Just because I play a minister's daughter on TV doesn't mean I am one! You have no idea what I've lived through. I haven't told you *everything* about my life!" Olivia and Camden found Heidi's indignation amusing and they both smiled and nodded as though one of them had just received the punch line of a rousingly good joke.

"Well, you sure don't act like a choir girl between the sheets," Blake said huskily. "If everyone knew how wild Miss Junior Idaho or Indiana or whatever redneck state you're from really was, you'd be on the cover of *all* the magazines."

"Shut up!" Heidi hissed. "Oh, let's just go. I'm not hungry anymore."

"Oh, babe," Blake purred. "I'm just messing with you. You know I think you're the most smoking-hot chick in the whole world."

"Notice he didn't mention brains," Olivia commented.

Camden smirked. "Or anything about her *burgeoning* talent."

Unaware of the acute attention being paid to her, Heidi slipped her thin arms into a white silk cardigan and then folded the garment across her high breasts. "Then why won't you introduce me to the guys?"

"The *guys* are not like my bandmates, Heidi," Blake growled. "They're not my posse — they're a bunch of ex-con fishermen and knife-carrying scumbags who'll do anything for a buck. Got it?"

"Then why are *you* hanging out with *that sort?*" Heidi asked and Olivia was pleased on behalf of her gender that the young woman had finally exhibited a hint of intelligence.

"Let's just say I'm making an investment in my future." Blake waved his hand in the air, rudely signaling for the check. "That's the end of the subject, Heidi. We're going."

"Well, I just hope you're not buying drugs," Heidi said with a sulk. "I don't approve of them, and besides, there's plenty of those back home."

"Right, like *you're* such an expert on the subject." Blake was openly derisive. "*You're* not the one who has to rock your ass off in front of thousands of people. You get to sit around between takes, getting manicures and drinking mocha soy lattes."

"No matter how much pressure I'm under, I'll *never* take drugs!" Heidi whispered as she stood. "So I hope that's not what your *big, secret* meeting at that gross bar is all about. If rumors about drugs or anything illegal affect my reputation, I'd be kicked off the show and my marketing value would go way downhill. I'm supposed to be a role model. Don't you care about *my* future? I have *two* films debuting this summer!"

Blake grabbed her roughly by the arm and propelled her past Olivia and Camden's table. "It's not drugs, babe, so get off your high horse. It's something much more dangerous than that," he muttered darkly. "And since I've gotta protect your *precious* rep, I won't tell you anything else, except that my plan is going to make me a shitload of money."

Camden stared after them, a greedy gleam in his eyes. "I wonder what bar he could be referencing?"

"If Heidi thinks it's gross and fishermen hang out there, then there's one likely choice. Blake is conducting his illicit business at Fish Nets. The establishment where Millay works."

"Olivia my dear, after we're done with our dessert, how would you like to —"

"Not a chance," Olivia cut him off. "Later this evening, after we're done here, I will be in my lovely house, clad in a pair of silk pajamas, cocktail in hand, watching *Masterpiece Theater*. I confess to having enjoyed myself tonight, but I have no intention of spending a single minute in a foul-smelling bar filled with men whose cologne is a mixture of smoke, sweat, and fish or with women whose clothes are either three sizes too small or veritably see-through. *Nothing* you say will convince me to change my mind." She placed her empty mug against its saucer with a firm clink. "I will never set foot in that disgusting place."

"Never say never," Camden said with an expressive wink.

Olivia felt an inexplicable tinge of anxiety as she headed into the kitchen to collect her thoroughly gorged poodle.

CHAPTER 3

The fog comes on little cat feet.
— CARL SANDBURG

The fog had always brought gifts to Olivia Limoges.

They were infrequent. And odd. Yet she knew they were meant for her. An aloof child, ever drifting along the shoreline near the lighthouse keeper's cottage, Olivia had spent endless hours turning over the slick husks of horseshoe crabs or collapsing holes dug by industrious coquinas. She poked at sand crabs with sticks and taunted seagulls with crusts from pimiento cheese sandwiches.

Olivia kept her gifts in pickle jars. She labeled each jar with the year on a piece of masking tape. Even now, at forty, she loved to twist the lid from one of the glass jars and pour the contents out onto the saffron and cobalt scrolls of her largest Iranian rug, releasing the scents of seaweed and ocean dampened sand. She'd lean over, her shock of white blond hair aglow in the lamplight, and finger a marble, a wheat penny, a star-shaped earring with missing rhinestones, a rusty skeleton key. Then, another year: a yellow hair barrette in the shape of a dragonfly, a fishhook, a one-shot liquor bottle with no label, a tennis ball, a steel watchband, a shotgun shell.

Today she took the metal detector along on her morning walk. She went out early, as soon as the fog rolled back, dressed in cotton sweats and Wellingtons. Haviland danced through the surf beside her as they marched north by northeast, Olivia swinging the detector back and forth like a horizontal pendulum as she inhaled the salt-laden breeze. Her Bounty Hunter Discovery 3300 issued a cacophony of vibrating clicks and murmurs that sounded more like the language of dolphins than something constructed of metal and electrical wire.

Haviland barked at a low-flying gull as the digital target identification on the Bounty Hunter's LCD display screen leapt toward the right, showing a full arc of black triangles. Olivia paused, removed her trench shovel from her backpack, and began to dig. She could have ordered a top-of-the-line detector — one with an attached digger, incredible depth perception, and the ability to function underwater, but she preferred the challenge offered by the simpler model.

"Help dig, Haviland," Olivia commanded her dog in much the same tone she used on the employees of her restaurant or the tenants of the buildings she owned downtown.

Haviland responded immediately, his front paws burrowing into the soft, damp sand. Olivia waited until the poodle had created a pile behind his hindquarters the height of a termite mound and then she began to shift through the sand too.

"Nothing. Let's see if we need to look deeper." Olivia leveled the detector over the hole and it chirped excitedly. She turned the volume down and nodded at her canine assistant. He resumed his work.

Then, Olivia saw a flash of metal beneath Haviland's right paw. "Whoa, Captain."

Haviland's liquid brown eyes were sparkling in the morning sun. Olivia grinned at the poodle, her blood quickening in anticipation of their find.

Rubbing clots of sand from the rectangular metal object, which was slightly larger than a matchbook, Olivia held her new treasure flat on her palm so that it might be bathed in the newborn light.

"It's some sort of box." She eased open the case and upturned it, shaking loose a sprinkle of sand. The interior was empty. Olivia closed her eyes and lifted the box to her nose. There were no lingering scents, no telltale remnants of a heady perfume or an exotic spice. "There are letters here, Haviland." She peered at the lid. "Something illegible and then the letters *E* period *M* period. Doesn't sound familiar. Ah! There may be some writing on the front too, but it's covered by splotches of rust. We'll have to soak this for a spell."

Stroking the soft curls between the poodle's ears, Olivia stood and slipped the small box into her pocket. "Breakfast time, Captain."

Haviland barked and the pair retraced their steps. The Bounty Hunter, now rendered mute as its owner was always satisfied with a single discovery, was slung over Olivia's shoulder like a rifle. The pair walked for a mile, Haviland trotting faster as soon as he caught the sight of the orange "No Trespassing" signs flanking the path that wound through the dunes toward Olivia's low country–style home. She paused to appreciate the sunlight dazzling against the bank of windows facing the Atlantic. The gray stonework seemed to absorb the hesitant warmth, and Olivia never failed to gaze upon her custom home without a feeling of deep contentment.

Haviland raced ahead of her toward the Range Rover, but Olivia pointed at the house. "It's not a Grumpy's day. We've got quite a list of errands to do."

Although she had a state-of-the-art kitchen with cherry cabinets, soapstone countertops, and a bevy of quiet and efficient appliances, Olivia wasn't much of a cook. Most mornings, she microwaved a bowl of instant oatmeal or grits, mixed the cereal with a thick pat of butter, and then rounded out her meal by eating a banana or a handful of pitted prunes. If she didn't feel like dirtying a bowl, she went to Grumpy's.

As Haviland pressed his wet nose against her leg, indicating an eagerness for his meal, Olivia rummaged around in her deepest cabinet. "I'll have you know that I only bought this double boiler for you, Captain. Your polenta will be ready in no time. What would Michel or I have done if I hadn't discovered such a glorious list of healthy recipes on that fantastic Coddled Canine website? Why right now, you might be eating *canned* dog food!" Haviland flattened his ears as Olivia crashed pots and pans. "We're lucky Michel doesn't mind cooking for you. He's told me you're to expect chicken liver dumplings for dinner. Ah, here's that double boiler."

After stirring together the mixture of cornmeal, milk, and Parmesan cheese and leaving it to simmer, Olivia sat down in front of her MacBook. She pushed her partially completed critique of Camden's chapter to the far side of the desk and directed her mouse to Google's home page. The rectangular container she and Haviland had unearthed on their walk was now soaking in vinegar, but she had brushed off enough of the heavy clots of rust using baking soda and a toothbrush to reveal an acronym reading, "G.E.M." Olivia took a bite of a soft, overly ripe banana and typed the letters into Google's search box.

"Global Electric Motors. That's a bit too modern for this object, I'd say. Graphical Environment Manager. A relatively new term. So is this reference to documentation for PCs." She continued to scroll down the list of results, bypassing references to gem mining, gem shows, and the county of Gem, Idaho. "None of these fit."

Haviland put his paws up on the counter closest to the cooktop and sniffed.

"Your polenta! Forgive me, my dearest." Olivia removed the top saucepan and scooped the contents into a ceramic bowl on his elevated feeder. "It's still too hot. Let's rinse off our mystery box and see if the rust is gone while your breakfast cools."

The poodle watched eagerly as Olivia dumped the vinegar into the sink, rinsed the silver box, and gingerly dried it with a paper towel. Squinting, she eased back the lid and smiled. "Here's something! It says 'G.E.M. Brooklyn, New York. Made in U.S.A.' " She shut the lid and turned the case over in her hand. "Looks like a patent number here."

Olivia returned to her computer and refined her search. "Gem pawnbrokers in Brooklyn, Acme Smoked Fish on Gem Street in Brooklyn, Gem Auction Company. Brooklyn. No, no, no!"

After pouring herself a second cup of coffee and serving Haviland his polenta, she decided to switch tactics. Logging on to eBay, she typed in the exact words found inside the silver lid.

"Eureka!" she yelled and Haviland barked in excitement. "G.E.M. safety razor. Produced between 1912 through 1979 in Brooklyn. Formerly known as G.E.M. Cutlery Company of New York." Olivia showed her poodle their metal container. "This piece of steel is a shaver head, Captain. It's missing its blade and the handle too. According to this auction, it's worth a whopping twelve dollars."

Haviland lowered his head and closed his eyes, clearly ready for a post-meal nap. Olivia stroked the smooth metal of the shaver head. "Now, now. We don't do this for profit, Captain. You don't have to act so disinterested. It's the adventure we're after." She shut the lid of her laptop. "You lick your bowl clean, I'll get dressed, we'll put this little *gem* in a jar, and then we're off to the furniture store."

The sun had seared away all traces of the fog by the time Olivia turned from her gravel drive and climbed onto an empty stretch of gray blue asphalt the color of a heron's plumage. On the narrow street marking the northernmost end of the compact town of Oyster Bay, there was once a plethora of vacant stores and available parking spaces, but ever since *Time* magazine had hailed Oyster Bay as one of the nations "Top Ten Best-kept Vacation Secrets," their half-deserted berg had been overrun with tourists.

Pale-legged vacationers descended like a locust swarm to trample the natural beauty of the shoreline, watch birds through thousand-dollar binoculars, sample Southern country cooking until their buttons burst, and host drunken deep-sea fishing trips for their rich friends. In their wake, they left behind mounds of garbage, soiled linens, crisp, inconvenient hundred-dollar bills, and a sour taste in the mouths of the yearlong residents.

Despite this influx of new faces and businesses, Olivia had to drive for more than an hour to reach a decent furniture store. She quickly selected two sofas and a pair of oversized club chairs in warm fabrics, a room-sized sea grass rug, and breezy curtains in a shimmering ecru.

Trouble arose, as Olivia expected it to, when the designer informed her that the furniture would take eight to ten weeks to be delivered and that the items on the floor were absolutely not for sale.

"How would we be able to show how wonderful this sage and almond checkered fabric looks on our club chairs if it wasn't in the store?" the woman questioned rhetorically.

"Perhaps there is another equally attractive chair in your warehouse?" Olivia suggested, placing a fat roll of twenty-dollar bills into the woman's hands. "And I would *certainly* make it well worth the while of the gentlemen delivering my new furnishings if they could arrive at my cottage, say, by five this afternoon?" Placing her credit card and a calling card bearing her name, address, and phone number on the designer's desk, Olivia met the other woman's eye.

"I'm going to check on my dog," she announced. "I'll be back in to sign my receipt in a moment."

She had been right in assuming that the decorator wanted to examine the wad of twenties more closely before agreeing to the deal. Olivia was also confident that four hundred dollars in cash would sway most people into figuring out a way to break the rules, especially since no one would be the worse for the transgression.

After promising Haviland that her errand was almost complete, Olivia walked briskly back into the store, scribbled signatures on several pieces of paper, and then drove off in search of some colorful art.

"Don't worry. We're going to eat first, Captain. Should we be naughty today?"

Haviland knew perfectly well that naughty meant unhealthy and offered a jubilant bark. Thirty minutes later, the pair was seated at a patio table, enjoying the shade of the umbrella as they dined on tender cheeseburgers and thin, crunchy curls of fried onions.

After lunch, the poodle insisted on a brief squirrel-chasing session through the park before being dragged off to the next errand. Olivia was more than happy to comply. Thus far, the day had progressed with great promise. The mystery of their beach find was solved and the lighthouse keeper's cottage was almost renovated. All she needed now was some inspirational art, but the furniture store, with its Impressionist prints and unattractive modern art silk screens, had been a disappointment.

Oyster Bay wasn't quite cosmopolitan enough to support an entire gallery, but several local artists sold their works by displaying them on the brick walls of the local coffee and pastry shop. Olivia opened the front door to Bagels 'n' Beans and waved hello to the octogenarian proprietor, who was also one of her tenants. Her favorite one, in fact.

"I'm here to check out your art, Wheeler." Olivia and Haviland breezed past the "No Dogs" sign and began to scrutinize the grouping of paintings, sketches, and framed black-and-white paper-cut designs.

"I like the paper cuts of the herons, don't you?" Olivia pointed at the framed art hanging above the eatery's worn purple sofa.

70

Haviland snorted in assent. "Let's take the one of the three birds in the roost and the other showing them fishing in the cove. I particularly like how this artist made the tree branches. Spindly-shaped. They don't seem sinister to you, do they?" she asked her dog.

"More angular than sinister, I'd say," a man two tables down remarked.

Olivia turned to look at the speaker and recognized him right away. "Hello, Chief Rawlings." She glanced back at the paper cuts. "I've never seen such delicate work."

The chief of the Oyster Bay Police Department nodded. "My sister Jeannie will be mighty pleased to hear you say that. Nothing sinister about *her*, that's for sure. I don't think she's had a negative thought since 1965."

"What happened in 1965?" Olivia couldn't help but ask.

"I was born." The policeman laughed and took a sip of his coffee. "And spent the next sixteen years making her life a living hell. Who'd have thought we'd be the best of friends now."

Olivia took a second look at the lawman. Stocky and wide-shouldered, with dark hair going gray above the ears, Rawlings didn't come across as the type of man to have a female as his closest confidante. In fact, whenever Olivia saw him in public, he was always accompanied by at least one other equally bulky officer. Rawlings and his officers tended to swagger down the street as though the heavy Maglite banging against the right hip didn't equally balance the weight of the gun resting just above the left hip. Today, he wasn't in uniform but wore a loud Hawaiian shirt covered by yellow pineapples over a pair of wrinkled brown shorts.

Returning her attention to the art, Olivia only took a brief glimpse at the watercolor landscapes hung above a row of small cafe tables. With their soft illumination and pastel hues, the pictures of gardens, shorelines, and children playing on the beach were fine, but didn't hold her interest. The next pair of paintings was very large and looked to be oils.

The first showed a row of boats tied to the dock. Their sails were unfurled and it appeared as though their bowlines were about to be set free from the cleats holding them in place. Rows of colorful flags streamed from the masts, reminding Olivia of medieval pennants. People moved about the boat decks and the surface of the dock with a tangible energy. The picture conveyed a feeling of happy anticipation as well as an invitation to freedom. It was as if the boats were only waiting for the viewer to board before being launched into the sun-drenched water. She found herself wishing to be among the sailors waiting to embark.

The second painting was a contrast in calm. An old-fashioned bicycle, the kind Olivia had once pedaled into town as a young girl, had been left on a solitary stretch of beach. The kickstand kept it propped upright and its front tire was pointed very subtly toward the surf. Again, the painting conveyed an invitation to the viewer, a promise of leisurely days and a release of responsibility. Olivia felt infused by serenity by simply gazing at the scene.

"We'll take these too, Wheeler!" Olivia shouted over her shoulder to the hearing-impaired shop owner. "They're just what I was looking for," she murmured happily to herself.

Without having been asked, the chief plucked the canvas of sailboats from the wall. "I painted these, so the least I can do is take them to your car. After you, Ms. Limoges."

"*You're* the artist?" Olivia glanced at the initials in the lower right of the painting left on the wall in surprise. *How can someone wearing such a horrid shirt create such appealing art?* she thought, puzzled.

Rawlings slid the painting into the back of the Range Rover. "I've only been at it since my wife died. Jeannie thought it would do me good, but you're only the second person to buy one. Maybe you're just trying to get on the good side of the law." He pretended to glower at her. "After all, I saw where you parked the other day. You'll have to explain your *handicap* to me sometime." He then gave her a friendly wink and ducked back inside the coffee shop to retrieve the rest of Olivia's purchases.

"Oh Lord, is he flirting with me?" Olivia whispered to Haviland and the poodle cocked his head to the side. "I think he winked at me at the last Planning Board meeting too."

Somewhat discomfited by the chief's attentions, Olivia quickly told Rawlings that she needed to stop by the new bookstore before heading back home to meet the furniture truck. The lawman placed the rest of the paintings in the SUV and gently closed the hatchback.

"Through the Wardrobe," Rawlings said as he leaned an elbow on Olivia's side mirror. "Good name for a bookstore. I was there earlier," he informed her. "You're mighty busy these days, Ms. Limoges. Rumor has it you're remodeling the lighthouse keeper's cottage — even offering it to our local writer's group to use. That's quite generous of you." He gazed at her through the open window, his brown eyes glimmering with humor. "Are you planning to join those folks? Pen the next bestseller?"

Now Olivia was certain the chief was being more friendly than necessary. "I'm mulling it over, Chief. But right now, I need to get these paintings home. Thank you for loading them, but if you'll excuse me . . ."

"You need to go home *after* you visit Mr. McNulty, you mean," Rawlings reminded her with a teasing smile. "He had some fine recommendations for me."

"And what do you read? Police procedurals? Mafia thrillers?" Olivia lightly mocked the lawman as she turned on her engine.

Unperturbed, the chief pointed his finger at her. "I see you tend to pigeonhole, Ms. Limoges. I read everything, including the books you mentioned, but my latest Amazon box contained some classic literature, poetry, and cookbooks. But it looks as though my online ordering is over now that Mr. McNulty's here. Have a nice day, ma'am." With a subtle bow, the chief walked away.

"Remarkable. Our chief is an interesting

character," Olivia announced and then drove to the western fringe of town where Flynn McNulty had converted the ground floor of a former commercial fishing supply warehouse into his new bookstore. Upon passing through the wooden doors, Olivia expected her olfactory senses to be assailed by the taint of old fish and saltwater, but she smelled Murphy Oil Soap instead. The inviting aroma was only the beginning of the pleasant surprises. Without doubt, she had stepped inside a reader's paradise.

The front portion of the store contained oversized antique wardrobes. Standing shoulder to shoulder, these massive pieces of vintage furniture had their doors thrown open, inviting browsers to glance inside at the treasures held within. Rare books, coffee table books, art books brimming with color plates, and signed first editions took residence in the polished interiors made of walnut and southern yellow pine. Small framed signs describing the contents of each case had been tastefully mounted in the center of each wardrobe's crown molding.

"I'm hoping to see your works in this armoire one day." Flynn had appeared silently next to Olivia. He now gestured at a stunning English oak arts and crafts wardrobe that bore the sign: "Coastal North

Carolina History / Local Authors."

"Where did you find all of these incredible pieces?" Olivia asked in admiration.

Flynn gazed at his collection with pride. "Several belonged to my aunt. The rest I found in antique malls, thrift stores, or at auctions. It took me over a year to clean them all up, and if this place shows a profit, I plan to keep on buying. So far, only the front of the store has wardrobes, but one day, I'd like every book to be displayed like these sections." He held his arm out in front of his body. "May I give you a tour?"

Olivia paused. "That depends on how you feel about dogs entering your shop."

"Well-mannered canines are welcome."

Pleased by his answer, she asked him to wait a moment while she retrieved Haviland from the Range Rover.

"Come in, Captain. We can add this to the list of places that recognizes the superiority of your breed."

Barking with eagerness, Haviland bounded toward the door and then sat on his haunches, as if to show Olivia that he would be calm and dignified inside the place that smelled, to his finely tuned nose, faintly of fish.

Flynn knelt and held out his hand. "Flynn McNulty. And you are?"

Haviland offered Flynn his right paw.

"This is Captain Haviland," Olivia made the introductions.

Flynn grinned. "Limoges and Haviland. A fine match. Do you collect porcelain by chance?"

"I have a few pieces," Olivia replied enigmatically as they walked deeper into the store. Here, standard wooden bookshelves had been bolted into the wall around the perimeter. To the left, Flynn had arranged works of fiction and to the right, nonfiction. The center of the room contained a grouping of upholstered chairs, end tables, and an enormous coffee table. The table was built with a glass top. A drawer slid out from beneath the glass and Flynn had cleverly displayed magazines for sale within the drawer.

"All you need now is a cappuccino machine," Olivia commented.

"You haven't read the sign next to the register yet." Flynn jerked his head toward the front room. "Free coffee with any purchase." He placed a hand on Haviland's head. "I can see I'm going to need to buy a jar of dog biscuits as well."

Haviland licked Flynn's hand and smiled at him. The trio continued into the back of the building, where a curtain of shimmering fabric made of floor-to-ceiling rainbow stripes created a distinct separation. To gain entry to this area, one had to pass through a particularly wide wardrobe whose feet had been cut down. The doors were propped open and held fast with rows of string tied with colorful bows.

"Those look like kite tails," Olivia said, fingering a red and white gingham bow.

Flynn's eyes twinkled, but he said nothing.

Together they walked through the wardrobe and stepped into a world of color. Above their heads, kites, model airplanes, papier-mâché balloons, and glittery stars hung from invisible threads. Beanbags in primary colors were dumped haphazardly on a rug designed to resemble a large box of crayons. Beneath a sign reading "Fantasy Land" was a wooden chest stuffed with pirate hats and eye patches, fairy wings, sparkling wands, and tiaras. Under a sign in gold script that said "Dr. Seuss Stage" was a wooden puppet theater complete with a box of Dr. Seuss character hand puppets. Another station, called "Wild Adventures," featured a table shaped like a crocodile surrounded by four plush chairs in the form of a lion, a monkey, a zebra, and an elephant. Instrumental music featuring flutes and oboes filled the room with an aura of magical serenity.

Olivia was impressed. "Every mother in Oyster Bay is going to be here when word gets out about this room. And the free coffee." She made a mental note to tell Laurel.

"I certainly hope so." Flynn surveyed his handiwork and folded his arms in contentment. "Feel free to browse around and let me know if you need anything."

Olivia walked around the entire adult section again. She didn't have much time, but she wanted to buy something from Flynn to show her support. Suddenly, she spied a section of gift books and was attracted to a group of writing journals. The blank pages were lined and the top of every page featured an inspirational quotation on the art of writing. Olivia scooped up six journals and a coffee table book called *Outer Banks Edge: A Photographic Portfolio* and brought her purchases to the register.

With three customers ahead of her, Olivia had the chance to study Flynn further. He wore a navy polo shirt over khakis and a pair of leather sandals. His movements were relaxed and his smile seemed genuine as he thanked each patron and handed them a disposable coffee cup.

"Pour yourself some of the Wardrobe

House Roast," he ordered good-naturedly. "And next time, feel free to bring your own coffee cup." He pointed at a rack holding a single coffee cup showing a cardinal sitting on a dogwood branch on a field of cobalt. "Just label it with permanent marker and I promise to take them all home to the dishwasher every night." He winked at Olivia. "I hope you've got a not-so-fine porcelain mug to bring in here."

"I'm sure I can dig up a suitable cup," Olivia replied, stunned by the realization that two men had winked at her in the same afternoon. And while Flynn was both interesting and attractive, it wouldn't do to express undue interest without getting to know him better. For all Olivia knew, the bookstore proprietor was happily married. His ring finger was bare, but she was aware that the lack of jewelry meant nothing. For all she knew, he had a life partner, eleven children, two hamsters, and a parakeet. Putting on her business face, Olivia smiled pleasantly. "Perhaps you can introduce me to some new historical fiction writers when I return."

"I believe I'm up to that challenge," Flynn remarked, handing her a receipt and a coffee cup. He then turned his attention to the next customer.

Olivia frowned as she eyed the large coffeemaker. She doubted that the bookstore brew would be to her liking. It certainly wouldn't be made from Kona beans, but for some reason she didn't want to offend the good-looking bookstore owner, so she poured herself half a cup. Adding a splash of cream, she took a sip and forced herself not to grimace. The flavor wasn't unappealing, but it was far too weak for her tastes. Taking the unfinished cup outside, she furtively tossed the remnants into the flower bed.

CHAPTER 4

Everyone has talent. What is rare is the courage to follow the talent to the dark place where it leads.

— ERICA JONG

The furniture movers were standing, arms folded in irritation, in front of the lighthouse keeper's cottage when Olivia pulled up behind them.

"Hello, gentlemen. I trust you haven't been waiting long." Without pausing for their reply, she unlocked the front doors and hurried inside, eager to inspect the transformed building for the first time. Taking a brief glance at the polished wood floor, she entered the old living room first.

Her decision to cover the dark walls with Benjamin Moore's Wilmington Tan, with a bright white trim on the windows and wainscoting, had given the room an instant lift. The antique-style bronze sconces and ceiling fan, which spun in a lazy, almost hypnotizing circle of maple blades, added to the room's new warmth. Olivia was pleased by the transformation.

Stepping back outside, she waved at the disgruntled deliverymen and then proceeded to boss them about until the rug was placed in the exact center of the room and her paintings were hung with mathematical precision. Just as both men were close to throwing their leather gloves on the ground and storming off, Olivia handed them each an envelope containing one hundred dollars in tip money and then inquired if they minded moving some potted ferns from the back porch of the main house.

"You'll have to put them in the truck. They're heavy as anchors."

The men fingered their five, crisp twenties and agreed to the one final task. Soon, they were gone completely and Olivia sat alone in the cottage, which seemed cleansed of poor choices and bad memories.

The past is buried, she thought, pulling Camden's chapter onto her lap. She uncapped the green pen Harris had given her and continued where she had left off the night before.

Bradley Talcott put his feet up on the

counter in front of an illuminated makeup mirror. His metal-studded boots knocked aside containers of face foundation, brown eye shadow, and black eyeliner as well as an empty bottle of Absolut and a vial of amphetamines.

"It's time to rock, bro." The spiked-haired drummer rattled his sticks against the doorjamb. "We got a hot crowd out there."

Tossing a lit cigarette onto the counter, Bradley stood. "We could be bigger than this, damn it! I'm sick of playing these shitty clubs. It's time for a tricked out tour bus and twenty-five, sold-out, big-city shows a year."

"But your punk-ass old man didn't give you the cash to back a tour, dude, so get on that stage and start singing." Seeing the flash of anger in his bandmate's eyes, the drummer retreated a step. "Come on, man. Just think about the fine booty we get to tap after the show."

The drummer departed and Bradley languidly rose to his feet. He leaned into the mirror and snarled at his reflection. "I'm not going to live like this much longer. I'm no kid. I'm in control of my own future!"

With abrupt vehemence, he pushed the contents of the counter onto the floor. Vials of pills and makeup bounced off the floor, but the vodka bottle shattered in a loud crash. Bradley looked at the result of his rage with satisfaction. He bent over to retrieve one of the shards and, after examining his face in the fragment, muttered, "I am in control."

Then he strode from the room, the triangle of broken glass still clutched in his hand.

Olivia tapped the end of her pen against her lip. She reviewed her notes on the earlier sections of the chapter in which she had complimented Camden on the strength of voice in the first six pages and how well he had conveyed the emotions of his characters. She also suggested that he might incorporate more setting details and questioned the choice of Bradley Talcott's name.

Isn't that rather close to the young man's real name? she had written on page one.

Frowning, Olivia put down her pen and walked over to the window. She checked her watch and then waved at Haviland. "Let's grab some dinner before our fellow writers appear."

An hour later, the members of the Bayside Book Writers began to arrive. Harris was the first to use the polished brass knocker in the shape of a starfish. It looked just like the necklace belonging to Olivia's mother and Olivia felt it was a fitting memorial to the person she'd cherished most.

When she opened the cottage door to welcome Harris inside, he unsettled Olivia by giving her a hug and a quick, friendly peck on the cheek.

"This place is awesome!" he said, the ruddy skin on his face deepening a shade as he removed his arms from Olivia's shoulders. "It's the perfect setting for discussions. We are going to accomplish things here!"

"That's what I was going for," Olivia replied with a smile, surprised at how much she had wanted Harris to respond exactly as he had. She hadn't realized, until the moment the first Oyster Bay member had entered, how much she was looking forward to this meeting.

Millay appeared shortly afterward, wearing a shredded Japanime T-shirt and a purple miniskirt. Her hair was now black and blue and had been styled so that the ends fell in sharp points against her neck. "I hate fresh paint smell," she said by way of hello. "But it sure beats the diner. I used to walk out of there reeking of bacon." She looked around. "Cool colors."

Olivia nodded at the compliment. She offered the pair wine or iced tea, telling them to help themselves and then settled into one of the club chairs. She felt that it was important not to act as hostess.

"Camden's a pretty good writer," Harris said as he poured himself tea. "I'm a bit nervous about you guys seeing my stuff after reading his work."

As he chose a seat, Laurel entered the house, her cheeks tinged pink and her wheat-colored hair escaping from a loose ponytail. "Sorry I'm late! It was really hard to get out of the house. The twins dumped their bowls of spaghetti all over the kitchen floor and I had to help the babysitter get them into the tub." She glanced around the room, her forehead creased with worry. "Were you waiting on me?"

Millay frowned. "You're not late, but Camden is. You know he likes *dramatic* entrances." She filled a wineglass to the brim, her blue and black bangs falling into her eyes as she looked down. "This is going to sound whacked, but I *swear* I just saw him as I drove past Fish Nets."

"Doing what?" Olivia inquired. "Aren't we here to critique *his* chapter?"

Blowing the bangs from her eyes, Millay shrugged. "Maybe he wanted to toss back a shot before we ripped into his writing."

Olivia doubted that. "Then you saw him

go inside?"

"Yeah, pretty much." Millay swished wine around in her mouth as though she were using mouthwash. "He was reaching out for the door when I drove by. *If* that was even him, but I don't know too many other guys who'd wear a pink shirt and white pants."

"We'll give him fifteen minutes. Twenty at the most. That should give him plenty of time to finish whatever he's doing in that place," Olivia stated crossly. She'd been anxious for Camden's opinion on her redecorating and was disappointed to have to wait for his special brand of enthusiastic praise.

"This cottage is lovely." Laurel cradled her glass of Chablis and looked around appreciatively. Digging a sheaf of crumpled pages from what appeared to be a diaper bag, she inquired, "Do you all think Blake Talbot is *really* like Camden's character? I mean — the drugs, the girls, the drinking — that seems like regular rock star behavior, but Bradley seemed really *dark*."

"And angry," Harris agreed.

The group talked animatedly about Camden's chapter until Olivia finally interrupted by saying, "This is ridiculous! We're starting the critique without the author."

Harris checked his watch. "Guess his

fifteen minutes are up."

"Kind of like fame," Millay muttered under her breath. "Well, let's go drag his white-pants-wearing ass out of Fish Nets. For once in my life, I did my homework. I put time into this thing and I'm not letting my efforts go to waste." She shook the paper sheaves.

"I've always wanted to see the inside of that bar," Harris stated sheepishly. "But my friends are all afraid to go there."

Laurel also seemed frightened by the suggestion and looked to Olivia for guidance.

Olivia recalled her declaration that she'd never cross the bar's threshold, but she was so befuddled and irritated by Camden's behavior that she decided the gossip writer owed them an explanation. Hadn't she gone through plenty of energy and expense to prepare this cottage for *his* writing group?

Rising from her chair, like a monarch preparing to utter a declaration of war, she pulled her car keys from her pocket and gave them an angry shake. Her poodle leapt to his feet at the sound. "Come along, Haviland." Olivia marched to the front door. "We're going into town."

Millay led her friends into Fish Nets with the sort of pride one exhibits when inviting another person into a well-ordered and attractive home. Olivia was relieved she'd decided to leave Haviland in the car because she was certain he would have been unhappy over having to breathe the smoke-polluted air while walking on such a disgusting floor. The gray cement had turned nearly black with the sticky grime of spilled beer, cigarette ash, discarded chewing gum, and mucus. It was a foul film that could never completely be cleansed off.

The decorations were exactly what one would except in a bar named Fish Nets. Cracked buoys, faded life jackets, and life rings no doubt stolen from dry docks up and down the North Carolina coast were haphazardly grouped with an array of plastic lobsters, fish, and rusty, menacing hooks. Photographs of sports fishermen exhibiting their finned prizes by the gills were nearly obscured by thick coats of ash-flecked dust.

"Any sign of Camden?" Harris asked nervously as they all looked around.

Millay was right, Olivia thought. *A man with white pants and a pink shirt would never blend in with the bar's regulars.*

Fish Nets was filled with Oyster Bay's working-class citizens. Some of their faces, the fishermen in particular, were dark and wrinkled as walnut shells. The women had long stringy hair, tight jeans, and generous amounts of exposed cleavage. The conversation of the patrons closest to the door came to an abrupt halt when the group of writers arrived.

"These *your* friends, Millay?" A fat woman with a rose tattoo curling up the side of her neck laughed.

"Hey, Darla. Yeah, they're with me, but I gotta go talk to Mack, so catch you later." Millay wove her way toward the bar and began to shout at the bartender over the music, which was louder on the other side of the room.

As there were no speakers where Olivia stood, she could not have misheard the old man in a pair of stained overalls. "If it ain't Willy Wade's lassie. All grown up now, ain't ya? I'd know that white hair and those ocean eyes anywhere. You still lookin' for your papa, girlie?" He took a deep draught of his beer. " 'Cause he ain't ever comin' home. The fog carried him back to the sea. It's how men like us are meant to go." He pointed a gnarled hand at Olivia. "You can't take from the sea all your life and not have 'er claim somethin' as payment. 'Tis always been that way."

Stepping away from the man, Olivia crossed her arms protectively over her chest and rubbed at the goose bumps that had sprouted across the surface of her skin. The man drank his beer and stared at her. She never thought she'd be so relieved to see the indigo tint of Millay's hair appear before her.

"Mack didn't see Camden himself. He was too busy, but he heard Camden was in the alley, which seems kinda weird," Millay said with a frown. "There's nothing back there but the Dumpster, empty kegs, and the *scratch, scratch* of mongo rats slinking around."

Laurel uttered a little groan. "I'm not too fond of rats."

"I'm not either," Olivia sympathized. "But we've come this far. Lead on, Millay."

Avoiding the sharp, curious eyes of the fishermen, she propelled the young woman forward and then trod closely on Millay's heels as the crowd parted before them, casting unfriendly looks their way.

The back door was unlocked. As Millay pushed on it, the solid metal slammed against the exterior brick wall with a loud clang. A cloud of smoke escaped from within and quickly mingled with the salt-tinged night air. The rear of the building was dark and the sky was moonless. Olivia could barely make out the shape of the

Dumpster twenty yards away and she certainly saw no sign of Camden. All was silent.

"There's no one here now," Harris pointed out, looking to the left and right.

Laurel repeated the motion. "Are there any lights back here?" she asked Millay.

"Yeah. Right he—" Her words were cut short. "Well, there *used* to be a light. The bulb's been smashed." She kicked at some fragments with the tip of her boot.

Olivia didn't like the sound of that.

"Someone did that recently?" Laurel knit her hands together. Her voice sounded shrill and small in the darkness.

Millay shrugged, as though acts of vandalism were a natural part of the bar environment. "It was fine as of two this morning. I should know. *I'm* the one who took out the trash."

Harris turned to the right and began to walk the length of the building. The others followed, but Olivia moved off to the left. Something propelled her in the opposite direction.

Around the corner of Fish Nets, in a narrow alley separating the bar from the pizza parlor next door, she found Camden.

His back was against the wall and his head sagged over his chest. Even in the dark, Olivia knew that the black stain spread across the center of Camden's shirt was blood. For a moment, she couldn't shake the thought that the slick blemish covering his upper torso resembled a pair of distorted butterfly wings.

The amount of blood and the slackness of Camden's body told Olivia that her friend was dead — that his throat had probably been slit. She waited for a powerful feeling of horror or grief or anger to flood her, but she was completely overtaken by numbness.

Suddenly, she was a girl again. She saw the police car pull in front of the house, saw the pair of solemn officers remove their hats, heard the exchange of mumbles in the hall as the news was delivered to her father. She watched from her bedroom window as he walked down the path to the dock, heading toward the dinghy — a bottle of whiskey in one hand and her mother's purse in the other. He rowed away without even glancing up at the cottage where his daughter was facing the greatest shock of her young life. Alone.

Olivia shook herself free from the grip of memory but couldn't move a muscle. She was paralyzed by the numbness, trapped between the past and the present.

She didn't know how long she stood staring down at Camden's body when Millay's voice finally pierced the stillness. After releasing a string of high-pitched expletives, the younger woman grabbed on to Olivia's arm, hard.

"Olivia!" She tugged until the older woman blinked and pulled away. "Don't lose it on me! There's something written here! Look!" Millay flicked a lighter and tiptoed closer to the wall.

Olivia watched as a weak circle of light illuminated three lines of text, written in glistening black spray paint. The two women read it to themselves.

"What the hell *is* that?" Millay spluttered indignantly.

"Haiku. A Japanese-style poem following a set of strict rules," Olivia answered robotically and then, her mind regaining a sense of focus, sent Millay away to forestall the others from seeing Camden's corpse and to call for help.

Forcing her eyes on the glossy, spidery letters, Olivia tried to detach herself from the knowledge that the body of someone she liked and admired was slumped on the ground before her. As if Camden were still alive, she whispered to him, "Your murderer is a member of the literati."

She dug out a pen and a small notebook from her purse and copied down the poem.

Even when heavy footfalls alerted her that she was no longer alone, her eyes — flickering with a bright anger — remained fixated on the words on the wall.

His words are silenced —
An orchard in winter, where
Apple seeds slumber

CHAPTER 5

Dying is a very dull, dreary affair. And my advice to you is to have nothing whatever to do with it.

— W. SOMERSET MAUGHAM

Olivia felt a blanket being draped over her shoulders. It was made of coarse, gray wool and its semi-stale odor reminded her of the horse blankets she'd placed on the curved back of her favorite mare at boarding school.

Clutching the rough fabric together at the base of her throat, she turned to meet the solemn stare of Chief Rawlings.

"I understand you found Mr. Ford's body. Do you feel up to answering a few questions, Ms. Limoges?"

After a pause, Olivia nodded. "Yes."

The chief placed a strong hand on her upper arm and pivoted her, so that her line of sight fell away from the gossip writer's sprawled form. His touch made her aware of the other people milling around the alley. It seemed that suddenly, like a colony of ants erupting from underground, uniformed men and women were everywhere. They were accompanied by bright lights and sharp noises — the cacophony of expressionless professionals doing their jobs in the midst of a scene that had rendered Olivia Limoges completely immobile in its awfulness.

Camera flashes erupted like lightning, footsteps echoed in the tight space between the buildings, and a dozen voices spoke in low, urgent whispers as radio crackles from the hips of the policemen fired into the night air like gunshots from a small-caliber weapon.

"Did you see anyone else here with Mr. Ford?" the chief asked her.

"No, just him, the way he is now." Olivia looked toward the end of the alley, where the lights from a police cruiser cast blue shadows into the narrow opening. "We only came down to the bar because he didn't show up for our writer's group meeting." Her confident and straight-backed posture sagged by a fraction. It was subtle, just a marginal slump in the shoulders, but Chief Rawlings was the type of man to notice such a small detail.

He studied her on the sly, but Olivia could sense his scrutiny and she shrunk a little further inside herself. She knew he was aware that this was not the first time someone had discovered her, all alone, in the middle of a frightening tableau. She had been found by a passing fishing trawler when her father disappeared, shivering in the bottom of a rowboat, and when they brought her back to Oyster Bay's docks, half the town had been there to witness her pathetic disembarkation from the vessel. Her grandmother had been among those waiting onshore. After giving Olivia a cold, unpracticed embrace, she swept the orphan into her chauffeured Lincoln and drove right out of Oyster Bay.

Olivia knew the chief had lived in Oyster Bay for most of his life, and for a moment, she wondered if he recognized her as the bedraggled, towheaded, and barefoot girl plucked from the fog. If so, he made no indication, his features creased in genuine concern. "Look here, Ms. Limoges. My boys and I are going to have our hands full questioning the bar patrons," he remarked gently, his eyes sweeping over his industrious officers. "Why don't you run on home and get yourself something warm to drink? Maybe a hot cup of spiked coffee or some brandy? I'll send someone by to take your statement later. You've been through enough for one night."

"I could certainly do with some scotch," Olivia murmured in relief. She removed the blanket from her shoulders and folded it into a neat square. "Thank you, Chief. I really have nothing useful to tell you at the moment, but I'll gather the other writers and try to come up with a comprehensive statement." She pushed the blanket toward him and gazed at him intently, her navy blue eyes black, mournful pools. "Please find out who did this to Camden." She didn't let go of the blanket even as his hands reached up to accept it. "I didn't know him that well, but *nothing* he did justifies this cruel and *undignified* death. Please . . ."

The chief walked with her toward the alley opening. "Believe me, I won't rest until I know what this is all about. This is my town too, ma'am, and I won't stand for this. Now go home, Ms. Limoges." His exerted his authority softly. "I need to focus on other matters."

Olivia obeyed, moving toward the parking area where she'd left the Range Rover. Part of her wanted to climb in her SUV and race home, pour a glass of Chivas Regal, and crawl into bed. That side of her didn't want to speak calmly and clearly to one of Rawlings' officers. That side wanted to ignore the doorbell, pull the covers over her head, and wash away the image of Camden's body, slumped against the brick wall like a discarded department store mannequin, by overindulging in both booze and sleep.

Yet the other, conscientious side knew she bore a responsibility. She owed it to Camden to make the right choice, and she needed to do anything possible to aid the lawmen in their search for the killer. As she strode toward the parking lot, the shock began to gradually give way to anger. When she saw the rest of the writer's group gathered around her car, her mind became clear.

"We're allowed to return to the cottage," she told them, disliking the coldness in her voice. "Someone from the police department will be by to take our statements later on."

The other writers were visibly relieved to be able to stay together and escape the dark. Olivia turned away from them in order to check on her dog.

Haviland barked out a cheerful greeting at the sight of his mistress and Olivia pushed her fingers through the crack in the passenger window, comforted by the rough moisture of her poodle's tongue. "Oh,

Captain," she murmured to her dog and tried to keep her voice from cracking.

No one else spoke. Laurel was crying and Harris had his arm around her. He looked wide-eyed and pale, while Millay's gaze was fastened on the ground. Her arms were crossed around her chest in a protective posture. No one seemed keen to move just yet.

"Listen," Olivia began again, forcing gentleness into her tone. "Someone did this to him. To Camden. I know we're all trying to understand what happened tonight and *nothing* makes any sense at this moment, but we have to clear out and let the chief do his job." She removed her car keys from her purse. "And we need to help by writing down anything that might be important while it's still fresh in our minds."

"I'm scared!" Laurel exclaimed, her lips quivering. "What if the murderer's still around? He could be in the bar or driving through one of our neighborhoods this very second! He could know *us* or have *seen* us with Camden!" Her eyes darted around the parking lot. "Who would do that to another human being? Millay said his throat . . ." She couldn't continue.

Olivia reached out and put a hand on Laurel's shoulder. "Don't think about that now. We'll focus on any details we know about Camden. About his life, not his death. Okay?"

The tender touch seemed to make Laurel cry all the harder and Olivia felt herself whispering, "Hush, hush," as though she were trying to calm a bereft child. "Come on, everyone. We'll go back to my place and make some coffee. Let's get out of the night."

That last statement echoed with Laurel. "That-that sounds good," she stammered. "I'll call Steve from the cottage so he won't worry."

Everyone piled into Olivia's SUV. Haviland stepped onto the center console and nuzzled Olivia with his head. She put an arm around him, and for a moment, buried her face in the fur of his neck, inhaling his familiar scent of wet sand and fresh soil and eucalyptus shampoo. When she released her hold of the poodle, she felt as though the ground had finally returned beneath her feet.

"To your seat, Captain," she ordered while blinking back tears. She buckled his safety belt and turned toward home.

Back at the cottage, she asked Harris to switch on the gas logs in the living room fireplace and for Millay to brew a pot of strong coffee. Laurel went straight for the phone set up in the small office adjacent to the living room. Olivia winced as she listened as the distraught younger woman sought solace from her husband, only to be denied.

"Is that all you have to say to me after what I've been through?" she queried pitifully. But Steve's reply obviously triggered something in Laurel and with a shout of anger, she slammed the phone receiver back into the cradle.

"I'm sorry," she told Olivia as she exited the office. "I just could *not* take one of his lectures on how I belong at home. Not tonight, no sir!"

Olivia nodded, pleased to see that Laurel had more spunk than one might credit her with. "I understand. Why don't you sit down in front of the fire and I'll get you something warm to drink. We could all use something to steady our nerves."

As she hadn't supplied the cottage with shot glasses, thinking they'd hardly be necessary for informal meetings, Olivia poured splashes of Chivas Regal into disposable coffee cups and distributed them to the others.

"Down the hatch." Millay raised her glass and tossed back the contents without as much as a flinch.

Harris tried to emulate the motion, but couldn't help from grimacing slightly after he'd swallowed. Laurel held her nose, downed her drink, and slapped the empty cup on the end table beside her.

"I'd like another, please," she said in a stronger voice.

Olivia shook her head as Millay stood, heading for the bottle. "Why don't I stir a little into our coffee this time around? We have to stay awake and alert in order to make our statements."

Hands cradling cups of laced coffee, the writers positioned themselves close to the fire and to one another. Each of them silently called Camden to mind.

"He was so charming." Laurel spoke first. "Everyone he met liked him from the get-go. Who'd want to hurt him?"

"Maybe he was simply in the wrong place at the wrong time," Harris suggested. "The crowd in that place looks like they could turn rough pretty quickly."

Millay snorted. "Yeah, like lightning-strike quick. I could pick out a half a dozen fishermen who might snap because you looked at them sideways. Shit, six or seven of them are totally capable of killing somebody. But to write poetry afterward? That's not their

106

MO. Seems more like a deranged college prof on an acid trip to me."

"But what was Camden doing in Fish Nets in the first place?" Laurel demanded. "It's not like he'd go there to make new friends."

Olivia couldn't help but smile. "If you're referring to Camden making sexual advances to one of the patrons, I can't see that happening either. Millay? Are you certain you saw him enter the bar?"

Running slim fingers through her blue and black hair, Millay exhaled loudly in vexation. "No. Like I said *before,* I only saw him reaching out for the door handle. Then I drove past. I just figured he was buying cigarettes or something." She shrugged. "I was, like, a mile away before I could even believe it was *him.* Camden and Fish Nets didn't go together, ya know?"

"Our eyes see what our brain expects them to see," Harris said in her defense.

A flicker of admiration entered Millay's dark eyes. "Exactly." She turned back to Olivia. "I wish I did know if he went inside for sure, but I don't. I'll ask around once the cops leave. No one's going to tell them a thing. Those guys keep things close to the chest."

Laurel shifted in her seat, tucking her legs

beneath her and smoothing out the fabric of her khaki linen trousers. Backlit by the flickering flames in the fireplace, her hair glowed like a golden crown and she instantly seemed years younger. Suddenly, the visage of another, even younger woman sprang into Olivia's mind.

"Wait a moment," she said, nearly rising to her feet. "Camden and I listened in when Blake Talbot was discussing his plans for yesterday evening with his girlfriend. From what we overheard, Blake intended to meet some people at Fish Nets."

"And since Camden's writing a book based on the Talbot family, he might have gone down there to find out what Blake had been doing there?" Laurel deduced.

Millay shook her head. "No way a rich kid like Blake shows up at my bar. *His* kind does *not* hang out there. They'd be at The Cleat and Anchor or the Dorsal Fin, guzzling their microbrews and checking out the waitresses while they stuff their faces with calamari or lobster bites or whatever you eat when you make more dough than all the drinkers in my bar put together."

The other writers took notice of the proprietary tone in Millay's voice.

Olivia cleared her throat. "No one's assuming one of your regular, ah, patrons, is responsible for Camden's death, Millay. On the contrary, I can't see that any of those men and women would have had a connection with him at all. Whoever did this wanted to make a point. Thus, the poem."

"What did it say?" Laurel asked nervously.

"Something about orchards and apples," Millay replied angrily. "A bunch of crap that made absolutely no sense!"

Recalling that she'd written the haiku in the small notebook she kept in her purse, Olivia dug it out and reread what she had written, frowning over the odd, horticultural imagery.

"What if Camden never went inside?" Harris wondered aloud, his eyes fixed on the shivering flames. "What if he found some clue in the alley?"

"You may be on to something there, Harris. Blake implied that the 'business dealings' he planned for last night were rather on the shady side." Olivia laid the notebook on the sofa and Millay instantly picked it up and began to study the poem. "Perhaps Camden found something not meant for his ears."

"Or his pen." Millay stabbed at the paper with her index finger. Olivia noticed that the young woman's nails bore the remnants of a deep purple polish and were clipped very short, as though to prevent her from chewing them. "The first line of the poem says, 'His words are silenced.' "

A little gasp escaped Laurel's throat. The fear in her eyes shimmered in the firelight. "That can only mean one thing," she breathed. "The killer knew what Camden did for a living."

"And there aren't too many people in Oyster Bay who'd be threatened by the appearance of a celebrity gossip writer," Harris pointed out. "Except maybe Blake or one of the other Talbots."

Olivia gestured at the notebook in Millay's hands. "Either Blake Talbot's educational background included instruction on how to pen this particular form of poetry, or he had dealings with another person who couldn't afford to be exposed and has been watching Camden's every move."

"Someone who created an impromptu haiku?" Harris seemed doubtful.

There was an authoritative rap on the front door and Olivia turned her head toward the sound but made no other move. She was too busy thinking. "It doesn't read like a spontaneous piece of writing. It feels specific, tailored, and . . ." She glanced anxiously at the other writers. "Premeditated."

■ ■ ■ ■

The blast of the foghorn woke Olivia the next morning. The deep, resonating noise caused her to imagine a trumpeting leviathan surfacing from the cold depths of the sea.

Still weary from the night before, she stayed in bed another thirty minutes, listening to the steady, repetitive tolls as the horn warned incoming vessels of the proximity of the shallows.

To Olivia, the sound was as familiar as the beat of her own heart. She remembered, after she'd moved away, how the noises in other parts of the world failed to offer the same level of comfort as the rush of the incoming tide, the blare of a foghorn, the high squawk of a gull, or the clanging of a ship's bell.

Haviland jumped up on the bed and burrowed under the covers in search of his mistress's hand. Olivia stuffed it under the pillow, knowing her poodle would lick her palm until she rose and served him breakfast.

"Five more minutes," she promised, briefly reaching out to scratch Haviland beneath the chin. She watched the tangerine-colored light filter through the bare glass of the master bedroom's wall of windows.

The foghorn fell silent and Olivia continued to pat Haviland, thinking of Camden.

Last night, when she'd answered the knock on the door of the lighthouse keeper's cottage, a fresh-faced officer named Cook had strutted in. He assessed them with a cocky glance and bossed them about as though they were schoolchildren. He'd taken their statements and asked a few standard questions, but his mind was clearly elsewhere. Olivia had the feeling the young lawman viewed his being sent out to the lighthouse when the real action was happening downtown an insult to his abilities.

Irritated by his arrogance and disinterest in their observations, Olivia strongly suggested he radio Chief Rawlings and track down Blake Talbot as soon as possible.

"Officer Cook." Olivia walked over to the policeman and did her best to stand even taller than her five-eleven frame. "You might be handing the chief a suspect on a silver platter. Camden Ford was our *friend* and we want to see justice done. We've told you all we know, now please share our information with your superior."

Cook bristled at her choice of words and

informed the writer's group that he knew how to do his job.

Millay rose from her position on the couch and came to stand next to Olivia. "Then prove it! Stop pissing around here and find out what Blake Talbot was up to over the last twenty-four hours!" she shouted. "I believe that's called 'chasing down an alibi' in cop talk."

Listening to Millay, Olivia had to fight to keep from smiling.

Thus bullied by the pair of aggressive women, Cook retreated, but only after issuing a final command that the Bayside Book Writers needed to make an appearance at the station first thing in the morning to review and sign their official statements.

"We'll be there," Harris promised. He opened the door and practically shoved the truculent officer out.

After Cook had left, Laurel began to weep again. "I'm sorry, everybody. I'm just so tired. All I want to do is put on my nightgown and sleep for a week. It's selfish, I know, but I'm scared and mixed up and mad all at once." She gazed at Olivia with moist eyes. "I wish I could be strong like you."

"Go on home," Olivia had answered quietly. "There's nothing else we can do tonight, and though it might not show, I'm every bit as muddled and shaken, I assure you."

As the tumult of emotions reflecting the onset of grief assaulted the writers, they said good night to one another and dispersed.

Now, only a handful of hours later, Olivia watched the light turn from an orange pink to a yellow-tinged white. Finally, she kicked off her covers and went into the kitchen to brew coffee. Haviland sat in front of the door, waiting to be let outside.

"Make it brief, Captain. I'm going to fix your breakfast and we'll have a quick walk before we have to go into town."

Olivia removed a covered casserole dish filled with organic ground beef cooked in beef broth from the refrigerator. She put water on to boil and poured herself a cup of coffee. While she waited for the water, she placed a bowl of instant grits in the microwave. By the time she'd cooked a cup of rice and mixed it with some fresh peas in a large stockpot, she was done with her cereal. As soon as Haviland reappeared, panting and shaking his ears friskily, she served him his meal and then walked out to the deck to eat a peach.

She listened to the rush of the waves curling onto the shore and relished the ripe, tender fruit. She felt a sudden, unexpected pang of guilt for experiencing such a moment of pleasure and peace.

"Poor Camden," she whispered into the faint, salty breeze.

Later, she and Haviland took a brisk walk along the shoreline and then Olivia changed out of her sweatpants and dressed in black cotton slacks and a chartreuse scoop-neck T-shirt for her trip to the station.

As she neared Main Street, the bells from the Methodist church began to chime. A second later, those from the Baptist church rang out and the two melodies overlapped each other. Instead of sounding disjointed, the effect was that of a melodious echo and Olivia rolled down her window in order to welcome the music into her car.

On such a morning, she thought, *it doesn't seem possible that last night truly happened.*

The Oyster Bay Police Department had been located in the same charming brick building since the late forties. Complete with large arched windows and a façade covered by ivy, it stood across the street from the modern, boxlike two-story building that housed the sheriff's department and the county jail.

One could walk out the side door of the police station and arrive at a small square

115

with neatly trimmed grass, carefully tended flower beds, sets of wooden benches, and a flagpole flying both the American and the state of North Carolina flags. Just beyond this tidy little park was the county courthouse. Renovated within the last fifteen years, the courthouse was a Greek-revival structure with a cornerstone dated 1836. It was whitewashed brick with chunky white Ionic columns and a frieze carved with an image of the state seal. By far the most impressive building in Oyster Bay, it basked in the early summer sun as though enjoying a well-deserved day of rest.

"You can accompany me into the station, Captain," Olivia informed her delighted poodle as she pulled into a spot near the courthouse. "They have a K-9 unit, after all, so they can't protest your presence. Do you remember Officer Greta? We ran into her during your last grooming appointment."

Haviland barked excitedly. "Quite an attractive and intelligent German shepherd, I would agree. But she's on the clock when she's here, Captain, so no flirting. This is all business. Understood?"

Snorting his assent, Haviland trotted next to Olivia. He'd never taken to a leash and, from the time he was a puppy, had re-

116

sponded to verbal commands with incredible acuity. Since her return to Oyster Bay, Olivia had been chastised about leash laws by policemen, fretful mothers, and a bevy of deliverymen (the most vocal being a terrified UPS driver), but she would rather pay a host of fines than force her poodle to wear such an undignified contraption.

"My dog is smarter than most humans," was her customary answer, but if someone persisted in lecturing her on leash laws, Olivia would launch into a list of classes she and Haviland had taken to ensure that he'd received top-level training in both hand signals and voice commands. If she felt especially talkative, Olivia would brag about Haviland's agility and tracking abilities, citing the number of awards he'd won in the canine classroom.

The locals had grown accustomed to seeing Haviland walking alongside his mistress, so when the pair entered the station, their gaits perfectly matched, the female desk sergeant blinked in surprise but said nothing. Olivia wondered if she had Chief Rawlings to thank for receiving no argument regarding Haviland's presence in the building.

"I'm here to give a formal statement about last night," Olivia informed the middle-aged woman wearing a snug uniform. "I'd prefer to see Chief Rawlings if I may."

The woman shook her head and set her lips into a firm, uncompromising line. "Sorry, but he's real busy."

"Of course," Olivia capitulated and took a seat in one of the lobby's uncomfortable wooden chairs. Haviland sat on his haunches next to her right leg, his soft, brown eyes alight with curiosity.

Five minutes later, Olivia looked up to see who would be taking her formal statement and was most unhappy to be met with the surly visage of Officer Cook.

"Long night?" she asked by way of greeting.

"Yeah." The policeman eyed Haviland distrustfully for a moment, even though he'd seen the poodle the evening before, and gestured for Olivia to follow him down the carpeted hallway.

They passed by several offices and when Olivia spotted a placard with Chief Rawlings' name, she peeked around the partially closed door. The chief was on the phone, but he caught the movement from the corner of his eye and waved her inside.

Without bothering to alert Officer Cook that she was deviating from the current course, Olivia stepped into the office, waited for Haviland to pass across the threshold, and closed the door.

"Yes, sir," Chief Rawlings spoke solemnly into the receiver. "I'll send an officer to collect you at the airport. He'll be there by the time you land. Again, I am truly sorry to be the bearer of such news. Yes. Good-bye."

Replacing the receiver, the chief pressed his hands over his eyes and sighed. "I haven't had to make too many of those phone calls during my tenure in this office, thank the Lord, but they are the greatest challenge of this job."

Olivia examined the lawman's stained and wrinkled uniform shirt, the shadow of an auburn beard darkening his chin, and the discoloration under his eyes. As he sipped from an oversized coffee cup, his head fell into a strip of sunlight pouring in through the window blinds. For the first time, Olivia noticed that the chief's hair was tinged with hints of red and that his hazel eyes resembled the muddy green of a deep woods pond.

"Were you speaking with a family member? A relative of Camden's?" she inquired respectfully.

Rawlings shook his head. "Mr. Ford's wallet held no clues in that area, but there was a business card for a publicist based in LA.

I called her last night and she informed me that Camden's emergency contact was his, ah, partner. Mr. Cosmo Volakis is already en route here. Of course, it will take him most of the day, seeing as he's coming from the west coast, but I got the sense he caught the first flight out. Poor guy. It'll be the longest plane ride of his life, I'd imagine."

There was an impatient tap on the office door. Rawlings shot Officer Cook a questioning glance.

"I was *supposed* to take this woman's statement, sir. Then, she just up and disappeared on me." The young man gave Olivia an accusatory stare.

Frowning, Rawlings said, "I'd like to speak to *Ms. Limoges* personally, Cook. I'll return her to you when I'm through. In the meantime, I'd like you to get an update from the coroner."

"Yes, sir!" Cook immediately brightened and Olivia was reminded of the policeman's youth. He probably hated dealing with paperwork and had joined the force in search of action and excitement.

"Were you able to question Blake Talbot?" Olivia asked once they were alone again.

"Mr. Talbot had little to tell," Rawlings grudgingly admitted. "He provided us with an alibi and then gave me his lawyer's number in case I should have anything further to discuss." His face darkened. "I can tolerate the Talbots' money, their attempts to buy up every spare acre in Oyster Bay, and even the lack of imagination of that new condo development, but I cannot stand rudeness. And *that* boy! Well, let's just say I'd have loved to put him over my knee and teach him some manners."

Olivia smiled. "Some discipline would probably do him good." She reached down and stroked Haviland's curls. "Did you find any helpful witnesses? Did Camden actually go into the bar? What business did Blake have there?"

Rawlings drew in an impatient breath. "Ms. Limoges, this is an open case and I'm not at liberty to discuss it with a civilian. I shouldn't even have said what I just said." He sank back in his chair, as though his spine was too tired to support the weight of his torso.

The chief's words settled for a moment. Rawlings looked out the window at the park and Olivia looked at him. There was something appealing about his gentleness and intelligence.

"It doesn't sound as though you've got any solid leads," Olivia remarked dejectedly. "Yet this crime is so unlike our town. The gruesomeness, the poem, the risk of being seen in the alleyway. It's as though the killer wanted publicity."

Rawlings raised his hand to stop her from continuing, but Olivia plowed on. "I really *liked* Camden Ford, Chief. I liked his energy, his ability to bring people together, his verve. All I want is to assist in any way I can. Our writer's group . . ." She paused, noting how good it felt to use such a pronoun. "We can work on unraveling the mystery of the haiku. Who better to help with a literary conundrum? Officer Cook?" Her tone was derisive. "Or us?"

"I'm no novice when it comes to poetry, Ms. Limoges," Rawlings reminded her of his propensity for reading verse for pleasure.

"And I wouldn't doubt you could solve a poetic riddle during normal circumstances," Olivia conceded. "But you'll soon have the media to face, evidence to examine, and hopefully, witnesses to question. Surely it is not outside the bounds of the law to allow well-meaning civilians to put forth a few theories about this particular clue."

She could see Rawlings relenting. "I suppose there's no harm in that." He handed her a business card. "My cell phone number is listed here. Feel free to call me anytime."

Olivia rose. "I can find my way back to

Officer Cook." Haviland got to his feet and leisurely joined her in the doorway. As Olivia reached out to grab the handle, something prompted her to turn back to Rawlings. He was regarding her with his kind smile. "And if you need to talk to someone about the case, when you're off-duty of course, stop by The Boot Top. I'll buy you a drink."

His smile grew warmer. "Thank you, Ms. Limoges. Before this is all said and done, I may just take you up on that offer."

Olivia found Officer Cook at a cluster of desks in a large room at the end of the hall. Harris was seated across from him.

"Hello!" Harris beamed, clearly welcoming the sight of a friendly face.

"I'm glad to see you," Oliva said and sat down next to Harris. She noticed that the red flush across her friend's cheeks, nose, and forehead was exacerbated. It looked raw and irritated. No doubt stress caused Harris's skin condition to become more pronounced.

It's such a shame, Olivia thought. *He'd be quite handsome without that red face.* She made a mental note to ask the aesthetician at the spa she frequented in New Bern if there were treatments available to alleviate the symptoms of rosacea.

"Sign here. We'll call you if we need more information." Officer Cook slapped a piece of paper on his desk. After Harris signed, Cook dismissed him without so much as a thank-you.

"May I speak to my friend for a moment?" Olivia inquired and then, without waiting for Cook's permission, took Harris by the elbow and led him several steps away from the desk. "Do you have all of Camden's chapters?"

Harris shook his head. "No, we just have the one. I know he wrote more, but I've never seen the rest of his work. Why?"

"Because if Blake Talbot has anything to do with Camden's death, the reason might be hidden in Camden's writing." Olivia cast a glance over her shoulder. Cook was scowling at her while tapping a ballpoint pen impatiently against his computer keyboard. "Perhaps by getting to know *Bradley Talcott* more intimately, we might discover what recent scandal Camden was investigating regarding the Talbots."

Harris turned the idea over for a long second. "That seems like a real possibility. Are you going to tell the cops?"

"Yes, but I also think *we* could assist the authorities by reviewing the manuscript ourselves. Where was Camden staying?"

"At The Yellow Lady." Harris touched Olivia's arm. "But we're not going to be allowed in his room, are we? Isn't that room and all Camden's stuff, you know, off limits now?"

"Not to Mr. Cosmo Volakis. He was Camden's partner and he's on his way here from LA." Olivia's eyes narrowed with determination. She leaned toward Harris and whispered, "Set up an emergency meeting of the Bayside Book Writers. Anytime is good for me, but make sure *everyone* can attend. *I'm* going to offer my chauffeuring services to the good officer here, and, come hell or high water, I intend to get ahold of a copy of Camden's work-in-progress for us to review."

"How can you be so confident?" Harris's tone was a mixture of admiration and doubt.

"Because Camden's lover is going to want justice, even more than we do. And I cannot go on living my everyday life knowing that someone is out there, walking the streets of Oyster Bay, breathing the sea air and letting the sun fall on his face, when Camden isn't. Camden's life has been stolen from him, in *our* town, and we have to do everything in our power to see that the killer pays for what he did."

Harris clenched his jaw and nodded, his

eyes filled with resolve. Olivia caught a glimpse of the mettle coexisting with the young man's kindness. Turning toward Cook, Olivia pasted on the most winsome smile she could muster.

"I am *so* sorry to keep you waiting, Officer," she gushed. "I know you must have a dozen tasks of *real* significance to complete today. Please. Tell me what you need me to do."

Looking quite satisfied, the officer leaned back in his chair, laced his fingers together, and tried his best to exude power and authority. "I just need you to review and sign your statement, Ms. Limoges. I doubt there's anything else *you* could do to help *us.*"

Nodding humbly, Olivia said, "There may be *one* little errand I could run on behalf of the Oyster Bay Police Department, ensuring your talents or those of another valuable officer aren't wasted providing limo service for the victim's *boyfriend.* I hear he's on his way as we speak."

Cook looked torn, but clearly he wanted to see some real action and he didn't feel like acting as a chauffeur would qualify.

He took a manly swig of soda. "All right, Ms. Limoges. You can pick him up, but I'm gonna tell you how it's gonna play out and you're gonna follow my *exact* directions. Understand?"

"Of course." Olivia smiled demurely and gave Officer Cook her undivided attention.

CHAPTER 6

Parting is all we know of heaven and all we need to know of hell.

— EMILY DICKINSON

Upon leaving the station, Olivia found she didn't feel like going home. She was restless, but most of Oyster Bay's businesses were closed on Sunday, so there was little to do but attend church services or go out to eat. Olivia didn't want to do either, so she decided to stop by her restaurant and busy herself with mindless paperwork.

The Boot Top Bistro had recently added a Sunday brunch to its list of offerings and the churchgoers were streaming into the restaurant as Olivia and Haviland pulled into the parking lot. Plump matrons in pastel skirt suits led their pressed and polished families like clucking hens gathering chicks to the feed pile. Glowering teenagers, pained over being separated from cell phones, iPods, and handheld video games, trailed after the rest of their kin as though hoping to appear unrelated to those who caused them such acute embarrassment merely by existing.

Normally, the sight of so many patrons filing into The Boot Top would have put Olivia in an agreeable mood, but she felt completely out of sorts. It wasn't only Camden's tragic death that bothered her, but the feelings of powerlessness that accompanied his murder.

Bursting into the kitchen through the back door, Olivia was greeted by her staff, but she merely waved them off and headed for her office, a tiny, windowless room next to the dry goods pantry. Michel followed her, Haviland right on the chef's heels, clearly hoping to receive a savory treat.

"I do have something for you, my friend. *Une moment.*" Michel smiled at the poodle but wouldn't pet him while he was in the midst of food preparation. "Olivia, I heard what happened to your writer friend." Michel worriedly studied his employer. "Are you sure you want to be here? Georges has things well under control."

Georges served as both maître d' and general manager.

"Last time I checked, this was *my* restaurant and I could come and go as I pleased!" Olivia snapped and then immediately relented. "My apologies, Michel. I shouldn't be directing my ire at you. I simply cannot stand to sit around, idle, and hope for things to turn out as they ought."

Michel nodded. Another type A personality, he understood her need to take action. "The police don't know your friend, do they? He's an outsider?"

"Camden? He was a gossip columnist from Los Angeles." She pictured Camden's silk shirts and flawlessly creased trousers. "Though I'm sure most of them noticed him. He was rather flamboyant for our conservative little town." Absently, Olivia pressed several pencils into an automatic sharpener and then, satisfied with their sharpness, lined them up neatly on her desk calendar. "But I see what you're saying — that it would be easier to find his killer if we really knew Camden Ford. Unfortunately, I consider myself his most recent acquaintance, so I need to squeeze as much information as I can out of the person who knew him best."

Michel looked intrigued. "Who would that be? His mother?"

"His lover. I'm picking him up at the Raleigh-Durham airport early this evening,"

Olivia answered and then grinned slyly as an idea struck. "Michel, darling, how would you like to assign one of your assistants a *small* task? As a personal favor to me?"

Bowing from the waist, Michel said, "Anything for you. You need only ask."

"I'd like a picnic dinner of sorts. A basket brimming with the type of delicacies to loosen the tongue of a stranger." She looked up at the chef in appeal. "Can you make it fancy yet comforting?"

Her unusual request seemed to please Michel to no end. He stood a fraction taller and straightened his pristine, white hat. "I'll see to it myself. Robbie and Jeremy are perfectly capable of making omelets Florentine and crab Benedict. *This* requires a delicate hand." He displayed the briefest of sulks. "I know these brunches are profitable, but they're rather unadventurous for someone of my talents."

Olivia glanced at him with a trace of amusement. "You don't have to work Sundays, Michel. I already told you that. You work too much as is."

"It beats being at home," he murmured, and Olivia knew he was referring to his recent breakup with his girlfriend. Personally, she felt the end of his affair with a married woman was a good thing. Besides,

Michel was a born optimist, and despite the lovers' drama-rich parting, he wouldn't be down for long. Even now, he quickly shook off his melancholy and turned his thoughts to what he knew best: food. "Let's see. I think I'll pack some crisp herb crostini with goat cheese, avocado stuffed with chicken salad and dill, cubed watermelon and mango with a lime drizzle, and perhaps a few macaroons dipped in dark chocolate. Linen napkins, small bottles of Perrier — all gracefully arranged in a deep, wicker basket. We have one around here some-where."

Rising, Olivia placed her hand on Michel's arm. "You're worth every cent of the exorbitant salary I pay you. Make sure you pack enough for three."

Michel shook his head. "I'll wrap up something else for the Captain. Neither fruit nor macaroons are to his taste."

Olivia laughed. "Of course not. Now get back in that kitchen or I'll make you operate an omelet station out in the dining room."

Flipping a dish towel over his shoulder, Michel blew air noisily through pursed lips. "You wouldn't dare. The first sign of a rolling cart with fixings for Belgian waffles and I'll walk right out the door."

"Don't worry. I wouldn't dream of insulting the staff in such a way. Food preparation belongs in the kitchen. Still, the restaurant does seem rather full. Perhaps I should raise the brunch prices? I don't want to take any business away from Grumpy's."

Michel left Olivia to her musings. As soon as she was alone, she logged on to her computer and typed the first line of the haiku written over Camden's body into Google's search box.

" 'His words are silenced,' " she mumbled to herself as an assortment of results appeared on the screen. "No matches. How about the second line? 'An orchard in winter.' "

She studied the links to photographs of orchards in winter and selected a page of color shots showing an apple orchard covered in snow. One of the images, called "First Frost," depicted the trees' barren branches encased in a layer of ice. The snow around the trunks was at least a foot deep and was unmarred by a single blemish. No footprints, animal tracks, or shovel cuts spoiled the pristine, blinding white surface. Olivia enlarged the picture and sat staring at it for several moments. The absolute silence of the scene was almost palpable. She could feel herself there — in the cold, beneath the gray sky. The more her eyes fixed on the image, the more clearly she could sense the stark loneliness of being the only human being around for miles.

Someone dropped a metal bowl in the kitchen and the clanging brought Olivia out of her reverie. She rubbed her arms, wondering if the air-conditioning was set too low or if the pictures of snow and ice had made her feel cold.

" 'Apple seeds slumber,' " she whispered and clicked on the next image, which captured the twisted, sharp branches of a single tree. In fact, the limbs looked as though they'd been whipped so harshly by a persistent wind that they'd bent back upon themselves. The photo created feelings of anxiety, as though the tree was in agony. Olivia had never realized that an apple tree could appear frightening, almost violent, but this one did. She exited the website and returned to the original search results.

Her quest for apple seed references led her to pages of recipe listings and advertisements for preschools, eateries, and gardening supply companies. At the bottom of the third page, there was a link to an article on the hazardous nature of cyanide. Olivia read, fascinated, about the dangers of ingesting the poison. When Haviland entered the room, licking his chops with the utmost satisfaction, she pointed at the screen.

"Listen to this, Captain. Cyanide works by preventing the blood from carrying oxygen, so a person dies quickly from asphyxiation. And even though mystery writers often describe it as having an almondlike scent, cyanide can also be completely colorless and odorless." She sighed. "It also requires a huge amount of pulverized seeds to poison someone, so I don't see any connection between cyanide and Camden's death. The apple seeds must mean something else."

Olivia absently stroked her canine companion. "Are you thinking what I'm thinking? That the haiku wasn't just about Camden? Perhaps it was a warning to others. Camden's 'words were silenced.' He was killed and therefore silenced. Because of death, he was also totally still, like an 'orchard in winter,' but that last line . . . it's almost as though the apple seeds were waiting. Do you think there will be another victim? That someone will be poisoned?"

Haviland rested his snout on her leg. Olivia stroked his head and cooed, "Don't worry, Captain. I'm just thinking aloud."

Olivia was aware that she was trying to reassure herself as much as her poodle.

After two more hours of futile research, Olivia had no clearer idea of the haiku's meaning. She'd refreshed her memory of high school English literature classes, in which she'd once known that haiku were poems made up of three lines containing five syllables in the first and last lines, and seven syllables in the second line. She was also reminded that one of the four seasons was usually referenced in the poem and that haiku were written using simple language so that a large audience could understand the imagery, yet still be awakened to a unique perspective of a familiar object, setting, or emotion.

What seemed like new information was the requirement of something called a *cut*. Appearing in the first or second line, cutting was meant to divide the short poem into two sections. Each section could have a different meaning, but the overall poem would remain cohesive. The line containing the cut would end with distinct punctuation such as a colon or a dash.

"Camden's killer is no fisherman — or a very well read one," Olivia remarked to Haviland as she drove west toward Raleigh. "He placed a cut in the first line *and* used proper punctuation according to the rules of haiku. His syllable count was also exact. I must find out more useful information about Blake Talbot. I wasted a good hour sifting through fan pages and Hollywood claptrap. The only interesting tidbit I came across was that his rock band is named Blackwater."

Haviland turned his head and stretched his neck as far over the center console as he could, avidly sniffing the air.

"You're being impolite, Captain. It is *not* time to eat. Is this how you're going to behave when Mr. Volakis is in the car?"

The poodle gave an apologetic bark and resumed his seat.

"According to Wikipedia, Blackwater is a military company based right here in the beautiful state of North Carolina." Olivia resumed her lecture. "How do you think the employees of this private security corporation feel about five spoiled twenty-two-year-olds screaming in microphones while garbed in designer fatigues and diamond-studded dog tags?"

Haviland made a rumbling noise in his throat.

Olivia laughed. "Oh, so you *did* hear the title track I played from their latest CD. I was hoping you'd be under Michel's butcher block by then, the sounds of Blackwater happily obscured as your favorite chef hacked merrily away at hapless carrots and cucumbers.

"Don't worry," she assured the poodle. "I'm not going to play a single note from 'Wreckage' ever again. Let's listen to the rest of our *Ancient Evenings* audiobook. It'll help refresh the Egyptian setting for Kamila's chapter involving . . ." She trailed off, her hand frozen on the volume knob. "I hadn't thought about my writing future, Captain. I wonder if the Bayside Book Writers will continue without Camden?"

Haviland cocked his head, giving his mistress a version of the canine shrug.

Feeling gloomy, Olivia drove the rest of the way in silence, surrendering herself to the melodious voice of the narrator as he led his listeners through the climax of Norman Mailer's tale of reincarnation set in 1100 B.C.

Upon arriving at the airport, Olivia parked in the short-term lot and informed Haviland that he'd need to wait in the car. Haviland frowned and turned his face away when Olivia reached out to pet him.

"There are limits to where you can go, Captain. I might get away with trotting you around Oyster Bay, but we'd get in trouble if we went strolling into the terminal like we owned the place."

Giving his mistress a cold, hard stare, Haviland settled down on the seat and closed his eyes.

Inside the air-conditioned terminal, Olivia joined a cluster of limo drivers waiting on one side of security. Withdrawing her own sign from her purse, Olivia stood stiffly upright next to a driver dressed in an inexpensive black suit, white shirt, and midnight blue tie.

"Excuse me." Olivia smiled at the man. "Could you tell me whether the US Air flight from Los Angeles has arrived yet?"

The driver's southern upbringing dictated he come to the aid of a woman in need. "Let me run over and check the board, ma'am. Be back in two shakes. You just wait right there." Returning quickly to his spot, he said, "The flight's landed. Probably take ten minutes for the passengers to deplane and for them to walk to this area." He noticed her sign. "You expectin' family?"

"No. I've never seen this man in my life," Olivia answered. "He's coming to attend a funeral, I'm afraid. He isn't expecting to be picked up and I'm worried he'll rush right by me."

Bowing slightly, the driver said, "Ah, I

doubt anyone would miss you, ma'am, but I could hold up the sign for you if you'd like. I know you're tall for a lady and all, but I've got that chauffeur look about me. Wouldn't want this fellow to pass you by."

Olivia handed him the sheet of cardstock with gratitude. She wanted to be able to take brief measure of Camden's lover before he became aware that he wasn't actually being picked up by a member of the Oyster Bay Police Department. Fortunately, Mr. Cosmo Volakis was easy to identify. The moment he exited the corridor adjacent to the security check, Olivia knew she was looking at Camden's significant other.

Of average height and build, Cosmo had a thatch of glossy black hair, an unlined, olive-skinned face, long, feathery eyelashes framing chestnut brown eyes, and a firm, masculine jaw. His lips were as plump as a supermodel's pout, his chin was dimpled, and his nose, though slightly hooked at the tip, gave him an air of distinction. He wore a cobalt dress shirt, a checked blazer, tailored jeans, and Italian calfskin loafers. A Louis Vuitton garment bag was slung over one shoulder and a pair of sunglasses peeked out of his breast pocket. Every woman within range glanced at Cosmo with appreciation. Several cast him openly flirtatious smiles, but he was too focused on locating his method of transportation to pay his admirers any heed.

Olivia noticed that despite the tumult of emotions he must be experiencing, Cosmo seemed outwardly calm. Still, he approached the driver beside her with hurried strides and introduced himself in a pleasant, musical voice. Olivia detected more than a trace of anxiety as he confirmed his identity.

"Are you bringing me to Oyster Bay?" he asked, perplexed. Obviously he'd been expecting to see a policeman's uniform.

"Welcome to North Carolina, sir!" the driver told Cosmo. "I'm actually just helping this lovely lady here." He pivoted toward Olivia. "Ma'am, here's your weary traveler."

Cosmo blinked in surprise and Olivia promptly inquired, "Do you have any luggage?"

"Just what I'm carrying." He stared at Olivia in frank confusion. "And *you* are . . . ?" Apprehension spread from his voice to his eyes.

Gesturing for him to follow her, Olivia murmured, "I'm a friend. Now, let's get outside in a hurry. I don't like having to leave my dog in the hot car."

Cosmo's expression of initial astonishment slowly dissipated as he moved to keep pace with Olivia. He switched his thick garment bag to the other shoulder so that it wouldn't be a barrier between them and studied her as they walked. "Are you with the Oyster Bay Police?"

"No. I assumed the chief and his officers had more pressing matters to take care of, so I volunteered to collect you. I hope you don't mind."

Once outside, she held out her hand to Cosmo. "I'm Olivia Limoges. Camden and I had just formed the beginnings of what I believed would have become a long and fulfilling friendship when his life was stolen away." She held out her arm, indicating they should cross the street while there was a lull in traffic. "Coming here to meet you was the only useful thing I could think to do in his memory. Besides, I thought it might be easier for you to talk to me during the two-hour ride since I actually cared for Camden, in lieu of some blasé young policeman who didn't know him from Adam."

"That *would* have made things even worse," Cosmo readily confessed. "If things can get any worse." He paused and glanced up at the sky. "I was also dreading the idea of riding with a policeman just taking care of official business. He probably would have

142

insisted on small talk to fill up the silence and would have refused to tell me anything about Camden's . . ." He trailed off, his expression pure misery.

Olivia opened the back door of the Range Rover. "About his case?" she finished for him. "I'll tell you all I know, which isn't much, I fear. Haviland? You cannot sit in the front seat. Haviland? Up!" When the poodle didn't move, Olivia scowled. "Just this once, Captain. You'll get a reward from the picnic basket, I promise."

Haviland's ears perked at the word "basket" and he launched himself into the backseat. Olivia removed the seat protector from the passenger seat, transferred it to the trunk and tried to relieve Cosmo of his garment bag. "Please. Allow me," he insisted.

Consenting, Olivia removed the take-out containers Michel had packed, noting with a grin that Haviland's was labeled in Michel's neat script. She placed the poodle's meal on a napkin on the backseat within reach of Haviland's quivering nose and then handed a meal to Cosmo.

"I own a restaurant in Oyster Bay and my chef has prepared these treats for our ride home. I haven't traveled recently, but from what I remember, the airlines have replaced any semblance of an in-flight meal with a sprinkling of peanuts or a package of six tiny pretzels."

Cosmo nodded but made no move to open the parcel. "Thank you, but I haven't eaten all day. I don't know if I can swallow anything."

Olivia started the engine and maneuvered the Range Rover out of the parking area. "Try a few, small bites. Not to sound like a cliché, but you'll need to keep up your strength. You can't help Camden if you fall to pieces." She opened a napkin with a flourish and let it fall gently on Cosmo's lap. "There you are."

Both human and canine passengers ate in silence as Olivia exited the airport and began heading east toward the ocean. She crunched on her portion of herb crostini with goat cheese, but her inability to offer comforting words or maternal assurances to the young man beside her eventually put her off her food. As Cosmo focused on the passing scenes out the window, his beautiful profile was a portrait in anguish. The sky was morphing from its summer day yellow blue haze to a reluctant charcoal.

Nearly an hour into the ride, Cosmo ran his hands through his wavy locks and sighed deeply. "I'm ready to hear the horrible details now. Can you tell me what happened to my Cam?"

Olivia did. Succinctly and as painlessly as possible. However, there was no way to soften the specifics regarding the cause of death and when Cosmo's eyes grew moist, his agony evident as he heard how his lover had been killed, Olivia's own eyes filled with tears. Swallowing hard, she immediately tried to distract him by reciting the mysterious haiku.

"Does anything about that poem seem familiar?" she asked him gently.

Cosmo pressed a handkerchief to his eyes. "No! *No!*" He sobbed into the fabric. "None of this makes sense!" His shoulders shook and he turned away from her again.

He grew calm quickly. "Forgive me, dear lady. When the police chief called me, this seemed like some mixed-up nightmare. Part of me thought I'd fly here and find out they'd made a huge mistake. It would be some other beautiful gay man who got killed, not my Camden. But hearing it from you . . . now I know he's really gone. There's . . . God, I feel like there's a hole in the middle of my chest. Like I've died too."

Wordlessly, Olivia removed her right hand from the steering wheel and found Cosmo's. She squeezed his soft flesh and he grabbed her hand in both of his and clutched it against his chest, just above his heart. "Tell me! What *monster* could have done this to him?"

Olivia shook her head. "I don't know. Camden didn't mention making any enemies in Oyster Bay? Conflicts?"

"No!" Cosmo was crushed to have no helpful information to share. "He was digging up dirt on the Talbots, but he was *happy* doing the research. Last time we talked, he was full of ideas for this book of his. Said his publicist already had a publishing house drooling for the thing. Did you know about the novel?"

"Yes. I've read one of the chapters. Camden was a gifted writer." She carefully reclaimed her hand. "Did you read the Milano Cruise stories before they were published?"

After a pause, Camden's lover grinned. "Only the seriously juicy ones. I'm no good at writing, but sometimes I could get Milano a story or two. I'm an interior designer to the stars, so Camden was always careful to make sure none of the scandalous tidbits could get traced back to me." He gestured toward the trunk, his youthful face infused with pride. "That garment bag? A castoff of Sharon Stone's."

Olivia wasn't one to swoon at the mention

of a celebrity's name, but Cosmo looked so forlorn and eager for praise that she did her best to appear impressed. "You must be *very* talented."

"Oh, I am." Cosmo's smile grew. "Cam and I — our stars were on the rise." He touched Olivia on the elbow so that she'd meet his eyes. "I'm not going back to LA without answers. My future was with Camden and now that's gone. Just like that!" He snapped his fingers. "I can't even *think* about living through another day until the evil creature who stole my best friend away is caught!" He put his head in his hands and sighed. "Could you help me find a decent place to stay? I don't have anywhere to go."

"There's really only one decent option in town. That is, if you want to avoid the tourists and their boisterous children. I'll get you a room at a bed-and-breakfast called The Yellow Lady."

Cosmo leaned heavily against the headrest. "Ugh! Creaky floors and saggy mattresses covered by old quilts. Nosy innkeepers and housemaids going through my pockets? There's nothing more modern?"

"Oyster Bay is a town in transition, I'm afraid." Olivia was struck by an inspiration. "I have a cottage on my property. It's small, but it has a kitchen and a living room and overlooks the ocean. Do you think you'd be more comfortable there?"

"*Do* I? Oh, I'd so rather be away from prying eyes and close to you. I've never needed a friend as much as I do now!" Cosmo gushed sincerely.

Simultaneously flustered and pleased by his boyish need, Olivia began to give commands to the phone installed in her car's dashboard. "Call The Yellow Lady," Olivia ordered. As the computer complied, Olivia told Cosmo, "You'll have to stay there tonight. The cottage isn't set up for guests and I'll need to buy a bed first thing tomorrow. I'd also like to be there when you go into Camden's room. My friends and I, the ones from Camden's writing group, believe there could be a clue within the pages of his manuscript."

"The book about the Talbots? Do you think he was killed because of some connection to that family?" Cosmo's voice was tight with anger.

"I don't know, but here's why *I* view Blake as a suspect." She repeated the conversation she and Camden had overheard between Blake and Heidi St. Claire.

Cosmo shook his head. "Blake may pretend to be tough with his black leather pants, wallet chain, and shiny combat boots, but he's almost as soft as I am. But from how Camden's talked about that boy, I could believe he'd pay someone to do something horrible. He's got plenty of money to burn."

"Not enough for a tour bus, if Camden's fictitious account is accurate," Olivia remarked.

"Well, the word on the street is that Daddy Warbucks doles out a monthly allowance and Blake isn't happy with the amount. Dean Talbot is his son's manager, you know, so he controls the band's finances."

This was news to Olivia. "I thought he was in real estate."

Chuckling dryly, Cosmo said, "Honey, he's got his hands in more pies than the pastry chef at Spago." He paused. "That's one of Wolfgang Puck's restaurants."

"In Beverly Hills, yes. I've eaten there."

Cosmo sighed again, this time with relief. "Thank God I've got you! I thought I'd be surrounded by the cast of *Deliverance*!"

"Hardly. In any case, Camden paved the way for you by charming half the town. Even the Republicans loved him."

"That's my Cam," Cosmo whispered.

They fell silent for a while. Olivia had left

the interstate and the Range Rover was now cruising down an empty two-lane highway. Cosmo cracked his window and inhaled, closing his eyes so that his long lashes lay against the smooth skin of his cheek. "I smell the ocean."

I want to protect this boy, to shield him from further harm, Olivia thought, feeling relieved she'd invited him to stay on her property. Not only would it keep the Bayside Book Writers in the investigative loop, but she could watch out for Cosmo. No one could approach her house or the lighthouse keeper's cottage without Haviland's knowledge, and Olivia's private school education had taught her marksmanship with both bow and arrow and hunting rifle. She could load and fire the Browning BPR rifle she kept in the downstairs coat closet with lethal precision.

"This is our county line," she informed Cosmo.

Haviland shuffled restlessly in the backseat, having napped during most of the trip. "Slept off your dinner a bit, Captain?" Olivia teased.

The poodle barked once in reply, his mouth smiling at her reflection in the rearview mirror.

As they passed through town, Cosmo

wrung his hands together. "Are we going to pass by the place . . . ?"

"Not tonight," Olivia replied firmly. "You're exhausted. It's time for you to have a drink and go to bed."

"Yes. That sounds like the thing to do." Cosmo exhaled. "You're an angel, Olivia. Thank you."

Olivia couldn't help it. She laughed aloud. "An angel? Now, *that's* a first."

CHAPTER 7

He is dead and gone, lady,
He is dead and gone,
At his head a grass-green turf,
At his heels a stone.

> — WILLIAM SHAKESPEARE
> (HAMLET, ACT IV)

After a night of troubled sleep, Olivia rose just as dawn was breaking over the water. A pale light seeped into the sky, followed by a washed-out sun. Already the summer haze was sitting on the land like an animal resting on heavy haunches. Only the ocean breeze kept Oyster Bay's residents from being completely weighed down by humidity, though the northern tourists sweated so copiously that they often needed to change clothes twice before lunchtime.

After breakfast, Olivia and Haviland took their customary walk on the beach. The poodle raced after gulls and sandpipers, did some cursory digging in clam holes, and frightened crabs into scuttling for cover in the white-bubbled foam feathering the shore. Haviland's mouth hung open in a joyful smile and his bright eyes darted from the moist sand to the grass-speckled dunes to his mistress. Olivia smiled back at him, taking in deep breaths of ocean air. It had taken decades of travel and a dozen different addresses for her to realize there was nowhere else on earth she'd rather be than on the beach she ran across as a child.

Once the pair had walked a little over a mile, Olivia climbed a small rise and settled on the sand. Hugging her knees against her chest, she sat still as a stone as the sun bathed her face.

She thought of Camden and Cosmo and their life together in Los Angeles and wondered what it would be like when Cosmo returned home alone. She could almost see him passing through the clean, chic rooms of their apartment, picking up photographs, listlessly shifting throw pillows, opening and closing the refrigerator — anything to avoid the empty truth that his friend and lover would never enter the space again. Eventually, Cosmo would be confronted by the scent of his lover lingering on a bathroom towel or clinging to a silk shirt hanging in the closet and then the beautiful young man would crumple to the floor, a piece of cloth pressed against his face, as grief asserted itself with overwhelming power.

"But he can't really begin to mourn without closure," Olivia murmured to herself. "Oyster Bay is a small town. *Someone* knows *something* about this death. I just need to ask the right people the right questions." She brushed away the stirrings of melancholy as she shook loose sprinkles of sand from her gray yoga pants.

Haviland trotted over and licked the side of her neck, gracing her with one of his rare, gentlemanlike kisses. She cupped his ears in her hands and pressed her face against his soft cheek. "Come on, darling. We've much work to do."

Their morning walks were always restorative, and by the time Olivia pulled the Range Rover in front of the cheerful yellow Victorian with the wraparound porch and the lavender front door, she felt as though she had an abundance of strength of will to share with Cosmo. The Yellow Lady was one of the most beautiful houses in Oyster Bay and Olivia felt there was no rival in the entire county for its wild and colorful gardens.

Though it was nearly ten o'clock, Olivia half expected to learn that Cosmo was still asleep, so she'd come prepared with a James Michener novel and a plump nectarine in case she had to wait. But not only was Cosmo awake, he was showered, immaculately dressed in pressed khakis and a hot pink polo shirt, and dining heartily on the inn's bountiful breakfast spread.

Annie Kraus, co-owner of The Yellow Lady, hovered at his elbow. She placed a steaming cup of black coffee next to Cosmo's plate and solicitously arranged a creamer of steamed milk and a porcelain sugar bowl adorned with silver sugar tongs within easy reach. After giving him a maternal pat on the shoulder, she passed behind his chair in order to adjust the blinds so that the burgeoning sunlight didn't fall across his eyes.

Olivia had met Annie and her husband Roy several times. As business owners, all three were involved with the chamber of commerce. Roy and Olivia were also committee members on the town's Planning Board. Despite the fact that the meetings were often tedious, Olivia enjoyed being in the know about the changes occurring in Oyster Bay and she suspected the Krauses shared her pleasure over being able to direct those changes through their voting power.

One of the pine floorboards creaked, announcing Olivia's presence. Annie looked up and produced a tentative smile. Annie and Roy had purchased The Yellow Lady shortly before Olivia's return and Olivia sensed they were still uncertain what to make of the attractive and imposing female entrepreneur. Having been married for more than two decades, Annie seemed slightly wary of unattached women, as though she believed it unnatural for a woman to remain single and childless. Annie was fifteen years older than Olivia and had been raised by religious parents who placed great value upon both marriage and procreation. When the youngest of her four children left the nest, Annie didn't have anyone to cook or clean for, so it seemed only fitting to continue those tasks for paying clientele.

"Good morning, Ms. Limoges," she greeted Olivia formally. "Would you care for some coffee? My dear guest is on his second pot." She beamed at the young man.

Cosmo stood and quickly held out a chair for Olivia. As she grew closer, he pulled her into a brief but gentle embrace. "I can see why Camden loved this town," he declared. "Roy and Annie have been such darlings.

And the room — gorgeous! Crisp, cotton sheets, fluffy white duvet cover, a pillow-top mattress, and not a framed needlepoint in sight. It looks like something *I* would have designed."

Olivia thanked Annie for the coffee. She added some of the steamed milk, stirred, and took a sip while studying Cosmo over the rim of her cup. "This is delicious coffee," she said after swallowing the rich, creamy brew.

It was the right thing to say. Annie's stiff shoulders relaxed and her smile became genuine. "It's the beans. They're pure Kona and I grind them fresh every morning." She paused. "I know you're used to fancier food than this, but you're welcome to breakfast too."

"The biscuits are to die for," Cosmo said, pushing a basket toward her. "If I eat like this, I'll have to get elastic-waisted pants."

Annie swatted at him with the corner of her apron. "I'll have you know that *some* of us have been wearing those for years." Her tone was indulgent.

"I already had Raisin Bran and a banana, but if I'd known this is what you serve your guests, I would have skipped breakfast and gotten here sooner." Olivia saluted Annie with her coffee cup.

"Would you sit down for a minute, Annie? *Please!*" Cosmo pleaded. "I know we talked a bit last night — actually, I blubbered and you listened — but could you tell Olivia what Cam was like on . . . his last day?"

Hesitating, Annie smoothed her apron and looked to Olivia for guidance. Olivia gestured at the seat across from her own as though they were gathered in her dining room and not Annie's.

"Mr. Ford was a charming gentleman," Annie began. "Kept his room ever so tidy, complimented me on my cooking (though he never ate any sweets or bread or whatnot — he was very health-conscious), and he was always humming or singing. He just filled this house up when he was in it. You couldn't help but smile when he was around. He was a real ray of sunshine."

Olivia nodded. It was an apt description of Camden. "Did you see him on Saturday?"

"Only in the morning and for a few minutes in the evening when he came in to change his clothes." She directed a smile at Cosmo. "He wore such lovely things. Ironed them himself too. Of course, I offered to do that for him," she added defensively. "We aim to coddle our guests here at The Yellow Lady, but Mr. Ford said ironing helped him think, so I left him to it."

"Well, I hate ironing," Cosmo replied in an attempt at humor, but Olivia noticed that he'd put down his utensils and seemed unable to eat any more of the biscuit, thick-sliced bacon, or ripe strawberries on his plate.

Annie patted the tablecloth close to Cosmo's hand. "You don't need to worry about a *thing* while you're here, dear." Sensing Olivia's impatience, she finally answered the original question. "Now I could tell that Mr. Ford had been doing his best to get to know folks from our town, from fishermen to librarians to little Dixie Weaver. He also talked on his cell phone *quite* a bit." She flashed a look at Cosmo. "Please understand. I make it a point to give my guests their privacy, but because this whole house doesn't get the best reception, Mr. Ford often talked out on the front porch and I'd hear bits and snatches now and then. When I was tidying up and such."

Olivia didn't buy this explanation for a moment. Annie was clearly an inquisitive innkeeper. "Did you hear any *bits and snatches* on Saturday?" she asked.

"All I know is that while he was talking on the phone, he wrote down the name of our little park south of town — the one right on the river with the bird plaques and that old Civil War cemetery. If you can even call it a cemetery. It's just a few graves, really." She shrugged. "Mr. Ford planned to visit the park that very afternoon, though he wasn't wearing the right shoes, if you ask me." She clucked her tongue in disapproval. "He also told the person on the phone that he was real interested in what he had to say and would like to meet in person. And I only know this much detail because Mr. Ford came to me in search of pen and paper. I didn't hear anything else."

"Well, that's quite a comprehensive tidbit," Olivia mused aloud and turned to Cosmo. "Was Camden a nature lover?"

"Of course not." Cosmo grimaced at the idea. "The man *hated* the outdoors. Give him air-conditioning and double-paned windows or he'd complain like a starlet who's lost her sunscreen! In LA, Cam only went outside for Starbucks or the newspaper."

"Therefore, going to the Neuse River Community Park would be out of character?" Olivia pressed.

Cosmo leaned forward on his elbows. "As out of character as *me* going to a women's fashion show to ogle the *models* instead of the clothes." He shook his head. "I'm assuming there'd be *bugs* at this park too?

160

Mosquitoes? Ticks?" He shivered in distaste. "He'd only go there if he could borrow a hazmat suit!"

"I don't think our souvenir shop keeps those in stock." Olivia took a sip of coffee. "Truly excellent brew, Annie." The innkeeper flushed. "Can you tell us anything else? What was Camden's mood when he came home to change for the evening? And what time was that?"

Annie looked out the window. "Let's see. I was in the kitchen making scones to put in the freezer. I had to stop to register the Parker couple and ring Roy to carry their luggage upstairs. That must have been around six because the scones were already in the oven when I saw Mr. Ford." She tapped her watch. "Must have been a bit after seven when he came down from his room. He'd been in jeans and a cotton shirt that afternoon, but he was fresh as a spring day in white pants and a pink shirt. He smiled and gave me a friendly wave but didn't stop for a chat like he usually did. Still, his eyes were twinkling, like a kid on Christmas Eve. He was real worked up, like he couldn't wait to get where he was going."

Cosmo sighed. "So he wasn't scared when he left. Cam wanted to see this person. But

he didn't meet a *person*. He met a *monster!*"
His voice cracked and his eyes filled with
tears.

Pushing her chair away from the table,
Annie got up and put an arm around Cosmo
and squeezed. The young man leaned back
into her pillowy chest. Olivia also rose. She
and Annie exchanged a look. They both
knew Cosmo needed to be taken under
someone's protective wing and Olivia hoped
her face portrayed her relief over sharing
the responsibility with such a capable
woman.

"I think you should stay at The Yellow
Lady," Olivia whispered gently to Cosmo.
"You're perfectly safe here and Annie and
Roy can care for you better than I ever
could. If you stayed in the cottage, you'd
have to cook your own meals, make your
own bed, and you'd be all alone. Besides, I
don't even own an iron."

Cosmo waved his hands in front of his
face and blinked away a fresh round of
tears. "I have *got* to get a grip!" He sniffed
several times. "Okay. Since you two insist,
I'll stay here and be spoiled, but don't you
try to disappear on me, Olivia Limoges!"

"The thought never crossed my mind. I'm
only a phone call away and in this town, it'll
never take me more than fifteen minutes to

get to you," Olivia assured him. "Now, can we peek in Camden's room?"

Annie shook her head. "The chief gave me strict instructions to leave it be. Cosmo already asked me to look inside for Mr. Ford's computer, but it's gone. He always left it square on the writing desk, with his phone and a notepad lined up right beside it. Neat as a pin, that one was."

"There are no printouts of his manuscript either," Cosmo said dejectedly. "Annie was nice enough to check. I just couldn't go in. The cops must have it all."

Olivia fell silent. Not only did she need to acquire a copy of Camden's work in progress, but she now wanted to know the identity of the caller feeding Camden information regarding the town park. At the moment, she couldn't think of a single connection between the Talbot family and a seldom-frequented community park. Luckily, there were several locals who might be able to enlighten her.

Cosmo took hold of Olivia's hand. "You go on ahead with CSI Oyster Bay. I've got to make . . . arrangements. I can't stand the thought of my darling Cam spending another day lying on some cold piece of metal." His eyes filled with tears again. "The least I can do is buy him the most decadent, velvet-lined coffin ever made and cover him with heaps and heaps of flowers."

"I could drive you over to Woody's Funeral Home," Annie offered kindly. "You shouldn't have to do that task on your own."

"Oh, you're a treasure!" Cosmo exclaimed with relief. "It's going to be a very small affair. After all, Cam's family cut him out of their lives the day he came out. That was almost *twenty years* ago. Can you *imagine?* They don't even realize what a wonderful person they've missed knowing — *I* got the best of him."

He hid his face in the napkin for a long moment. "Enough!" He resurfaced and sniffed. "I have to face Oyster Bay's men in blue at one o'clock *sharp.*" Cosmo's gaze returned to Olivia. "I *must* be assertive with these people if I want to find out if they have any idea who did this. I simply *cannot* go through another day imagining that sick bastard walking around out there. Do they still use the electric chair in this state?"

"Do your best to speak directly to Chief Rawlings," Olivia counseled. "And might I suggest you change your shirt into something a little less —"

"Gay?" Cosmo guessed wryly.

"I was going to say 'pink.' " She grinned and pulled out another business card from her purse. She'd written both her mobile and home numbers on the back. "Call me if you need a ride to the station. I've got a decent measure of influence in this town and I'll make certain you're treated with the consideration and respect you deserve."

Annie began placing dirty dishes on a lacquered tray. "You'll do well with Ms. Olivia watching your back, young man. But it's *my* job to see that you're up to all this, which you *won't* be if you don't finish your breakfast. At least eat some strawberries and polish off the bacon."

Cosmo saluted. "Eat protein. Change shirt. Stop blubbering. Yes, yes, mommy dearests. Whatever you say."

Olivia left the inn and drove straight to Bagels 'n' Beans. She ordered Wheeler's home-brewed orange iced tea and then asked him if he had a minute to spare for a chat. She selected the table closest to the back door where she was least likely to be overheard. Her seating choice also allowed her to view Chief Rawlings' newest paintings. Haviland, clearly sensing there were no treats to be had in a room smelling, to a dog at least, of burned cocoa beans and rubbery dough, went to sleep.

Wheeler finished making soy lattes with

no foam for a pair of tourists, gave them a gummy smile when they stuffed a few bills into the tip jar, and then shuffled over to Olivia's table. He pointed at the paintings. "You gonna snap these up too?"

Though the nearest painting was of a subject Olivia would not choose to display, she had to admit it was charming. It depicted a little boy in overalls standing alongside an ice cream truck. The whole truck wasn't in view — only one of the wheels and the colorful menu board. The boy, who was barefoot and generously freckled, gripped a dollar bill in one hand and had the other shoved deep into the pocket of his denim overalls. His eyes gleamed as he gazed longingly at the tempting images of orange creamsicles, Astro Pops, ice cream sandwiches, king cones, strawberry shortcake bars, and chocolate éclair bars.

"It's well executed," Olivia told Wheeler. "But I like this other one better. Do you know the woman?"

"Aye. Sawyer's wife, Helen, that is. Died a few years back. Caught the cancer."

Olivia had never heard the disease described as catchable before, but Wheeler had spent the better part of his life trolling for tuna across the Atlantic, and like many of

Oyster Bay's older fishermen, had developed a unique dialect of blended accents and phrases.

"I don't recall hearing Chief Rawlings' first name before," Olivia answered as she studied the painting. It was a simple scene showing a woman reading. She was reclined in an Adirondack chair with a hardcover propped open on her knees. Her intelligent eyes were opened wide, her expression one of guilty pleasure. The nail of her index finger was held captive between her upper and lower teeth and her lips curved in a slight, secretive smile. The woman was not beautiful, but it was difficult to turn away from her animated face. Olivia immediately liked how the picture championed the notion that time spent reading was a treasure to be cherished.

"Wheeler, you met Camden Ford, didn't you?" Olivia turned away from the art. "He was visiting from California."

"The writer fellow. Acted girly." Wheeler grunted. "Dressed girly too."

"Yes, Camden did prefer pastels," agreed Olivia. "Did he ask you any questions about Oyster Bay or any of the people here?"

Wheeler nodded. "Sure enough. Wanted to know when those houses first started goin' up on the bluff. I told him they slapped them up in no time like everythin' they build these days. The first real storm and those things'll blow over like a feather in the wind."

"Talbot Fine Properties at work," Olivia muttered.

"He wanted to know about those folks too. Daddy Talbot was in here a time or two this spring. Never talked to him direct though. He's got helpers to order his drinks, fetch him a cookie, and stir the sugar in his coffee. Wonder if they wipe his ass for him too." Wheeler gave a dry chuckle.

"Was Camden interested in any other subjects?"

Wheeler pulled a damp cloth from his pocket and began to wipe the table. Olivia moved her elbows off the surface and watched as the old man's hands moved in slow, careful circles. The motion seemed to help him think. "He wanted to know about the soldier graveyard — if there was livin' kin to the boys buried there. I reckon there are a handful of folks sharin' names with those written on the stones, *if* you can read 'em anymore. I haven't been out there in years, but even way back they were almost picked clean by the weather. Not too much can stand up to bein' scrubbed clean by wind and sun and sand."

168

The park again, Olivia thought, mystified.

The tinkle of the sleigh bells dangling from the front door hinge caused Wheeler to lift his head. "No more chitchat, Miss 'Livia." He leaned closer to her. "But I'm right glad you came in. I wanted to thank you for not raisin' the rent this year. I'm doin' fine, but I had to hire another kid for the summer and I wanna pay the boy a decent wage or he'll be off cuttin' grass instead. I gotta have decent young folks for the evenin' shift 'cause I can make it here at five A.M. every day, but by three o'clock I gotta go 'cause I'm all done in."

"Five in the morning? You're amazing, Wheeler," Olivia told him. The octogenarian winked at her and returned to his station behind the counter.

Outside, the humidity hit with full force. The wet, languid air shimmered above the asphalt, distorting the images of parked cars and storefronts across the street. Olivia removed her sunglasses from the crown of her head and put them on. She poured water from an insulated cup into Haviland's travel bowl and placed it on the ground beneath the nearest awning. When he was finished drinking, she belted him into his seat, put down all the windows, and headed south. Olivia loved the heat and had never quite grown accustomed to more than a hint of air-conditioning.

The Neuse River Community Park had never been a popular place. Olivia had been dragged there in elementary school to identify the bird species portrayed on the colored plaques lining the walking paths. She had found the assignment dull and pointless, as most of the children had been able to name the birds since they could talk. Unlike school, which at least had a playground, the park's pluses were limited to walking paths (grass-pocked trails of sand) and a few picnic tables. There were no restrooms and the water fountain had been rusted beyond use. The benches were made of coarse wood that zealously dislodged splinters into their bare thighs, and the single gazebo had been covered by layers of excrement left by mischievous Canada geese.

"Not much has changed," Olivia commented to Haviland before he lurched forward, dashing after a pair of startled mallards.

Allowing the poodle his canine pursuits, Olivia took a cursory look at the closest plaque. The photo of the royal tern was too faded to appear regal any longer. Its orange beak was now a muted brown and the black tail feathers were a dull, watery gray. The font describing the bird's habits and habitats was no longer legible. Here and there, a letter would show itself clearly, like a tiny fish rising to the surface of a pond to feed.

Strolling past the gazebo, she noted the weathered structure had been used as a carving board. Names, initials, expletives, and symbols covered every inch of the tired wood, adding to the park's atmosphere of neglect and disuse.

Haviland rejoined her and together they mounted the steep flight of cracked cement steps leading up to the small cemetery. Midway in the climb, Olivia caught her toe on a fissure that nearly split one of the steps in two. Looking ahead, she noticed how the three steps nearest the top were swollen and split due to the pressure being forced upon them by the roots of a mature swamp chestnut.

Olivia reached the top and was surprised by the realization that there was no handrail for the flight of stairs leading up to the graveyard. Approaching the cast-iron fence surrounding the space, she paused. Seven white headstones were lined up in two rows — one of four, one of three — beneath the shelter of another old chestnut tree. Grasping a fence finial in each hand, Olivia stared respectfully at the weathered stones.

Unlike the rest of the park, the secluded little graveyard was carefully tended. The grass had been mowed, the fence had recently received a fresh coat of black paint, and when Olivia eventually pushed open the narrow gate, it swung inward on well-oiled hinges. There was a bronze plaque set in cement just inside the gate. The plaque read, "Lest We Forget. Our Boys Sacrificed All," and was surrounded by a ring of miniature Dixie flags.

Treading softly, Olivia approached the headstones. As Wheeler had said, the text carved into the surface had nearly been sanded smooth by wind and time, but three of the graves in the back row still proclaimed their occupant's names.

"James Greenhow, Henry Bragg, and Wallace White," Olivia whispered. "Lest we forget." Haviland sniffed at the graves and gave his mistress a quizzical look. "Why would Camden be curious about this place?" Haviland barked dismissively. "Good point, Captain. He was researching the Talbots, not the park. So why would the Talbots be interested in this place?" She gazed around and then inhaled sharply. "The *park!* It must be thirty acres." Her dark blue eyes swept over the deserted landscape. "Situated on the picturesque Neuse River. Minutes from town, minutes from the beach . . . I can almost write the brochure. Of course! The Talbots want to buy this land!"

Turning on her heel, Olivia closed the gate gently behind her and strode to the Range Rover. She dug her pocket-sized planner out of her purse and, after jotting down the names she'd read on the gravestones to research further later on, examined the notations on the calendar page. "The Planning Board meeting isn't until the end of the month. If the town of Oyster Bay's been approached about placing this parcel up for sale, it'll be coming up for vote at the township committee meeting first. I wonder when that's being held."

Her cell phone vibrated in the cup holder in her center console. Picking it up, she noted the missed call had come from Cosmo's phone. She immediately returned his call.

"I'm with the chief," Cosmo informed her, sounding deflated. "He's getting me a coffee and a glass of chocolate milk for himself. Can you believe that? What kind of cop drinks chocolate milk? Aren't they supposed to be caffeine addicts by day and raging alcoholics by night?"

"Do you want me to come down?" Olivia asked. "I can be there in ten minutes."

"No, no." Cosmo sighed wearily. "They haven't arrested anyone yet. Not a single soul saw Cam go inside the bar and only *one* person noticed him on the sidewalk. It's like Cam was invisible that night. And their lone witness was already up to his gills in whiskey. Not *exactly* the picture of reliability. It's *too* awful!"

Olivia tried to distract Cosmo from becoming morose. "Did you ask Chief Rawlings about the cell phone and the laptop?"

"No comment on the phone, but he's letting me look at the laptop right now, but only because I promised to tell him if I saw any unusual files or emails," Cosmo answered. "The emails are purely social and there are a few of mine on there I don't want *anyone* to see!" He was clearly agitated over the invasion of his privacy. "All of the Milano Cruise files are here and some facts on your darling little town. What you wanted me to look for is here too. Cam saved his manuscript under the name, 'Book.' How *uncreative* of him! I'm emailing it to you this *second*, and then I've got to go. I hear Rawlings down the hall and I don't want him to catch me. Bye!"

The connection was severed.

"Well done, Cosmo," Olivia said aloud, relieved that her work email address was printed on The Boot Top Bistro's business card. Anxious to begin reading Camden's manuscript immediately, she turned on the engine and backed out of the parking space. The speed of her reversal formed tornadoes of dust that briefly obscured her view out the windshield.

CHAPTER 8

The writer's duty is to keep on writing.
— WILLIAM STYRON

Olivia forwarded the email containing Camden's manuscript to the members of the Bayside Book Writers. She then opened all the windows in her spacious living room, switched on the overhead fans so they spun languidly overhead, and got comfortable on the sofa with half a tumbler full of Chivas Regal. She spent the evening carefully reading the dead writer's work, only taking a break to eat a quick dinner of Michel's famous sweet potato vichyssoise and a spoonful of chilled chicken salad mixed with grapes over a bed of chopped lettuce and tomatoes.

The moment she was finished reading, Olivia began to call her fellow writers in order to plan a lunch meeting for the following day. She phoned Laurel first, assuming the young mother would need to make babysitting arrangements, but Laurel insisted she'd have to bring her children along.

"Tomorrow's Tuesday. Steve'll be at work and I can't hire a sitter unless we're going out together for a date night," she explained without embarrassment. "He's a dentist but he just bought into a practice. I don't understand it, but he says we really have to watch every penny. And the twins cost *so* much! The way they grow out of clothes and car seats — and they seem to eat all the time! I never thought having kids would be this expensive."

Plans foiled, Olivia tried to think of a suitable location in which four adults could hold a serious conversation while a pair of demanding, hyperactive toddlers played in relative safety. She tried to picture them in the lighthouse keeper's cottage but found the thought incredibly distasteful.

"There's the playground at the beach," Laurel suggested.

Olivia predicted that the screeches of dozens of children would repeatedly interrupt their concentration. "We couldn't talk to one another effectively sitting on those benches because they all face the playground. We need to gather around some kind of table," Olivia reasoned. "Not only that, but an outdoor meeting at noon in June might be a tad warm."

"I don't mind. I love the heat," Laurel said.

Olivia was pleased to know that another Oyster Bay native loved the summer weather as much as she did. "I do as well, but Millay doesn't seem overly fond of daylight and I think the UV rays would be too harsh on Harris's skin."

"You are *so* considerate," Laurel gushed and then went *tsk, tsk* with her tongue. "Our Harris is *such* a handsome guy if you look beyond that rash, don't you think? I wish there was a product to help clear up his face. I can only imagine the effect his condition has on his confidence."

"He seems to possess a solid level of self-assurance," Olivia remarked, but even as she spoke she scribbled a quick note to call the spa in New Bern the next morning.

Laurel made a noncommittal noise. "Only around us. He hasn't had a date since his high school prom and I think his social life exists totally in cyberspace. Facebook and Twitter and places like that."

Olivia's glance wandered to her copy of Sunday's *Oyster Bay Gazette*. The local weekly, which went to print Saturday evening and was therefore mercifully free of

178

any dramatic headlines regarding Camden's death, featured a black-and-white photo and a front-page article about Flynn McNulty and Through the Wardrobe.

"Laurel!" Olivia tapped the photograph of Flynn leaning against one of his armoires, his arms crossed over his chest as he smiled warmly for the camera. "I know where we can meet. Do your sons enjoy books?"

Laurel laughed. "They like chewing on them and hitting each other with them. Does that count? Oh! I've heard about that new bookstore from my Mommy and Me group. With the dress-up stuff and the puppets, there's a chance the twins might stay relatively calm."

"I'll bring a large bottle of ether just in case," Olivia murmured, sending Laurel into peals of laughter.

The other members readily agreed to join them at the bookstore. Harris reminded Olivia that he only had an hour lunch break and then told her how he'd spent most of Sunday reading up on the Talbot family. Being savvier about Internet search protocol, he'd also been more successful than Olivia in retrieving background information on Blake Talbot. He hadn't stopped with the youngest son, however, and was prepared to present biographic summaries on the entire family.

Olivia called Millay last, and though the younger woman complained she'd normally still be abed at noon, she seemed anxious to discuss Camden's chapters.

"Will you have time to read them?" Olivia asked her. "Are you working tonight?"

"Yeah, I'm here now. You can only hear me because I'm in the supply closet looking for toilet paper. Totally glam, huh?" She snorted. "But Mondays are slow. Between my breaks and the lulls that'll come when the guys get too riled up over some stupid NASCAR race to drink, I'll get it done." Millay sounded determined. "Even if I have to stay up until dawn, I'll be ready to contribute. And I'm going to see what I can weasel out of my regulars during my shift too. They'll talk to me, especially if I don't water down their whiskey as much as I usually do."

Olivia was impressed by Millay's commitment. "That a girl," she told the bartender. "And be careful."

Millay blew air out through her lips. "*Please.* Those men would rather have sex with me than murder me and I don't intend to let them do either. See you at noon and make sure there's coffee. Lots of it."

Recalling Flynn's unpalatable brew, Olivia

frowned. "Don't worry, I'll bring a thermos."

"Then I'll bring a flask," Millay said and rang off, leaving Olivia to wonder if the young woman had been serious.

Camden had written nearly one hundred pages of the book he had entitled *The Tarnished Titans.* The writing was fluid and filled with vivid imagery, but Olivia found the lack of chronology confusing. Chapter one described the sheltered childhood of the "Talcott" siblings, and just when Olivia felt as though she was developing a sense of each of the five family members' personas, Camden focused chapter two solely on Don Talcott.

Don, who was undoubtedly the titan referred to in the book's title, was easily the most interesting character. Raised in a blue-collar Brooklyn home, the young man had gotten ahead by any means possible. After spending four years running errands in one of Manhattan's premier investment firms while he took night classes toward a business degree, Don was finally awarded a desk and assigned the miserable task of cold calls. As luck would have it, the ambitious Talcott was a born salesman and his exceptional skill at "dialing for dollars" earned him the attention of the firm's board of directors. Ten years later, he was one of them.

Don married the beautiful Broadway sensation, Lana Alexander. At nineteen, Lana's decision to become Mrs. Donald Talcott immediately resulted in the death of her career. Pregnant three times in less than five years, Lana remained secluded with her progeny behind the tall, ivy-covered fence surrounding their Long Island estate while Don paraded a host of young models, fresh-faced debutantes, and high-class prostitutes into New York's chicest nightclubs and restaurants.

The book's next few chapters centered on the Talcott children. According to Camden's claims, the two boys and one girl were reared primarily by a Hispanic nanny until they were old enough to be sent away to boarding school. Lana spent most of their childhood checking in and out of rehab centers in New York, Beverly Hills, Texas, and across Europe. The last chapter focused on Bradley and was the only chapter already read and critiqued by the Bayside Book Writers prior to Camden's death.

"There's nothing specific about what kind of education Blake received," Olivia said to Haviland as she pulled into a parking space across from the bookstore. "I was hoping to learn that the boy had written poetry since grammar school or something equally obvious. Maybe Harris can paint a more complete picture."

As she reached for the shop's brass door handle, her cell phone rang.

"It's Annie Kraus. I thought you might have tried to reach Mr. Cosmo on his mobile. You see, he left it in the dining room and it plays a little song every time it rings, and since I just happened to see your number on the screen, I wanted you to know he's all right." She finally took a breath. "Well, he's not exactly in good shape, but he's here at the inn."

Olivia relaxed her outstretched arm. "Thank you. I've called him several times since yesterday afternoon but assumed he wanted some time alone so I let it be."

"He's been sleeping most of the time away." Annie sighed heavily. "The poor boy was completely done in what with the funeral home and then his trip to the police station." She paused. "I'm afraid I didn't do him any favors. I brought him a nice bottle of Merlot to go with his lamb chops. He polished that one off and asked for another to take to his room. I couldn't refuse him — the sweet, sad, sad boy."

"A few hours of oblivion were probably a

gift to him," Olivia stated. "When he feels like himself again, tell him he can call me if he'd like a drink or a meal at The Boot Top."

"Will do," Annie replied. "I'm going to brew some peppermint tea and slice up an apple and a banana. The fruit soaks up the alcohol and the tea gives the body back some of its pep. Mr. Cosmo will be right as rain by this afternoon. Nothing beats my mother's magical hangover remedy."

"I'll keep that recipe in mind." Olivia said good-bye and stepped into the bookstore, where she immediately collided with Chief Rawlings. He automatically reached out and held on to her arm, as though she needed to be steadied. But Olivia hadn't lost her balance and now the two stood, their chests centimeters apart, frozen for a moment. To Olivia, the chief's touch and the proximity of their bodies became instantly intimate.

Shocked by the realization that she felt completely at ease being so close to the lawman, Olivia immediately took a step back. She looked down at the chief's hands, searching for evidence that he'd been shopping for books in the midst of a murder investigation.

"I'm glad to run into you, Ms. Limoges." Rawlings kept his tone formal, but his eyes appraised her warmly. With the full force of the midday sun illuminating his face, Olivia could see the lines on the chief's forehead, like river symbols on a primitive map. Crinkles deepened the corners of his eyes, indicating he smiled easily and often. Olivia couldn't help but wonder if he'd had any reason to express humor since Saturday night. Today, his eyes were less the brownish green of pond water and more like sun-dappled tidal pools.

She broke eye contact. "This is hardly where I'd expect to find you, Chief," she said stiffly, discomforted by the pleasure she'd taken in examining his features. Holding the door open for Haviland, she allowed the poodle to stand in front of her like a canine barricade.

Rawlings made room for Haviland, his mouth curving into the shadow of a grin. Just as quickly as it had surfaced, the hint of amusement was gone. "I thought Mr. McNulty might be able to offer some enlightenment about our strange poem. I was able to find general information about haiku, but the deeper meaning of the spray-paint poem is making my head swim." Frustration hardened the line of his lips. "Have you had any ideas?"

Olivia shook her head. "I'm going to meet with my friends now to discuss that and other things," she answered elusively. "Was Mr. McNulty helpful?"

Rawlings hesitated. "He thought it felt unfinished. Not the poem itself, but the message of the poet. Specifically, Mr. McNulty felt there was a sense of pause in the last word, 'slumber.' A pause in lieu of closure."

Looking over the chief's shoulder at the bookstore proprietor, Olivia nodded. "I'd have to agree with that assessment. I too felt alarm over the seasonal nature of the poem. If this haiku is meant to represent winter, then will a spring follow?" She shook her head, as though trying to dispel the fear. "Without knowing his motive, I can't see why the killer wrote a poem at all. But the possibility that his message hasn't been completed worries me."

Rawlings nodded. "Me as well. I see those three lines whenever I shut my eyes."

Behind the checkout counter, Flynn thanked his customer, noticed Olivia, and waved at her. She felt a quickening in her blood as their eyes met and, for a brief moment, wondered if Flynn McNulty would make a good candidate for a casual affair. "It's too bad this store didn't open sooner," she said, returning her gaze to the chief. "You'd know the name of every person who reads verse in this town."

"I've got an officer at the library as we speak," Rawlings answered and then reached down to allow Haviland to sniff his palm.

Olivia glanced at her watch and, seeing she was a few minutes early for the meeting, succinctly told the chief about Camden's interest in the Neuse River Community Park. "So if you go through his cell phone and review the list of ingoing and outgoing calls, you'll know who was feeding him information on the locals and our prime tracts of land."

Rawlings looped his thumbs under his belt. "We will be questioning an individual regarding a series of calls to Mr. Ford's phone." He turned back to Olivia, humor twinkling in his eyes. "Any other suggestions, ma'am?"

Thinking about the township meeting, Olivia wished she'd had the foresight to check the agenda printed in last week's *Gazette* before leaving her house. "Not right now, but perhaps after my friends and I exchange ideas we'll come up with something useful."

"In that case, I'd like to accept your offer of a drink. Would Wednesday evening do? That gives your group twenty-four hours to come up with theories about the haiku's meaning."

Olivia felt relieved they weren't to be entirely excluded from the investigation. "Yes. I'll be at The Boot Top from four o'clock on." A movement near the door caught her eye. It was Harris. The young man exchanged polite greetings with the chief and then looked at Olivia expectantly.

"Is anyone else here?" he asked.

The chief answered. "If one of your writers is the mother of twin toddlers, then *she's* here." He smiled and opened the door. "If you all can work around those two, you've got more discipline than a platoon of marines."

Harris stared after the departing policeman. "Does he have any leads?"

Olivia shook her head with regret and she and Harris walked to the back of the store. Upon entering the rainbow-hued children's area, their ears were accosted by dual howls emanating from behind the wooden puppet theater.

"Give Mommy the sippie cup. Give it to Mommy, please," Laurel cooed, her face hidden between the red curtains. "Dermot, do *not* hit your brother with the owl puppet. Dallas! Stop that this minute! Be my good baby boys? Please?" Laurel sounded close to tears. "Do you want Cheerios? If you want Cheerios you need to give Mommy the sippie cup."

"What's with the freaking noise?" Millay croaked from behind Olivia and Harris. Dressed in a gauzy, mango-colored sundress, her streaked hair hidden beneath an orange bandana, Millay looked more exotic and lovely than ever.

It's as if she just stepped from a Gauguin canvas, Olivia thought as Millay moved behind the puppet theater with swift grace.

"Listen, you two," she whispered urgently. "The grown-ups need to have a secret meeting. There are *monsters* coming and we need to stop them! If you want us to beat the monsters, then be *very* quiet." She reached out to a rather stunned Laurel, gesturing at the diaper bag. Laurel handed her two baggies filled with oat cereal and raisins. "This is magic food. If you hide back here and eat super quietly, then you'll turn invisible and the monsters won't be able to see you."

"Monsters are not real," Laurel rapidly assured her children, who remained secreted behind the theater. "Ms. Millay's just playing a game with you."

Two pairs of wide eyes peered through the curtains as Millay took a seat on one of the miniature ladder-back chairs. Olivia rewarded her young friend with a full thermos of coffee. Harris folded up his long legs and settled onto the floor. Olivia pulled the only adult-sized chair against the dress-up chest. She opened the manila folder containing the incomplete manuscript and cleared her throat. "I have a feeling our time is limited, so let's get started. Did anyone find a clue after reading Camden's book?"

Harris removed a stack of paper from his own folder. "There wasn't enough info on Blake Talbot in that single chapter Camden wrote about the now-famous rocker, so I did some digging on the computer." He passed out copies of the printouts. "All three Talbot kids attended The Hotchkiss School in Connecticut. It's one of the top prep schools in the country, and even when the Talbots went there, it cost close to thirty grand per kid."

"Damn!" Millay exclaimed. "I wonder if they'd like to adopt a nice half-Asian girl. I could use thirty Gs. Do you know what kind of sweet ride I could buy with that much cash?"

Laurel put her fingers to her lips. "Language please."

Harris stopped staring at Millay and continued. "Here's why I'm telling you about the school. Both Blake and his sister

Diana were really into creative writing. Blake wrote songs for his dorm band the whole time he was at Hotchkiss. Some of his lyrics were published in the school's literary magazine. Diana was the editor of the mag. For two years. She wrote short stories and poetry." He put the notebook on his lap. "I called the English department and pretended to be a prospective parent. They definitely teach haiku and there's no doubt that at one point, all three Talbot kids were familiar with haiku and could write that kind of poem."

Millay reached over and chucked Harris in the arm. "You *called* the school? Way to go, man! You've got a bigger pair than I thought!"

Harris's cheeks blazed crimson.

After quickly checking to see that the noises coming from behind the puppet theater were giggles and not the spasms of a child choking on raisins, Laurel pulled a mangled mass of paper from her diaper bag. As she flipped through the sheaves, Olivia was impressed to see that Laurel had not only highlighted passages, but had also written small, neat notes in the margin of every page.

"I thought it was sad how each one of the Talbot kids tried to make their daddy proud." She turned to a particular passage and smoothed down a wrinkled corner. "But it seems like only money could impress him. Listen to this section in Diane aka Deirdre's chapter: '*Her sweet sixteen party was the talk of Long Island's nouveau riche. Her guests received Tiffany jewelry party favors, her dress was designed by Vera Wang, and her chocolate truffle cake shaped like a Louis Vuitton purse was made by the executive pastry chef of Tavern on the Green.*

'*The compliments flowed like the champagne, with Don's sycophants tripping over themselves to pay tribute to his only daughter. The pudgy-fingered and corpulent businessmen proclaimed the girl regal as a princess, graceful as a prima donna ballerina, and as fine-boned as a French supermodel. And while Don accepted the praise with a nod here and a forced smile there, Deirdre grew more and more enraged.*'"

Laurel pointed at the page. "She yells at the guests, saying that she wants to be known for her brains and talent — that it won't be her brothers who'll continue the Talcott business legacy, but her."

"I remember that scene," Olivia said quietly. "Her father mocks her in front of everyone and tells her he'd never let a woman run the show. In fact, he didn't consider any of his children capable of taking over the family business."

"They're quite the Shakespearean family," Millay added. "Rich, beautiful, and power-hungry. Mix in a heavy dose of hatred, resentment, and jealousy, and you've got a tragedy in the making. The dad rules them like an American King Lear, knowing no one will dare stand up to him for fear of losing their allowance."

Harris stared at her. "How do you know so much about Shakespeare?"

"I went to one of those fancy, fascist boarding schools too," she answered cryptically and then hurried on. "In Camden's last chapter he described how Blake's character wanted to be in control of his own future. Remember how angry he was? At the end of the scene, he stared at the broken glass like he was planning to do something violent."

Laurel nodded. "That's true! He also said, *Time to take control.*"

"The line implies Blake is ready to get out from under his father's thumb," Olivia pointed out. "Perhaps he wants to break away from both parents, as it seems his mother was incapable of providing much in the way of parenting. He may be just as bitter at her for being negligent. And you're right, Millay. If we can believe Camden's interpretation, these children are all very angry."

"So how would murdering a gossip writer grant them revenge against a controlling father and a neglectful mom?" Harris wondered aloud. "Could they even have known Camden was working on this book?"

Setting a copy of *US* magazine on top of the dress-up chest, Laurel pointed at a photograph on the bottom left of the cover. "I don't know about the rest of the Talbots, but the oldest son, Julian, isn't a threat to anybody but himself. Here he is being escorted into a drug-treatment center by his . . . entourage." She seemed pleased by her word choice.

Olivia craned forward. The image provided a close-up of the profile of an ashen-faced young man wearing mirrored sunglasses and a black baseball hat.

"I read the whole article," Laurel gushed excitedly. "No official comment from the Talbot camp, but Mrs. Talbot came to visit Julian soon after he was admitted. According to this writer, the two have grown close over the last few years."

"I can't believe she's still married to that cheating scumbag, Dean. I would have hooked his favorite appendage up to a pair of jumper cables by now," Millay growled. "Must be no prenup."

Harris picked up the magazine and flipped through the pages until he found the short article proclaiming Julian Talbot's humiliation. "He tried to follow in his father's footsteps, but it looks like he couldn't handle the pressures of Wall Street. Cocaine addiction, outrageous debt, a few DUIs — this guy's in trouble."

Olivia sighed and Haviland raised his head from where he'd been happily napping behind a blue beanbag. "Millay, did you learn anything significant at work last night?"

Millay began picking at her cuticles. "Fish Nets was buzzing, that's for sure. I heard some of the narrow-minded crap I expected. Six or seven of our hillbilly homophobes were saying, 'Now there's one less fag in the world,' but most of the people were rattled." She kept her eyes fixed on her hands. "It takes a lot to shake these guys. They've all stared death in the eye out on the ocean, but this is a death they don't recognize. This had nothing to do with storms or waves, but a straightedge and a poem. They don't get it and neither do I!"

She glanced up at the kites as though wishing she could climb aboard one and float away, her eyes glistening.

"One of your patrons saw Camden, didn't they?" Olivia asked softly. Millay's shoulders stiffened. Olivia leaned forward and hardened her voice. "With whom, Millay?"

"Look, it might just have been the booze talking," Millay spoke after a lengthy pause. Seeing that she was backed into a corner, she sighed and went on. "Davie Malone *thought* he saw Jethro Bragg talking to Camden outside the bar."

Laurel squeaked. "Outside? As in . . . in the alley?"

Millay nodded her head miserably. "Yeah. Camden never stepped foot inside Fish Nets. Davie saw Camden and him at the mouth of the alleyway. No one saw Camden after that. But Jethro's not the killer. Trust me. He's not the type to take a man down in an alley, let alone spray paint an obscure type of poetry on the wall."

"I appreciate your loyalty to your, ah, clients, but Chief Rawlings will need to know this," Olivia said, holding Millay's gaze. *Why does Jethro Bragg's name sound familiar?* she wondered. She was pretty sure she didn't know the man. Millay met Olivia's dark blue stare and shrugged. "I'll tell the chief, but he won't be able to do anything about it. Jethro goes away for days at a time to work over the clam beds, and his boat's gone. His motor boat, that is. He lives on a houseboat — it's docked right at the marina. I walked to the slip this morning to ask him if he'd spoken to Camden. Jethro's not there."

"How do you know he didn't just zip out for a spell?" Laurel inquired innocently. "Steve takes out our whaler whenever he wants to blow off steam."

Millay didn't have a chance to respond because the puppet theater suddenly tumbled backward and two boys began to scream as though they'd fallen into a wasp nest.

Olivia expected Laurel to fly to their rescue in a fit of hysterics, but she calmly righted the wooden structure and dug the twins out from under a pile of endangered animal puppets. Gently laying several spider monkey puppets aside, Laurel pulled Dermot free from the plush mound and, after giving him a quick kiss, told him to sit on the yellow beanbag. Once Dallas had been extricated, hugged, and sent to the green beanbag, a peaceful silence descended upon the space.

"Nicely done, Mom," Millay said with a grin and then became serious again. "And to answer your question, I *know* Jethro's clamming because he always flies a flag from his houseboat when he's away. It's how he tells people he's not home."

"Flag?" Dallas piped up from his cushioned seat. He sounded as though he was speaking from the bottom of a sinkhole.

Millay walked over to the little boy's side and squatted down beside him. Closing one eye tightly, she screwed up her mouth and growled, "Aye, matey. A pirate flag!"

The child's eyes grew round with wonder. "I like pirates! They have booty!" he cried and everyone laughed.

Not a bad declaration, Olivia thought, smiling. *For a troll.*

"Sorry, but I've got to get the twins home for lunch," Laurel said and began to cram cups, empty baggies, and a package of wipes into her diaper bag. She shouldered the bag and gave Olivia a questioning look. "What do we do now?"

"We continue with our writing, for starters," Olivia answered with conviction. "Camden would have wanted that. Who's next in line to be critiqued?"

Millay raised her hand and saluted. "Me."

"It'll be nice to read your work after what's happened. We could all use a little fantasy right about now," Harris said, and once again, Olivia was impressed by the

198

young man's kindness.

Scowling, Millay replied, "This is dark fantasy, my friend. Just because I'm writing about mythical creatures doesn't mean my chapter will be full of sunshine and giggles."

"Well, that's a relief," Laurel shot back. "My life is *so* overloaded with sunshine and giggles." Her boys began to laugh at the silly face their mother was making and the writers couldn't help but join in.

Olivia could see the twins were getting restless. "So, we'll comment on Millay's chapter and we'll keep our eyes and ears open. Talk to people. Keep thinking about that damned haiku. If anything comes up or one of us happens to track down Jethro Bragg before we meet on Saturday, let's get in touch with one another." Olivia rose and Haviland immediately jumped to his feet. The twins, who hadn't noticed his presence before, became instantly curious. Approaching the poodle without the slightest indication of caution, they reached out their plump hands and roughly grabbed Haviland's curly fur.

"Doggie!" one of them shouted.

Before Olivia could decide exactly how to detach the human barnacles from her friend, Laurel took a plastic purple squirt gun out of her bag and aimed it at her sons.

"Let go of the nice doggie *right now* or I'll spray you! Remember, if the magic water hits you, you won't be allowed to go to McDonald's *ever* again!"

The twins obeyed instantaneously.

"Perhaps you should write a parenting book," Olivia told Laurel on her way out. Laurel smiled sheepishly, suddenly looking like a young girl herself.

"I know threats aren't the best parenting method, but sometimes you just do what you can."

"I wasn't being sarcastic," Olivia assured her friend. "I'm impressed with your calm and effective techniques. There are worse things than bribing kids with Happy Meals once in a while."

Flynn was placing bookmarks in a spinner rack when the writers appeared in the front of the store. Olivia waited for her friends to leave before speaking to him. "I'd like to get Laurel's boys a few books about pirates. Are there any available for their age level?"

Tossing the bookmarks aside, Flynn gestured for Olivia to follow him back to the children's section. "Are you their fairy godmother?" he teased.

"Certainly not," Olivia replied. "I'm merely an adult who realizes that the only chance they have of growing into decent human beings is by becoming enamored of books. Laurel can't afford new ones, but I can. It's as simple as that."

Eyes twinkling, Flynn selected several board books from a lower shelf. As he did so, Olivia chose two macaw puppets and added them to the books in Flynn's arms. "Those too." She pointed a finger at him. "And no more references to fairy godmothers or I'll be forced to sic my dog on you."

Haviland curled his upper lip, exposing a row of pointy, white teeth.

Flynn's fingers paused over the cash register. "I'm sorry. I shouldn't poke fun at you after what happened to your friend. I'm not normally insensitive. Please accept my apology."

Olivia knew everyone in the small town would have heard about the murder by now, but she couldn't help bristling a little. "No matter how private the pain, it becomes everyone's business in a town as small as this. Skeletons don't stay in closets in Oyster Bay. They're brought out and paraded through the streets."

Accepting Olivia's credit card, Flynn held the plastic in his hand and gave her a sympathetic look. "Sounds like you know about this custom firsthand." He waited for her to respond and when she didn't, he turned away in order to tender the sale. "I suppose it's a good thing I've got such a dull past," he stated airily, clearly trying to lighten the mood. "You can't get into too much trouble trapped in cubicle land for half your life. Borrow someone's stapler and not give it back, jam the fax machine, use the last of the powdered creamer at the coffee station — that's about as far as you dare go."

When Olivia reached out to take the bag, Flynn's fingers folded over her hand. "Remember, I'm new to Oyster Bay. Keep your secrets locked away from me as long as you want. I only want to see what you'd like to show me."

Unused to hearing such frankness, especially delivered by such a handsome and charismatic man, Olivia found herself at a loss for words.

When a mother carrying an infant in some kind of sack across her chest approached Flynn in search of a book called *The Baby Whisperer,* Olivia politely excused herself and left the store.

Outside, the air was twenty degrees warmer and stiflingly moist. Haviland blinked against the sun's glare and cocked his head at his mistress.

"All right, so I'm flustered!" Olivia

snapped. "He *is* very good-looking and it has been quite some time since my last —"

Haviland barked.

"Point taken, Captain. My mind should be on other matters." She hastened to the Range Rover. "But there's no need for you to act jealous either."

Ten minutes later, Olivia parked in the employee lot of The Boot Top and, giving her kitchen staff the most cursory of waves, went straight back to her office. Haviland perched firmly in the threshold, thereby increasing his chance of being fed choice tidbits by Michel.

Olivia called her aesthetician in New Bern and listened as the woman recommended several products to render Harris's skin condition less irritating.

"I'm in search of something more permanent than a topical cream," Olivia explained. "We're talking about a good-looking boy here, but because of this issue, he probably hasn't had a proper date since high school. And he'd be a real catch. Harris would treat some lucky girl like a queen."

The aesthetician laughed. "Then send him my way!"

"Can you help him or not?" Olivia was impatient to get to her computer.

"Only if you bring him into the spa," the

woman replied sweetly. She never seemed bothered by Olivia's abruptness. "I can see if he'd benefit from a series of laser treatments or IPL, which stands for intense pulse light. I can't prescribe a treatment over the phone."

Olivia wondered how she'd ever raise the subject to Harris. She didn't know him well enough to pull him aside and embark on a discussion about his facial rash, let alone drag him to a posh spa in New Bern to have it treated by a laser while she footed the bill.

"I'll find a way," Olivia promised.

Next, she pulled up the website for the *Oyster Bay Gazette* and searched for an announcement about the township committee meeting. By law, the time, place, and items to be discussed had to be posted for the public prior to the meeting. The notice had appeared in last week's paper and could also be found on the library bulletin board and on the town's website. Olivia easily found the link on the *Gazette*'s online site, opened the PDF file, and began to read.

"The meeting is *tonight*," she murmured under her breath. "Here it is! Listen to *this!*" she shouted, breaking Haviland's trance. He leapt up and barked nervously. "Committeeman Johnson proposes a discussion followed by a vote to sell the Neuse River Community Park land to Talbot Fine Properties for a sum of eight and a half million dollars."

She leaned back in her chair, lacing and unlacing her fingers together as excitement and anxiety coursed through her blood. She could feel it rushing through her heart, surging through her extremities as she rose from her chair. "The Talbots want a bigger piece of Oyster Bay." Taking Chief Rawlings' card from her wallet, Olivia picked up the phone and began to dial his number. "The question is: How far will they go to get it?"

CHAPTER 9

I will be the gladdest thing
Under the sun!
I will touch a hundred flowers
And not pick one.
— EDNA ST. VINCENT MILLAY

The smell accosted Olivia as soon as she stepped through the poppy red double doors of the Edward Thatch Middle School. Ammonia, sweat, and greasy food mingled with an animalistic odor of surging hormones. Like all large public buildings, the polished laminate floors still looked dingy beneath rows of dust-covered fluorescent ceiling lights. Without windows, the school's central hallway could belong in any hospital, mental institution, or low-security correctional facility across the country. Only the self-congratulatory trophy cases and forcibly cheerful bulletin boards identified the corridor as being a part of a building dedicated to learning.

Olivia followed the sound of murmuring voices, relieved to have left Haviland at home. Not only would his olfactory senses be overwhelmed but the impassioned arguments she expected to take place during the meeting would also cause her poodle far too much anxiety.

Previous notices listed the township meetings as being held in Classroom 105, but as Olivia passed the room, she noticed the door was shut. A purple sign had been hung across the narrow window slit, announcing that the meeting had been moved to the auditorium.

To Olivia, the word "auditorium" conjured an image of cushioned seats, velvet curtains, crystal chandeliers, and flashes of gilt. Having left Oyster Bay before middle school, she had never actually seen the Edward Thatch auditorium.

"It'll be just like Lincoln Center, I'm sure." Olivia chuckled to herself. "Instead of amateur productions of *The Wizard of Oz* or *Cheaper by the Dozen,* the citizens of Oyster Bay are surely treated to stellar performances of *Aida* and *Tosca.*"

Turning down another locker-lined hallway, the murmur of conversation swelled. The meeting hadn't started yet and townsfolk were standing in clusters outside the cavernous room, heads bent as they rapidly exchanged opinions. Words ricocheted off the sand-colored cement walls in a sharp staccato. Already Olivia could see tension in the furrowed brows and balled fists of those waiting just outside the propped auditorium doors.

Suddenly, the clang of a bell blasted through the wall-mounted speakers, cutting through the clamor as the adults jumped to attention, their memories triggered by the sound. Though some of them hadn't trod a public school hallway for nearly forty years, the local business owners, lawyers, Realtors, shrimpers, stay-at-home mothers, waitresses, builders, and barbers responded to the signal as if they were still clad in letter jackets and poodle skirts.

The townsfolk chose seats quickly, arranging themselves by cliques just like the school's current students. Despite the fact that she had always kept herself apart from such groups, Olivia couldn't help herself from searching for a familiar, comfortable face. Therefore, she was delighted to feel a tug on her arm and to look down at the darkly tanned, heavily made-up face of Dixie Weaver.

"Have they started yet?" Dixie licked her

finger and scrubbed at a smudge on the top of her left roller skate. In addition to the milk white skates, Dixie wore boys' tube socks, a plaid miniskirt, and a navy sailor top. Her feathered hair had been styled into high pigtails and she held a Blow Pop in one hand.

Dixie noticed Olivia's appraisal. "I'm channelin' Britney Spears's first video. You probably never saw it, but that's because you don't have teenage boys. I can lip-synch the whole thing and Grumpy loves me in this outfit. Can you spot him in this herd?"

Scanning the crowd, Olivia noticed Annie Kraus and her husband Roy in the second row. The B&B proprietors smiled in greeting. Olivia waved her hand briefly, her gaze drawn to the man sitting next to Roy. His appearance was similar to Roy's as both men were tall and lean with dark hair and eyes, and Olivia assumed the man was likely Roy's brother. But while Roy's face was rounded by rich foods, his brother's was gaunt and more weathered, like those of the fishermen in the room. His lips were drawn together and an unpleasant thought seemed to have settled between his creased brows.

Tearing her gaze from the discomfiting visage of the stranger, Olivia spotted Grumpy toward the back, a few rows shy of the rear wall and the enormous painting of Blackbeard standing at the prow of his ship, *Queen Anne's Revenge.* Blackbeard, also known as Edward Thatch or Edward Teach, was an unusual personage to choose when selecting the name for a middle school, but Olivia liked the choice. She imagined that children caught between childhood and young adulthood could identify with the romanticized version of Blackbeard's life, which elevated his supposed skill, smarts, and wiliness to legendary heights. To these confused and insecure youths, the rebellious nature of the eighteenth-century pirate, who plundered from North Carolina to the Caribbean and had rousing parties with fellow buccaneer Charles Vane along the banks of the Pamlico, was cause for idolization.

"He's up there." Olivia showed Dixie where her husband was seated.

Dixie scowled. "Now how does he expect me to climb up all these damned stairs with my skates on!" She sighed. "Men. Thick as mules, I swear."

Following Dixie was a slow process. She'd stop every few aisles in order to chat with the person seated at the end of each row and only hurried when Mayor Guthrie picked up a handheld microphone and called the meeting to order. He rapped on the podium with a wooden gavel and then quickly stepped aside to allow one of the local ministers to recite an opening prayer. By the time the audience bowed their heads, Dixie and Olivia had finally taken their seats.

After the Pledge of Allegiance, Oyster Bay's portly mayor called for the minutes of prior meetings to be approved and the townsfolk settled down for a long wait. After completing mundane business such as passing a proposal for a universal speed limit within the downtown area, voting on the budget for mosquito and litter control, salary increases for certain town employees, and a review of the maintenance contract for the parking lots serving the public beaches, the committee members were ready to discuss the final proposition of the evening.

It had taken an hour and a half to get to the agenda item of interest. During that time, in which the townsfolk coughed, fidgeted, cracked gum, knitted, snacked on beef jerky or hard candies, and muttered softly to one another, Olivia had noticed a man carrying a laptop slip into the auditorium wearing an expensive tailored suit and a politician smile.

Committeeman Earl Johnson rose to his

feet. A hush fell over the crowd as he took the microphone from the mayor. A good-looking man in his mid-fifties, Earl owned the marina and the general store supplying the rising numbers of boaters stopping overnight in Oyster Bay's sheltered cove. Genuinely liked by almost everyone in town, Talbot Properties had won the right man to their side. And since Earl was the person putting forth the proposal for a vote, Olivia wondered if the marina would soon be expanding.

Earl smiled as he tapped on the microphone and then stuck one hand in his pocket. His casual dress and posturing seemed to relieve some of the apprehension in the air, but the sheen of perspiration on his brow gave away how important the proposal was to the committeeman.

"As many of you know, our little town has been experiencing quite a growth spurt. *Time* magazine put us on the map and now people want to vacation here, live here, and start businesses here." He held out his arms in a brief shrug. "I know change isn't always neat and tidy and isn't always welcomed by all. But it's coming to our town, that much is certain."

He paused and Olivia was impressed by his sense of timing and calm delivery. "This past year, as a result of Oyster Bay's population boom, we've seen some exciting new businesses open." He consulted his notes. "Recently, some of our long-vacant retail spaces have been transformed into a boutique clothing store, a bookstore, and my favorite, a toy store named Animal Crackers."

This earned him a few chuckles. Even though Animal Crackers wasn't housed in one of Olivia's buildings, the revitalization of those adjacent to hers were a boon. Most of her rentals had been filled by boutiques she was more than happy to patronize. She especially liked Possessions, an upscale consignment store, and Palmetto's, a woman's clothing store specializing in colorful, washable cottons in stylish cuts and colors. The last lease she'd signed had been for The Potter's Wheel. The owner, a master potter from western North Carolina, planned to sell his own wares while conducting workshops for both children and adults. At first, Olivia had been reluctant to house a business requiring three kilns capable of reaching two thousand degrees, but the potter had showed her how some simple renovations to the back room could safely accommodate the equipment. In the end, her own willingness to support the arts had allowed her to be swayed into agreeing to the potter's terms.

"More and more folks have decided to call Oyster Bay home — even if just for the summer months," Earl continued. "And this means we need more houses for them to live in. Talbot Fine Properties has made the town an offer for the Neuse River Community Park land. They plan to develop this land into a housing complex called Cottage Cove.

"Cottage Cove will feature single-family homes, townhouses, and an apartment complex. There will be a clubhouse, a pool, tennis courts, a putting green, and jogging trails. As you can see on the agenda, the town has proposed to sell the land for eight and a half million dollars. The grave sites at the current park will be relocated to the Confederate burial site at the Third Street Methodist Church. This transfer will occur with the utmost dignity. And there's more." He held out his hand. "But I'd like Max Warfield from Talbot Fine Properties to personally show you the rendering of Oyster Bay's brand-*new* park."

The crowd rumbled with displeasure as Max took the microphone from Earl. The Talbot representative grinned self-effacingly and Olivia got the feeling he'd been in this situation many times before and it didn't bother him in the least to meet the hostile eyes of the locals. In fact, the confident set of his shoulders indicated that he relished the opportunity to convince people that his company wasn't a villain, but the savior of their unsophisticated town.

"Yes, I'm the bad guy," he began in a honeyed voice and several women called out "amen" in response. He smiled at the shadowed faces before him. "Now that we've established that, please hear me out. When I show you what I've got here, you might just change your mind." He tapped his laptop, which was hooked up to a projector. "Yes, Talbot Fine Properties would like to build a lovely community of homes on your park land, but my company does not want to leave the town without a park. Therefore, in addition to paying nearly nine million dollars for the old park land, we're prepared to include a new and improved park as part of the final proposal."

Earl Johnson, Debbie Hale (one of the female committee members), and Mayor Guthrie did their best to appear pleasantly surprised by this revelation, but Olivia wasn't fooled by their act and she suspected few of the townsfolk were either.

"Allow me to show you the new and

improved Talbot Community Park." Max nodded at a man stationed by the door. With well-timed synchronicity, the lights went out the same moment the projector was turned on, revealing an architect's drawing on the large screen occupying center stage. The image was rendered from a bird's-eye view and was carefully labeled.

"Look! A real playground!" a woman whispered to her neighbor as the next image showed a stylized drawing of the children's play area. "It's wonderful!"

Indeed, the playground featured two sets of swings, a sandbox, a teeter-totter, and an enormous wooden castle structure complete with firemen's poles, slides, monkey bars, and a rock wall. A small building housed restrooms, a vending machine area, and three water fountains at different heights. Benches surrounded the mulched area, and the covered areas with picnic tables looked like old-fashioned bandstands with their striped roofs and wide-planked floors.

The next image displayed a map of paved walking trails and dirt tracks reserved for mountain bike enthusiasts. The final slide featured a generous parking lot bordered by a white split-rail fence and landscaped flower beds. Upon entering the park, one would be greeted by a flowing fountain featuring a statue of a jumping dolphin.

"We don't have dolphins here, Mack!" one of the men called out.

Max smiled. "Pretend it's a blue heron then. I've seen them flying over the Ocean Vista condos." He gestured to his underling and the lights were turned back on. "So there you have it, folks. A new park, nine million dollars added to the town budget, and an attractive community of homes for those looking to relocate to Oyster Bay. I can assure you that these are tasteful, quality homes built to blend in with the traditional style of the area. Thank you for considering this proposal."

There was an immediate explosion of excited chatter in the room. Mayor Guthrie resumed the podium and banged his gavel.

"We're going to vote on this proposal tonight, so if any members of the public would like to ask questions or voice your concerns, now's the time. Please raise your hand and wait to be called on so everyone can be heard in an orderly fashion."

Dixie snorted. "In other words, we'd best behave ourselves or we'll have to sit in detention."

A burly man wearing a sweat-stained T-shirt and dirty khaki shorts stood up. Without bothering to wait for the mayor to give him permission to speak, he shouted, "It's a damned disgrace to move those graves! Those boys died fightin' for this place. They *bled* for us. And now we're gonna dig 'em up like they're some kind of weeds and stick 'em in the ground someplace else?" He turned to face the audience, his face dark with anger. "Don't they deserve peace? My great-great granddaddy's buried at that park. You'd best not touch a splinter of wood on his coffin or you're gonna have to answer to *me!*"

Several people jumped to their feet and clapped loudly as the rest of the crowd tittered, wondering how the refined committee members would handle the man's overt threat.

"They're having the time of their lives," Dixie remarked with a fond smile. "A few rounds through the gossip mill and the story will have him draped in a Confederate flag and holding up a photograph of his great-great granddaddy."

"Or a gun," Grumpy murmured in agreement.

Olivia's eyes were on the broad back of the man who had spoken. "Who is that?" she asked Dixie.

"Jethro Bragg," she answered readily. "Quiet type. Clam-kicker. He's a war vet.

Been in Iraq and Afghanistan. He had a house and a girlfriend when he got deployed, but lost them both while he was on tour overseas. She lives with an insurance salesman now." Dixie sighed. "Jethro saw a lot of hard things when he was away — lost some of his friends to a car bomb. I can see why the idea of movin' those soldiers troubles him."

Olivia knew the weight of loss and fought against feelings of sympathy for Jethro Bragg. After all, he'd been the last person to see Camden Ford alive. Olivia stared at the man and wondered if his eyes were haunted by more than loss. Perhaps something even darker lingered there, a shadow of horrible deeds. "Is he a fisherman?" she asked Dixie.

"Nah, he's one of those quiet types. Doesn't like to work with a crew. He's been a clam-kicker ever since the war. Before that, he was a land surveyor. He must still know folks in the field, since he came here tonight ready for a fight, so this whole thing was no surprise to him."

Her gaze still fixed on Jethro's back, Olivia thought about the profession he'd chosen. Clam kicking was a method of netting clams by using the backwash from a motorboat propeller to force the clams to the surface. It was a lonely occupation. Jethro would only have to talk to another person when it came time to sell his catch.

He's a man who likes to be alone with his memories, she thought. *Or worse. A man crippled by the past.*

As Earl Johnson made his way to Jethro's side in order to speak to him in calm, soothing tones, the mayor called upon a plump woman in the middle of the audience. "I think this idea is wonderful! Nobody ever goes to that old park anyhow. Have you all seen it lately? It's a disgrace. Me? I'd love to have that new playground. Not only do we get bathrooms, but we can also have church picnics in those nice covered areas. We shouldn't look a gift horse in the mouth, people!" She gestured at Jethro and spoke with pointed gentleness. "Now, I'm not saying I like the thought of moving those boys, but as long as it's done with respect, then why not lay our soldiers to rest in the churchyard? Why not give them a Christian burial while giving our living children a fine, safe place to play?"

Her statement was followed by a smattering of applause from the crowd and an enthusiastic nod from the minister onstage.

Several others made speeches for and against the sale of the park, but the combination of parents, outdoor enthusiasts, business owners, Realtors, and those engaged in all facets of the construction trade made it clear that Talbot Fine Properties was welcome to continue building in Oyster Bay.

Earl Johnson, who had returned to his seat after being shoved aside by Jethro Bragg, gripped the microphone and announced that it was time for the committee members to vote. "Who's in favor of this proposition?" he asked.

Without hesitation, all five members raised their hands and said, "Aye!"

A unanimous decision.

Mayor Guthrie beamed, pumped Max Warfield's hand, and stepped to the podium for his final address of the evening. "We can't get our shovels out yet, folks. The Planning Board will need to make the final call on this proposal next week. It's up to them to debate the amount of green space or storm water drainage required for the new development, but I have every confidence that Talbot Fine Properties has seen to every tiny detail."

He and Max Warfield exchanged smug nods. At that moment, Olivia felt an extreme dislike for their mayor.

"In the meantime," Mayor Guthrie continued — he was a man who loved the sound of his own voice, "might I suggest you bring

the family down to our Twenty-Sixth An-
nual Barbeque Cook-off this weekend?
Yours truly has been working since last year
in hopes of winning the Best Beef Rib
category. Come on by and bring a lobster
bib. It's going to get messy! Good night!"

The committee members were the first to
leave. Though buoyed by the outcome of
the meeting, all five had full-time jobs and
were eager to get home. The mayor stayed
to field any remaining questions from his
constituents and Olivia wondered how
many times she'd be approached by townsfolk about the proposition before the Planning Board meeting.

She leaned over Dixie. "Looks like our
vote is going to be a topic of interest,
Grumpy. I bet the diner will be filled with
curious folks between now and next Tuesday, all wanting to know if you're planning
on saying aye or nay."

The short-order cook shrugged. "I'll vote
for the new development, though I doubt
Talbot's homes are any better built than our
double-wide. When it comes down to it,
Dixie and me got a pile of bills high as the
lighthouse. Between the diner and the kids,
the only way I'm gonna be able to pay them
is if more folks eat my food."

Dixie's taciturn husband had never strung

so many words together in Olivia's presence before. "Perhaps you should raise your prices," she suggested.

Grumpy shook his head. "Don't wanna drive off the workin' man. I gotta cook for *some* folks like me so I don't feel like somebody's servant. 'Sides, most of the fishers have eaten and gone long before the suits are even awake."

Olivia nodded in agreement, gathered her purse, and stood up. It felt good to stretch her long legs.

"How about you, 'Livia?" Dixie asked with a smile. "You wanna expand your territory? Buy up a few more town blocks so these new folks will have places to shop? Maybe get their toenails painted? Eat some sushi?"

Not for the first time, Olivia was grateful that Dixie didn't resent her wealth or her success in business. The other woman seemed to genuinely admire her for her achievements and this esteem made her a rare friend indeed.

"I don't know," Olivia answered honestly. "The proposal seems most attractive on the onset, but the idea of relocating the graveyard does trouble me a bit. I also have concerns about the limited green space I saw on those renderings for Cottage Cove."

She fell quiet for several seconds. "With only five of us voting on such a major issue, I'd like to do a little more research before reaching a decision."

Dixie spun the wheels of her left skate around and around as she mulled over Olivia's response. "Fair enough." She elbowed Grumpy. "Come on, babe. We gotta go home and see which of our kids is on fire, hanging from the ceiling, or has run away."

Laughing, the couple wished Olivia a good night. Grumpy took his wife's arm and helped her down the stairs. Olivia exited at the other end of the row and was a few steps from the bottom when she noticed Chief Rawlings.

He wasn't in uniform, but he wasn't wearing one of his typical Hawaiian shirts either. In dark jeans, a light blue collared shirt, and a houndstooth blazer, he was hardly recognizable. As though sensing her eyes on him, Rawlings looked up and smiled, but he glanced away quickly, fixating on the man standing before him.

"I was wondering if you and I could sit a spell and talk." He spoke to Jethro Bragg with utmost courtesy. Rawlings' words were as relaxed as his dress, but his tone was laced with authority. Olivia was close enough to hear them clearly.

Jethro shook his head and growled, "Look, I didn't touch a hair on that queer's head, so we don't need to *talk*."

"Please come on down to the teacher's lounge with me. I'd appreciate your help concerning Mr. Ford's movements the night he was killed. This is an unofficial request. I'm just trying to get a picture of that night, that's all. Will you give me a few minutes of your time?" Rawlings' humility gave Jethro pause. But when it looked as though the clam-kicker wouldn't cooperate, Rawlings put a hand on the other man's shoulder. "Come on, man. I don't want to go home and put on my uniform. I'd rather not have to turn all the lights on at the station for just you and me. No need to make our electric bill any higher. Besides, there's no coffee, so what do you say?" He held out his hand in the direction of the hallway as though assuming Jethro would comply. After a moment's hesitation, he did.

Olivia glanced at her watch. It was half past nine and she was tired. As much as she wanted to wait for the chief outside the teacher's lounge, the vision of her peaceful home and the lulling call of the surf won out over curiosity.

Her evening wasn't over yet, however. She ran into Annie, Roy, and the stranger Olivia took to be Roy's brother in the hallway.

"How's Cosmo?" Olivia asked Annie.

"Better. He took a nice long walk on the beach this afternoon and the sea air did him good. I laid out a nice afternoon tea for him." She colored. "We don't normally fix food other than breakfast for our guests, but I feel like Mr. Cosmo is more like family than some sightseer. Besides, I just couldn't send him out in search of a snack in the state he's in."

Olivia admired the innkeeper's generous spirit. "Your care is exactly what he needs right now." She turned her body slightly in order to include Roy and the unfamiliar man in the conversation. "How are you, Roy?"

"Good, but busy," he replied. "We're into the season full-swing now. Booked solid until October."

Roy didn't appear inclined to linger any longer, but Olivia's inquisitiveness prompted her to thrust out her hand toward the man standing next to Roy. "I don't believe I've seen you around town before. I'm Olivia Limoges."

"Atlas Kraus, Roy's brother," he answered, briefly squeezing her hand.

Annie gave her brother-in-law a nervous smile. "Atlas is staying with us for the season. We just can't handle all the work so it was a real blessing when he called Roy and said he'd like to stay with us awhile. Atlas is real good with his hands. He can build, repair, or restore almost anything!"

Olivia could sense a current of unease underlying Annie's praise. Atlas dipped his head in acknowledgment of the compliment while Roy shifted on his feet. He was obviously eager to get on his way.

They don't want Atlas too involved with the inn, Olivia thought, listening as Annie described the breakfast she had planned for the next day.

She watched the body language of the three people. Annie was gripping her own fingertips as though trying to hold on to a sense of control, Roy's eyes shifted everywhere but avoided looking at his brother, and Atlas was studying Olivia, his dark gaze alert and unblinking. Of the three, he was the most composed. He leaned against the wall, pressing his wide shoulders onto the cool cement, his muscular arms folded over his chest.

"Roy says that you're one of the five people who'll vote on this thing next week," he said. "Must be pretty exciting to be so important."

"Like the mayor stated, Oyster Bay is

certainly growing," Olivia answered enigmatically. "Did you relocate from a similar town or are you a city man?"

"I've lived in both," Atlas replied with equal ambiguity.

"And have you always been a fix-it man?" she asked, hoping to provoke more information from him.

Roy's brother remained unfazed. "Construction jobs, mostly. I go where the towns are experiencing a building boom like this one. I've moved around a lot."

Olivia didn't like the picture the term "building boom" called to mind. She loved Oyster Bay the way it was. Sometimes the lack of amenities was an inconvenience, but the coinciding absence of traffic jams, monolithic superstores, and ugly office parks more than made up for the occasional long-distance errand.

"Do you plan to work at The Yellow Lady and do construction jobs as well? That'll be quite a full plate," Olivia said.

Atlas shrugged and looked away. "There aren't any openings with the crew building the condos on the bluff, but I might be able to land a spot if this new development goes through. I plan to be the first guy in line when they hand out the job applications." He turned back to her and smiled. "So keep me in mind when you vote, okay?"

"Sure," Olivia replied and bid the Kraus family good night.

She passed the teacher's lounge and noted a crack of light at the bottom of the closed door. Pausing, she heard the even bass of the chief's voice followed by Jethro's angry rumble. The words were unclear, however, so Olivia didn't linger.

Outside, she was met by a pleasant breeze. The humidity had receded, leaving in its wake a clear sky filled with crisp stars and a bright sickle moon. As Olivia drove beyond the town limits and later turned off the paved road onto the sandy track leading to her home, she noticed the bank of luminous clouds hanging just above the horizon.

Their silver hue seemed especially celestial against the ebony sky. Upon reaching her house, Olivia opened the sliding door to the deck, released Haviland, and together the pair meandered through the dunes to the beach.

For a long while, Olivia stared at the moon-illuminated clouds, thinking they looked like an ideal setting for a fairy tale castle, or the colossal abode of Jack in the Beanstalk's giant, or perhaps the pristine, white-marbled temples of Olympian gods.

"I met a man named Atlas tonight," Olivia

said to Haviland. "Either his parents shared a love of maps or they expected him to have enough strength to hold up the world. It's some name."

Haviland barked and held his nose high, sniffing the air.

Olivia had always adored Greek mythology and reread Bulfinch's collection every two or three years. "Atlas was the son of a Titan, brother to Prometheus and Epimetheus," she spoke to the night-darkened waves. "As punishment for joining in the war against the Olympians, he was condemned to bear the weight of the sky on his shoulders for all time. Because of his assignment, the Titans Earth and Sky would never again be able to meet. Never again would they embrace."

She glanced above the ridge of clouds to the star-sprinkled heavens.

"What is Atlas Kraus's burden, I wonder?"

Olivia stood at the edge of the surf, reviewing the evening's events. Would the next day see the resolution of Camden's case? What might Jethro Bragg's anger reveal? Why had he been talking to Camden? Why were Annie and Roy on edge? How would the Planning Board vote next week?

"Let's go in now, Haviland. We'll come back bright and early tomorrow. Perhaps we'll take out the Bounty Hunter and dig for treasures. For now, I just want sleep."

That night, she had the dream — the dream in which her mind returned to the last time she saw her father. These were not photograph-clear images, but flickered scenes stretched and bent and distorted by time.

The dream walked a tightrope between memory and nightmare.

Olivia was nine years old. There were her tan, skinny limbs, her favorite blue boat shoes with the untied laces stained by mud and grass, and the T-shirt with the unicorn iron-on — faded and cracked from repeated washes. Her hair was stringy and tangled, hanging down the sides of her face like a fisherman's net. It hid the fear in her dark blue eyes.

She was on her father's trawler heading toward the open sea. It was the eve of her tenth birthday and the night sky was clouding over. Her father stood at the helm, guzzling cheap whiskey and grumbling to himself. He seemed to have forgotten she was there. Cold, Olivia wrapped an old sweatshirt around her shoulders. It was pink and smelled of salt and fish, but it was still a comfort.

The night wore on.

Suddenly, her father swiveled, his hands

leaving the wheel as his eyes flashed with rage. Snatching the sweatshirt from Olivia's grasp, he cursed her, using language she'd never heard him speak until after her mother's death. But every time the whiskey flowed, he searched for words that would wound his daughter. Words that would form scar after scar.

"It's your fault!" he snarled at Olivia. "She's dead because of you."

The black sea seemed to rise with his anger, and for the first time, Olivia was terrified he would strike her. He'd raised his calloused and weathered hand above her many times, but the blows never landed.

Springing out of his reach, Olivia scrambled into the dinghy tied to the side of her father's boat. She jerked the rope securing it to the larger vessel from its cleat and leapt aboard. Ignoring her father's wrathful threats, she pulled in the wet mooring line and began to row in the opposite direction.

The clouds multiplied, obscuring the little craft in a shadow of dense, protective fog. After rowing until her arms ached and the blisters erupted on her palms, Olivia slept. When she woke, she looked around at the dark and unreadable ocean. It still felt like night, but there were no stars, no moon, no horizon line to distinguish the ocean from sky.

There was only the fog.

Hours later, a shrimper heading out with the dawn light found the drifting dinghy and brought the mute girl back to dry land.

She never saw her father again.

CHAPTER 10

When one's character begins to fall under
suspicion and disfavor, how swift, then, is
the work of disintegration and destruction.
                                    — MARK TWAIN

The dream clung to Olivia like a sweater
slung over the shoulders. Though night was
long over and the dawn had brought light
and heat and a high tide, Olivia couldn't
wait to get out of bed and escape the air of
her room. The darkness might be gone, but
the space was crowded by the memories the
dream had conjured.

Gathering her metal detector and the bag
holding her folding trench shovel and nylon
dishwashing brush, Olivia followed Haviland as he raced to the beach in a blur of
black fur.

As she walked past the lighthouse keeper's
cottage, Olivia glanced at the window of her
childhood room, half expecting to see her

child self gazing back at her. But the glass only reflected twinkles of sunlight. The day was simply too fresh and full of promise to be held captive by the past, so Olivia turned her face toward the ocean, slipped on her headphones, and felt the presence of the dream dissipate.

She walked along the flat sand for three quarters of a mile and then headed away from the water's edge into the dunes. It was more challenging to walk there, but she hadn't hunted this deep around the grass-covered sand before.

Swinging the Bounty Hunter's disc back and forth, Olivia listened carefully to the chirps and blips, ignoring the low sound signaling pull tabs or nails. Finally, a high-pitched bleep indicated the possibility of a buried coin and Olivia removed her trench shovel from her bag and began to dig up the heavy sand. About a foot down, the tip of her tool struck something metal. Olivia tossed the shovel aside and reached into the damp hole with her fingertips.

Haviland appeared like a phantom from behind a dune and sniffed at the pile of displaced sand.

"Just a shotgun shell," Olivia told him, placing the find in her bag. "That makes four this year."

Standing up, Olivia surveyed the flat ocean. "I think we'll bend the rules a bit this morning. Let's walk back by the road and see if we can discover something more interesting."

Trotting up to the unpaved track, Haviland happily searched the unfamiliar scents along the side of the road, his nose quivering with excitement.

Olivia hadn't gone more than fifty yards before the metal detector indicated another coin possibility. However, after digging through the less yielding soil, she unearthed a second shotgun shell.

"Was someone picking off your relatives with a twelve gauge?" she demanded crossly of a curious gull and shoved the spent shell in her bag.

Overtly disregarding her customary rule to stop after a single find, Olivia continued to move the Bounty Hunter back and forth in a gentle sweep as she and Haviland turned toward home. A few hundred yards along the road, the buzz signaling yet another coin echoed in Olivia's ears. She almost ignored it.

Haviland barked impatiently. He was ready for his breakfast, but Olivia wanted the ground to provide a distraction from Camden's death, the upcoming Planning

Board meeting, and her inability to complete the chapter describing Kamila's reception by Pharaoh's other concubines.

"We'll go to Grumpy's this morning, Captain. *If* you help me dig."

Together, the pair set to work. After moving about a foot of dirt, Olivia sat back on her heels and wiped the sweat from her brow.

"Nothing!" she shouted in annoyance. Rising, she scanned the displaced soil with the metal detector and, when the panel blinked red, spooned the dirt into a sifter. Furiously shaking the dirt free, she ended up with several large pebbles, a twig, and a corroded circle the size of a penny.

Surrendering, Olivia dumped the unknown coin into her bag and increased her pace so that by the time she reached her house, she felt completely spent. After refreshing Haviland's water bowl and taking a quick, tepid shower, Olivia grabbed her laptop and drove into town.

Dixie had a sixth sense when it came to her regular customers. She always seemed to know when they'd arrive and what they were in the mood to eat. Olivia's usual table by the window had been wiped clean and set up with gleaming utensils, a spotless coffee cup, and a glass of tap water without ice.

Haviland jumped onto the booth across from Olivia and, after greeting Dixie with a toothy smile, focused his gaze on the passersby on the other side of the window.

"Florentine egg-white omelet for you, ma'am?" Dixie asked, her small hands looped under a pair of pink suspenders. The unlikely accessory was clipped to the waistband of a purple crinoline skirt, under which Dixie wore a pair of white spandex shorts. Frowning, she held up her pointer finger. "Nope. You don't feel like eggs today. You want some comfort food. Something sweet and buttery. Am I right?"

"As usual," Olivia agreed. "I'll be decadent and have the Oyster Bay French Toast."

"With a side of carcinogenic bacon?"

Olivia smiled. "Yes, please." She examined the pieces of fabric covering her friend's forearms and elbows. "Are those arm socks?"

"Arm *warmers*," Dixie corrected. "They're all the rage with the teenage girls. I borrowed my daughter's just to see what all the fuss was about. Any luck on this morning's treasure hunt?"

Haviland issued a muffled bark.

"Two shotgun shells and a coin. The

coin's soaking, but from what I could see, it's an Indian Head penny. Can't read the date yet."

Dixie shook her head. "That's a lot of effort for a penny, isn't it? No wonder you stay so damned thin. Let me put your order in and then I'll come back and fill you in on some gossip you'll find *very* interesting." With a wink, she skated off to the kitchen.

Booting up her laptop, Olivia tried to immerse herself in her ancient Egyptian setting. She imagined Kamila bathing in a cool, shallow pool filled with floating lotus blossoms. Afterward, she'd rub her skin with costly oils and drape herself in the thinnest linen shift. Sitting on a low stool in the morning's sunshine, Kamila would comb out her long, black tresses as she watched an ibis strut around the lush, private garden.

Just as Kamila was attempting to make friendly overtures toward a group of three older concubines, Dixie returned with Olivia's bacon and a platter of meat and eggs for Haviland.

"So," Dixie began. "You know Grumpy's got a cousin who works at the airport?"

"Grumpy's got a cousin working in every profession in the county," Olivia remarked.

Dixie smirked. "Probably three counties. But *this* cousin likes to tell us when the fancy planes come in. He keeps a list of them in a notebook. Writes down the rich or famous passengers whenever he can recognize them." She paused, waiting for Olivia to sample her bacon. "Guess who flew in as early as the cock crows this morning?"

"One of the Talbots?" Olivia deduced.

Looking disappointed, Dixie scowled. "You're no fun. How'd you know that?"

"Our writing group has been researching the family. Dean likes to appear and soften up the locals prior to any vote that might influence one of his bigger projects. He's got less than a week to butter up all the Planning Board members. I guess the Ocean Vista condos weren't grand enough to get him down here," Olivia remarked. " 'Course, we all approved that development in a flash. It was the first time somebody realized Oyster Bay was a real gem. Shows you how smart Talbot is. He decided to build before that *Time* article was ever written."

A ring sounded from the pick-up window and Grumpy's quizzical eyes searched out his wife. Seeing her positioned for a good long chat, he pointed at the platters of food and then turned away to focus on his grill.

"Be right back." Dixie skated off to deliver

tall stacks of pancakes to the patrons seated in the *Phantom of the Opera* booth. She whisked back to the kitchen, grabbed Olivia's order and two stainless steel containers of warm pure maple syrup and, after depositing the first with the pancake eaters, returned to Olivia's table.

Easing the heavy porcelain platter onto the table, Dixie said, "Don't see that Talbot's got too much convincing to do on this project either. Grumpy and Roy are voting for the new development and you know damn well Ed Campbell is going to say aye. After all, he'll be signing a load of new loans for the folks who want to buy those houses. Shoot, Ed'll probably be made president of the bank before they finish pouring the first foundation."

Chewing on a piece of soft, cinnamon-laced French toast, Olivia silently agreed. "That leaves Marlene and me and whether the two of us have issues with the lack of green space or the displacement of wildlife doesn't much matter, does it? Cottage Cove is going through. It only takes a majority to pass a proposal and the majority will vote in favor of this one."

Dixie chucked Olivia on the arm. "Don't sound so down. Think of the treasures you could find when they start digging up the park land."

Olivia immediately envisioned the grumbling excavators as they crunched the soil with their metal teeth. Thinking of an excavator biting through the crumbling steps and collapsing the iron fence surrounding the tiny graveyard forced her to put her fork down.

"How did you find out how Roy was going to vote so quickly?" she asked Dixie, hoping to expunge the image of the decimated burial site from her mind.

The customers in the *Cats* booth were signaling Dixie for their check. She smiled and nodded at them but didn't move. Turning back to Olivia as though she had all the time in the world, she leisurely continued their conversation. "Annie and Roy and that brother of his were parked right next to us last night. We couldn't help but trade thoughts on the proposal."

"I met Atlas Kraus after the meeting as well. He seemed . . . odd." Olivia was fishing, hoping Dixie would reveal her take on the stranger. Olivia trusted her friend's ability to read people.

"Not odd. I can warm up to odd. *I'm* odd. You havin' a dog for a best friend is odd. No offense, love." She blew a kiss at Haviland. "Annie told me that her brother-in-law used to have a family of his own in Idaho or Iowa. Wife left him and took their kid to another state. Told him not to call or visit. Ever. Can you imagine? Anyhow, word is he hasn't been the same since." Dixie pulled a sympathetic face and began to skate away. Looking over her shoulder, she paused. "He's got a damaged look to him, but maybe this town can heal him like it's been healin' you."

With Dixie's words echoing in her head, Olivia left Grumpy's and drove straight to The Yellow Lady. Cosmo waved to her from the front porch, looking refreshed and comfortable. He was seated in one of the cushioned wicker chairs and had his feet propped on a pillowed ottoman. He cradled a mug of coffee in both hands and a selection of newspapers sat on an end table nearby. A stack of eight-by-eleven typed papers rested on his lap.

"Good morning, Goddess of the Carolina Coast." Cosmo set down his coffee, clasped the papers against his chest, and jumped up in order to kiss Olivia on both cheeks. He then performed a sweeping bow in Haviland's honor, but the poodle was more interested in finding a shady spot to rest than in flattery. His belly stuffed, he waddled over to one of the mammoth potted ferns, stretched out beneath its emerald fronds, and closed his eyes.

"Excuse Haviland's rudeness. He overindulged this morning. But you're looking well," Olivia informed Cosmo pleasantly as she took the seat on the other side of the end table. The wicker creaked and crackled as she settled into the chair. She placed her forearms on the armrests, frowning. She didn't like furniture that protested over having to bear the weight of a human body.

Cosmo waved off her compliment. "If I let Annie feed me one more comfort meal you're going to have to transport me in a pickup truck bed. Go right ahead and line it with hay. Then a nice, talking spider can write words in her web to spare my being turned into Greek sausage links!"

Olivia laughed.

The two of them fell silent for a moment, listening to the buzzing of insects and the sound of a lawn mower rumbling in a neighboring yard.

"I hear they're questioning a suspect down at the police station," Cosmo said softly and caressed Camden's pages. "Some man named Jethro. Do you know him?"

"I didn't know he'd been taken into custody, though I was aware that the chief had questions for him," Olivia answered after a moment. "Jethro's an army vet. He makes his living selling clams and oysters. Resides on a houseboat and generally keeps to himself."

Cosmo's lovely eyes turned dark. He suddenly squeezed them shut in pain. "Why would he hurt Cam?"

Olivia's gaze traveled beyond the porch to a bed of calla lilies and lantana. "Honestly, I can't see why he would, but I don't know him personally, Cosmo. I do have a hard time believing he reads or writes poetry, but the chief must have his reasons for considering him a suspect."

"There must be thousands of those little poems out in the world, Olivia." Cosmo gestured at the packet in his lap. "There's all kinds of creative writing for the taking on the Web. Maybe the poem wasn't an original. Maybe this Jethro is some kind of plagiarizing psychopath."

Choosing her words carefully, Olivia said, "You raise a valid point about the poem. I shouldn't have assumed it was original just because I couldn't find it on the Internet. You may also be on target regarding Jethro." She paused, considering. "He may be unstable. He may even suffer from post-traumatic stress disorder. Still, I can't help but wonder why he'd randomly attack Camden. There's no connecting factor between the two men." Olivia thought of Millay's strong conviction that Jethro wasn't involved in the murder. She had to talk to her soon and find out once and for all why the young bartender had such unshakable faith in Jethro's innocence.

Cosmo raised both hands into the air. "Do you think only LA has crazies? There are broken people everywhere! In every apartment complex, every mansion, and every house — even the floating kind." He sank back into his seat and took a deep breath. "Anyway, this is all trickle-down gossip delivered by the friendly, neighborhood mail lady. I want to go down to Chief Rawlings' office *this* minute and find out if he's beaten a confession out of this . . . person."

At first, Olivia thought Cosmo might be joking, but one look at his face confirmed that he was completely serious. She reached over, ignoring the complaining wicker, and grabbed his hand. "The chief may still be interrogating Jethro or searching his boat. He isn't going to provide you with specifics. It's more likely Rawlings will politely send you on your way and you'll be more stirred up than before." She squeezed his hand. "Come to The Boot Top for dinner tonight.

I'm having drinks with Rawlings beforehand. Any information I can wheedle out of him during the cocktail hour will be yours for the hearing over a bottle of my finest wine."

Sighing theatrically, Cosmo relented. "*Fine.* I have work to do anyway. When I checked my voicemail yesterday, I had a message from the agent to that *American Idol* star. I can't remember his name at the moment. I don't watch those silly reality shows. *I* prefer *fantasy.*" He wiggled his eyebrows. "Well, this rich, handsome singer wants his *Malibu* beach house to remind him of a southern beach, so I'm going to spend the morning collecting seashells and taking a *billion* photographs."

"You should visit the town's new bookstore as well," Olivia suggested. "The owner's name is Flynn McNulty and he has some gorgeous coffee table books on Coastal Carolina with one-of-a-kind color plates." She rose and snapped her fingers lightly. Haviland got to his feet, blinking sleepily, and leaned his head against her leg. Her hand automatically reached down and stroked the soft fur of his ear. "I'll send one of my employees to pick you up at eight. Good luck with your research and if you do visit the bookstore, Through the Wardrobe,

247

do *not* drink Mr. McNulty's coffee."

Cosmo, who had stopped in the act of raising his coffee cup to his lips, paused. "Is there such a thing as bad coffee? If I can drink *Starburnt* I can drink anything."

"If you say so, but I felt it was my civic duty to warn you. See you tonight." Olivia smiled and walked away.

Olivia returned home to work on her latest chapter and to check on the soaking coin. She let Haviland loose in the yard and removed the penny from its vinegar-based solution. Scrubbing the remaining debris from the surface, she rinsed it off beneath a gentle flow of warm tap water. The penny felt slightly thicker between her fingers than a modern penny.

Excited, Olivia grabbed a jeweler's loupe from her desk drawer and moved to the window. Holding the coin beneath the magnifying tool, she could see the distinct profile of an Indian Head penny. Though the edges of the coin were well worn, the raised silhouette was in good shape. The native's mouth hung open as though he was in a state of shock and his eye sockets seemed dark and haunted. Olivia traced the feathers of his headdress with her fingertip.

"Eighteen sixty-three. So you were around

to witness the War Between the States." She turned the coin over, enjoying the feel of the aged copper and nickel.

Closing the penny in her fist, a thought popped into her mind. She opened the pocket calendar she kept in her purse and flipped to the notes she'd taken after visiting the cemetery at the Neuse River Park the day before. The name Henry Bragg leapt from the page.

"That's why Jethro's name sounded familiar!" she exclaimed as she noticed Haviland's face at the deck door. She let him in without taking her eyes from the notebook. "Henry *must* be Jethro's relative. And with Jethro being a veteran, I can understand why he'd feel passionate about the graveyard being disturbed."

Removing the lid of a jumbo pickle jar, Olivia dropped the coin and the shotgun shells inside. The metal objects clinked against the vintage razor case she'd collected a few weeks ago and the stainless watchband she'd found last time she and Haviland had ventured forth with the Bounty Hunter.

Olivia stared unseeing at the trinkets. "Camden *must* have discovered something beyond the fact that Talbot Properties wants to build this housing development. He *must* have learned something about Blake Talbot's dark business deal. But what? How does the park fit in? How does Jethro fit in?"

Haviland whined and placed his front paws on the edge of Olivia's writing desk, nudging the computer mouse with his nose.

"You're right, Captain Task Master. No more procrastinating. I'll read Millay's chapter before I work on my own if that's suitable."

Sitting upright, Haviland stared at her expectantly. Olivia retrieved Millay's document from the Bayside Book Writers file on the computer. Haviland cocked his ears as Olivia read aloud.

"Tessa didn't want to die.

"She stood on the cliff edge, looking down at the surging sea. Her black hair wriggled free from its silk band and flowed out behind her like a pennant. The wind whipped at the voluminous skirts of her white Initiate gown, but Tessa was too frightened to feel the cold.

"She was one of many. Two hundred Initiates would be pushed from the cliff top this dawn.

"Most would meet their death in the freezing waters far below, their bloated bodies washing to shore hours or even days later.

"Thirteen young girls would not die.

"Thirteen young girls would fly.

" 'It's in your blood, lass,' her nanny told her as she laced up the back of her white dress. 'You are not destined to drown this day.'

"Tessa could feel the rapid breathing of her Pusher. Standing a foot behind her, his warm exhalations fell onto the pale skin just under her left earlobe. The Priestess of the Initiates began to chant in a clear voice that was carried to every girl and hooded Pusher by means of powerful magic.

"The man behind Tessa took a step toward her. She drew in a quick breath. A pair of strong hands closed around her arms.

"She stiffened. Her time was running out faster than the grains of sea salt in her nanny's hourglass.

" 'Do not be afraid, beauty.' The man's rough whisper momentarily distracted Tessa from the ancient words of the Mistress. 'It'll be over soon, for better or for worse. May the gods show pity on you lasses.'

"Then, he lifted his voice so that it mingled with the Priestess's and those of the other men. 'You fall or you fly. We keep the blood pure. This is the way of the Gryphini. This is the way of the Gryphon Warriors.'

"The man pressed his hands against Tessa's shoulder blades.

"He pushed her off the cliff."

The sound of the ringing phone jolted Olivia out of the narrative. She hadn't realized that she'd edged closer and closer to the computer screen as she read Millay's opening paragraphs. Haviland was watching his mistress intently, waiting for her to continue.

Irritated, Olivia checked her caller ID and recognized Michel's number.

"We have a problem," he announced. "Our entire order of shrimp was delivered less-than-fresh for the second time in a row. I refused to accept it and will never buy from those bastards again, but I can't leave now to visit the docks. Olivia, I *must* serve my shrimp grits with prosciutto this evening. A little bird told me one of the food editors from *Coastal Living* plans to stop by the restaurant this evening. You've *got* to get me the freshest, plumpest, most succulent shrimp in the sea and you need to get it *now!*"

Olivia glanced at her watch. "Never fear, Michel. I'll take care of our crustaceous dilemma."

Reluctantly, she printed Millay's chapter in hopes of reading it before bed. Next, she hurriedly selected a pair of black slacks, a shimmery lightweight pullover in silver, and a pair of metallic sling-back sandals from her bedroom closet. She hung the ensemble on the dry cleaning hook in the Range Rover.

"To the shrimp docks we go, Captain," she said and opened the passenger door for Haviland.

The poodle jumped into the car, his puffy tail waving in excitement.

Roaring down the dirt road, Olivia left a screen of dust and sand behind her. The shrimp docks were ten minutes south of town and Olivia worried that the trawlers would either still be out on the ocean or would already be emptied of their payloads. The majority of the shrimpers left before dawn to return late in the afternoon. Olivia was hoping to catch a crew just pulling into the dock. As luck would have it, that's exactly what she saw as she parked in a hasty slant in the gravel lot.

"We've got cash," she murmured as she removed a bank deposit envelope from the glove compartment. "And we've got ice." She glanced at the large cooler in the back of the Rover. "You'd better wait here, Captain. These macho men might exhibit poodle discrimination and I can't afford to return without shrimp."

Haviland fixed his eyes on the dock, eager to accompany Olivia.

"Don't worry. I'll leave your window completely open just in case you need to leap out and sink your teeth into one of their calves."

The poodle leaned forward in his seat and stuck his snout into the salty air.

Normally, Michel oversaw the purchase of fresh food for The Boot Top, but Olivia often accompanied him on his trips to farm stands, herb gardens, and various commercial fishing docks. Michel was meticulous in his selections. He poked, prodded, and scrutinized every piece of fruit, cut of beef, or squirming lobster with an agonizing slowness. Even Haviland grew impatient with Michel, nudging him on the hip with his black nose in a futile attempt to hurry the persnickety chef along.

Confident that she could be as discerning as Michel, Olivia walked down the dock, shielding her eyes against the winking reflection of sunlight bouncing off the water. The roar of the incoming trawler's motor died down and the vessel coasted toward the dock. With feline grace, a man with a faded baseball hat leapt from the bow onto the dock, a bowline held loosely in his hands.

Ignoring Olivia, he secured the line to a cleat and then raced to the stern to catch another rope. Three men shouted companionable orders to one another, and within minutes, the *Clara Sue* was docked.

"Good haul?" Olivia asked the older man she assumed to be the captain.

"Can't complain," he answered gruffly.

Having spent the first ten years of her life with her fisherman father, Olivia knew the man's response indicated a full hold. "I'm Olivia Limoges. I own The Boot Top and I'm in desperate need of fine, fresh shrimp."

"Aye. I know who you are." The man paused in his preparations to unload and stared at her, his deep-set eyes softening as he did so. "You favor your mama. She was a real looker."

For the moment, Olivia forgot her purpose in coming to the docks. "Did you know her well?"

"Nah. The missus and me would cross paths with her and your daddy from time to time. She always had a kind word for us. Was a real lady, she was."

"Thank you," Olivia spoke after a long pause. "I don't remember much about her, so whenever I come across someone who does, those memories are a gift to me." Embarrassed by her own candor, she looked away toward the blue blur where the sky met the ocean.

"The waters we fished today were the same color as your eyes, miss. We caught some mighty fine shrimp there." The captain offered her a tentative smile. "How can I help you?"

Olivia explained how much shrimp she required and that she needed it loaded into her cooler immediately. She and the captain quickly agreed on terms.

"And I have a bonus here to show my gratitude." Olivia handed the money to one of the mates. The man removed the bills and began to count them.

The captain's eyes slid over to the money and then returned to Olivia's face. "You've got class, miss, just like your mama did."

A warm feeling flooded Olivia's heart. She handed the captain a business card. "I'd like you to be our primary shrimp supplier." She focused her attention on the captain. "If you contact my chef, Michel, he'll see to the arrangements."

The captain and his two mates expressed

no obvious satisfaction over her offer, but the slight straightening of their shoulders and the flicker of light in their eyes told Olivia they were pleased. Times were never easy for a fisherman, and a steady buyer created both an element of pride and provided a small measure of relief from constant monetary worries as well.

Back at The Boot Top, the kitchen was a cyclone of activity. Pots bubbled and knives flashed as two sous chefs chopped cloves of garlic, mushrooms, and scallions. Michel flew around the room, barking sharp commands, tasting sauces, and consulting his food-stained recipe notebook. Her employees were pink-cheeked and frenzied. Olivia smiled. All was as it should be in the kitchen of a five-star restaurant.

"Don't look so smug," Michel cautioned, reading her expression. "We need stellar reviews if we want to remain the best restaurant on the coast. Those shrimp had better be perfection."

"You won't be displeased," Olivia promised. She and Haviland headed for her office. After replying to several emails, she was just about to review the week's menus when one of her waitresses tapped on her door.

"Ms. Limoges? There's a man asking for you. I think he's the chief of police, but I'm not sure."

"Thank you, Lisa." Olivia checked her watch. "How did it get to be five o'clock? You can stay here, Captain. I'm sure Michel will give you a few nibbles of shrimp after he's had a smoke break."

Haviland looked hopeful. The poodle was very fond of fresh shrimp but was treated to them very rarely. Even then, he was only allowed a few, as Olivia didn't consider shrimp good for his diet.

In The Boot Top's luxuriant ladies' room, Olivia hastily changed into her spare outfit, ran a brush through her white blond hair, and put on mascara and lipstick. Briefly wondering if she smelled of shrimp, she rubbed on a dab of scented hand lotion kept on the counter for patrons' use.

Satisfied with her appearance, Olivia slung the bag containing her other clothes onto the chair in her office and marched out to the dining room to meet her guest. Chief Rawlings stood at the bar, a martini glass in his hand. He and Gabe were engaged in a casual conversation and Olivia reflected that most people seemed completely at ease in the lawman's presence.

It must make him good at his job, she thought. *To get to the bottom of a crime, he needs to listen to people's stories. The more open they are, the more details he's given to sift through.*

Upon seeing Olivia, Rawlings immediately put down his drink and took her hand in his. He studied her and seemed to like what he saw. For a moment, Olivia was afraid he'd kiss the back of her palm, but he merely squeezed her hand and then gently let go.

"Gabe makes an excellent vodka gimlet. I believe it's the best I've ever had." He smiled at the bartender. "And I've had quite a few."

Olivia glanced at the chief's inexpensive but meticulously pressed suit. She wondered if he had dressed up on her behalf and wasn't quite certain how she felt about the possibility. Gabe handed her a tumbler of Chivas Regal and she led the lawman to a small bar table flanked by leather club chairs.

"I'm glad you came early, Chief. I'm having dinner with Cosmo and I doubt you'll want to be here when he arrives. He's sure to want an update on Camden's case."

Rawlings traced his finger down the bowl of his chilled glass. "Please call me Sawyer. I'm off duty tonight."

Olivia's brows rose over the rim of her tumbler. She took a sip, wondering if Rawlings was hinting that he didn't plan on discussing the investigation with her. She decided to feel him out. "Is Jethro Bragg a suspect in Camden's murder?"

"Life in a small town. I've got more leaks in my department than an inflatable raft stuck on a coral reef." He sighed in resignation. "Yes, Jethro is a suspect."

"He's familiar with haiku?" Olivia asked incredulously.

Rawlings' shoulders moved in a slight shrug. "That's unclear. We searched his houseboat and he's got books on a variety of subjects, including poetry. He's had a library copy of *The Norton Anthology of World Literature* checked out for a year."

"Imagine the late fees," Olivia quipped. "There must be more substantial evidence against Jethro than the volumes on his bookshelf."

A flash of annoyance crossed Rawlings' features. "He followed Mr. Ford into the alley. Mr. Bragg is overtly antigay. He warned Mr. Ford to leave his town or face the consequences. He made several incriminating remarks."

Olivia watched several emotions flicker over the chief's face. She leaned closer to him. "You don't think Jethro's the killer, do you? You believe he's capable of killing and has probably taken lives while serving in the army, but you don't truly think this crime fits him." She didn't wait for his reply. "But having him in custody makes people feel better. The mayor. Camden's partner. The local press. It gives you some breathing room."

"That's a long list of assumptions, Ms. Limoges." Rawlings smiled thinly. "Mr. Bragg is being detained because he became violent during questioning. He has no alibi for the night of Mr. Ford's murder and spoke with a great deal of hostility against the victim."

"So no one saw Jethro go inside Fish Nets? He was just nearby, in the alley?"

The chief shook his head. "He never went in. When I asked him to recall his movements for the entire evening, he refused to cooperate. When pressed, he became violent." He stared at her curiously. "Any breakthroughs on your end?"

"No," Olivia reluctantly confessed. "We have no idea what the haiku means other than the killer needed to silence Camden."

Rawlings made a noncommittal grunt.

Gabe walked out from behind the bar and wordlessly served them another round of drinks. A middle-aged couple walked into the bar area, heads bent toward each other, hands interlaced. The man pulled out a padded leather stool for his wife and then asked Gabe for the wine list. Even without looking at the couple, Olivia knew they were from out of town by their New England accents. She gave them a friendly smile. Well-to-do tourists always ran up a nice tab at The Boot Top.

Olivia was just about to turn back to the chief when two men came in. She recognized the one on the left wearing an expensive suit and confident smile. It was Max Warfield. The Talbot Properties employee was laughing robustly in response to something his older, more attractive companion said, but Olivia sensed the humor was insincere.

"I believe we are about to be graced by the presence of Mr. Dean Talbot," Rawlings whispered.

"Then let's be as inconspicuous as possible," Olivia replied. "I'd like to eavesdrop on their conversation."

Rawlings grinned. "You shoot straight from the hip, don't you? Now I know he's got plenty of female fans, but do you have a crush on him too? Sure he's rich, powerful, and handsome, but he doesn't strike me as your type."

"He's not," Olivia hissed, eying the real

estate tycoon from her peripheral vision. Dean Talbot had the bronzed, unlined skin of someone who regularly frequents both tanning salons as well as the plastic surgeon. His hair fell in thick, silvery waves and he was lean without being too thin.

More interested in examining the screen of his BlackBerry than his surroundings, Dean settled into the chair behind Olivia while Max stepped up to the bar to order their drinks.

"And get me some peanuts or something. I'm freaking starving," Dean commanded. His voice was nasal and tinged with a Brooklyn accent.

Olivia saw Max's shoulders stiffen and silently wondered if the man resented the orders he was given. The moment Max set a tumbler in front of his boss, Dean popped out of his seat. "I'm going to take a leak. See to those peanuts, would you?"

Before Max could answer, Gabe come around from behind the bar with a glass dish filled with a mixture of cocktail pea-nuts, sesame sticks, and wasabi-dusted dried peas. Max, who was busy dialing a number on his cell phone, nodded at the bartender. As soon as Gabe turned away, Max spoke angrily into the phone.

"Are you sure you've picked the right guy?

He's already screwed up big-time! Have I backed the wrong horse? You *said* you had it all worked out!" He paused. "Yeah, it passed, but there's still the damned Planning Board."

Olivia and Rawlings exchanged curious looks.

"Look, kid. You know why I agreed to this. Just hold up your end and everything will be fine. And remember, you can't do anything without *me.* If I get so much as the slightest vibe that you're trying to screw me over I will crush you like —" Max immediately stopped speaking. Olivia heard him snap his cell phone shut.

Raising her tumbler, Olivia could see Dean returning in the reflection of the glass. Behind her, she heard the rattle of ice and a loud swallow as Max took a deep sip of his gin and tonic.

"Ah, snack mix!" Dean exclaimed as though Max had presented him with a chest stuffed with fine jewels. "What would I do without you?"

"You'd be just fine, sir," Max replied affably.

Dean laughed. "You're probably right." There was a pause in which Dean likely consumed several handfuls of the snack mix. "I saw the most interesting movie trailer during my flight down," he said next. "I think Blake's little girlfriend was the star. Pretty little thing, though I prefer my women to have more curves and more . . . experience. You seen her TV show? That girl is going places."

Their talk ventured into the realm of movies and television and Olivia no longer bothered to listen in.

Rawlings glanced at his watch. "I shouldn't keep you. I know you have dinner plans." He pushed his empty glass away but made no move to stand. "There's something I've been wanting to ask you, but it never seemed to be the right time."

Olivia's heart drummed. Was the chief going to make a romantic overture? Or inquire about her painful past? She wrapped her long, elegant fingers around her tumbler and nodded in encouragement.

"I value your opinion, Olivia, and before I made a fool of myself in front of your writer friends I wanted to see whether your critique group would welcome another member." He cleared his throat. "Meaning me, of course."

This was hardly the question Olivia had expected. Relieved, she let forth a rare giggle. "But we're the Bayside *Book* Writers, Chief, ah, Sawyer. Don't you write poetry?"

The chief's cheeks flushed slightly. "I *read* many genres, including poetry, but I started penning a mystery a few years ago and I'd love to bring it out of the drawer and see what the group thinks of the first few chapters."

Olivia believed Rawlings would make an excellent addition to their group. After all, with Camden gone, Harris was the only remaining male. Besides, Olivia was particularly fond of the mystery genre. She didn't enjoy them as much as historical fiction, but they ranked a close second. "I don't see why not," she replied. "I'll run it by them prior to this Saturday's meeting."

"Good." Rawlings stood up and gave her a little bow. "Of course, if I am invited to join, I'd prefer to be there as a civilian. Just another struggling writer type. I won't even bring a gun."

"That's fine." Olivia smiled. "If the need arises, you can borrow mine."

CHAPTER 11

It is not time or opportunity that is to determine intimacy; — it is disposition alone. Seven years would be insufficient to make some people acquainted with each other, and seven days are more than enough for others.

— JANE AUSTEN

Two days later, Jethro Bragg was still being held in a county cell. The townsfolk vacillated between quietly believing in the local man's guilt and complaining vociferously that the police had arrested Jethro in an act of discrimination against fishermen.

"The cops always point the finger at one of us when somethin's wrong!" Olivia heard a fisherman call to another at the Exxon station.

The second man shook his head in disgust. "Whoever killed that queer was a yellow belly. He weren't one of us. We go at it face-to-face — look our enemy in the eye when we take him down. It ain't our way to creep up on a man like that."

Olivia considered this exchange. The fishermen were right. The killer must have wanted to surprise Camden, to rob him of his life with stealth and quickness. Yet there was an element of cowardice to the murder that wasn't in sync with Jethro Bragg's character. She'd seen him at the meeting. He'd spoken his piece against the new development and wore his heart on his sleeve while doing so. He was a former soldier and proud of his heritage — hardly the type of man to attack an unarmed stranger in the dark.

"No, the *real* killer wanted to remain anonymous to his victim, yet he wanted to get public attention by writing the poem," she mused as she filled the Rover's tank. "A person of contradictions." Inside the car, she turned to Haviland. "Is Jethro Bragg that complex? I don't think so. They've got the wrong man, Captain."

Haviland stuck his head out the window and watched the fishermen drive off in nearly identical Ford pickups. He let loose several short barks, a sign of agreement.

Olivia was just offering Haviland an organic dog treat when her phone rang. It was Cosmo.

"I can't stay here another day!" he exclaimed into the phone.

"What's happened?" Olivia shoved the treat bag inside the center console.

"Nothing! Nothing besides the fact that my best friend in the world is dead and gone! Gone!" he shouted. Olivia could hear a dry sob through the phone. "Oh, I'm sorry. It's just starting to sink in. I woke up in a strange bed with the sun pouring in through the windows and the sound of birds twittering outside and I . . . can't . . . stand . . . it another second! I need car horns and smog, people speaking Spanish, and my own pillows. I want to go home!" He exhaled loudly. "There. I've said it. I feel like the biggest heel, but I want to go home now."

Olivia understood. She couldn't imagine two places more opposite in nature than the city of Los Angeles and the town of Oyster Bay. "Of course you do. There's nothing wrong with your wanting to leave this place. Go home if you want to. It doesn't mean you loved Camden any less if you do. How can I help?"

"You *are* an angel." Cosmo began to cry. "I want to take Cam with me, so I've decided to have him cremated. I just can't

269

leave him here, Olivia. I can see letting him drift away on a wave in the Pacific, some-place nice like Carmel or Malibu, but not in this ocean! This isn't his home either."

"Has the chief released Camden's body?" Olivia inquired gently.

Another sniff. "I met with Rawlings first thing this morning. They checked him . . . his body over carefully, but there were no clues. Apparently the monster who killed him wore gloves and a mask. There are no fibers or fingerprints or any of that stuff you see on those TV crime shows." His voice broke. "Poor Cam must have been so scared to see that creature rise out of the dark. What was he *doing* in that alley? Stupid, darling Cam! Look what you've done to us!"

Olivia could hear Cosmo banging on something. "Cosmo!" she shouted, reeling him back into their conversation. "What about the killer's handwriting? Is it being analyzed?"

After a pause, Cosmo answered. "Yes. Photos were sent to some state lab. It'll take *weeks.* At least that's what Rawlings told me."

Unable to think of what other information the chief might have volunteered to Cosmo, Olivia said, "Would you like me to help with the arrangements? I know Annie took you to the funeral home, but do you need someone to stand beside you during the cremation?" She hoped he'd refuse her offer. She couldn't think of anything she'd rather do less than bear witness to Camden's funeral pyre.

Cosmo didn't answer immediately.

"I need to do this by myself," he finally declared. "It's not that I don't want you there, it's just that this act is the last thing I have of him that's all mine. And then I'm booking a flight out of here. I know that sounds cold, but they have a man in custody and I can't *do* anything else for Cam. I wanted to take in everything about this town because it's where I lost him, but now I've seen it and I'm ready to go."

"I understand. In fact, I'll drive you to the airport." She hesitated. "And know that I won't forget about Camden *or* his case, Cosmo. I promise you that."

"I know." His voice grew stronger. "That's why I feel free to leave."

Cosmo departed later that same day. He tearfully hugged Annie good-bye and kissed Roy on the cheek after the older man had loaded Cosmo's garment bag and newly purchased souvenir duffel bag into Olivia's car. Atlas was on his knees spreading pine

271

straw in one of the perennial beds, but he put down his tools and stood up in order to properly wave good-bye as the Rover drove away from the inn.

Opening his window, Cosmo yelled, "Go get 'em, tiger!"

Olivia watched Atlas's figure recede in her rearview mirror. "What was that about?"

"He's interviewing with Talbot Properties today. Roy's been keeping him plenty busy, but Atlas would rather work building new houses." Although Cosmo looked washed out and weary, he managed a thin smile. "With all those shirtless men in tight jeans, who wouldn't?" He patted the top of the cardboard box containing Camden's ashes. "Remember those two who redid our bathroom, darling? Simply gorgeous! Beautiful, strapping Italians in white overalls." He glanced out the window, remembering, and his face lost some of its drawn look. "Cam and I didn't want to leave the apartment for a second! I think we ate out of cans for three days until we finally had to go out for more coffee. One cannot survive without coffee, no matter how magnificent the asses on the men bending over your tub are!"

Laughing, Olivia felt a lightness course through her. She was suddenly certain that Cosmo would recover from this blow.

Losing Camden would scar him, change him, and haunt him, but he was capable of living a full and colorful life despite his lover's violent death. The realization comforted Olivia.

As though sensing her thoughts, Cosmo reached over and squeezed her arm. "How long did it take you to get over your parents' death? I know you've never brought it up, but Annie told me they died within a few years of one another. Poor you."

Olivia suppressed a surge of anger over being the source of idle gossip once again. After all, it was almost a given that Annie would tell Cosmo about Olivia's past. Perhaps the innkeeper hoped to let the young man know he wasn't alone in his grief. Perhaps Cosmo wanted to get a more complete picture of the woman who'd recently befriended his lover. Either way, Olivia knew she needed to stop being so prickly when asked about her personal history.

"My mother left our house in order to pick up my birthday present during the onset of a hurricane," Olivia began. "She'd left it at the library — that's where she worked. After she'd gotten it from her office and returned to the car, a strong gust of wind gave a rotting telephone pole a fierce push." She swallowed. It never grew any easier to talk about the next part. "It fell, smashing right through the windshield. They say she probably didn't even know what hit her. Her death was instantaneous. I turned seven the next day."

Cosmo covered his mouth with his hand. "Oh! That's horrible!" He tightened his hold on the cardboard box in his lap. "Why didn't she wait? It was a *hurricane* for crying out loud."

Olivia shrugged. People had been asking her the same question since her mother was laid in the ground. "Around here, one can grow complacent about storms. They're such a part of our regular rhythm. Living on the coast, hurricanes and tropical storms are commonplace." She smiled wanly. "They're like unwelcome relatives. Sometimes, we don't give the weather the respect it deserves. This hurricane was only a category two by the time it reached Oyster Bay, and us locals can get pretty cocky about anything under a category three."

"Not *me*." Cosmo paled. "Give me a nice earth tremor anytime!"

"My father understood storms," Olivia continued as though Cosmo hadn't spoken. "He tried to stop her. It was the biggest fight they'd ever had! My mother usually listened to him, but she wouldn't back down this time. The last image I have is of her blowing me a kiss as she ran out to the car."

Cosmo's eyes were glistening. "What was the gift? The one she drove through a hurricane to bring you?"

Olivia glanced at Haviland's image in the rearview mirror. His eyes had been closed, but even in sleep he seemed to sense her need. He lifted his head and met her gaze, as though saying, "I'm right here."

"It was a puppy," Olivia answered. "And before you ask, he was on the front seat of my mother's car when the pole fell. He lived, but I wasn't allowed to keep him."

"Why not?" Cosmo was shocked.

"Because he survived," Olivia whispered.

A silence descended and the passengers listened to the sound of road passing beneath the tires. After a few miles, Olivia said, "I have Haviland now. The finest dog ever born. Not only that, but I believe Michel has packed us another bountiful lunch. Would you mind reaching for the picnic basket? It's behind my seat."

Cosmo graciously accepted the change of subject. "I'll tell you *one* thing, my dear. If you ever want to open a restaurant in LA, I'll be your first investor. That shrimp prosciutto risotto Michel made the other night will live on in my dreams."

"We aim to please," Olivia replied, pleased by the compliment.

For the rest of the ride, Olivia questioned Cosmo about his decorating ideas for his new client. As he talked, Cosmo distributed the courses of their delectable lunch. The Rover's occupants dined on curry glazed duck legs, vegetable tortillas, succulent peaches, and truffles until they were satiated.

At the airport, Cosmo insisted Olivia drop him curbside.

"I'd make a scene otherwise," he told her. The pair embraced next to the Rover.

On the return drive, Olivia thought about what Cosmo's life would be like during the next few months. She visualized his first days alone. He'd take a cab from the airport and, after a stiff drink or two, fall asleep, too tired for the tears he'd expected to shed. The following morning he wouldn't want to get out of bed. He'd linger there, replaying memories in his mind. But after a few hours he'd grow bored or hungry or be forced by other physical needs to rise.

Later, he'd open the fridge and smell the milk. It would be sour. The fruit would be spoiled and the cheese tinged with green. Not really hungry, he'd end up making toast with butter and jam just to see what food tasted like. He'd try to concentrate on at least one article in the paper, but reading would be an exercise in futility. He'd throw out the rotten food and take the trash to the street. Eventually, perhaps not until nighttime, he'd go out to the grocery store and empty the mailbox.

The next day he might have cereal because there was milk now. He might eat a banana. The small victory of having replaced the ruined food would be enough to encourage him to shower and, perhaps, to water the plants.

Cosmo would drink too much and talk aloud to Camden for hours on end. When Camden wouldn't answer, Cosmo would rage and then, his anger spent, he would weep. But each day he'd wake up and eat something. He'd get dressed. He'd drink orange juice without the vodka. One day, he'd finally venture out to his local Starbucks, the dry cleaners, and the outdoor market. He'd open a few letters and return a few calls. He would begin to live again.

"Cosmo will be fine," Olivia told Haviland. "Give him a year and he'll be on the cover of every interior design magazine on the rack."

Haviland looked out the window and

whined.

"I'll miss him too. And Camden. There's no one like them in Oyster Bay," she said as she approached the town limit sign. She glanced at the billboard featuring the Ocean Vista Condos and muttered, "Oyster Bay's changing, Captain. Who knows what our little population will look like in ten years."

Picturing dozens of Talbot Fine Properties building projects springing up all across town like mushrooms after a long rain made Olivia feel glum. It was Friday evening. Her restaurant would be filled with lively laughter and tantalizing aromas, but she didn't feel like being there. At home, her unfinished chapter waited for her, but she wasn't in the mood to write.

She was restless, craving something different. She wanted company — to share a bottle of wine and quiet the tumult of thoughts whirling around in her head.

If only for a short while.

Without being fully conscious of her actions, Olivia parked across the street from Through the Wardrobe. She approached the front door just as Flynn was turning the dead bolt with his key. Seeing her, he smiled.

"You caught me! I'm closing a full hour early." He gestured at the periwinkle sky. "It's just too nice a night to be stuck inside."

Olivia followed his gaze and nodded. "Dry though. I could use a cold drink."

Flynn studied her face. "I'd love a beer, myself. Where should we go?"

Hesitating, Olivia wondered if what she planned to say would turn out to be a grave error in judgment. Still, the sultry air and hazy moon convinced her to follow through on her impulse. Shrugging idly, she said, "How about your place?"

Flynn's Caribbean-style cottage was located on a sleepy street not far from Through the Wardrobe. Olivia and Flynn had shared a few drinks on his back patio. The drinks had led to a kiss, which quickly became heated, but Olivia wasn't ready to explore anything further with the attractive bookstore owner. Despite Flynn's coaxing and cajoling in hopes that she would stay a little longer, Olivia firmly said good night a few minutes shy of midnight. Seeing any further attempts at persuasion were futile, Flynn walked her through a jade green living room decorated with murals of tropical fish and waited on the front porch until she was inside her car.

Once she'd pulled away from the curb, Olivia whispered to her poodle, "His décor is wanting, I know." She laughed, feeling weightless and invigorated.

Olivia spent the remainder of the night in her own bed and woke early, stretching her long limbs languidly beneath her cool, white cotton sheets.

After taking a walk, Olivia finished critiquing Millay's chapter. She was impressed with the younger woman's imagination and the unique voice that grew stronger with each page. Having never enjoyed the fantasy genre, Olivia found herself eager to read more of *The Gryphon Tamer,* though one of her first recommendations was that Millay come up with an alternate title.

Your current title calls to mind a circus performer wearing sequins and brandishing a long whip, she wrote on Millay's draft. She went on to praise Millay's use of voice, the success of the suspense created by the opening scene, and her pacing. Olivia's main criticism was that Millay needed to tone down her use of alliteration and provide more description about the gryphon's lair.

Overall, an excellent start. You have definitely captured my interest! She scribbled at the end of the chapter. *I am curious to discover what happens now that Tessa has been claimed by her gryphon.*

While Olivia worked, the morning sky had grown overcast. A front was moving in from the south and by afternoon, an exhilarating summer thunderstorm would set upon the town of Oyster Bay. The rain would carry the smells of the deep ocean and childhood and everyone would welcome its arrival. Even the tourists would smile as it fell, watching from porch rockers or from covered balconies as they sipped coffee and propped paperbacks on their thighs.

As Olivia placed Millay's chapter into a folder, the phone rang. Flynn's voice rumbled through the speaker, his low baritone sounding like a distant train or the surf splashing over a jetty of stones. Olivia gravitated toward it but made no move to pick up the phone. Flynn kept his call brief, merely thanking her for last night and inviting her to join him for dinner. Olivia wasn't ready to see him again just yet, so she deleted the message the moment he was finished speaking.

"Let's take another look at the specs for the proposed housing development, Haviland. We can have a picnic lunch in the old park's gazebo while it's still standing."

Haviland sat on his haunches and raised his eyebrows high, questioning her decision.

"Why, you ask? Because if I feel like going to war for the current park I'd like to be armed with all the information I can get my hands on. I can't influence Ed Campbell, our local mortgage man, but I could possibly sway Roy or Grumpy."

Yawning, Haviland turned toward the door.

Irritated by this show of disinterest, Olivia scowled. "I should have adopted a nice mixed breed from the ASPCA! He might have been more polite. You don't have to be so cross just because you had to eat dog food for breakfast. You *are* of the canine species, Captain, regardless of how intelligent you are."

Haviland ignored her. The two drove into town without making eye contact and only when Olivia stopped at Bagels 'n' Beans to buy an egg salad sandwich on a sesame seed bagel did the poodle attempt to make amends.

Placing his nose against her palm, he nudged her hand and then opened his liquid brown eyes wide as she glanced down at him. "That teddy bear look might work on old ladies and little children, but you're not fooling me for a second."

Wheeler overheard the exchange and, grinning, prepared a turkey and cheese lettuce wrap for Haviland even though Olivia hadn't asked for one. As he was particularly fond of the poodle, he added two pieces of bacon to the dog's customary order.

"This is to go, Wheeler," Olivia said.

"You havin' lunch outside?" the old man asked. "There's gonna be a storm within the hour. The ache in my left hip says it's movin' fast, so get this down your throat by one o'clock, ya hear?"

Olivia smiled. With all the barometric body parts in Oyster Bay, no one needed The Weather Channel. The locals had ancient ways of predicting the weather and they seemed to be far more accurate than anything Doppler radar could produce. Olivia trusted Wheeler's hip, the pouf in Dixie's hair, and all the fishermen's forecasts without question.

"I'm just going to the Neuse River Park," she answered. "I haven't spent much time there since I've been back and I'd like to sit there awhile."

"You gotta figure out which way you're gonna vote," Wheeler stated as though he had second sight. "Sittin' a spell will make things clear, I reckon."

Olivia shook her head in wonder. "You're nearly as informed about Oyster Bay's goings-on as Dixie."

Shrugging, Wheeler placed a paper bag filled with the two sandwiches, a plump apple, and half a dill pickle on the counter. "I just keep my antenna up, is all." He held on to the bag and met her gaze. "That real estate man has been lookin' for you. The slick Yankee fellow who's too high and mighty to order his own coffee."

"Dean Talbot." Olivia wasn't surprised. Even though his proposal was likely to pass, the man was shrewd enough to feel out every member of the Planning Board. "If he comes in today, go ahead and tell him where I've gone. I'll be at the restaurant after the park. I'd rather *not* have him knocking on my door at home."

Wheeler nodded. "I know you can take care of yourself, Miss Olivia, but you watch out for that one. He's used to gettin' his way. I've seen men like him before. They can turn from snake charmer to the snake quick as a lightnin' strike."

Moved by Wheeler's concern, Olivia reached across the counter and touched the man's leathery cheek. "Don't worry. I know how to handle snakes," she stated firmly. "Especially the ones that come out into the open."

Haviland snarled as if to remind the pair of humans that he was no pushover either. Both of them laughed, breaking the serious mood. Wheeler moved away to serve his next customer and Olivia headed for the town hall. She dashed inside to pick up a copy of the drawings of the proposed community park as well as current maps showing the town's utilities, water, sewage, and zoning data.

She was carefully studying these maps in the shade of the Neuse River Park's vandalized gazebo when a rental car pulled in next to the Range Rover.

Haviland, who had settled down at Olivia's feet in order to digest his sandwich, leapt to his feet, his hackles rising.

It was an unusual reaction on the poodle's part and Olivia steeled herself for a confrontation. Haviland must have sensed an aura of animosity from one or both of the car's occupants.

Max Warfield and Dean Talbot slammed the doors of their black Lincoln Town Car and glanced around the park as they attempted to locate their quarry. Olivia remained still, watching them.

As usual, Max wore a tailored business suit, but Dean was more casual in tan slacks, a green polo shirt, and hiking boots. As he drew nearer, Olivia could see that the baseball hat he wore was embroidered with the logo of an exclusive golf club in Scotland. His mirrored sunglasses made it impossible to tell what he was thinking as he headed Olivia's way. Max followed closely behind his boss, dabbing at his perspiring brow with a wad of tissues.

"You're a hard woman to find," Dean stated without preamble as he mounted the gazebo's first step. "May I come in, Ms. Limoges? I don't want to interrupt your meal."

"Do what you like," Olivia responded ungraciously. "This is public property. At least for the time being."

Haviland bared his teeth.

The real estate tycoon looked at the poodle with disingenuous amusement. "Does your dog see me as a threat?"

Olivia folded up the map she'd been studying. "I don't know. Are you?"

"Not at all. Our proposition is sound." He gestured at the maps. "However, I'm glad to see you doing your research. It makes our job easier when we're dealing with informed board members." Dean leaned with deliberate nonchalance against the support post, and Olivia was satisfied to keep a measure of space between them. Being on higher ground than the ambitious real estate mogul and his crony made Olivia feel as though she had an advantage. Haviland's proximity also solidified her sense of confidence. She wasn't afraid of either man, but this was her town they sought to change and she wanted to come to a decision without their influence.

"Since you've come all this way to see me, I'll tell you exactly what I think of your proposal. While the new park seems to be quite people-friendly, it does not provide an equitable habitat for the wildlife that will be displaced from the current park. There is a great deal more marshland here." She watched their faces closely for signs of irritation or anger, but both men kept their expressions guarded. "And I cannot approve of the burial ground's destruction. I think you should build around it. If someone doesn't want to live in a house too close to it, then surround the graveyard with additional green space." She tapped one of the maps. "I consider Cottage Cove's current amount to be minimal, at best."

"You've raised valid points, Ms. Limoges, but surely you agree that this new Talbot community means homes, jobs, and revenue for Oyster Bay," Dean replied pleasantly. "The fishing industry is waning. As a native of the town and the daughter of a fisherman, I'd have thought you'd want new opportunities to be available to the men who work from sunup to sundown and still can't make ends meet."

Olivia flushed. *He's done his research,* she

thought, doing her best to quell a surge of hostility.

"Your tenants and employees will all benefit from this project," Max Warfield added smoothly. "I'm sure you're more interested in their futures than in the nesting locations of a few birds."

"I hope that isn't the tack you took when speaking to Marlene Gibbons." Olivia took a sip of Wheeler's sun tea. His secret was that he steeped fruit-flavored tea bags in the open air for hours. On any given sunny day, one could walk behind his eatery and find rows and rows of covered glass pitchers lined up on a pair of old card tables. No one else in Oyster Bay could rival the flavor of Wheeler's iced tea. Today, the tea was peach flavored and tasted like bottled summer.

Dean gazed around the park, a smug smile tugging at the corners of his mouth. "We have something to offer *everyone*, Ms. Limoges. For example, Talbot Fine Properties has decided to add a feature to our new park. Would you care to see it?"

Olivia inclined her head and Max stepped into the gazebo, his nervous eyes fixed on Haviland.

"He won't bite unless commanded to do so," Olivia remarked coolly. "At least, not usually."

Skirting around the poodle as though Haviland might suddenly lunge forward and sink sharp teeth into the costly material of his pant leg, Max unfurled another bird's-eye view of the new park and tapped on a section of green toward the lower right-hand corner. Olivia wasn't sure if the man was addressing her or Haviland when he said, "This space is specifically for dogs."

"Yes, I can read the words 'Dog Free Play Area' quite easily," she said. "So this is an open field where dogs are welcome to play unleashed?"

Dean's smile grew larger. He came a little closer, fearful of scaring the fish he believed to be so near his sharp hook. "Exactly! There will also be garbage cans with disposal bags available, agility equipment for the dogs to exercise on, and a wading pool for those hot paws."

"A lovely touch." Olivia silently wondered if Haviland would condescend to join his furry kin in a communal pool. "Do you have a dog, Mr. Talbot?"

Sliding his eyes toward Haviland, Dean stuck his hands in his pockets. "No pets for me. I practically live out of my suitcase."

Olivia produced a sympathetic look. She wanted to prove that she'd done her own share of research. "That must be hard on your wife."

Dean shrugged. "Oh, I think my other half is happiest when I'm hundreds of miles away. We both have our own hobbies and interests. That happens in a marriage sometimes."

Derailed by his frankness, Olivia broke eye contact. "The dog area is thoughtful. They don't have a comparable play space at the moment and the public beach isn't always the most practical solution, what with little children playing nearby and waste issues and such."

"Look. I'm not asking you to commit to our project this second," Dean continued amiably. "I'd just like you to consider the benefits alongside your concerns. Fair enough?"

Max made a move to collect the drawing, but Dean raised a finger, instantly halting the forward motion of his employee. Olivia noticed he was not wearing a wedding ring.

"I'll be in town until next Wednesday, Ms. Limoges. Would you care to have dinner with me over the weekend? I promise not to discuss business matters." He smoothed a nonexistent wrinkle from his shirt. "It would be purely platonic — a chance for me to learn about Oyster Bay from a business owner's perspective."

"I'm not the only business owner in town."

"But I'd prefer to share a meal with an attractive, intelligent, and sophisticated woman. I may be married, but I can still admire beauty."

"Married with three children," Olivia pointed out. "Are any of them involved in the family business?"

Dean's face darkened for a moment, but then he shook his head in exaggerated disappointment. "My kids aren't interested in my field. One son deals with investments, my daughter is into fashion design, and my other son is a musician. I guess I didn't play enough Monopoly with them when they were little."

"So Mr. Warfield must be the heir to the throne," Olivia remarked flippantly, but she'd chosen her words with care.

A disdainful light entered Dean's eyes. "Max would be perfectly capable," he said pleasantly. "But I'm not planning on retiring anytime soon."

"I believe I had the honor of having your youngest son frequent my restaurant recently. Forgive me, but I don't remember his name," Olivia lied.

"Blake?" Again, the flicker of disapproval. "Well, we *do* own a house here and the kids are free to use it." He paused and asked nonchalantly, "What do you mean by 'recently'?"

Olivia rubbed her temple as though trying to remember. "He and a lovely young woman dined at The Boot Top about two weeks ago."

"I see." Dean fell silent and Max shifted uncomfortably.

After packing up the debris from her lunch, Olivia stood. "I should be getting back to the restaurant." She held out her hand. "I'd love to have dinner with you on the condition that you allow my chef to prepare something special for us. I have plans this afternoon, but we could dine later this evening if that suits you?"

Dean took her hand and shook it gently. "I accept your terms and look forward to our evening together." He placed his hand over his heart. "And I solemnly swear not to talk about the proposal. Not one word."

The two men retreated in haste, shooting nervous glances at the sky. During the past half hour, it had become thick with gun-metal gray clouds, which seemed too heavy to hold their burdens much longer.

Haviland began to pace around the gazebo. He'd never been fond of thunder and Olivia knew he wanted to be safe at home before the storm broke. Olivia let him hop into the Rover and then asked him to be patient for a little longer.

She jogged up the dilapidated steps toward the little graveyard. The breeze had given way to a more persistent wind. The tree branches swayed like the arms of a dancer, and the tiny Confederate flags shivered as though cold.

Olivia opened the gate and stepped onto the soft grass with care. She noticed someone had gathered wild phlox and placed a single stem at the foot of each of the seven graves. The purple, tissuelike petals were crinkled with thirst but still gave off a faint sweet scent.

Someone else besides Jethro Bragg cares about this place, Olivia thought.

She got on her knees in front of Henry Bragg's headstone and stroked the smooth rock. There was a stillness to the place, a sense of deep peace Olivia rarely experienced anywhere but at the water's edge and within the confines of her home.

The wind curled under her white blond hair and flipped it upward. It felt like the flutter of bird's wings against her face. A feathery caress. It was as if the souls of the men buried beneath her had descended on a current of warm air and, moments before the rain began, blessed her with their presence.

"I won't let them destroy this place," Olivia whispered, her fingers tracing the shallow letters carved into the stone.

In her mind, she was seeing another name on another tombstone.

Olivia was still kneeling there when the rain came.

CHAPTER 12

I think that I shall never see
a billboard lovely as a tree.
Perhaps, unless the billboards fall,
I'll never see a tree at all.

— OGDEN NASH

"Aren't gryphons part lion and part snake?" Laurel asked Millay later that evening.

Millay took a sip of coffee and shook her head. "That's a chimera. A chimera has a scaly tail that ends in a serpent's head. On the other end, you've got a lion's head and a goat's head kind of growing out of the back of the neck. I think chimeras are way cool, but for my story, I needed an animal with only one head. It'd be tough for Tessa and the others to find room on a creature's back if it had *two* heads." She waved her hands around as she spoke, her silver thumb rings catching the light. "Besides, I like the gryphon's combination of the lion and the eagle. What's a goat head going to do in the middle of a battle? Ravish a flower garden?"

The writers laughed.

"You know your mythological beasts and you did a great job describing the gryphon as both a potential weapon and a possible friend." Harris turned to the third page of Millay's first chapter. "I really like this part, after Tessa's been pushed and her gryphon catches her in his talons and flies her into his cave."

He held up Millay's second page and read, *"Despite the piercing light of the full moon, the cave was mostly in shadow. The gryphon's gold eye gleamed as he assessed his new rider. He watched the blood seep into her gauzy white dress where his scythelike claws had bit into the flesh of her waist. The coldness of his gaze sparked a flicker of fear in Tessa's belly. She had heard tales of what happened to girls who did not instantly bond with their gryphons. Trembling, Tessa moved toward the creature, awed by his tawny fur, the shimmering feathers of his wings, the massive legs and muscular back, and the daggerlike curve of his beak. She sunk to one knee and bowed to him."*

The group let the words settle over them for a moment. It seemed a fitting segment to listen to as the light waned outside the cottage. Laurel had requested an early evening meeting, as her parents were coming to town after dinner and she wanted to make sure the twins were presentable before their arrival. Millay's shift at Fish Nets began at eight, so she seconded the motion to begin the meeting at five thirty instead of six thirty. Olivia had left a message about the time change with Chief Rawlings the day before, but he had neither returned her call nor showed up for the meeting. She was surprisingly disappointed by his absence.

Returning her attention to the notes she'd written beside the passage where Tessa dropped to her knees near the gryphon's nest of dried grass, Olivia raised a question. "The bones scattered about the corner of the gryphon's cave — animal or human?"

"Eeew!" Laurel squeaked. "You can't have Tessa's rescuer be a flying, feathered, people-eater! This is a young adult book, not a Stephen King horror novel!"

Millay patted Laurel's knee. "Relax, Mama Bear. It's a pile of cow bones. I've got a scene in the fourth chapter that shows the gryphon feeding. I wanted to get the point across that these creatures aren't oversized, cuddly plush toys. They're wild animals and fierce warriors. They can be cold, brutal, and unpredictable. *And* they're total carnivores."

"You need to portray them in this light if the reader is to believe that a gryphon is capable of winning a battle against a dragon," Olivia agreed. "I'm looking forward to reading what kind of bonding goes on between Tessa and her beast. For example, how will she convince him to attack something that breathes fire?"

Harris fidgeted. "Yeah. Um, about that whole dragon thing . . ."

Flicking her black bangs out of her eyes, Millay stared hard at Harris. "You're well-schooled in the fantasy genre, so tell me, is there a better creature to pick as the enemy than a dragon? They're like the fantasy world's equivalent of an A-bomb."

In order to avoid meeting her penetrating gaze, Harris drew a series of spirals on the margin of his paper. "It's just that some of your details are a little bit cliché. Tessa and her friends are dressed in white robes. The dragon riders are all good-looking but vicious women dressed in black. They remind me too much of the riders in Anne McCaffrey's books." He hesitated and then plowed on. "And the descriptions of your dragons seem a lot like those of the ring wraiths from Tolkien's trilogy."

Laurel interrupted. "I know who Anne

McCaffrey is! *The Dragonriders of Pern* was on my summer reading list in high school. I checked it out of the library thinking there'd be lots of hot guys rescuing princesses," she added with a giggle, clearly hoping to dispel the hostility radiating from Millay. "And even though I'm not as experienced as Harris about these kinds of books, I see his point. Can you change the dragons into something else? It seems that it would be pretty tough to beat a creature that breathes fire unless Tessa knows some powerful magic, and though she's strong and brave, I get the sense that she's still kind of finding her way."

Millay screwed up her lips, still staring at Harris. "What do you suggest? I don't want anyone thinking my stuff is *cliché*."

Harris, who had obviously given the subject serious thought, responded immediately. "Well, if you want to maintain your aerial battle scenes, then why not use a wyvern? They're reptilian, but usually smaller and less massive than a dragon. You could make yours really different. More like a snake with wings. No legs and no breathing fire."

"Sounds like a viper," Olivia added. "I can picture a black, forked tongue."

"A poisonous, winged viper?" Millay's

face brightened as an image formed in her mind. "With curved fangs and an anvil-shaped tail. That *does* sound more interesting and even *more* sinister than your everyday dragon." She jotted down some quick notes and then flashed Harris one of her rare smiles. "You're pretty good at this critique stuff. Thanks for being straight with me."

Harris blushed with pleasure over the compliment. The pronounced ruddiness of his cheeks reminded Olivia that she still needed to find a way to get the young man to New Bern in order to have a consultation with her aesthetician.

"I know this is only the first chapter, but I thought it was a really good beginning," Laurel praised Millay. "If I read this right, Tessa and her gryphon were born connected to each other, even though they didn't know it. So when they speak to each other, do they do that telepathically?"

Millay nodded. "That's why the dialogue's italicized."

"One last question." Laurel quickly checked her cell phone to ensure that she'd received no calls over the last half hour and then asked, "Is the gryphon going to be called 'the gryphon' the whole time or will you give him a name?"

"He and Tessa have to seek out his name. They have to succeed in a series of minor quests before they'll be ready for battle." She shrugged. "Though to be totally honest, I've been having a hard time coming up with a name. Every one I've tried out sounds like a brand of organic cereal or a STD. If you guys have any ideas . . ."

Harris leaned forward eagerly. "I have this awesome book that lists the names of all the minor mythological figures. Medieval ones too. I bet you could find something by blending parts of those names together."

"Cool. Can you bring it by my apartment tomorrow?" she inquired lightly. "I'll feed you pizza."

Harris tried to keep his delighted smile under control. Olivia suspected even without the offer of pizza, an invitation to Millay's home had him flying high. "Sure," he answered with nonchalance. "I can swing by around six."

Grinning at her two friends, Laurel folded Millay's pages in half and tucked them in her purse. "Speaking of names, what are we supposed to call the chief when he joins us? *If* he joins us, that is. I feel like I'm going to say Chief or Mr. Rawlings no matter what! I'm still calling our pediatrician Dr. Davis even though Steve and I have been to dinner with his wife and him a bunch of times!"

"The chief's first name is Sawyer," Olivia replied as she rose to replenish her empty coffee cup. "I don't know why he's not here, as he seemed quite sincere about joining us. He even sent me an email saying he'd finished critiquing your chapter, Millay. My only guess is that he got tied up at work. Things aren't exactly sleepy in Oyster Bay these days."

Her words immediately forced the writers into silence. Each of them recalled their last meeting in the cottage and how it had ended with the discovery of Camden's death. Laurel hugged herself as though she was suddenly cold, Harris began to doodle again, and Millay's expression turned mournful, making her seem incredibly young and fragile.

Olivia walked over to the window and watched the surf curl onto the shore. The sun hung low in the sky — an amber disc surrounded by streaks of heron blue clouds and a dusky, lavender haze of humidity.

It was nearly half past seven. Millay and Laurel both needed to leave, but neither woman seemed keen on ending the evening's fellowship.

The buzzing of Olivia's cell phone suddenly became the center of attention. She had placed the gadget on the glass-topped coffee table and now, as it vibrated, it slid sideways across the slick surface, looking more animated than a rectangle made of mere metal and plastic. Lurching centimeter by centimeter toward the edge of the table, the shiny black device took on the persona of a robotic insect. Laurel swung her knees away from its approach, staring at it with distrust.

"Are you going to answer that?" she asked Olivia.

The chief's number surfaced on the phone's sulfur-hued screen. "It's Rawlings," Olivia stated flatly, but her stomach clenched. Her body seemed to sense that something ominous was approaching — that the writers' peaceful time together was about to be invaded by unwelcome news.

Gripping the phone, Olivia flicked it open. "We've been wondering what's kept you, Chief," she began with forced levity.

Over a cacophony of background noise, Rawlings' words burst through the receiver. "Dean Talbot is dead."

Of all the things the chief might have said, Olivia had expected this statement the least. The blunt delivery also surprised her. "Talbot? How?"

Again the droning filled the space between

them before he had a chance to answer. "Looks like he fell and broke his neck. I'm at the scene now."

Olivia turned away from the anxious glances of her fellow writers and focused on the rolling water outside the window. "Where?"

A pause. "The Neuse River Park. At the foot of the stairs leading up to the graveyard."

Recalling the dilapidated steps, Olivia could envision how someone might snag the toe of a shoe on one of the deeper cracks or stumble forward on the uneven cement. Still, it was difficult to picture someone with Dean's acuity falling to his death. The man was both athletic and agile, and it seemed too coincidental that he would meet his demise at the very place he planned to demolish. Besides, Olivia didn't much believe in coincidence.

"What was he doing there?" she asked, speaking as much to herself as to Rawlings.

"*My* question exactly." Rawlings' tone was steely. "Specifically, I'd like to know why you appear in Mr. Talbot's appointment book? He's got the entire evening blocked off and the only thing written across the hours spanning from eight o'clock to midnight is *your* name."

Olivia stiffened. "There's a simple explanation for that."

"When I'm done here, I'd like you to share it with me. Until then, stick close to the phone." Rawlings hung up.

Frowning, Olivia turned away from the window. "There's been another death," she told her friends, though it was obvious from the slack expressions on their faces they had already guessed as much.

"Another *murder?*" Harris's voice was hushed.

Laurel reached over and covered his hand with her own.

Millay stood and slipped her purse onto her shoulder. "Can you just skip the extraneous details and hit us up with tomorrow's headline?" She shrugged her shoulders self-effacingly. "Sorry, but I've gotta go."

Olivia was untroubled by the younger woman's bluntness. "Apparently, our visiting real estate mogul, Dean Talbot, fell down the steps at the community park. His neck was broken and he's dead. That's all I know," Olivia said.

The writers exchanged anxious glances. Millay glanced at her watch and moved to the door. "Was there a poem?" she asked, her hand on the knob.

"Rawlings didn't mention one. It looks

like an accident at this point," Olivia stated reassuringly.

Millay looked dubious. "I need to motor. Text me if you find out anything more. Otherwise, I'll have to wait for one of the customer's wives to call in with the news and *that* version will be so exaggerated that I won't know what really went down."

Olivia gathered her own purse and keys and signaled to Haviland. "I'm going to the park to see for myself. The chief wants to talk to me and he's sure to be tied up until late tonight."

Harris cocked his head, reminding Olivia of Haviland when the poodle sensed something wasn't quite right. "You don't think he fell, do you?" He hurriedly picked up his loose papers, pen, and journal and gathered them to his chest. "I'm coming with you."

Laurel's eyes widened. "Well, I'm *not*. Sorry, you two, but I do *not* want to lay eyes on a dead man. Even a rich and famous one. I still can't sleep after . . ."

Olivia patted Laurel's shoulder. "*I'm* not going to the park out of morbid curiosity, let me assure you. I need to know if Dean's 'accident' has anything to do with Camden's death, and if I can observe the chief while he's still gathering information, he might let a valuable insight slip."

"Chief Rawlings doesn't think Dean tripped?" Laurel began to look a little pale.

"Publicly he does. Privately, who knows? I'm just looking at the situation logically," Olivia said. "Camden discovered some unsavory connection between someone in the Talbot family and their proposed development, and I believe that information cost him his life." She reached down, her hand searching for Haviland's soft head. "Now Dean Talbot, a shrewd, ambitious, and possibly dangerous businessman lies dead. And *I* don't think he tripped."

"If Talbot *was* killed," Harris said as he fished his car keys out of his jeans pocket, "the murderer isn't acting like he did before. If it's the same person, he's really sly. It's like he's created two different — what's the word? — signatures. Camden's death was obviously a murder, but Talbot's death looks like an accident. No blood, no poem, and I'm assuming no witnesses . . ." Harris fell silent as he continued to ponder the possible differences.

"*If* this is his second murder, then yes, the killer is both intelligent and crafty. He is also *not* Jethro Bragg. After all, Jethro's in jail. If Talbot was 'helped' down that flight of steps, then Camden's murderer is still at large," Olivia remarked with soft anger.

The fear they'd all been able to suppress since their friend had been killed resurfaced with renewed strength. Wordlessly, they gathered their things and avoided one another's eyes. It was no comfort to see the dread they felt echoed in one another's faces.

Olivia opened the cottage door and mutely led the shaken writers into the descending night.

Olivia and Harris took separate cars to the park, but neither of them was allowed to step foot beyond the entrance sign. An officer stood, hands on hips, and informed them in a tone that allowed no room for argument that the park was closed until further notice. When Olivia stretched the truth by insisting the chief had requested her immediate presence, he gave her and Haviland a quick once-over and then spoke into the radio attached to his shirt.

"I'll come to her," Rawlings' voice crackled through the speaker.

"You'd better go," Olivia told Harris. "I'll call if there's a need for us to get involved."

Harris glanced at the massive policeman straddling the pathway leading into the park.

"Are you sure? I could stay . . . keep you company." He gave Haviland a pat on the head. "I know you've got your trusty hound with you, but two-legged friends have their uses too."

Olivia smiled. "Thank you for the chivalrous gesture, but the chief just wants to know why Dean Talbot planned to have dinner with me tonight. I don't know what *Talbot's* intentions were, but I agreed to break bread with him because I wanted to ferret out more information on Blake, the new housing development, or anything else that could be relevant to Camden's death."

"Won't the chief be ticked off when you tell him you planned to investigate on your own?" Harris asked nervously.

"I'm not going to confess that latter bit to him," Olivia admitted. "In any case, it makes sense that I'd be questioning Talbot about the development. After all, our Planning Board meets in three nights. Now go on with you. If you don't hear from me tonight, call me tomorrow. There's something unrelated to tonight's incident that I'd like to discuss with you."

Harris raised his eyebrows. "Sounds interesting."

"That's a good word for it," Olivia said, and then wished Harris good night.

Less than a minute later, the chief's figure detached itself from a shadow of trees toward her left. "I thought we could talk now," she called as she moved forward to meet him, ignoring the threatening posture of the junior officer. She lowered her voice as Rawlings drew alongside. "I wanted to set your mind at ease about why my name was written in Mr. Talbot's appointment book, and since our writer's group meeting has ended, here I am."

Rawlings tugged a flashlight from his utility belt and pointed it in the direction of the gazebo. "Let's take a seat."

As they walked, their footsteps were obscured by the noises of nighttime creatures. Frogs, owls, crickets, and dozens of other insects filled the darkness with their musical autographs. A mild breeze ruffled tree leaves and whispered through the reeds by the riverbank. A whir of mosquito wings buzzed behind her ear and Haviland snapped at an unseen invader near his hindquarters. Fireflies blinked like miniature stars all around them.

"It seems too peaceful for someone to be lying dead so close by," Olivia murmured. Rawlings remained quiet, his eyes moving away from Olivia's face as he watched a white moth flutter across the beam cast by his flashlight.

Once again, Olivia was struck by how

comfortable she felt with the policeman. He knew how to relish a precious moment of tranquility and beauty, even when it did not appear at what others might deem a suitable time. In fact, she reflected, most men would fill the silence with demands, explanations, or boasts, but not this man. He knew how to be still and Olivia admired that quality.

"I was sitting right here when I last spoke to Mr. Talbot," she said and proceeded to tell Rawlings of her exchange with Dean and Max Warfield. She omitted nothing and went so far as to include the mens' expressions and postures as she observed them during their conversation.

Rawlings watched Olivia intently as she spoke, and when she finished, he simply nodded.

"It's strikes me as unlikely that Dean Talbot fell down those stairs," Olivia stated plainly.

Surprisingly, Rawlings dipped his chin in mute agreement. "At the moment, however, we have no evidence to tell us otherwise. What I've got is a dislodged hunk of cement, traces of cement embedded in the soles of Mr. Talbot's shoes, and a corpse with a broken neck." He sighed. "This will be the last time I'll be gazing at fireflies for a while. Once the media gets wind of this . . ." He left the thought unfinished.

Olivia felt a pang of sympathy for the chief. "Have you talked to Max Warfield yet?"

Rawlings nodded. "One of my officers paid him a personal call. Mr. Warfield was entertaining a young lady in his hotel room all afternoon. He was still, ah, preoccupied, when my man arrived. The coroner believes Mr. Talbot experienced his fatal slip between three and four o'clock."

"So if it *was* murder, both Warfield and Jethro Bragg are in the clear."

Groaning almost inaudibly, Rawlings scratched his neck. "Actually, Mr. Bragg was released yesterday. His handwriting was not a match with that of the spray-painted poem. There aren't many forensic handwriting experts doing graffiti analysis, but I happen to know one of the best. Though his report wouldn't be admissible in court, it reaffirmed the conclusion I'd already reached. Jethro was not our man, and no matter what anyone believed, we had no solid evidence against him."

Olivia raised her eyebrows. "He was merely in the wrong place at the wrong time?"

"He finally confessed to being drunk and

sounding off at Mr. Ford. He doesn't recall precisely what he said, but Mr. Bragg thought Mr. Ford was in the employ of the Talbots. Judging by his dress, accent, and mannerisms, he assumed Camden was in favor of relocating the graveyard. Before he was deployed to Afghanistan, Jethro was a land surveyor. One of his former coworkers told him about the Talbots' grand plans for the park, so he's been stewing over this project for a long time." Rawlings rubbed at a crease in his uniform pants. "He remembers telling Mr. Ford that all queers should burn in hell, but he never touched him. In fact, Jethro would have been free to leave on Wednesday if he hadn't spit a mouthful of hot coffee right in the face of Sergeant Barrett."

"Did the handwriting analysis provide you with any clues about the real killer?" Olivia asked, her interest quickening.

After studying her face for several seconds, Rawlings opened his notebook and directed his flashlight beam to the white page. "Based on the space between the lines, the angular nature of some of the letters, the narrowness of other letters, et cetera, the killer is likely a single male. An aloof, independent, self-serving, dissatisfied, and frustrated individual. A man filled with hidden aggression." He paused, tried to interpret his own scrawl, and then continued. "There seems to be an irregularity between the handwriting and the content of the poem. According to the analysis, the handwriting belongs to someone who knows hard work, even drudgery. A laborer. It doesn't jibe with the writing of an academic type or the type associated with a poet or an artist."

So much for Blake Talbot being the killer, Olivia thought, bewildered. *I bet the Talbot kids haven't done a day's labor in their lives.*

"I'm not telling you anything you won't read in the paper. Except for the handwriting analysis. Keep those details to yourself, if you would." Closing his notebook, Rawlings stood. "I'm sorry to have missed the meeting tonight. Whose work will we be critiquing next week?"

"My head will be on the chopping block next. I should think the press would have come and gone by then, so hopefully you'll be able to join us." Olivia gestured at the shadowed land spread before them. "I wonder who will take over the running of Talbot Fine Properties now that Dean is dead."

A voice crackled through the chief's radio.

"They're ready to move the body now, sir. Over."

"Meet you at the entrance, Mullins. Over and out." Rawlings let his eyes linger on the dark woods beyond the gazebo. "I plan to find an answer to that question," he replied. "It could be telling or it could be that some elusive board of directors is waiting to take the reins." He placed a hand on Olivia's elbow and led her out of the gazebo. "I'm sorry your dinner plans were ruined, even if you were only on a fact-finding mission."

Olivia shrugged. "Regardless of what elaborate speeches Dean planned to make tonight, I would have and still plan to vote against the proposal as it stands. I'm opposed to the relocation of the graveyard." She turned to Rawlings. "Chief, I'm certain the development is the reason behind Camden's death. He found out something about the Talbots that would put a stop to this project. And someone wants the project to go through at any cost — even murder."

Releasing her elbow, the chief gave her a hard stare. "When you have as many millions as Dean Talbot had, you don't go around hiring killers to ensure your projects are brought to fruition. If Oyster Bay voted no, Talbot would have just moved on to the next town. There are dozens just like ours up and down the coast."

Olivia's ears seemed to filter out the majority of the chief's argument, focusing only on the phrase "hired killer." "That would explain the handwriting discrepancy," she muttered too softly for Rawlings to hear.

The pair left the gazebo and headed back to the park's entrance.

"Thank you for coming with such expediency, Ms. Limoges," the chief said as they approached the waiting ambulance. The hint of amusement in his voice was occluded by the grim look in his eyes as he watched the paramedics push a loaded gurney into their vehicle. After bidding Olivia a brief good night, he walked off to query one of his officers.

Olivia and Haviland stayed where they were. Unwittingly, Olivia caught a glimpse of the lower half of the body. The feet were splayed beneath a white sheet, stretching it from toe to toe so that it appeared as though Dean Talbot had a fin.

"He wouldn't have made a good merman," Olivia informed the night air. "That man loved land. He wanted to own it, carve it up, and leave it unrecognizable. Land can't fight back the way the sea can." She rubbed Haviland behind the ears and turned away from the ambulance. The poodle rubbed his chin along her leg and barked twice. "Yes, Captain. We'll go see Michel now."

As she drove toward the welcoming illumination of town, Olivia whispered, "You're out there, aren't you?"

CHAPTER 13

O, wind, if winter comes, can spring be far behind?

— PERCY BYSSHE SHELLEY

On Monday morning, Olivia and Haviland were enjoying breakfast at Grumpy's when they noticed Laurel jog past the window, pushing a double stroller. Her ponytail streamed behind her like a palomino's mane.

"Look at her go," Olivia remarked to Dixie. "Seems more like hard labor than exercise. That contraption must weigh more than Laurel does."

"In about twenty minutes she'll go flyin' by again. Does the same loop every Monday, Wednesday, and Friday. She's runnin' late this morning though." Dixie glanced at her purple Swatch. "She's usually come and gone by the time you drag your lazy ass in here for coffee and eggs."

Scowling, Olivia held out her empty mug. "Fortunately, I'm not forced to wake up at dawn to attend to the endless needs of young and helpless humans. It's one of the many reasons I'm relieved to have avoided motherhood. Might my lazy ass have a refill, please?"

With a toss of her feathered hair, Dixie skated off for the coffee carafe. "You've been holdin' out on me," she murmured upon her return.

Olivia watched the steam from the carafe rise over the table, only to be obliterated by the downdraft created by the languid whirling of an overhead fan.

The diner was full of strangers. Olivia recognized only the elderly couple in the *Starlight Express* booth and a middle-aged woman reading a Barbara Kingsolver novel at the counter. Judging by their dress and the bulky camera bags partially tucked underfoot, the remaining patrons were journalists and photographers.

"That's a rather vague statement," she said to Dixie, observing as the curl of white cream she poured into her coffee morphed into a warm, pecan hue. "Haviland and I did find something on our walk this morning, but it's not interesting from a monetary standpoint. See for yourself."

Olivia passed Dixie the quarter she and Haviland had dug up on the beach. There had been an extremely low tide that morning, providing a rare opportunity to use the Bounty Hunter over areas of sand normally covered by water.

"It's just one of them state quarters." Dixie was unimpressed. "New Hampshire. 'Live Free or Die.' I find these every night sweepin' up."

"Turn it over," Olivia directed.

Amused, she watched as Dixie's thin eyebrows climbed up her forehead. The morning sun highlighted the shimmery purple shadow covering every centimeter of skin from Dixie's lids to her ruthlessly plucked brows. "It's like somebody just took an eraser to it," she breathed and ran her fingertips over the quarter. "But that's not what I was hintin' at when I said you were holdin' out on me. Let me get these city folks their food and I'll be back to worm the details out of you."

Dixie plunked the quarter onto the table. As she'd pointed out, one side was engraved with New Hampshire's Old Man of the Mountain and the state motto, but the reverse was utterly blank. There wasn't the slightest indication that George Washington's profile had ever been etched into the front of the coin. No words remained. Not a single letter had escaped the scouring of sand and sea. It was smooth as glass.

Olivia slipped the anomaly back into her pocket and sipped her coffee, watching Dixie deliver platters of omelets, peach pancakes, and Belgian waffles to customers. She then slid side dishes of hash browns, sausages, bacon, and baked apples onto any available space remaining on each table. Once her customers were busy eating, she skated backward to Olivia's booth and did a neat half-turn inches away from Haviland's paw. "Now, for the good stuff. I heard tell you paid a visit to a certain gentleman's house the other night." She grinned, her bubblegum-colored lip gloss twinkling. "And didn't leave again 'til midnight."

Olivia couldn't help but laugh. "Let me guess. One of your bevies of relatives lives on the same street as Flynn McNulty." Her smile quickly disappeared. "If only one of them was around to witness Camden's murder. Or Dean's fall."

"Fall? Feed me another one." Dixie snorted. "That's not how a man like him goes. Take that with a grain of salt, mind you, because I've only seen him a time or two, but he seemed like one sure-footed fellow. He ate lunch here on Thursday so he could ferret out how Grumpy was going to vote come Tuesday night." She gazed out the window as she remembered. "I liked that he didn't sugarcoat his reason for coming in. Just asked us straight out. Grumpy told him just as plain that he was votin' in favor of building that development. Talbot and his buddies ate up every bite of their burgers, thanked us, left the biggest tip I've ever laid eyes on, and then went about their business."

Dean was smooth, Olivia thought. Dixie and Grumpy weren't easily impressed, especially by outsiders.

"I won't mince words with you either," she told her friend. "I'd like to talk Grumpy into rejecting the proposal." She raised her hand to stop Dixie from interrupting. "All I ask is that the two of you spend a few, quiet moments in the graveyard in the park. If you still want to support Cottage Cove as it stands, fine, but I'd like the proposal to be altered to allow the cemetery to remain untouched. Consider backing me up on this point. I'm going to talk to the rest of the board members when I'm done here."

Dixie jerked a thumb toward the dining area behind her. "There aren't going to *be* any quiet moments at that park for any of us! Every inch of that place will be on the news, in the papers, and on the Web by tomorrow. Grumpy's cousin told us that the Talbot kids have being arriving since Sunday. Each one in their own little jet. Isn't that too cute?"

Olivia laid the fork laden with omelet back on her plate. "Can you find out *exactly* when each of them landed? I'm specifically interested in when Blake Talbot arrived and if anyone met him at the airport."

"I'll make you a trade. Flight information for Flynn information." Dixie produced a theatrical wink before pushing off from the table. Propelled forward, she dropped off two checks, collected empty dishes, and zipped through the kitchen's swinging door in the time it would have taken another waitress to tie on her apron.

Smiling, Olivia returned her attention to her omelet. She was just about to take a bite when Laurel's flushed face appeared at the diner's window. Before Olivia could wave, Laurel raised her fist and knocked loudly on the glass. As she gestured feverishly for Olivia to come outside, her lovely face crumpled and tears slipped down her cheeks.

"Haviland! Something's wrong!" Olivia shoved the diner door open. Haviland burst out in front of his mistress and immediately began to scan the street for threats. Laurel had turned the stroller away from the sun. The twins were both sleeping, their heads tilted at what looked to Olivia like supremely uncomfortable angles against the blue fabric of the jogging stroller.

"What is it?" Olivia took Laurel by the elbow, fearing that the younger woman might collapse at any moment.

Laurel gulped. "I saw it! At the bulletin board by the town hall. I saw the . . . the . . ." Her words tumbled from her mouth as she fought for air.

Olivia couldn't make sense of her friend's jumbled phrases. "You need to get out of the sun and drink some water. Come inside."

Shaking her head, Laurel wouldn't release her grip of the stroller handle. "It doesn't fit through the doorway. Too wide."

"Wait here." Olivia strode into Grumpy's, slapped some money on the table, and grabbed her purse and her water glass from the table. Several reporters cast her interested glances but were too captivated by their food to pay her any real heed. Outside, Olivia handed the water to Laurel. "Take small sips." She waited while Laurel complied. "I'm going to push the boys under the pharmacy's awning."

Mutely, Laurel allowed Olivia to claim her position behind the stroller. Olivia gave the vehicle a light shove.

"The brakes are on," Laurel whispered and stepped on a lever with her heel.

Olivia maneuvered the sleeping children farther up the block and then insisted Laurel sit down on one of the pharmacy's wide steps. Laurel drank down half of the water, then passed the glass back to Olivia. Her hands were trembling.

"Take your time." Olivia pivoted the twins out of the sun and sat down next to Laurel, keeping a firm hold on the stroller's oversized front wheel. "You ran past the bulletin board outside the town hall and saw what?"

Laurel nodded. "I don't usually stop to read the notices, but I got a cramp as we were going by. There was a bright red piece of paper tacked up there. I needed to catch my breath, so I started to read it." She wiped her perspiring forehead with the bottom of her pink Adidas shirt. "It's another poem, Olivia. I couldn't even tell you what it said, but I know it meant something bad. It . . . the words turned my blood cold."

Olivia was dumbstruck for a moment. "Another haiku?"

Laurel glanced at her sleeping children. "I didn't count the syllables, but it was three lines long. It sounded a lot like the other one. Like the same person had written both poems. Olivia, it felt . . . evil."

"Was it handwritten?"

"No. It was typed." Laurel pushed a damp lock of hair off her forehead. "Would you call the police? I really need to go home and sit down."

"Let me give you a lift." Olivia felt acutely protective toward the younger woman. "You've had a shock. I'm worried about you walking home."

"I doubt there's a pair of car seats in that Range Rover of yours," Laurel replied with a weak smile. "I'll be okay now that I've told you. I know you'll handle this better than I ever could. Will you call me after you're done with the chief?"

"Of course." Olivia waited for Laurel to rise to her feet and begin walking the stroller at a slow, controlled pace before hustling to her car. She dialed the chief's number as she headed for the town hall, irritated by the clot of traffic caused by vacationers in search of parking spaces and journalists on the lookout for photo ops. Rawlings didn't pick up his cell phone so Olivia left him a brief message.

Several minutes later, she drove the Rover into the crowded town hall lot and selected a spot reserved for jurors only. She stuffed her phone back in her purse and pumped her long legs double-time until she reached the bulletin board. There was the poem, just as Laurel had described.

Olivia read it once, and then twice, before copying the lines down into the notebook she always kept in her bag. She then read them aloud to see how the words, once spoken, grew in power:

Cherry branches bow —
Petals pushed into the wind
Pale as a new moon.

From the bottom of her purse, her phone chirped. Olivia glanced at the number. "Chief? I know you've probably got your hands full answering questions for the media, but you need to take a quick walk down the block. I'm standing at the bulletin board in front of the town hall and there's something posted here you must read immediately."

"What is it? I can't leave the station whenever the fancy strikes me," Rawlings replied impatiently as phones rang noisily in the background.

"It's a poem, just like the one written above Camden's body. It may also be a clue that Dean Talbot's death was no accident," she whispered urgently. "You might want to bring an evidence bag with you. I'll stand guard until you get here."

She could hear the creak of the chief's chair. "Give me five minutes."

Before he could hang up, Olivia felt compelled to give him what was probably an unnecessary piece of advice. "And you don't want the press following you here. Trust me. If you have a back door, then use it."

Olivia waited on a nearby bench as Rawlings read the haiku. He then directed an officer to dust the entire metal case for prints before opening the lid to remove the sheet of red paper with a pair of tweezers.

"The font makes it look almost like real handwriting," Officer Cook remarked as he examined the bag. "This guy knows enough about computers to use a special font."

Another policeman peered over Cook's shoulder. "How do we know it's by the same person? Someone could be screwing with us."

Rawlings crossed his arms over his chest. "The poem is part of a sequence. First winter. Now spring. But what should cause us to view this poem as a possible piece of evidence is the word *pushed*."

Cook held out the bagged poem as though it were a contagious virus. "Oh man," he breathed. "The real estate guy from the park?"

"Precisely. And this piece of information *must* stay between us, gentlemen," the chief warned in a tone that demanded obedience. "Until we know more, we will still refer to Mr. Talbot's death as an accident — whether you're talking to the press, your mama, or your fishing buddies. Is that clear?"

The officers faced their superior and said, "Yessir," in solemn unison. Rawlings, satisfied with their response, began to issue calm, firm commands to his men. As he spoke, Olivia stared at the dozens of fingerprints being highlighted on the surface of the bulletin board's glass case. Black smudges covered the entire area. Some of the prints overlapped, forming moths and spiky bat wings reminiscent of Rorschach's inkblot images. As a sergeant applied a final sweep of black dust across the glass, he shook his head, the enormity of his task settling upon his shoulders.

Rawlings placed a hand on his officer's back. "One at a time, Marshall. One at a time."

Once his men had been dispersed, their

ever-raucous radios crackling as they moved off, the chief sat down next to Olivia. He stared at the square of bulletin board cork from which the poem had been removed.

Olivia opened her notebook. "The spring poem." She traced the lines with her fingertips. "It fits the parameters of traditional haiku. While it's not a given that the author of this poem killed Dean Talbot, there is no doubt in my mind that this person wrote the winter haiku." She glanced around the square. Lawyers, clerks, local government officials, secretaries, tourists, and citizens walking dogs or pushing strollers meandered over the sidewalks or stopped to chat in the shade of one of the mammoth magnolias.

Rawlings observed the environment as well. "Another public place. Someone must have seen him unless he tacked the poem under the glass in the middle of the night."

"Why not leave it with Dean's body?" Olivia asked. "And isn't that case locked?"

"The lock is about as secure as a young girl's diary. You could easily jimmy it with a penknife. In any case, it was unlocked." He jerked a thumb toward the town hall building. "The officer I sent inside to begin questioning the employees has already reported back. According to one of the clerks, the last person to place a notice on the board forgot to lock it. Apparently, she forgets quite often."

Olivia stared at the poem again. "Harris was right. This killer is wily. Careful too." She gripped the edges of the notebook until the cardboard collapsed beneath her fingers. "A monster dressed as a man."

The chief rose. "He'll give something away. He has a goal and anything that threatens his goal enrages him enough to kill. I need to figure out what he wants and as much as I'd like to do that sitting on this bench, I must get back to the station. I am counting on your discretion. Good day, Ms. Limoges."

Releasing the notebook, Olivia watched Rawlings walk briskly across the grass. She felt sorry for the chief. He had limited manpower and resources and he was undoubtedly angry, frustrated, and embarrassed that he'd yet to discover the identity of the killer. Now Oyster Bay was overrun with reporters, and sooner or later, news of the second poem would leak out and Rawlings would feel the pressure to solve the murders tighten like a noose.

Olivia pulled out her cell phone and explained what had happened to Harris. "We need to meet. Come to The Boot Top tonight. We can have privacy in the banquet

331

room and order off the menu. It's my treat." She paused, listening to Harris's question. "Yes, I'll get in touch with Laurel and yes, I'd love for you to call Millay. And, yes, I'll make sure we have *plenty* to drink."

After lunch, Olivia paid brief visits to her fellow members of the Planning Board. At The Yellow Lady, she found Roy perched on a steel ladder at the back of the house, cleaning out the gutters. Thrilled to have an excuse for a break, he listened to her suggestion regarding the preservation of the graveyard and readily agreed.

"Talbot Fine Properties shouldn't raise too much fuss about having to move the putting green. That's a sound solution you've come up with, Ms. Limoges."

Roy wiped at his face and Olivia noticed the sweat stains on his T-shirt.

"Shouldn't Atlas be giving you a hand? This looks like a major job." Olivia craned her neck to take in the gutters above the second story.

"He's out truck shopping," Roy replied lightly. "I think he's about done being the odd-job man around here. Luckily, it's summer and I can get a few kids to help out. It's what we've always done before." He grinned. "I'd better get back to this. Annie's honey-do list is as long as my arm."

Olivia smiled sympathetically at him.

Satisfied by her conversation, Olivia stopped by the Neuse Community Bank next. Her talk with Loan Manager Ed Campbell wasn't as fruitful, however.

"A change like that is going to cost Talbot Properties a pretty penny," Ed explained. "They'll have to level the ground, run a line to install the irrigation system, add a bunch of French drains to keep the greens dry when there's too much moisture, et cetera, et cetera."

"It's worth a few extra dollars to keep that cemetery intact," Olivia argued, but she could see that Ed was unwilling to challenge the Talbots' proposal by the slightest fraction.

Knowing Dixie would speak to Grumpy and that Marlene planned to vote against the resolution no matter what adjustments were made, Olivia spent the remainder of the afternoon in her office at The Boot Top reading the online articles about Dean's death. She knew she shouldn't be surprised by how quickly information was collected and dispersed via the Internet, but she was. Papers from across the country featured stories of the real estate tycoon's "tragic death" on their homepages. Links to dozens of photographs showing Dean and the rest of the Talbot clan were prominently featured on Yahoo! and Google.

As she watched video clips of the Talbots, Olivia paid careful attention to any appearance of Max Warfield in the footage. She then muted her iMac's volume and studied the facial expressions and body language of anyone who routinely appeared in public with Dean Talbot.

"No one liked that man," Olivia informed Haviland as pleasant aromas drifted in from the kitchen. "Look at his kids. They're all partially turned away from him. None of them will look him in the eye. They probably felt inferior all their lives and their wounded pride and lack of affection eventually turned into anger. The mother is never at any of their public outings. Year after year, she hid at home or was checked into some rehab center, so Dean was the only parent available to receive the full share of his children's ire."

Olivia turned her attention to the articles she'd printed out from the Internet, picking up the top sheet. "Dean's controlling share of Talbot Fine Properties goes to Blake Talbot," she reread the sentence she'd highlighted. "I can see why he didn't pick the older son if he's got a cocaine problem, but why Blake? The daughter clearly has the business smarts while Blake sings in a rock band. Dean didn't trust him to manage the band's money, yet he entrusted him with a multimillion-dollar corporation? It doesn't make sense."

Having exhausted her search on the computer, Olivia walked out to the bar and turned the wall-mounted television to *Headline News*. As she waited for the top of the hour, in which the show was certain to lead off with a story on Talbot's death, Olivia read through her notes once more.

"Blake Talbot had the motive, if not the means to kill his father. He has the necessary skills to write poetry. And he is definitely possessed of a darkness of spirit. Listen to this song lyric, Haviland."

Haviland sank to his belly and lowered his head to his paws.

"Stop that. I'm not going to sing!" Olivia remonstrated. " *'I'll push you into the black water. Fish are gonna swallow your last breath. I'm gonna tear down your towers and rip down your signs. People are gonna remember my name. You shouldn't have tried to hold me, fool. You shouldn't have tried to keep me down. Look at me. I ain't no sheep, man, I am the wolf.'* "

Groaning, Haviland rolled onto his side.

"Well, you have to imagine the verse accompanied by pounding drums, feverish electric guitar strumming, and a heavy dose of screaming by a group of young men with gelled hair and leather pants." She examined the lyrics. "None of the stanzas rhyme, but the lines of the chorus do. More sheep/wolf imagery there. Do you see what I mean, Captain? If this kid wasn't holding a serious grudge against his father, then I'll start drinking wine from a box."

Gabe's arrival interrupted her musings. He greeted her and then began his preparations behind the bar. Olivia silently observed as he sliced lemons, limes, and strawberries. Considering his profession, Gabe was a calm and unassuming young man, but Olivia found his quiet friendliness refreshing and so did the regulars that liked to sit at his bar.

Millay and Harris appeared at The Boot Top at half past five and joined Olivia at the bar. Harris looked puzzled while Millay, whose black hair was bright yellow at the tips, tried to put on her signature expression of cool disinterest. However, she quickened her pace upon seeing Olivia and a spark ignited in her eyes, belying her eagerness to discover why an emergency meeting had been called.

Before Olivia had time to say hello, Laurel burst into the room.

"I am the mother of two-year-old twins, you know!" she said, slamming her purse onto the bar's polished surface. "I can't just leave the house every other night. I have responsibilities!"

Grinning, Millay slung an arm around Laurel. "Rough visit with the parental units so far?"

Laurel's shoulders slumped. "They're my in-laws, actually, though they make me call them Mom and Dad as if I don't already have a pair of my own." She sighed heavily. "The *good* news is they just closed on one of the three-bedroom Ocean Vista condos so I'll have free babysitting any time I want."

"And the bad news?" Olivia was already ordering Laurel a glass of wine. Gabe poured a glass of the house Merlot and then headed to the kitchen to fetch olives and pearl onions.

After taking a generous sip, Laurel cracked a thin smile. "That they've moved here, of course! Oh, I know I should be happy to have the help, but I can *never* do anything right in Steve's mother's eyes. She always knows *just* how he likes things and *now* she seems to have the twins all figured out too."

"Don't let her push you around. Your

husband and kids are *your* family. Be nice, but do things *your* way," Harris advised and Olivia wondered how often he'd had to stand up to bullies as he grew into manhood.

Laurel patted his arm gratefully. "Well, let's look at that haiku so I can get back home before she Cloroxes every inch of the nursery."

Olivia, who privately thought disinfecting Dallas and Dermot's potentially germ-infested room sounded like a very sound idea, handed out copies of the new poem. She then poured wine for the rest of the group and led them to the table where she'd last sat sharing a drink with Chief Rawlings, preferring the bar's intimate setting over the formality of the banquet room.

"Oh, yeah, that Talbot dude was pushed all right," Millay said after reading the haiku. She drank down half her wine in one gulp. "But you'll be happy to know that Jethro Bragg is *definitely* in the clear as a suspect in Camden's murder. He and Missy Gordon — she's a trashy redhead who has a thing for men who've been in the slammer, even if it's just the drunk tank — came into Fish Nets around three o'clock on Saturday. According to my boss, they were all over each other. They left before I poured out my first Bud of the night, but the word on the street is that Jethro's hands were *way* too busy investigating Missy's body to be killing anyone or writing poetry. I didn't tell you guys before because I swore not to. We're talking the hand-on-the-Bible kind of promise."

"Who cares about your promise?" Olivia stood over the younger woman, holding the wine bottle out of reach, her blue eyes dark with anger. "All along, we've been trying to figure out what happened to Camden and you kept this quiet?"

Millay had the good sense to look abashed. "Missy's married, okay! But her marriage is a big secret. I'm the only one who knows and I don't spill secrets people tell me when they're wasted. Besides, if her three-hundred-pound truck-driving husband came back after two months on the road and found out about her and Jethro, there would have been another murder in Oyster Bay, *capisce?* Missy's better half is a recovering alcoholic, so he doesn't come into the bar, but if I ratted on his wife, Missy would have known I'd opened my big mouth. I figured Jethro could provide his own alibi without me having to betray anyone." She grabbed the bottle from Olivia's hand. "Anyway, I *told* you Jethro didn't do it. How about a little trust next time?"

Stunned by the news, Olivia watched wordlessly as Millay filled her wineglass to the brim. "I admire you for being true to your word," Olivia finally said. "But your decision allowed the police to waste time and energy." Surprised to see Millay's eyes grow moist, Olivia dropped the subject. What was done was done. She had to remember that Millay was young. She'd truly believed that her actions were noble. Olivia touched her briefly on the shoulder. "Jethro doesn't seem to have known much peace in his life. I'm relieved he won't have to spend any more time behind bars."

"It also means there are no suspects for Camden's murder," Harris pointed out. "Or Dean's. It's not like I wanted Jethro to be guilty, but knowing he's innocent means the cops still don't have any leads."

"We'd better be careful of tossing assumptions around so quickly," Olivia said with more bite than she'd intended. "This second poem isn't public knowledge, so let's keep our thoughts between ourselves and try to come up with something helpful for the police, shall we?"

The four writers studied the poem. Millay and Laurel took pens from their bags and began to make notes or scribble questions in the margins and on the bottom of the paper. Harris read the haiku several times and then wandered off to gaze out the large windows overlooking the harbor where dozens of mast lights winked and shimmered as moored boats swayed gently in the current.

The sky was caught between day and night — peach and melon stripes were being chased away by periwinkle and cobalt blues. Harris lifted his eyes to look at the first stars of the evening, which had awakened and were burning through the lingering clouds.

"What is the connection between Camden and Dean?" Harris spoke without turning. "Camden came here to gather dirt on Blake. Then he was killed. Dean came here to make sure his project would go through. Then he was killed and —"

"And his shares of Talbot Properties go to Blake," Olivia interjected.

"But Blake *wasn't* here!" Laurel protested. "Blake was long gone before Camden's death. We saw that concert footage of him playing in Vegas, remember? And, if what I read in the paper is right, he left in the middle of his band's tour and flew in yesterday. I guess his siblings are on their way, too."

Millay punched some buttons on her iPhone. "It's true. Blackwater was in concert in Sin City on Saturday. Here's a YouTube video of Blake testing out the mic before the performance. Look at the time it was filmed."

Olivia peered at the screen, a little awed by what Millay had been able to discover using a mobile phone. "The medical examiner thinks Dean was killed between three and four in the afternoon. Whoever pushed him has probably been in Oyster Bay since Camden's murder."

"What about that Max Warfield? He seems sly enough to fit the profile." Harris pointed at his untouched wine. "Do you have any of that Gaelic Ale? That stuff is really good."

"Max was shored up in his hotel room with a woman. That's his alibi for Dean's murder." As Gabe was still in the kitchen, Olivia went behind the bar and popped the cap from one of Highland Brewing Company's most popular products and removed a chilled pint glass from the small refrigerator under the bar. She served Harris his beer and the other writers watched as the foam bubbled near the rim of the glass without so much as a drip escaping.

Laurel made a growling noise. "This is so frustrating! What Oyster Bay local would want to help Blake Talbot become even richer?"

"A poor one," Millay replied tersely.

"We're talking about slitting a man's throat! It's got to be about more than just money," Laurel argued.

Olivia stopped tapping the stem of her wineglass and studied her friend. "I think you're on to something, Laurel. Money is a motivator, but I agree that the killer must benefit in another way from Blake's advancement. There's got to be something personal about these crimes. He's not shooting them in some private place. He's makes a statement, but what is he trying to say?"

"Maybe the killer wanted revenge against Dean," Harris suggested. "Man, I wish Camden could have just spelled out what he discovered and put it in his manuscript. There's nothing incriminating in those pages. I've read them a dozen times by now."

Delicately draining her glass, Laurel placed it on the table. "Someone must have noticed the creep outside the town hall. I see the same people whenever I'm out for a run. I know who's a tourist and who's starting a new exercise routine, who's running late, and who wears the same shirt every Wednesday . . ." She shrugged. "You get my point. Anyway, we should talk to Flynn, the bookstore owner. He runs every day and he's out early. Even earlier than me."

Olivia felt the fine hairs on the back of her neck stand up. "I'll have a discreet talk with him. Right now if I can. You all stay for dinner. I'm going to catch Flynn while he's locking up for the night."

Laurel stood. "I can't stay, but let me know if I can help in any way."

"What about you, Millay? Should we keep the wheels turning here?" Harris asked with a hopeful smile.

Millay handed Gabe her empty wineglass and ordered an apple martini. "Sure, I'm off tonight. As long as Olivia's buying, I'll stay until we figure out who this bastard is."

Harris shot Olivia a look of appeal.

"Just go easy on the Dom Pérignon," Olivia responded and followed Laurel out the door.

Chapter 14

We long for an affection altogether ignorant of our faults. Heaven has accorded this to us in the uncritical canine attachment.

— George Eliot

The sign posted on Through the Wardrobe's front window claimed that the shop would open promptly at nine every morning but might close anywhere between the hours of five and seven, depending on the "whims and temperament of the management."

Despite the seriousness of her errand, Olivia grinned upon reading this declaration. She pushed open the heavy wooden door to the sound of tinkling bells and was surprised to hear a woman's voice call out, "Welcome to Through the Wardrobe!"

A woman in her early thirties in a form-fitting flowered sundress looked up from her task of gathering a long vacuum cord.

From the manner in which the pretty brunette wrapped the cord from palm to elbow as a veteran sailor would coil a length of rope, Olivia wondered if the younger woman could move about a boat with the same show of grace and ease.

"Can I help you find something?" the brunette asked, using the gentle drawl indigenous to the Carolinas.

Olivia pasted on a friendly smile. "I was looking for Mr. McNulty, actually. There's something I wanted to ask him. I'll only take a few minutes of his time as I've left my dog in the car." She gestured toward the front door while inhaling the pleasing aroma of orange-scented furniture wax. "I'm glad to see he's found some help. This place needed a woman's touch."

The woman looped the cord neatly onto the hook on the vacuum cleaner's body and held out her hand. "I'm Jenna Watts. I've seen you around town, of course, but it's a pleasure to meet you in person. Flynn's out back taking care of the garbage. Just go through the stockroom. I hope you don't mind if I let you find your own way. I don't like to leave the register unattended." She glanced out the window. "And I'll make sure to keep an eye on your beautiful dog."

Upon first seeing her, Olivia had been

fully prepared to dislike Flynn's new employee, but instead found herself disarmed by Jenna's pleasant, practical nature.

And why would I care that Flynn hired such a pretty woman? she asked herself. *I have no claim on him.*

The only customer in the store was a teenage boy enveloped in one of the upholstered chairs. His nose was buried in a graphic novel and he had a stack of similar works piled up on the coffee table in front of him. Olivia suspected Jenna would have to politely tell the absorbed reader the store was closing if she wanted to go home before midnight.

Olivia walked through the deserted children's section and passed through a set of double doors leading to the stockroom. The space was dimly lit and contained a rolling cart, stacks of cardboard boxes from Ingram and other book distributors, and cardboard book displays sent by various publishing houses in order to highlight the works of some of their bestselling authors.

The sounds of Bob Seger's "The Fire Inside" burst forth from the radio. The appliance was angled so the speakers faced the cement door leading outside. Olivia walked toward the open door but paused to examine Flynn's CD collection first. She found people's tastes in books and music to be very telling. Flynn's selected artists included Bob Seger, Bruce Springsteen, the Eagles, Lynyrd Skynyrd, The Who, Bread, Creedance Clearwater Revival, Miles Davis, Ella Fitzgerald, and John Coltrane. When her eyes fell on the last pair of CDs in the small rack, she took an involuntary step backward. Flynn owned both of Blackwater's albums, even though his musical taste didn't seem to reflect an interest in Blake Talbot's brand of punk rock.

Olivia opened each of the jewel cases and pulled out the CDs. No notes or scraps of paper bearing sinister instructions fluttered to the floor. She replaced the two CDs, feeling foolishly paranoid and acutely anxious all at once.

What do *I really know about this man?* she thought as she moved forward to find him.

Stepping over the threshold, Olivia saw him and abruptly stopped.

Flynn had stripped off his button-down shirt and hung it from the handle of a small moving dolly. Clad in a snug white T-shirt that accentuated his muscular arms and back, Flynn was engrossed in breaking down empty boxes. Wielding a box cutter, he sliced through packing tape using deft, deliberate movements. He then stomped heavily on each box, driving the heel of his foot against the cardboard so that it collapsed in a single, defeated motion.

Olivia focused her gaze on Flynn's face, watching the tight clench of his jaw and the fixed determination in his eyes as he worked. After finishing another three boxes, he sheathed the box cutter, put it in his pocket, and reached for the bottle of beer he'd had sitting in the shade of the Dumpster. Looking up, he spotted Olivia in the doorway.

Time crawled as he stared at her without seeming to actually see her. It was as though his mind had been miles away and had been suddenly forced back to the here and now. Blinking, a hesitant smile appeared on Flynn's face and he headed toward Olivia, signaling that he needed to turn down the radio's volume. She stood aside as he came into the stockroom and switched off the music, perturbed by the vacant look she'd just seen in his eyes.

"Are you one of those people who don't believe in the modern device known as the telephone?" His tone was playful, making Olivia doubt whether she was reading too much into the far-off thoughts of a man busy with menial labor.

"I prefer to speak to people in person," Olivia replied. She glanced outside. "Are you almost finished?"

Flynn hesitated and then nodded. "I've done enough work for today. Have you had dinner yet?"

"Actually, that's why I'm here," she said. "Do you have plans for tonight?"

"Only to fire up the grill so that I can prove to my neighbors that I'm a real man even though I don't own a pickup or a chain saw." He gave her a pleading look. "Having a beautiful woman on my patio won't hurt either, so if you like Italian sausages, corn on the cob, and watermelon, I've got enough for two."

"Well, if your cooking abilities are anything like your decorating tastes . . ." Olivia trailed off, recalling the interior of Flynn's house.

Flynn's laugh bounced off the cement walls "Let me just lock up back here and tell Jenna she can scoot. Did you get a chance to meet her on the way in?"

Olivia nodded. "Yes, she's lovely. However, she might be too nice to kick out your last customer. He looks like he'd like to spend the night here."

"The teenager reading graphic novels?" Flynn asked. "That's Alan." He flicked a life-sized cardboard cutout of Dan Brown on the nose. "Alan will leave when I start turning the lights off. Meet you out front."

Olivia browsed the poetry section while Flynn finished with his closing tasks. Once she'd returned to the Rover and began following Flynn to his home, Haviland whined in protest.

"This is a fact-finding mission," Olivia explained to the unhappy poodle. "And there will be sausages for dinner."

As though he understood the word sausage, Haviland bounded out of the car and across Flynn's lawn in a blur of black fur. He eagerly sniffed at all the shrubbery surrounding the front porch and then sat on his haunches on the welcome mat as though he couldn't imagine what was taking the humans so long to open the door and begin the food preparations.

"Good evening, Haviland." Flynn nodded at the poodle.

Olivia watched closely as her dog sniffed Flynn's hand and then turned away, disinterested. Apparently, Haviland's feelings hadn't changed. The poodle still didn't appear the slightest bit threatened by the man.

Relieved, Olivia walked into the living room and then laughed when the poodle began to bark at the three-dimensional tropical fish swimming across the kelly green wall. "Captain, it isn't polite to criticize another's person's taste in, ah, art-work."

Flynn looked appalled. "Hey, now! This isn't *my* taste. Those heinous fish came with the house, along with the atrocious paint colors. Come on, do you think *I'd* have a silver and purple bathroom?" He put his hand over his heart and groaned as though he'd been wounded. "My goal was to get the store straight before turning my attention to this place. Believe me, if those Little Nemos weren't fastened on there with industrial strength wall anchors, they'd have been at the curb from day one."

He walked into the kitchen and opened the refrigerator. "I've got soda, beer, tap water, or milk that's probably well on its way to becoming sour cream."

"A beer's fine for me," Olivia answered, thinking wistfully of the unopened bottle of Chivas Regal she had at home. "And a bowl of water for Haviland, please."

"Bowls are in the cabinet to the right of the sink." Flynn placed the beer on the counter and removed a package wrapped in brown butcher paper from the meat drawer. He loaded two ears of corn, unhusked, and several types of sausages onto a platter. As he walked through the living room, he suddenly stopped.

"I can't believe you thought I deliberately hung those fish. What *else* do you think I'm capable of, I wonder?"

There was a hint of displeasure in Flynn's voice. Olivia tried to lighten the mood by saying, "I'm hoping you'll enlighten me during our meal. Last time I was here, you told me about working for a pharmaceutical company in Research Triangle Park. Now tell me how you became a runner. My friend Laurel sees you pounding the pavement on a regular basis."

Out on the flagstone patio, Flynn lit the grill and a pair of tiki torches mounted to the backs of lawn chairs. "I know Laurel. She's the one with the cute twins." He shook his head. "I don't know how women run with those monster strollers. I can barely propel my own body forward." He put the sausages on the grill. "Truthfully, I love running. Not to be faster or stronger or for any of those health reasons. I just like to lose myself for an hour or so."

"I understand that feeling. Haviland and I do that every morning on our walks on the beach. But after you run, do you get to relax in the pages of one of your thousands of books?" Olivia inquired.

Flynn moved the food around with a pair of tongs. "I don't get much read at the store.

We have a steady stream of customers most days and believe it or not, I do have to restock and ring people up and —"

"Brew that odious coffee," Olivia teased. "Laurel said she notices the same people exercising in the downtown area. Apparently, there's an entire group of running addicts. Have you noticed that too?"

"Sure. People like schedules. Runners in particular. Me? I'm a morning runner. Can't do it at night and I'd melt if I went out midday." He shrugged. "I guess we're a particular lot, kind of like the folks who love my odious coffee." He swatted the air near her leg with the hot tongs.

"Did you happen to notice a guy posting a piece of bright red paper on the bulletin board outside the town hall this weekend?" She watched Flynn carefully for a reaction. There was none.

"Nope." He shook his head. "But I can be pretty clueless about things when I'm in the zone and I've got my music turned up loud. Is he important? This guy?"

"I'd just like to know the guy's name, that's all," Olivia answered cryptically and changed the subject.

As Flynn had no patio furniture other than flimsy lawn chairs, they ate on a blanket on the grass. Without the presence of an ocean breeze, the air felt especially cloying. It stuck to Olivia's arms and neck, inviting a host of bugs to circulate around her head as they searched out the source of her jasmine and gardenia perfume. Haviland didn't seem to notice the pests as he wolfed down a bratwurst and then gave Flynn his most poignantly imploring look.

"Forget it, Haviland. You're having vegetables when we get home," Olivia scolded.

"You can't stay?" Flynn asked casually, his eyes betraying his desire.

Though part of her wanted to linger, Olivia was too unsettled by the discovery of the haiku and the realization that Camden's killer had an agenda that possibly included more murders. On another night, she might have wanted comfort, to lose herself with Flynn, but tonight she wanted to go home. It was her goal to make a list of all of the facts and theories she'd accumulated about the murders and try to discern what the killer was after.

She wanted to think and after that, she wanted to sleep, wake up early, and think some more.

"I'm sorry, but with all these reporters in town, we're swamped at The Boot Top. I need to be up early tomorrow to lend a hand," she explained softy, doing her best to sound disappointed.

Together, she and Flynn carried their plates to his kitchen. Olivia rinsed while Flynn loaded the dishwasher. When he excused himself to use the bathroom before walking her to the car, Olivia meandered back into the living room. She noticed a white hardback with a pear on the cover sitting on a side table. Curious, she bent down and glanced at the title.

"*Haiku Mind: 108 Poems to Cultivate Awareness and Open Your Heart* by Patricia Donegan," Olivia read. She took a closer look at the page Flynn had marked with a Post-it note. It was a chapter beginning with what the author referred to as Allen Ginsberg's death poem.

To see Void vast infinite
look out the window
into the blue sky.

Olivia flipped through the book, scanning every haiku for the familiar lines of the winter and spring poems she had now memorized. When she heard the water rush through the pipes, she slid the book back onto the table and moved toward the front door.

Sensing her sudden discomfort, Haviland

whined.

Flynn appeared and patted the poodle's head. "Didn't mean to keep you waiting, my man." He held the door open for Haviland and then took Olivia's hand. "I really wish you didn't have to go."

Giving his hand a quick squeeze, Olivia plastered on a smile. "We'll get together again soon."

Outside, Flynn leaned his back against the Range Rover, preventing Olivia from getting inside. He reached out and slipped an arm around her waist, pulling her against him. His voice grew hoarse with hunger. "If I promise to feed those plastic fish to the equally unattractive colony of yard gnomes down the street, will you stay over next time?"

Laughing, Olivia kissed him lightly on the lips and disengaged from his grasp. "Maybe. Thank you for dinner. If being adept with a grill makes you more macho in your neighbor's eyes, then you are one hundred percent pure Grade-A male."

"Me Flynn Man!" Flynn stepped away from the car, beating on his chest like an ape. "Me get to interrogate *you* on our next date." He shuffled, primatelike, around the other side of the Rover and opened the passenger door for Haviland.

"Be safe!" he called out before closing the door and jumping nimbly onto the sidewalk.

Olivia pulled away from the curb and glanced at Haviland. "I find those parting words a bit unsettling, don't you?"

Haviland barked.

At home, Olivia kicked off her shoes and poured herself a generous splash of Chivas Regal. She let Haviland out for his nightly roam and sank onto the sofa with her notebook. She reviewed every detail she'd previously recorded about the deaths of Camden Ford and Dean Talbot.

Ripping out the pages containing copies of the two haiku, Olivia stared at the lines. She drained her drink and jiggled the melting ice against the walls of the tumbler. "Do you have a victim in mind for your summer poem?"

Olivia went into the kitchen for a refill and to treat herself to a few squares of dark chocolate. Chewing on the smooth, slightly bitter Belgian sweet, she paced around the spacious living room. "Bottom line: Blake Talbot has benefited from both deaths." She spoke to her reflection in the large windows facing the ocean. "Camden no longer has the power to write anything negative about Blake and the death of Blake's father makes

him one of the wealthiest and most powerful young men in the country."

Returning to her notebook, she circled
Max Warfield's name. "Do you benefit as
well? Has Blake promised you a bigger slice
of the pie?" Sighing, she tossed down her
pen. "But all the obvious villains have
alibis!" Her thoughts strayed to Flynn and
to the image of him wielding the box cutter.
"No, he can't be involved. He has no motive."

She continued to debate a host of pos-
sibilities aloud until she felt frustrated and
spent. Opening the French doors leading to
the deck, she called for Haviland. A refreshing breeze sprang up from the ocean, and
Olivia leaned against the railing, listening to
the gentle rush of the waves onto the sand.
Inhaling the salt-misted air calmed her
thoughts, but eventually she grew impatient
for bed.

"Come on, Haviland!" Olivia called again.

When another five minutes passed, Olivia
shouted again, an edge of irritation entering
her voice. She listened for Haviland's
responding bark, but the only sounds were
the water's whispers.

Annoyed, Olivia grabbed a flashlight from
the cabinet beneath the kitchen sink, stuck
her feet into the well-worn sneakers reserved

for morning walks, and stomped across the luminescent sand.

"HAVILAND!" she bellowed.

Slowly, her exasperation turned to concern. Haviland always reappeared within minutes of her first call. Even during daylight hours, when he was routinely distracted by gulls, crabs, and a host of interesting odors, he responded almost immediately to her commands.

Heading toward the lighthouse keeper's cottage, Olivia felt a tightness in her chest. Something was wrong.

At the same moment she felt that sharp stab of fear, the beam of the flashlight sought out a darker patch of black in the shadow cast by the cottage.

Olivia's heart nearly stopped. She broke into a run, her legs moving with agonizing slowness over the sand. She dropped to her knees next to her dog.

Haviland was lying on his side. He was utterly still and didn't even flinch when Olivia put her hand on his chest, nearly crying in relief as it inflated, albeit shallowly, with oxygen.

"What is it? What is it?" she demanded frantically, her fingers exploring his coat for signs of injury. There was no blood. None of his bones felt broken. Nothing indicated why he now lay unconscious in the dark. His collar was also missing.

Having taking several courses on administering canine first aid, Olivia gently peeled open Haviland's eye. She took in the glazed appearance as though from a great distance, and then parted the poodle's lips and pulled his tongue free, allowing him to breathe with slightly more ease. It was at that moment she saw a flash of red sticking out beneath Haviland's front paw.

Stomach churning out of fright and anger, she pulled the piece of paper loose and held it under the light.

"BACK OFF," it read.

Olivia dropped the note as though it had singed her skin and then shoved it into her back pocket before running as fast as she had ever run back to the house. She grabbed her purse and keys and sped down the hill, backing the Rover over the sand near the cottage until it was only a few feet away from Haviland. She opened the back and, heaving her dog into her arms, laid him down as carefully as she could. She checked once more for signs of breath and then covered his body with a blanket.

She did nearly eighty into town, dialing the local vet's number along the way.

"Hello?" Diane Williamson, doctor of

veterinary medicine, croaked. She'd clearly been asleep.

Fighting to keep her voice calm, Olivia explained how she'd found Haviland and that she was on her way to Diane's office. The vet, who lived in the carriage house behind the converted home where she practiced, reassured Olivia that she would be ready and waiting to receive her patient.

"Thank you." Olivia's words came out like a dry sob.

Barely pausing at red lights, Olivia passed slower drivers by crossing the double yellow line, swerved in front of meandering tourists, and even drove on the sidewalk to get around a double-parked convertible filled with teenagers.

Diane was standing in the doorway when Olivia backed into the driveway. The two women lifted Haviland onto a dog gurney and whisked him up the ramp and into the first of two examination rooms.

Olivia stroked Haviland's head while Diane listened to his heart. She inspected his eyes and gums and then gently opened Haviland's mouth wide and sniffed.

"What's the last thing he ate?" Diane asked.

"A bratwurst," Olivia answered shamefaced. She knew Diane disapproved of Haviland's diet. "It wasn't the sausage . . . ?"

"No." Diane straightened but left one hand on the poodle's flank. "His mouth smells like ground beef."

"Then someone else fed him that." Olivia's dark blue eyes blazed with a fierce anger. "Has Haviland . . . ?" She could barely formulate the thought let alone speak it out loud. "Was he poisoned?"

Diane hesitated and then shook her head. "No, I don't think so. There's no swelling, unusual redness around the eyes, ears, or skin, and no blistering in the mouth. I believe he's ingested some kind of sedative. Let me run a few tests to make sure." She turned away from her patient for a moment and touched Olivia's shoulder. "Trust me. He's going to be fine."

Olivia couldn't see through the tears. "He's got to be," she whispered. "The Captain is . . . half of my whole being."

The vet didn't respond. She'd already turned her attention back to the poodle. She didn't waste time asking Olivia to wait outside either, knowing full well she'd refuse.

Exhausted, Olivia perched on the edge of the room's only chair, watching every brisk and efficient move Diane made, but allowing the professional to work in silence. At some point, though she did not remember doing so, Olivia shut her eyes, leaned her head back against the wall, and fell into a light sleep.

Diane woke her with a gentle squeeze on the shoulder. "Haviland is stable. I ran a blood test and found that he did ingest sedatives. Too much for his body weight, but not enough to be fatal. He needs to rest for several hours, but he should make a full recovery and be his charming self in a day or so."

Olivia pressed her hands over her eyes. "Thank you," she murmured, too weary to infuse her words with the gratitude she felt.

"*You* should go home and get some rest too," Diane suggested kindly. "I'll call you as soon as he's awake."

"No. I won't leave him."

Diane smiled. "I thought you'd say that." She pointed at a door in the back of the room. "My office is through there. I've put a clean blanket and pillow on the sofa for you. You might as well sleep if you can. That's all Haviland will be doing."

Nodding, Olivia walked over to Haviland and stroked the fur behind his right ear. She leaned over and kissed him on the forehead and then simply stood there, watching the reassuring rise and fall of his chest. When she finally sank down on the plaid couch in Diane's office, something crinkled in her back pocket. She pulled out the small square of red paper.

"You have hurt the wrong dog, you bastard," she hissed. "I'm going to devote every resource, every thought, and every moment of my waking hours *hunting you down.*"

She stared at the note until the typed words blurred into black, beetlelike smudges and the bright red of the paper became the color of vengeance.

Olivia waited until six the next morning to call Rawlings. She'd slept a few fitful hours on Diane's couch, but it had been enough to allow her to spend the rest of the day in action. She planned to scour the area surrounding the cottage as soon as the light allowed for a detailed search and she wanted the chief and his men on the job too.

Rawlings listened to Olivia recall the events of the previous night and promised to be waiting in her driveway by the time she got home.

"I don't want you going inside until I check it out," he ordered.

Olivia complied, asked Diane's assistant to call the moment Haviland woke up, and drove to Bagels 'n' Beans. She requested a coffee and a sesame seed bagel with butter for herself and then placed an order for coffee, pastries, and a lunch tray of assorted sandwiches to be sent to Diane's office and to the Canine Cottage, the grooming business she owned as well.

"Give them the works," Olivia told Wheeler, handing him her Visa card. "Chips, cookies, sun tea, all of it. As a matter of fact, I'd like you to do this for them once a week for the rest of the month."

Wheeler scrutinized his customer's bloodshot eyes and drawn face and then scanned the length of the store in search of Haviland. "He's all right then?"

"He will be," Olivia replied, relieved Wheeler hadn't asked what had happened. She didn't want anyone to know that she and Haviland had become victims over the course of the night. She didn't want the town gossips spreading the tale about town, inviting the interest of the journalists present. Besides, playing the victim was a role she refused to accept.

Rawlings and two of his officers were walking the perimeter of her house when she pulled into the driveway. Olivia handed him the plastic baggie containing the note.

"My fingerprints will be on there," she said as he drew near. "I don't think you have mine on file, so I'll come in and be printed as soon as we're done here."

Accepting the bag, Rawlings read the warning and his eyes narrowed. "Why does he feel threatened by you?"

"I've been thinking about that. Yesterday, I paid brief visits to the other members of the Planning Board, asking them to reject the Cottage Cove proposal until it can be altered to include more green space and the preservation of the Neuse River Park's cemetery." Olivia unlocked her front door and stepped aside.

She watched Rawlings draw his gun, his eyes sweeping the kitchen. Without responding to what she'd said, he waved one of his men toward the living room. The third opened the coat closet and peered inside.

Olivia noticed that Rawlings had chosen seasoned men to accompany him and was satisfied to find him taking the incident so seriously.

"Clear!" he called from the living room and disappeared upstairs.

Impatient to get down to the cottage, Olivia occupied herself by prepping the coffee machine to brew to its full capacity.

When the chief returned, his gun was holstered. "There's no sign of an intruder and it doesn't look as though anything's been touched. Considering how tidy you are, Ms. Limoges, I'd think it would be obvious if someone had gone through your things. Would you care to check?"

Olivia shook her head. "No. It doesn't feel like anyone's been in the house. I believe I would know. Now let me show you where I found Haviland."

The sand and grass-covered area in the lee of the cottage offered no clues except for the faintest boot print. Even that was a disappointment, being a shallow indentation no bigger that a two-inch square. The ridges were similar to the boots worn by both officers, and though the chief squatted down and studied the mark carefully, Olivia wasn't hopeful that an arrest would be made based on a few lines in the sand. Half the men in Oyster Bay probably owned work boots that made similar imprints.

"There's no indication of where he put the ground beef," Rawlings commented, looking at Olivia. "Were you surprised to learn Haviland ate food given to him by a stranger?"

"First of all, there's no way that bastard got close to him until whatever drugs he fed Haviland took effect," Olivia protested. "He must have left out the meat nearby. If it smelled fresh and Haviland was hungry, which he was, he'd have eaten it. Despite the fact that his intelligence exceeds that of a great deal of Oyster Bay's residents, Haviland *is* a dog."

"He might have put the meat out closer to the water, sir," one of the officers suggested. "The tide would have washed away all traces of the beef before Ms. Limoges ever found the dog. Even if our guy fed him right here, the flies, ants, and gulls would have cleaned up the scraps hours ago."

Rawlings turned his face toward the sea. "Tonight's meeting is important to him. I think he's going to be there, as risky as that might be. He *needs* to see this thing come off without a hitch."

Olivia followed his gaze. "He could have killed me, Chief. I was a sitting duck out here. I think he's had a plan from the beginning. He knows his victims. I bet he's had four poems written, four faces in his mind, and a single goal all along. I didn't fit in his plan so he didn't hurt me, but he doesn't want me to spoil his vision either. That's why he gave me a warning I couldn't ignore. I just don't understand why he took Haviland's collar."

Rawlings rubbed his chin and spent a few moments quietly thinking. "He may also have a code. Don't kill women. Don't hurt the innocent. He knocked your dog out, but he didn't kill him."

"Close enough," Olivia growled.

Sending the two officers into the cottage for a quick search, Rawlings took Olivia's elbow and held it. "Is it too much to ask you to be careful between now and tonight's meeting?"

Olivia smiled at him. "Don't worry about me, Chief. I'll come into town to give you my fingerprints. Until then, I plan to find things to do at home." Her smile vanished. "Such as cleaning my rifle."

CHAPTER 15

In winter I get up at night
And dress by yellow candle-light.
In summer quite the other way,
I have to go to bed by day.
— ROBERT LOUIS STEVENSON

To her relief, Rawlings and his men declined Olivia's offer of coffee, leaving her free to take a hot shower. Afterward, her hair curling against her forehead and the side of her cheeks in damp tendrils, Olivia placed a call to Diane.

"Haviland's still asleep, but that's to be expected," the vet said. "It's not the drug-induced sleep he was in a few hours ago. In fact, he's dreaming. His paws are twitching as though he's out on the beach chasing sandpipers."

Reassured by this image, Olivia spread an old towel on the kitchen table and set out her rifle and gun cleaning kit. She switched on her living room stereo and felt a measure of the tension lodged between her shoulder blades slide away as the opening strains of Beethoven's *"Für Elise"* tiptoed into the room.

After pouring herself a large mug of coffee, Olivia laid out the contents of the gun cleaning kit like a surgeon organizing his instruments before a case. She looked over the folding ramrod, nitro solvent, gun oil, cleaning pads, and cloths and was satisfied with her supplies. Unloading the rifle, she carefully pulled the trigger off and then removed the bolt from the rifle body. She screwed together her collapsible ramrod, fed a folded cleaning pad through the hole, and dipped the tool into the solvent.

Gently easing the ramrod all the way into the barrel until it rubbed against the firing mechanism, Olivia worked the device in and out, stopping to change cleaning pads. Once the interior was clean, she dabbed a bit of oil on a soft cloth and began to wipe the pieces of metal on the outside of the gun. The task was calming. It gave Olivia a sense of control and as the music washed over her, she was able to focus on the riddle of the murderer's identity.

Max Warfield has got to be involved, she thought as she began to reassemble the rifle.

As soon as I pick up Haviland, I'm going to pay him a visit. And I think I'll bring my weapon along.

Out on the deck, Olivia stared down the barrel of her gun. She zeroed in on twigs or dark-hued rocks sticking out of the sand and then let her eyes drift across the sparkling water. Recalling Haviland's limp body lying in the dark, Olivia felt anger surge through her body — a fierce juxtaposition of the lazy roll of wavelets before her. Jaw clenched, she pumped the unloaded rifle and pressed the trigger, imagining a bullet puncturing the surface of the water, slicing through the blue gray depths until it drove beneath a layer of murk, forever embedded in the cold sea floor.

Having just cleaned the rifle, Olivia had no intention of sullying it by firing a round, no matter how much release she'd gain by doing so. Instead, she collected an unopened box of bullets, a covered bowl containing a healthy snack for Haviland, and a travel mug of coffee for herself.

At the police station, she informed the desk officer that her fingerprints were needed and, to her chagrin, Officer Cook appeared to take them.

"It's you again," he muttered, gesturing for her to follow him to the processing area in the building housing the jail. Neither spoke as they walked, but Cook glanced over his shoulder several times, as though a big, black poodle might overtake them at any moment.

Standing across from Olivia, the policeman rolled each of her fingers with the same roughness she imagined he'd use on the combative drunk driver. When he was finished, he tossed two packets of moist towelettes on the counter.

Olivia studied the young man dispassionately. She could only imagine the feelings of impotency the members of the police department must be experiencing with a pair of unsolved murders on their desks and a bevy of reporters crawling over every inch of the town.

"You'll get him in the end," she said as she began to clean her fingertips. As one moist cloth became stained with the blue purple ink, she ripped open a second. "He's not any smarter than you are," she continued, though she knew this might not be true. The killer had already established his intelligence by avoiding capture. "And what if he's not working alone? Having a partner should make him easier to catch. Chief Rawlings believes he'll be at the town hall tonight. If not him, then his partner." She held up a stained index finger. "Watch for the nonverbal signals, Officer. One of our own has been bribed or blackmailed by Blake Talbot or Max Warfield. Watch those two. *They* have alibis but the 'silent partner' in these murders may not have. And he *has* to have a tell."

Cook frowned and Olivia thought the young man was sure to turn truculent, but he surprised her by nodding. "I play poker every Friday and everybody's got a tell. Even me." He handed her a third towelette. "You gotta get it off right away. This ink stains worse than blueberry pie on a white napkin."

"Thank you, Officer Cook." Olivia finished scrubbing her fingers and then followed the young lawman back to the lobby. "I was wondering if you knew the date of Dean Talbot's funeral?"

"No, ma'am, but it won't be here in Oyster Bay," Cook replied. "They're takin' his body back to New York tomorrow where it belongs. The oldest son is handlin' it all. He's a real prize. He thinks we're all a bunch of dumb hillbillies, but we know a coke addict when we see one. I'll be glad to see the last of that family for a while."

Olivia grew thoughtful. "Dean died on Saturday, yet his funeral is Wednesday, which means it was likely delayed until the conclusion of tonight's meeting. Interesting. With the two of the three Talbot kids not yet arrived from New York, someone needs to stay behind to oversee . . ." She trailed off. It was definitely time to pay a visit to Max's rented condo. "Good luck, Officer. The citizens of Oyster Bay are counting on you." She smiled at the bewildered policeman and returned to the Rover, which was parked in the fire lane right outside the jail's front door.

Inside the stifling car, Olivia checked her cell phone for messages. Her face lit up as she listened to the voicemail from Diane. Haviland was awake and moving around and seemed to be no worse for wear.

By the time Olivia pulled in front of the vet's office, her stomach was rumbling. Glancing at the Tupperware on her passenger seat, Olivia knew she'd end up tossing its contents. Haviland was going to dine on ground turkey and raw chicken hearts — one of his favorite meals. They'd both lunch at The Boot Top.

One of Diane's employees must have noticed Olivia's car, for as soon as she stepped onto the driveway, Haviland was allowed outside. He bounded over to his mistress and stood up on his hind legs with a jubilant yelp. Olivia threw her arms around the poodle and then sank to her knees, laughing as she welcomed the frenzied kisses Haviland planted all over her face, neck, and shoulders.

"You smell nice," Olivia remarked. "Did they give you a bath?"

Haviland barked happily and curled his mouth into a smile.

Olivia couldn't seem to stop running her hands over the poodle's soft, black curls. He appeared genuinely unharmed, but it was reassuring to feel his healthy, wiggling body under her fingers. Finally, Olivia kissed Haviland once more on the nose and straightened. Tugging on her disheveled shirt, she placed her drool-covered sunglasses inside her purse and waved at the groomers who had paused in their work to witness the reunion.

Inside the vet's office, Diane's pretty young assistant tabulated the bill and then gestured at the paper plate bearing a sandwich and a pile of potato chips on her tidy desk. "Thanks for lunch, Ms. Limoges. You didn't need to do that. We just love taking care of Haviland. If all our patients were as well mannered as the Captain, our jobs would be a lot easier."

Pleased by the compliment, Olivia reached

out and cupped Haviland's snout in her palm. "Thank Diane again for me, would you?"

"I sure will. She'd see you both off, but she's in surgery." The woman lowered her voice. "Doris Fielding *finally* brought Muffin in to be fixed. That bitch has given birth to every feral mutt in this town. God love them, but each one of her litters is dumber than the last. It's high time for Muffin to close her legs and start acting like a lady."

Laughing, Olivia led Haviland out of the vet's and headed for The Boot Top. The moment the pair walked through the back door, Michel rushed over to Haviland and hugged the poodle's neck.

"I've been waiting for you, my friend." He cast a worried glance at Olivia but continued to address Haviland. "I heard what happened and have been cooking ever since." He removed a bowl from the warming oven and began tossing the contents with a wooden spoon. "This will restore you completely." He set the bowl down beneath Haviland's quivering nose and whispered in all seriousness to Olivia, "I hope the ground beef he ate was at least *organic*."

Olivia rolled her eyes. "I hardly asked the vet for an analysis, Michel."

She left Haviland in the kitchen happily

gulping down his lunch and went into the office to phone Dixie.

"Please tell me you are *not* callin' me in the middle of my lunch rush to talk about those Talbot kids and their airplanes," Dixie scolded.

"I am. When did they arrive and who were they with?"

Dixie sighed, but Olivia knew it was all for show. Dixie would keep her customers waiting until suppertime if it meant passing on a choice morsel of gossip. "Let me hand out some bacon burgers and grab my phone bill. It's all I had handy to write on when I was talkin' to Grumpy's cousin."

Putting the phone on speaker mode, Olivia began to sort through her emails. When Dixie picked up the receiver, she cleared her throat and spoke clearly so Olivia could hear her over the din of the lunch crowd.

"Blake Talbot flew in Sunday afternoon. His girlfriend was with him, that Heidi St. Claire from TV. My girls are wild about her. They say she's going to be bigger than Hannah Montana." She paused dramatically. "And guess where she and her man are right now?"

"Where?" Olivia asked, imagining the glimmer in Dixie's eyes.

"The love birds are *here!* In the *Evita* booth!" Dixie dropped her voice to an excited whisper. "They're both wearin' baseball hats and those big ole sunglasses that make people look like horseflies, but I know it's them. Okay, back to the report: The older brother and his wife flew in Sunday evenin' around six and then the sister and Dean's widow came in together around eight. No other flights. No other passengers. And don't you forget you owe me dirt on Flynn for this."

Olivia frowned. Every single Talbot was out of town when Dean had his fatal fall. "And Saturday? Did any private charters arrive?"

"Just two. One stopped for repairs before headin' down to Myrtle Beach and the second was full of guys on one of those corporate fishin' retreats. Nothin' dark and sinister, darling." She placed her hand over the receiver and shouted something. "Gotta go. See you tonight for the fireworks show."

"That's one way to put it," Olivia replied with a smirk, but Dixie was already gone.

Next, Olivia dialed the number to the rental management office of the Ocean Vista condos. The phone was answered by a woman with a musical voice and Olivia sweetly asked to be put through to the manager.

"Bert Long. Can I help you?"

Olivia introduced herself as the owner of The Boot Top and proceeded to outline a proposal to reward new condo buyers and long-term renters with a dinner for two at the restaurant. "We are the only five-star restaurant in the area, Mr. Long. I'm sure your clients would appreciate the incentive."

"I know *I* would!" the manager declared. "I've only been to your place once, but I swear I can still taste the lobster and the wine I enjoyed that night."

Knowing her fish was on the line, Olivia began to reel him in. "Do you recall the exact vintage?"

Bert recited the French label perfectly.

"Why don't I swing over with a bottle and we can discuss this in more detail?" Olivia suggested. "I need to pay a visit to one of your guests anyway. Can you tell me which unit Max Warfield is occupying?"

"Two-twelve. A two-bedroom unit with one of our finest ocean views," Bert answered, switching into salesman mode. "But Mr. Warfield isn't here right now. He always parks his rental car in front of the office to catch the shade and it's gone."

Suppressing her irritation that Max was

unavailable, Olivia said, "Would you mind giving me a call when he returns? I don't want to waste *your* valuable time and we're expecting a full house at the restaurant tonight. If you'd be kind enough to alert me, I'll have time to locate that bottle for you and perhaps bring over a sample of this evening's chef's special."

"Splendid!" Bert bellowed.

Olivia recited her number and then sat back in her chair, wondering what to do next. She opened her notebook and flipped through the pages, hoping some clue would leap off the page and allow her to identify the murderer. As time slipped by, bringing her closer and closer to the evening's meeting, she felt the helpless anger that had been growing within her since Camden's death swell like a cresting storm wave.

A copy of Camden's manuscript sat on her desk. She began to read it again, but couldn't concentrate on the typed words. Her restless mind instead traveled back to the moment in which she'd first met the charming and gregarious gossip writer at Grumpy's.

She continued to reminisce as she served herself a cup of decaf, and the strong, hot coffee helped quell the emotions warring within. Calmer now, Olivia was able to pick up the phone and place yet another call. This time, a phone rang on the other side of the country.

Cosmo answered on the sixth ring. "Olivia! I thought you'd forgotten all about me!"

"Of course not. I've been preoccupied but that's no excuse. I apologize for being neglectful." She did feel rather guilty for not checking on him sooner. "Did you hear about Dean Talbot?"

"Who hasn't?" Cosmo responded. "All of Hollywood is abuzz about Blakey boy. What will he do with all that money? The power? You see, when someone Blake's age has been handed the reins to a multimillion-dollar company, one of two things will happen. The little rocker will party like the end of the earth is coming and burn out like a B-movie actress, or he'll suddenly act older than his years to prove to the other power players that he belongs in their exclusive club. Blake's either headed for rehab — he can share a room with his brother and Mommy Dearest — or he's going to start wearing Brooks Brothers suits and cutting the ribbons of new hospital wings." He paused. "And if he legally hitches his star to Heidi St. Claire, those two will be a *serious* power couple. Brangelina will be old news."

Even though she'd read Camden's chapter on Blake, Olivia couldn't predict how becoming the majority shareholder of Talbot Fine Properties would impact the behavior of the young musician. "Never mind the Talbots. How are *you* doing?"

"Oh, I alternate between believing I can make it through this to wanting to fill my pockets with boulders and step off the end of the pier. Do you know how hard it is to find decent boulders in LA?"

Olivia smiled sadly into the phone. "It's going to take a long time, Cosmo."

"I know." He sighed. "I'm working a lot and that helps the daylight hours pass, but the nights . . ."

"Last forever," she finished for him.

Cosmo sniffed. "I swear. It's like a big, heavy cat jumps onto my chest the second I lie down. I can barely breathe, let alone *sleep.* I have never, *ever* been this tired. Or looked this bad! I'm avoiding mirrors altogether — isn't that shocking?"

"You are one of the loveliest people I've ever met and your grief is only going to add another dimension to you." She clucked her tongue. "I fear you're going to become *so* irresistible that your head will swell like a blimp and there'll be no talking to you."

A laugh boomed into the earpiece. "Oh,

that hurts. I haven't used those stomach muscles since I left Oyster Bay. If only you were here I could practice the laughing bit some more . . ."

"Call me whenever you want, even in the middle of the night," Olivia invited. "I'll put Haviland on the phone and he'll send that 'cat' on your chest running for his ninth life."

Olivia's call waiting signaled and she bid Cosmo a warm, but hasty good-bye. Bert Long was on the other line and was eager to inform her that Max Warfield had returned to his condo.

"Michel, I need an eatable bribe and I need it fast!" Olivia announced as she stepped into the kitchen. "I know you're busy but, ah, I see you have a fresh supply of truffles."

The chef threw his hands into the air. "If you hadn't been through what you'd just been through, I'd tell you to shove these truffles where the sun doesn't shine. Every table is booked for tonight and you want me to whip something up just like that!" He snapped his fingers. "Is it a picnic basket this time or do you require something more sophisticated, like individual dishes served in a lacquer box?"

"A simple truffle quiche would be perfect," Olivia replied breezily. "I'll leave you to it. Haviland? Let's take a quick walk while Michel's working his magic. I need to think about how to handle Max Warfield."

Instead of jumping to his feet when he heard the word "walk," Haviland continued to rest on the floor, his drowsy eyes tracking his mistress. Olivia studied him. "You're right. You shouldn't overdo it. But no more snacking either. I need your canine intuition to be finely honed for the remainder of today and your mind is at its sharpest when your stomach isn't stuffed."

Olivia left the restaurant and headed for the docks. The heat of the afternoon sunlight poured down on her head and shoulders, but she was remarkably comfortable. Born in mid-July, she was a child of summer and had always welcomed its arrival and rarely wilted even on the hottest of days.

Jethro Bragg's houseboat was at its slip, but the small motorboat he used for clamming was gone. As she stared at the water, listening as it lapped against the dock's wooden pylons, she wondered how Jethro had been coping since his release from jail.

An old man carrying a tackle box drew up alongside her. He jerked a gnarled finger toward the ocean. "If you're lookin' for Jethro, he's out collectin'. But you should come down to his oyster fry tonight. Five dollars a plate and you'll never taste a better bite of shellfish in your life. The boy's got the touch." He glanced sideways at Olivia. "And he's a good lad, no matter what some folks say."

"I would very much like to sample his cooking and I'm glad to hear that he's got loyal friends in town," Olivia answered honestly and continued on her walk. She turned away from the docks and walked around a dilapidated warehouse behind the marina. It had recently been put back on the market after the original buyer had been unable to secure the loan necessary to repair the faulty wiring and plumbing, replace the rotten roof, and remove the asbestos hidden behind the moldy walls.

Olivia stood still, carefully scrutinizing the two-story structure. It occurred to her that Oyster Bay could do with a lively casual restaurant. Brew pub meets crab shack. That would appeal to both tourists and locals. She shielded her eyes against the glare of the sun and continued musing. Balcony seating. Checkered tablecloths. Plenty of televisions in the bar for the sports fanatics.

With images of the boisterous eatery filling her head, Olivia returned to The Boot

Top to collect Haviland, a bottle of her second-best Bordeaux and a white cheddar and truffle quiche for Bert Long.

Michel handed her a white shopping bag for the food and the wine. "I don't know what you're up to, but it can't involve taking it easy since you need to bribe someone with my food. Don't you think you should go home and put your feet up after what happened last night?"

Olivia patted her chef's hand, which was covered with dozens of small scars and burns. "Thank you for being concerned, but the person I'm going to see might know who came after Haviland. Someone sedated my best friend, Michel. I could have lost him. There's no chance of my turning the other cheek."

"Be careful then." He pointed at Haviland. "And keep your guard up, Captain. We are way too busy to have the two of you sleeping it off at the vet's office again."

Noting the slight flush in his cheeks, Olivia wagged a finger at the chef. "So *that's* how you knew what happened so quickly! You're dating someone at the Canine Cottage, aren't you? No? Perhaps the lucky woman is Diane's pretty assistant? She's not married, is she?"

Michel picked up a cleaver and advanced

on her. "Don't you have some place to be?"

"I do." Olivia eyed the sharp tool. "And if I didn't have my rifle in the car, I'd ask to borrow that."

The Ocean Vista condos were completely booked. Most of the parking spaces were occupied by SUVs and minivans stuffed to the roof racks with pool floats, boogie boards, and beach toys. There were convertibles and pricey sedans here and there, but Olivia sensed the Ocean Vista properties catered primarily to families.

As she walked around the perimeter of the rectangular structure, searching for number two-twelve, Olivia could hear the joyful screeches and splashes of children playing in a pool nearby. The strains of Bob Marley floated from the same direction. The combined sounds formed a jubilant and carefree melody, yet Olivia remained unaffected by the atmosphere, her mouth set in a firm, determined line.

She walked quickly over the well-maintained property, noticing the drought-resistant annuals and the close-cropped beds of Bermuda grass. The condos were built of pristine white stucco that gleamed in the sunlight, providing an aesthetically pleasing contrast to the terra-cotta-style roof shingles. Taking note of the signs pointing vacationers to bike paths, tennis courts, pools, hot tubs, a miniature golf course, laundry room, fitness area, snack bar, as well as an arrow pointing to even-numbered rooms, Olivia climbed the next set of stairs and paused as she came to number two-twelve.

"Ready, Captain?"

Haviland shifted his weight from one leg to the other, inhaled, and faced the door. Olivia knocked. She listened for sounds from inside the condo but heard nothing. She knocked again.

"His car is here." Olivia knocked a third time, impatiently calling out Max's name. She sighed in exasperation and turned to her poodle. "Is he inside?"

Dipping his black nose to the floor, Haviland's snout connected with the cement in front of the door. Breathing rapidly, the poodle absorbed the fresh scents and then pressed his nostrils as far into the crack under the door as he could. He growled and took several small steps backward. Olivia watched him carefully.

"He *is* in there! Your nose is never wrong. Let's get Bert."

Olivia hastened to the management office, pausing only to grab the shopping bag containing Bert's treats from the Range Rover. Olivia felt the food and wine would immediately smooth her way with the manager.

Bert must have seen Olivia coming up the sidewalk, for he met her at the receptionist's desk, pumping her hand and smiling as though he were running for political office. He glanced nervously at Haviland but was too polite to question the poodle's presence.

"From my chef," Olivia said, handing him the bag. "And though it was my intention to discuss business with you right away, I'm afraid I am too distracted over my concern for Mr. Warfield to do so."

Bert ran a hand over his pink, bald head. "Oh? What seems to be the trouble?"

"I don't know," Olivia answered truthfully. "I knocked on his door several times, but he didn't respond." Seeing that Bert was unaffected by this statement, she decided to embellish. "I also tried his cell phone. Normally, I'd say he was merely in the shower or taking a nap, but I'm aware that he has a heart condition. In this heat . . ." She waved toward the wall of windows facing the parking lot and lowered her voice. "Sometimes these northerners don't take proper precautions."

"Isn't that the truth? You'd think they'd

never heard of sunscreen," Bert agreed and then fell silent, considering a course of action.

"I'd feel *so* much better if you'd try to reach him." Olivia touched Bert's shoulder. "What if he required medical attention and we didn't respond?"

That pushed the right button. Bert grabbed a set of keys and gestured for Olivia to follow his lead. Together, they marched to unit two-twelve without speaking. Bert gave an authoritative knock on Max's door and then dialed a number on his cell phone. They could hear Max's phone ringing from somewhere inside the condo.

Haviland growled again. Bert did a little sideways hop as though the poodle's teeth were aiming for his meaty calf.

"He's not directing that threat at you, Mr. Long," Olivia said soothingly. "Haviland senses something amiss on the other side of this door."

Paling, Bert knocked once more and then announced he was coming in. He turned the key and tentatively pushed the door open. Assaulted by a blast of air-conditioning, he and Olivia stepped into the disheveled living room. Crumpled clothes and towels were strewn on the peach-colored sectional. The surface of every table was littered with empty soda and beer bottles, newspapers, magazines, and deflated potato chip bags.

Frowning, Bert called Max's name again, but this time his voice carried an edge of disapproval.

"You'd better wait here," Bert cautioned as he took a quick glance around the equally untidy kitchen.

Ignoring the manager, Olivia made a gesture with her right hand. "Search, Haviland."

The poodle darted in front of Bert and as the two humans waited, they heard a deep-throated growl echo from the back rooms. Instinctively, Bert and Olivia froze, only resuming their wary gait once Haviland's growl changed into an urgent, high-pitched bark.

Haviland was pacing anxiously in the doorway to one of the bedrooms. Olivia looked over his head toward the bed. The rumpled covers had been shoved into a wrinkled mass toward the middle and the white cotton sheets were covered by at least six pillows, all tossed about as though the bed's occupant had spent a restless night. Max had smoothed out a section of the comforter, however, upon which he'd laid out a gray suit still encased within a dry cleaner's bag.

Olivia's eyes continued to sweep the room and came to an abrupt stop at the pair of club chairs positioned beneath the double windows overlooking the ocean. Max Warfield was in the chair nearest the bathroom. His held was tilted backward at an awkward angle. The rest of his body was unnaturally still.

"You were right! He's had a heart attack!" Bert lurched forward in Max's direction, but Olivia clamped both hands onto his arm, nearly forcing him off balance.

"We mustn't touch him," she stated firmly. "See that thing wrapped around his neck? That's a dog collar. *Haviland's* dog collar. And I doubt Mr. Warfield is wearing it voluntarily. Call 911. Mr. Warfield's been murdered."

Mutely, Bert retreated several feet, his eyes bulging with shock and fear. Unblinking, as though he suspected the corpse of making a sudden movement, the property manager punched the digits into his cell phone with trembling fingertips.

Haviland sniffed Max's hand and then growled again.

"Get his scent, Captain," Olivia told the poodle, feeling a fresh surge of rage course through her. "He was *just* here. The man who hurt you. He did this. Smell him, Haviland," she whispered fiercely over Bert's shaky conversation with the emergency operator.

As Haviland disappeared into the bathroom, Olivia absorbed as much of the scene as she could without approaching the club chair where Max had been killed.

Her eyes were immediately drawn to Max's face, for his tongue lolled from between his slack lips. Swollen and blue tinged, it looked like some grotesque alien insect, and Olivia felt momentarily overcome by repulsion. She forced her gaze downward, seeing the slumped shoulders against the cushioned back of the chair, the limp arms, and the casual outfit of shorts and a T-shirt.

Finally, she stared at Haviland's blue collar, which was fastened around the dead man's neck. The skin above and below the collar was a purplish red and marred with scratches, illustrating the desperation with which Max had fought against the object robbing him of oxygen.

The most unsettling detail of all was the reflection of the windows in the dead man's unblinking eyes. A halo of soft, white light fell across the glassy surface of his corneas, giving the impression that an otherworldly radiance was being released from within Max Warfield's body.

Bert was repeating the condo address in a much steadier voice when Olivia spotted the sheet of paper. It was a standard-sized sheet of white paper that had been neatly positioned on the table in front of Max's torso. Olivia wondered if those were the last words Max Warfield had seen before he died or if the murderer had placed the paper on the table afterward.

She walked forward four steps, leaning over the table as she removed her notebook from her purse. "The summer haiku," she murmured and read the three lines upside down.

The summer air is so thick
its almost too hard to breathe —
so don't bother to try.

"What are you doing?" Bert hissed, but Olivia didn't hear him.

Backing away from the table, she copied down the words of the poem, silently counting syllables as her pen recorded them.

"This is wrong." She reread what she'd written. "The lines are too long, the hyphen doesn't divide the poem into two parts, the nature imagery is overly simplistic, there are grammatical errors . . ."

Olivia sank down on the edge of the bed, causing Max's suit to slide into the depression created by her weight. "This poem was not written by the same person. Are there now two poets?" Chilled, she shoved the plastic bag away from her leg, stood up, and walked quickly out of the room. Haviland growled once more and followed.

"Ms. Limoges? Are you all right?" Bert called after her.

Olivia didn't stop until she was outside. She needed to breathe real air, as though her lungs weren't capable of processing the chilled, Freon-tinged air within the condo. Stepping away from the shade of the overhang, Olivia lifted her chin and closed her eyes, letting the sun bathe her head and neck and burn away the gooseflesh on her arms.

Bert touched her lightly on the shoulder, repeating his query.

Mechanically, she pivoted to face him, her eyes wide and unfocused. "He's off the leash. That's what the dog collar means. The killer's not following someone else's agenda anymore. Yet he likes the poems, the progression of the seasons, the orderliness of it all. And he's got one more season to go." She reached out for Haviland.

Bert dropped his hand from her shoulder,

frightened by Olivia's incoherence.

"Who is meant for autumn?" she asked, turning her gaze toward the blinding ocean.

CHAPTER 16

There's always a period of curious fear
between the first sweet-smelling breeze
and the time when the rain comes cracking down.

— DON DELILLO

Olivia waited for Chief Rawlings in Bert's
office. After turning Max's condo over to
the pair of officers responding to the 911
call, Bert had retreated to the only restroom, unscrewing the cap to a flask as he
slipped inside. His secretary paced around
the front sidewalk, her lips moving double-
time as she enthusiastically shared the news
of Max Warfield's death into her headset
phone. Meanwhile, her unattended office
phone rang with such noisy insistence that
Olivia felt like knocking on the restroom
door and demanding Bert share the contents of his flask.

Instead, she sat in the chair facing Bert's

impressive mahogany desk, stroking the back of Haviland's head and trying to ignore the ringing phone. She fixed her gaze on a promotional poster showing a sunset over the Ocean Vista condos. Staring at the green palmetto fronds, which had been painted into a slight curl in order to give the feeling they were being caressed by a gentle sea breeze beneath a mango- and raspberry-colored sky, Olivia tried to still her agitated mind.

Several thoughts vied for attention and Olivia began to record each one in her notebook. She became so engrossed that she didn't hear Rawlings enter the office. "Ms. Limoges." He spoke softly, trying not to startle her.

Arresting the motion of her pen, she looked up at him. "I'm sorry, Chief. I didn't come here today expecting to find Max Warfield's body. I know it seems like I've done my best to insert myself into your investigation . . ."

"Then what were your expectations? Why were you here?" Rawlings took a seat in Bert's chair, instantly asserting his position of authority.

Olivia felt it was the chief's prerogative to treat her with professional formality considering the circumstances. "Honestly, I believed Max Warfield knew more about the previous murders than he pretended. I simply couldn't get the phone call he placed at The Boot Top out of my mind. Max has played second fiddle to Dean for a *long* time. It seemed logical that a man his age and status might grow tired of being treated like a servant. I felt strongly that he must be involved at some level."

"Mr. Warfield's alibis were airtight for both murders," the chief argued. "Trust me, I checked and rechecked his movements, as he fit the suspect bill quite nicely. We've also been monitoring his financial statements very closely. There hasn't been a suspicious dime deposited to his accounts. On paper, Mr. Warfield is clean. And before you start pointing a finger at Blake Talbot as your next suspect of choice, allow me to inform you that we've had a tail on him all day. He never came near this location."

Olivia nodded in approval. "That's good, because someone seems intent on bringing down Talbot Fine Properties and Blake is now the new face of the company." She held up her notebook. "And even though I don't know the identity of Max Warfield's killer, I can tell you that he did *not* write all three haiku."

Rawlings shook his head slightly. "Today's

poem is clearly amateurish, yet the writer still got his point across. 'The summer air chokes,' just as *he* choked the life out of his victim."

"And the dog collar implies Max was someone's pet. He followed orders. If the killer obeyed another's command, then he's not willing to any longer." Olivia touched the place on Haviland's neck where the blue collar used to rest and the poodle looked up at her with inquisitive eyes.

"I've called in some help," Rawlings said. "Officers from the New Bern Police Department are on the way. They're going to go over every inch of that crime scene with some of my best men, leaving me available to attend tonight's meeting. The question is, will I be free to concentrate on identifying the killer or will *you* be conducting a personal investigation from the podium?"

Duly reprimanded, Olivia met the chief's cold gaze. "Haviland has the killer's scent down now and he can identify him! Trust me, the Captain earned perfect scores in all of his tracking courses. He has more training than your entire K-9 unit combined. Just let me have his collar back. The killer touched it." When Rawlings didn't answer, Olivia continued. "I don't know what this guy's stake is in this housing development and I still don't understand *why* he felt the need to threaten me. The Confederate cemetery is certain to be preserved — I've made sure the majority of the board will vote for the revisions to the proposal. But the housing project will be approved and that must be the killer's ultimate goal."

"Unless this isn't about Cottage Cove or the park or the graveyards at all." The chief scratched his chin thoughtfully. "What questions have you been asking that we haven't?" Rawlings wanted to know. "I want to see every word you've got written in that notebook. We're running out of time, Ms. Limoges. I cannot allow there to be a fourth victim."

"Of course. Please, take it." Olivia placed the notebook on the desk and wisely remained silent as Rawlings read.

The pair remained quiet for the better part of twenty minutes. Haviland contentedly napped in a corner and Olivia slowly developed an urge for a dose of caffeine. As though sensing her need, Rawlings put down the notebook and wearily rubbed his temples.

"I could use some coffee to help me think." Rising, he returned her notebook. "You've got an observant eye, Ms. Limoges." He offered the compliment with reluctance.

"But I can see that I haven't written anything to help you solve this mess." Olivia was disappointed. "Perhaps I could ask Mr. Long's assistant to brew us a pot of coffee. She seems to have extra time on her hands."

Rawlings nodded absently and then reached out to stop her. "One thing: How *did* you plan to worm information out of Mr. Warfield? He didn't exactly strike me as a man who would freely share his feelings with a stranger."

Olivia colored slightly. "Well, it was my intention to flirt with him a little and then invite him to the restaurant for a celebratory meal following tonight's meeting. I wanted to see his reaction when I brought up the amendment to the proposal. I thought I could also get him to tell me how he felt about Blake Talbot, his new boss."

"And you thought he'd have a crystal-clear look on his face or a quaver to his voice or he'd spill his guts and BAM!" He clapped his hands together, causing Haviland's head to snap off his forelegs in alarm. "You'd know he had something to hide? Just like that? Perhaps you stashed a recorder in your purse? Because he was sure to confess all his sins to you right then and there, right?"

Surprised by the chief's venom, Olivia backed away a step. As she retreated, her hip jarred the sharp metal corner of the chair arm and she winced, the pain inflaming her anger. "He killed a friend of mine and *then* he came after Haviland! Yes, I could have stayed at home and read about your progress in the *Gazette,* but I wasn't willing to be quite that passive! This man is running around *my* town doing whatever he likes to whomever he chooses, and I —"

"Oyster Bay is *not* yours, no matter how many buildings you own," Rawlings growled. "You are a *citizen* and it is my duty to keep citizens such as yourself safe! What if Max Warfield had had something to hide? He could have hurt you, Olivia!"

As he spoke her name, Rawlings grabbed her by the shoulders. His eyes were lit with a mixture of fear and longing and his fingertips pressed into her flesh as though he might pull her roughly against his chest.

Olivia, torn between indignation and a surge of inexplicable desire, wanted him to do just that, but the chief didn't have the chance to act as he was interrupted by the appearance of Bert Long.

"I . . . excuse me," Bert stammered and Rawlings released his hold of Olivia's shoulders. "My secretary has made some coffee and put out some food. It's not much, but I figured you might be here awhile."

Embarrassed to be caught nearly in the chief's arms, Olivia gave Bert a hard look. "Got any more of what was in that flask?"

Now it was Bert's turn to act discomfited. "Ah . . . no. Sorry. I've never seen a dead body before and I needed a little something to help me settle down. I didn't mean to be rude."

"Well, we're in Oyster Bay, so perhaps you'll grow more accustomed to seeing corpses. They seem to be piling up around here." Olivia glanced at Rawlings. "I assume we're done for the moment and that I can give my official statement tomorrow, being as there's not much time until the meeting?"

Rawlings nodded, his expression alternating between concern and irritation. Seeing him struggle to maintain a neutral look, Olivia was again reminded of the weight resting on the man's shoulders. She took a single step toward him. "Haviland could stop this man before he gets a chance to enact that final haiku," she said softly. "If the killer doesn't show tonight, then we're of no use to you and I vow to stay out of your way, but if he does, and Haviland can zero in on his scent, then at least you'll know exactly who to pursue. Just give us a chance. I know the collar is evidence. I won't handle it at all. I just need to open the bag and let Haviland smell it before the meeting starts. What's the harm in that?" When the chief didn't immediately agree, she broke eye contact. "Come on, Captain."

Haviland trotted out of the office ahead of his mistress, obviously ready to leave. Olivia said a short good-bye to Bert and then turned back at Rawlings once more. "This town needs us, Chief. All of us. If I can bring about a conclusion, no matter how clumsily, then I will."

Olivia expected a small crowd to congregate at the town hall — somewhere around forty people. Their meetings typically attracted a dozen or so regular attendees, but with Dean Talbot's death, she expected several members of the press to be on hand to record Blake's reaction to the board's vote. She then added a dozen nosy townspeople to her mental list, knowing that Dixie would have talked up the evening as a potential source of colorful entertainment.

At five minutes to seven Olivia parked in the mayor's reserved space. "Well, his *Honor* should be inside by now," she informed Haviland defensively. "And he's filled with

407

so much hot air that he should be able to float right into the building with minimal physical exertion."

Haviland just looked at her.

"Honestly, Captain, I didn't think this meeting would draw such a turnout. There must be something else going on in the square. A local band or a dramatic performance by that awful theater troupe. Look, there isn't an available parking space within sight." She gazed up at the sky, which had clouded over during the dinner hour. The darkness was deeper than usual and the ocean breeze carried a slight chill. Olivia grabbed an umbrella from the back seat of the Rover. "It's going to pour," she told Haviland. "You'll be glad we parked where we did in an hour."

Steeling herself against the uncertainty waiting within, Olivia opened the hall's front door. She was surprised to hear noise echoing from inside the meeting room which was at the far end of the building's main corridor. There was the expected murmur of adult conversation, but it was louder than she'd ever heard before, swelling into the hall like the buzzing of a thousand hives. These sounds were punctuated by the shrill giggles of a gaggle of preteen girls. The atmosphere permeating the building was electric. Haviland raised his snout, sniffing out the feelings of excitement and nervous anticipation flowing out of the meeting room like a pungent perfume.

As Olivia crossed the threshold, it took her a moment to adjust her eyes to the sight before her. Clusters of young girls holding signs, magazines, and digital cameras filled every imaginable space toward the back of the room.

A child Olivia judged to be about eight years old approached her and asked, "Is there, like, a limo parked out front?"

"Not at the moment." Olivia studied the child. She wore a striped tank top over a white T-shirt, a pair of denim shorts, and rows of multicolored yarn bracelets on both arms. "Why are all of you here?" She gestured at the fidgety, boisterous girls surrounding them.

The girl in front of her held up a copy of *Seventeen* magazine. Olivia recognized the cover model right away. It was Heidi St. Claire. "*Everybody* is waiting for her to show up. I saw her new movie this weekend, like, *three* times. She is *so* pretty and *such* an awesome dancer! I am *so* going to make my mom buy me some of the Heidi St. Claire clothes when they come out too."

"I see," was all Olivia could manage.

Ignoring the follow-up questions from the girl's companions, Olivia pushed her way through a knot of parents who were only attending the meeting to indulge the whims of their daughters. After reaching the other side of the room, she noticed that the first five or six rows of seats were occupied by the residents of Oyster Bay actually interested in the outcome of the evening's vote. Assorted members of the media were scattered around the room as well. This was to be Blake's first official action as the new face of Talbot Properties and the restless reporters were eager to put their best spin on the small-town Planning Board meeting.

Olivia finally reached the table positioned on a raised dais at the front of the room. This was the reserved seating for the board members. She dropped her purse and umbrella onto the floor, put her hands on her hips, and surveyed the audience. The majority of the crowd behaved as though they were at a social gathering. Raised voices and hearty laughter boomed from wall to wall. Those who had gathered to hear how the board would vote appeared to be growing more and more irritated at the feistiness of the Heidi St. Claire fan club.

Someone waved from one of the front

rows and Olivia recognized Laurel's sheen of blond hair. The Bayside Book Writers were seated together. Harris gave Olivia a hesitant thumbs-up while Millay saluted her. Having spoken to all three of them after leaving the Ocean Vista condos, Olivia knew her friends were prepared to spend the next hour observing the townsfolk seated around them. Haviland glanced at the audience a few times and then darted over to Grumpy and began to sniff his boots.

"Ain't no bacon stuffed down my socks, good buddy," Grumpy said and patted Haviland on the head. "Though I reckon my shoes smell like a kitchen, hm?"

Grumpy's work boots reminded Olivia of the tracks in the sand near the lighthouse keeper's cottage. She turned back to the townsfolk again but could only see the feet of those seated in the first row.

Even if Rawlings brings me the collar, will Haviland be able pick up the scent in this crush? Olivia's worries were interrupted by the arrival of Mayor Guthrie, who was flanked by two policemen. Walking behind that trio were a man and a woman wearing sunglasses. Olivia only caught a glimpse of the pair before the room exploded in a chorus of high-pitched screams and the cops quickly leapt in front of their charges.

411

Haviland, disturbed by the yelling and shrieking, retreated behind the table. Olivia took her seat and pulled the poodle against her, crooning into his ear. It seemed to take ages before the mayor appeared behind the podium and Blake Talbot and Heidi St. Claire settled into a set of reserved seats in the front row. As the burly policemen took up their positions at the end of each aisle, holding out stiff hands to stop the further encroachment of the hysterical young girls, a third made his way to Olivia's side. Wordlessly, he handed her a paper grocery bag and then joined his fellow officers.

Olivia peered inside. Haviland's collar rested inside a sealed plastic bag.

"Attention, please!" Mayor Guthrie shouted into the microphone. "Girls, please! Quiet down! Stop screaming! PLEASE!"

Somehow, the decibel level dropped enough for the mayor to speak without hollering. His cheeks were already flushed with heat and self-importance.

"I understand that many of you are excited by our special guests." The mayor beamed and Olivia was impressed by his tact. Clearly, Heidi St. Claire was the star attraction, but by using the word "guests," he made certain to include Blake Talbot as one of Oyster Bay's honored visitors. "Miss St.

Claire has *graciously* informed me that she is willing to sign autographs *after* our meeting is adjourned." Here, Guthrie had to pause while the girls went wild again. "So if you'd care to wait outside while we conduct our business . . . ?"

"No way! It's totally raining!" one of the older girls argued.

Olivia looked toward the row of windows lining the outer wall. Indeed, a steady rain had begun to fall, leaving slashes of water against the glass.

"It's blowin' sideways," Grumpy stated. "Lightnin' will be comin' along shortly." He smiled at his wife, who had nabbed an aisle seat in the third row. "Guess Dixie was right about there bein' fireworks tonight."

Seeing that none of the girls or their parents intended to wait in the hallway or on the building's covered portico, the mayor called the meeting to order. As he made a few incidental announcements, Olivia's gaze repeatedly swept over the crowd. She saw many familiar faces, including Wheeler from Bagels 'n' Beans, Annie from the B&B, and surprisingly, Officer Cook dressed in plainclothes. The young lawman was leaning against the wall, chewing on a plastic straw. He looked utterly bored, but Olivia could see that his eyes never stopped roving.

"Good boy," Olivia murmured and Haviland's ears perked up. "I was talking about Cook. I would never use such a simple adjective to describe *you,* Captain." She smiled as the poodle licked her palm and turned her eyes forward again.

Finally, Guthrie yielded the mike to Ed Campbell, the chair of the Planning Board. The loan manager was all smiles as he quickly reviewed the minutes from the previous meeting. Wasting as little time as possible, he reiterated the Talbot Fine Properties proposal to build the community of Cottage Cove and then called for a vote. Unlike the previous meeting, the Planning Board didn't have to open the floor for public opinion, so Olivia rose and announced, "I would like to suggest a revision to this proposal. One that would preserve the Confederate cemetery."

Ed Campbell had been anticipating the suggestion, yet he still frowned as he surrendered the podium.

Olivia succinctly explained how the majority of the board was in favor of the housing development, as long as the graveyard was protected and more storm drains and green space were added. She watched Blake Talbot as she spoke, but it was difficult to tell what he felt without being able to see his

414

eyes. However, when she suggested relocating the putting green, the muscles in his jaw tensed and his lips compressed into a tight line. He was clearly unhappy about the counterproposal. Heidi, who had removed her sunglasses upon sitting, put her hand on her boyfriend's and gave it a supportive squeeze.

I wonder if he knows about Max yet, Olivia wondered.

According to protocol, Ed had to call a vote on the original proposal, but all the members voted nay except for him. Shrugging with exaggerated resignation, he asked for a second vote to support Cottage Cove as long as a representative from Talbot Fine Properties agreed to the changes. None of the board members took advantage of their opportunity to voice an opinion on the proposal except Marlene, who raised her objections over the destruction of what she described as an irreplaceable ecosystem.

"Despite how *people-friendly* the new park would be," she remarked with quiet passion, "it cannot replicate the environment currently inhabited by dozens of plant and animal species!"

By now, the audience had grown tired of the topic at hand. The girls began to twitter with increasing volume over the staccato of the driving rain. Mayor Guthrie shot nervous smiles in Blake Talbot's direction while Ed Campbell stuck out his freckled forearm and tapped on the surface of his watch, rudely signaling for Marlene to wrap things up.

Ignoring him, she began to list the names of the bird species that used the current park as their nesting grounds.

Olivia continued to scan the faces of those before her. As her eyes came to rest on Heidi St. Claire, the starlet glanced to her right and her expression of polite boredom instantly transformed to one of shock. Her mouth fell open and her eyes grew round and dark with distress.

In a blink, Heidi had her face under control, her dull gaze once again resting on the American flag. Her training as an actress served her well, but Olivia's sharp eyes didn't miss how the young woman was lacing her fingers together so tightly that her hands trembled with the effort.

Who scared you? Olivia leaned her body forward. She could feel her heart swelling as the blood rushed through her body. It was as though every part of her being was suddenly aware of the killer's presence in the room.

And then, she saw him. He was a man she

knew by name, a man she'd spoken to, a man she'd smiled at, and he was easing his way out of the room along the side wall. Obviously, he hadn't wanted Heidi to see him, but she had.

I don't understand, she thought wildly. *Why would Heidi recognize* him?

As Marlene continued to point out the flaws of the new park from the perspective of a snapping turtle, Olivia dialed Harris's cell phone number. She willed him to meet her eyes as she held her own phone to her ear and tried not to slide her gaze to the left, where the murderer's retreat had been temporarily blocked by a trio of girls holding poster board banners reading, "WE ♡ HEIDI!!!"

Harris noticed Olivia and reached into his jeans pocket for his phone.

"Olivia?" he whispered.

"Can you find out if Heidi St. Claire is the actress's real name? Right now?" Olivia murmured, pivoting away from the audience and the inquisitive arch of Grumpy's eyebrows.

"You should ask one of her fans after the meeting. I bet they could tell you her favorite color, bra size, and blood type. Why are you asking *me*?" Harris clearly thought Olivia was losing her mind.

"Don't you have one of those phones that connects to the Internet? I need to know before I order Haviland to track down and attack Camden's murderer."

Harris didn't reply, but Olivia saw him swallow hard and then nod. Hanging up on Olivia, he leaned against Millay and spoke into her ear. Paling, she shot Olivia a sharp look of alarm and grabbed the phone from Harris's hand.

Olivia struggled to feign an interest in Marlene's monologue, but the words buzzed around her head like circling flies. She looked out the nearest window, where the outline of the closest building was obscured by the heavy rainfall. Thunder growled over the ocean and a single branch of lightning sparked in the charcoal sky.

Just as she was about to check on the killer's position again, her phone vibrated in her hand and words surfaced in the silver window. Harris had sent her a text message but Olivia had no idea how to retrieve the thing. She frantically pushed menu buttons and then forced herself to stop and inhale a deep breath. As the sound of the rain seemed to penetrate the room, Olivia located her in-box and read Harris's message.

Atlas Kraus is Heidi's father, the message read.

Atlas Kraus was the killer and he was in this room. Not only that, but his next victim was most likely in the front row and Cook was eyeing Olivia suspiciously. Yet where was Rawlings?

Olivia decided to act. She reached into the brown grocery sack and, not caring how much noise she made, pried open the evidence bag. Placing the collar beneath Haviland's nose, she whispered a command in his ear. "Haviland. Smell." As soon as he obeyed, Olivia pushed back her chair and snapped her fingers, causing Haviland to prepare himself to track the scent. Marlene stopped speaking, but Olivia gave her a sheepish smile and pointed at the poodle, as though he were to blame for their rude and abrupt departure.

She hadn't distanced herself from the podium by more than ten feet when she heard Ed Campbell grab the microphone with an anxious laugh. "You've raised several valid points, Marlene, but I think it's time to vote now, don't you?" Without waiting for an answer, Ed joked, "Ms. Limoges? Could you cast your vote before you run off?"

Making sure to meet Officer Cook's alert gaze, Olivia called an "aye" over her shoulder and then continued toward the opposite

419

end of the room, following Haviland's lead. To her relief, she noticed Cook circling around the back. Together, they'd corner their quarry.

As soon as Olivia reached the end of the first row, she bent over and cupped her hands, directing her voice at her poodle. "Haviland!" Pointing up the aisle, she commanded, "Find and attack!"

At the same moment Olivia was delivering her orders, Ed Campbell had announced the acceptance of the Cottage Cove proposal and was striding forward to shake hands with Blake Talbot. Ed then handed over the portable microphone and invited Blake to say a few words. Blake rose and took Heidi's hand. As the power couple turned to face the audience, it was as though a switch had been flipped. The girls recommenced their shrieks and squeals of devotion and surged forward, their camera flashes glittering like stars.

In the raucous confusion, the killer slipped from the room. A flash of black fur passed through the doorway immediately afterward. Haviland was in pursuit.

Olivia was not the least bit gentle as she shoved aside one crazed girl after another in a desperate attempt to see where her dog had gone. When she burst out of the room and into the hallway, she slammed right into Cook.

"Where is he?" she yelled.

Cook didn't pause to talk and Olivia ran with him until they reached an intersecting corridor. "I radioed the chief. Every exit's covered. This guy's going nowhere."

"I meant Haviland!" Olivia shouted. It was one thing for the poodle to confront the killer in a packed room with armed policemen nearby and quite another for Haviland to assail the man in some darkened room, or worse, outside in the blinding rain. "He could get hurt."

Jerking open an office door, Cook stepped inside and swept the room with his flashlight. A voice crackled through his radio. "He's not running," Cook declared with a satisfied smirk. "Stupid bastard. We've got him now."

Olivia ran to the windows overlooking the square and peered outside. She saw nothing but the shadows of tree trunks and the rain-blurred foliage.

"He won't run because his agenda isn't complete," Olivia said as she pushed by Cook. "His fourth victim is back in that room." She yanked on the knob of the next door. It was locked. "I think he wanted to make sure none of those little girls got hurt, but he's not going to leave until he's done what he came here to do."

"But then he's *definitely* gonna get caught," Cook insisted smugly.

Olivia grabbed the policeman's arm. "That's why he's so dangerous! He doesn't *care!* He's going to see this thing through no matter what!" She pulled on another door and called, "Haviland! HAVILAND!"

"Olivia! We'll help you find him!" Several running feet stopped short behind her. Laurel, Harris, and Millay had arrived.

"Leave this to the police, folks," Cook commanded, but the writers ignored him and quickly decided to search for Haviland in pairs. Her lips quivering as she spoke, Laurel bravely volunteered to accompany Olivia.

Olivia had never wanted to hug another human being as much as she wanted to embrace Laurel at that moment. She could see the stark terror in her friend's eyes, yet Laurel grabbed Olivia by the hand and started toward the men's restroom as though she were a warrior preparing to walk into an enemy ambush.

After a pause, Cook charged ahead of the two women. "The chief will skin me alive if I let anything happen to you, Ms. Limoges," he remonstrated sharply and ducked into the bathroom.

By the time they'd checked the bathrooms, the crowd was clearly moving out of the building to the location where Heidi agreed to sign autographs. Ushered down the hallway by their parents and a pair of officers, the actress's fans milled forward, their unhindered enthusiasm roaring down the hall like the waters of a flash flood.

Cook shouted a warning into his radio and Olivia couldn't help but wonder where he'd been hiding the device. Then, despite the fact that she rarely picked up her pace beyond a brisk walk, Olivia ran.

Laurel easily kept stride with her, and together, the two women burst out the double doors onto the portico a few yards ahead of the first group of fans. A dozen policemen were gathered around the perimeter of the porch, their shoulders taut, jaws clenched, and hands on holsters in preparation to draw their weapons.

"Did a black poodle come out here?" Olivia asked the nearest officer.

"No, ma'am," the man replied, looking past her toward the doors.

Olivia followed his gaze as the girls began to stream out into the open air. "Then the killer's still inside!" she shouted at him. Seeing he did not plan to respond, Olivia ran to Cook. "Haviland didn't come out. That means —"

"We need to go back in!" Cook immediately parted the crowd, his lips pressed against the radio's speaker.

"Stay here!" Olivia told Laurel and followed in Cook's wake.

Elbowing through the departing crowd, Cook approached a fellow officer and spoke hurriedly to him. Olivia couldn't hear their exchange but interrupted anyway. "He's got to be after Blake or Heidi. We need to get them out of here!"

The second officer jerked his head toward the meeting room. "Chief said to keep them in the meeting room until these civilians had cleared the building."

"Where is Rawlings?" Olivia demanded as the remnants of the audience walked past them.

The officer shrugged, but he looked worried. "He hasn't responded to our calls. Must have turned off his radio for some reason."

As they stood there, the last stragglers exited the building and the cops decided to join the ranks of those guarding the young celebrities. They never got the chance to re-enter the meeting room, however, for Heidi St. Claire strode into the hallway, brushing aside Mayor Guthrie's protests. "I promised to sign autographs!" she declared in a haughty tone she seemed to have acquired since Olivia first listened to her speak at The Boot Top.

"Come on, Heidi. Who cares if you blow off these hick kids?" Blake's tone was petulant. He pushed his sunglasses onto his forehead and grabbed his girlfriend by the arm. "Look, something's happened to Max. He didn't show tonight and he never even bothered to call. Finding out why he blew me off is more important than what you promised the peasants." When she didn't respond, Blake glanced nervously around the hall and then leaned over to whisper in Heidi's ear.

She scowled and shook him off. "No way am I going out the back! I gave my word to those fans and I plan to keep it!" She pulled away from him and walked more purposely up the hall.

Suddenly, one of the closed office doors flew open as Heidi passed by. A man emerged from the doorway and raised a gun, taking aim at Blake Talbot's chest. The primed policemen reached for their weapons but were seconds too late. Instinctively, Olivia reached out for Heidi, as though to pull her to safety.

The next few seconds passed as though everyone in that hallway were moving underwater.

Olivia saw the mouths of the lawmen part as they prepared to shout orders. She watched Blake's eyes widen in surprise and fear. As she had not yet turned, Heidi didn't know what was happening behind her back and had time only to experience confusion.

Cook raised his weapon and squared his shoulders. "Don't do it, man! I'll fire before you can get your shot off."

Olivia caught a movement in the darkness behind Atlas Kraus. Finally, her heart began to beat again. She allowed her lungs to exhale. All would be well. For there was Chief Rawlings standing in Atlas Kraus's shadow. Rawlings didn't move, didn't speak. His eyes were fixed on the killer. Poised to attack, he waited.

Staring at him in wonder, Olivia realized Rawlings must have snuck, crouched and catlike, through an adjoining office to emerge at the killer's back.

Heidi swiveled, saw the armed man in the doorway, and screamed. Atlas glanced at her, wounded by her reaction. "Don't worry, baby. I'm not going to let this scumbag bring you down." He then turned to face Blake again, but in the moment he'd broken eye contact with his target, two policemen had stepped in front of the civilian, creating a human shield.

"Back off!" Atlas gestured angrily with his gun, his lips curled into an animal-like snarl. "I'll shoot through you to get to him. I swear I will."

Olivia watched the muscles in his right arm constrict as he made to pull the trigger.

But Atlas never got the shot off, for as the threat was leaving his mouth and the tendons in his forearm were tightening, Rawlings was raising his nightstick into the air. In a swift, powerful stroke, the police chief brought it down on the killer's head.

The *crack* echoed down the hall.

CHAPTER 17

Do what we can, summer will have its flies.
— RALPH WALDO EMERSON

Olivia hadn't expected to dream.

At first, her sleep had been deep and untroubled, but as the dawn light crept over the ocean, strange and disjointed images stirred in the trenches of her psyche.

She was back in the town hall again, but this time she was alone.

There were no policemen or exuberant preteens or members of her writer's group filling the shadowy corridors. Haviland wasn't at her flank. Overhead, the fluorescent lights flickered weakly.

"Haviland?" Olivia called out in a disembodied voice.

She knew the killer was here. At the same doorway in which she'd seen Atlas Kraus standing hours earlier, she stopped and reached out a trembling hand to turn the knob.

"That's not your job," Chief Rawlings murmured behind her. She turned, letting her hand fall to her side and surrendering her position. Rawlings opened the door, stepped into the yawning blackness, and was gone.

A bark emitted from another hallway and suddenly Olivia was outside. It was no longer raining, but the poster board signs bearing messages of idolization for Heidi St. Claire were scattered across the glistening asphalt of the parking lot, their words smeared, their hearts and smiley faces bleeding into ugly, distorted shapes.

Haviland came racing from around the corner of the building, a billow of fog following behind. Olivia embraced the poodle, then turned to witness Rawlings burst through the double doors of the hall with such force that the brass door pulls slapped against the bricks like a thunderclap. He shoved a handcuffed prisoner forward, shouting for the bystanders to make room.

In the way of dreams, where logic and orderliness seldom exist, the town hall's portico, which had been deserted a moment ago, was crammed with people. Dozens of cops, reporters, and stunned townsfolk formed a tight knot Rawlings had to push his prisoner through.

Rawlings made his way to a waiting police

cruiser, his grim face bathed in blue light.

The captive kept his head bowed and his face completely shielded by the brim of his baseball cap.

Olivia felt a pang of anxiety. Atlas hadn't been wearing a hat, but the faded American flag emblem was familiar to her.

Rawlings placed a hand on his prisoner's head and eased him into the squad car. He shut the door with an authoritative push and turned to address the yelling multitudes.

Feeling that the chief had made a grave mistake, Olivia circled around the edge of the crowd, which seemed to be rapidly multiplying. It was as if the fog were carrying people on its back and depositing them in front of the building.

Olivia picked up her pace, feeling a growing sense of fear as the police car slowly pulled away from the curb. Running now, she checked to make sure that Haviland was beside her as she cut across the lawn, hoping to intercept the cruiser at the end of the parking lot before it had a chance to turn onto the main road.

Breathing hard, she pumped her long legs and arms. Her bare feet were chilled by puddled water and pierced by sharp stones. Her lungs burned, but she somehow managed to reach the corner as the police car made its right turn.

At that moment, the killer raised his head and looked out the window, his eyes finding hers.

"No," Olivia whispered in shock, for the face was not that of Atlas Kraus.

It was her father's.

When she woke, the sun's rays were already pounding down on the beach, erasing any evidence of last night's storm but for some scattered branches and a fresh infusion of green into the parched dune grasses.

Olivia let Haviland out, leaving the sliding door to the deck open. Shuffling into the kitchen, she watched the coffeemaker as it gurgled and burped, sending the heavenly scent of Kona beans into the air.

Once her mug was filled, she walked onto the deck in her bathrobe. She let the steady rhythm of the surf restore order into her world, smiling as Haviland lunged at a small ghost crab near the waterline.

She wondered briefly if Rawlings had had any sleep at all.

Hoping to postpone a mental review of the previous evening for a little longer, Olivia went inside for a second cup of coffee and the pickle jar containing the recent metal detector finds. She poured the contents out onto the teak deck table, touching the shotgun shells and lining them up in a neat row. Glancing up momentarily to witness Haviland's glee as he splashed through the shallows, she ran her fingers over the warm metal of the razor blade case, thinking that it wasn't too long ago that she'd found the old case and made the acquaintance of Camden Ford.

The connection between the object and the man was startling.

Camden's throat had been cut by a straight edge, like that of a razor blade, she thought and grabbed the next object she'd dug up: the Indian Head penny dating to the Civil War.

"The Confederate cemetery. That's where Dean Talbot broke his neck."

Genuinely unsettled now, she reached for the New Hampshire quarter and was whisked back into the town hall meeting room, witnessing the look of shock and fright on Heidi St. Claire's face as her eyes fell on the familiar but unwelcome face of Atlas Kraus.

"Her father," Olivia murmured, tracing the coin's engraving of the Old Man in the Mountain. It had been that fleeting glance, combined with the memories of Blake teasing Heidi for being from a farm state beginning with the letter *I* and Annie telling Dixie how Atlas had left a family behind in Iowa, that had allowed Olivia to identify the murderer.

Abandoning her treasures, Olivia walked down to the water's edge. The sand singed the bottom of her feet but she was grateful to be reminded that she was no longer dreaming. Stepping into the surf, she wriggled her toes into the wet sand and sighed.

"You've always taken care of me," she said softly, listening as the ocean acknowledged her remark by delivering a crest that tightened into curl and finished in a surge of bubbled foam. And then came another. And another. Blessed predictability.

Calling Haviland, Olivia meandered a little farther down the beach, keeping her feet in the moistened sand.

"Let's have a Grumpy's brunch," she informed her fur-dampened canine. Haviland bounded back toward the house at the suggestion. "Wipe your paws!" Olivia reminded him.

Inside, she took a long, hot shower but spent little time on her appearance. Donning a breezy, chartreuse linen sundress and a pair of well-worn flip-flops, she ran a brush through her white blond hair and ran a stick of moisturizing gloss over her lips.

Grumpy's was packed. Between the tourists eating a late breakfast, the locals enjoying an early lunch, and the exuberant members of the press, the only available seat was at the counter. To Olivia's relief, it was a single stool at the end of the row and the person occupying the adjacent stool was her friend Harris.

"Aren't you supposed to be at work?" she teased as she picked up the familiar menu.

Harris blushed. "I went in really early, actually. Couldn't sleep any more, so I figured I might as well work." He studied her face. "Are you okay? I know you were really scared when Haviland went missing."

Olivia did her best to look unperturbed by the memory. "Somehow, Atlas must have led him into one of the offices down the side hall and locked him in. In short, my brilliant dog was duped. For the second time, if one counts the drugged ground beef incident as well."

Haviland sniffed and turned his head toward the front window.

"I think you've offended him," Harris whispered solemnly.

"Nothing a rasher of bacon won't cure." Olivia waved at Dixie who had just emerged through the swinging kitchen door bearing plates loaded with cheeseburgers, meat loaf, sandwiches, and fried fish filets. She sighed. "The diner seems so unchanged, as though its occupants weren't aware of the three murders committed in our town. If only it were as simple as ordering one's next meal . . ."

Harris grinned ruefully. "I'm finding this chocolate milk shake very consoling."

"But it's not that easy," Olivia continued as though her friend hadn't spoken. "There will be statements to be taken and given, lawyers to engage, trials to drag on, and all the while, the insatiable hunger of the media."

Olivia fell silent. For once, she didn't know what she felt like eating. The idea of consuming eggs turned her stomach and the lunch platters were too gluttonous for her tastes. The salads were rather bland as Grumpy had a penchant for serving half a head of iceberg lettuce with a couple of cherry tomatoes and thick slices of yellow onions. Upon this leafy pile, he'd then scatter a dozen croutons and a sprinkle of bacon bits. Skipping the salad selections, Olivia tried to decide whether she wanted a fruit plate with cottage cheese or a tuna melt with a side of slaw.

Dixie appeared and plunked a glass of

homemade limeade next to Olivia's hand. "I know that look," she said. "You don't know what to order, do you? Don't worry, sugar. Dixie will fix you right up. Haviland too." She skated forward and took Haviland's snout in her small, wide hands. "I saw you go after that bad man. You are the bravest dog in the entire state of North Carolina. I'm going to have Grumpy fry up a nice, rare steak for you. Pour a little gravy on it and serve it with a side of my finest tap water. How does that sound, my hero?"

Haviland barked, causing the heads of all the outsiders to swivel in his direction.

"He's a workin' dog!" Dixie called out by way of explanation. "It's within his rights to be here, so don't be makin' any faces at him." She touched Olivia's back and stared down the journalists. "She's got a whole list of disabilities, this one. So say a prayer for her and eat your food."

Chastised, the curious diners dropped their eyes to their plates and instantly began to talk to one another about the weather. Olivia and Harris snickered as several exchanges about the heat wave circulated through the room as though the subject were being pushed around and around by the ceiling fans.

"Now I understand why you park in so

many reserved spaces." Harris grinned and took a slurp of his shake. He jabbed at an unyielding lump of ice cream with his straw. "So I've mentioned before that I write code for computer games, right?" The laughter had gone out of his voice. "Well, right now my team is busy creating the backgrounds for the game's dungeon scenes. If I had been working on forest scenes or village scenes or anything else, I probably could have trudged along just fine. But this morning, as I sat at the keyboard designing damp stone walls, prison cells with chains, and skeletons piled up on the dirt floors and hanging from rusty manacles, I had to get out of the office." He paused and touched his chin. "Suddenly, I just had to breathe some fresh air and have a chocolate milk shake."

Olivia nodded. "How's Millay?"

Shrugging, Harris flattened his crumpled napkin on the countertop. "It's hard to tell. She acts so tough, but I think there's a lot going on under the surface she doesn't want to let people see. She found the last haiku, you know."

This was news to Olivia. "Where?"

Harris seemed pleased to be the bearer of such an interesting bit of information. "Atlas must have dropped it in the meeting room. Millay thought she was just picking up some litter. She had already gathered up gum wrappers from those girls. I guess she has a thing against littering. Anyway, she picked up the paper and unfolded it and we both read the poem."

"Do you remember the words?" Olivia asked doubtfully.

Setting his phone on the counter, Harris pressed a few buttons and three lines of text appeared in the display window. Olivia read them aloud.

A rotten tree falls
Letting in enough light —
For the sapling to grow

"Autumn," she murmured. "This poem comes closer to following the rules than the summer haiku. It's interesting and rather disturbing that he wanted to improve as a poet." Her eyes returned to the first few words. "I take it Blake Talbot is the rotten tree. Atlas planned to shoot him and watch as his body toppled over like a felled tree. Then Atlas's daughter, the sapling, would receive more sunlight. No one would hold back her burgeoning rise to fame and fortune."

"Somehow, I don't think Heidi's feeling

too grateful at the moment," Harris concluded as Dixie arrived with Olivia's lunch. She placed a bowl of tomato soup and a plate containing a grilled cheese sandwich on the counter in front of Olivia. Whisking away the empty limeade tumbler, the intuitive proprietor set a steaming mug of hot tea next to Olivia's hand.

"Wrap your fingers around that. You need some old-fashioned childhood food, 'Livia. Never met a person on this earth who couldn't start mendin' after a bowl of soup and a grilled cheese sandwich." Dixie tucked a feather of blond hair back under her silver headband and dusted a crumb from her Little Miss Chatterbox shirt.

Olivia opened her napkin and smiled. "Dixie, you're a precious gem hidden amid the rocks."

Dixie snorted. "Tell Grumpy that. He's been promisin' to buy me a new 'rock' for going on ten years now." She elbowed Harris. "If a gal ever tells you size don't matter, she's lying."

Harris's cheeks burned red.

"Aw, lamb. You don't need to blush. I'm just messin' with you." Dixie was genuinely contrite.

"It's not what you said, ma'am. I've got a skin condition." Harris put his palms over his cheeks, looking miserable. "I look embarrassed or humiliated or like I'm suffering from heat stroke at least ten times a day."

Dixie turned to Olivia. "Such a handsome boy. Reminds me a little bit of Peter Pan." She put a hand on Harris's back but kept her eyes on Olivia. "There's got to be somethin' out there to fix his skin, am I right?"

"Actually, there is," Olivia answered brightly.

Harris shook his head "I've tried every topical medicine on the market. They don't work." He smiled at Dixie. "If I ever *do* find a girl to propose to, it'll mean she's gotten used to my face and likes me despite my rosy red cheeks. We'd be a modern age Beauty and the Beast."

Olivia touched his arm. "Personally, I'd prefer the Beast, but women your age aren't often as wise as those of us who've learned what matters." She and Dixie exchanged a wink. "And I'm not referring to creams or salves either. How would you feel about trying a laser treatment? On me, of course. It would be a favor to an aesthetician friend of mine. She's been searching for someone with your condition to use as a test case for her pulse laser." Olivia felt no shame in concocting such a flagrant lie. "What do you think?"

Harris's eyes glimmered. "Cool. A pulse laser? Kind of sounds like an episode of *Star Trek*. When can we start?"

"I'll call her right after lunch," Olivia answered casually, though she was truly excited over the idea of watching Harris's rosacea become a bad memory. "Let's keep it a secret too. We'll see if anyone notices when the Bayside Book Writers meet again."

Dixie skated off and returned fifteen minutes later with Olivia's check. Beneath the total she had written, "Softie!" followed by a goofy smiley face. Frowning, Olivia balled up the check and slapped it on top of a twenty-dollar bill.

"Come along, Haviland. Time to visit the chief. Perhaps we should have brought him a grilled cheese sandwich," she mused as she said good-bye to Harris and stepped outside. A pair of journalists moved to follow her, but Dixie skated in front of them, blocking their path and giving Olivia and Haviland ample time to escape untroubled, at least for the moment.

From a distance, the police station resembled an anthill. Uniformed policemen, important Oyster Bay citizens, and many of those present at the town hall the night before streamed in and out the front doors.

In addition, reporters and cameramen milled about the sidewalk. Awaiting an official statement from the chief, they passed the time smoking, speaking into cell phones, fiddling with their BlackBerrys, or accosting the more colorful locals as they left the station.

Olivia scowled in disgust as a woman wearing a pink suit dabbed at her heavily made-up face with a tissue. "I declare!" she drawled. "I won't be able to sleep a wink until that horrible man is put away for *life!* And to think he was here among us good, churchgoing folk the *whole* time. Poor Annie Kraus! She welcomes her brother-in-law into her home and how does he repay her? He kills one of her guests and then nearly ruins our chances of getting that nice new development built."

The reporter murmured a question and the woman squared her shoulders and declared, "Of course I'm relieved to hear it's still going through. I am a business owner, you know. Pink Lady Cleaners, that's me. We have two locations, here and —"

But the woman's plug was cut short when the reporter spotted Olivia and Haviland. Several cameras swung around to capture her image and she turned her head from the penetrating stares of their zooming lenses.

"Ms. Limoges! Ms. Limoges!" voices shouted, all vying for attention. "Is it true you aided the police in their investigation?"

"Is your dog a trained tracker?" another yelled.

"Are you romantically involved with Chief Rawlings?" she heard just before entering the relative quiet of the station's lobby. After checking in with the desk officer, she and Haviland sat down and curiously observed the comings and goings of familiar faces. Ed Campbell appeared from a closed door off the lobby. He nodded at her deferentially and then steeled himself to exit the building. Marlene Gibbons arrived in the lobby shortly afterward. Upon seeing Olivia, she came over to say hello.

"For what it's worth, I admire your passion concerning the preservation of our current ecosystem," Olivia told her.

Marlene's brows furrowed in anger. "Then why didn't you vote against the development? I thought you were on *my* side. And the environment's side."

"I am, but I'm on the side of the townsfolk first," Olivia retorted gently. "This development will create dozens of new jobs. Plenty of people need those jobs. As much as I like birds and snapping turtles, these people are my neighbors. They *need* this."

Releasing a weary sigh, Marlene rose. "I'd always choose animals and plants over people. I just see them as being more worthy of existence, I suppose." She smiled ruefully at Haviland. "You're a fine example of such a noble creature. I wish I'd brought of few of my pets with me today. I'd have felt much more confident with my iguana sitting on my shoulder." She ruffed Haviland's ears. "Now I'm going to have to fend off the press with sharp words instead."

Olivia wished Marlene good luck and resumed a pose of patience. However, she quickly grew restless as the station continued to hum with activity.

Finally, Officer Cook strode into the lobby and waved for her to follow him to his desk.

The young man's appearance betrayed his exhaustion. The puffy skin around his eyes, his stubbly chin, and his rumpled uniform indicated an all-night shift.

"I should have brought you coffee," Olivia began, attempting friendliness.

Cook waved off the suggestion. "I've had so much I can hardly hold my pen. I'm gonna fall flat on my face when I finally get home, but it'll be worth it. I told you we'd nail the bastard."

Olivia studied the smug gleam in the officer's eyes. There was no way to explain to someone half her age that there was nothing to celebrate. Many lives had been destroyed or altered beyond repair. The arrest of Atlas Kraus would never restore the damage already done. Instead, she dipped her chin ever so slightly, gifting Officer Cook with a show of respect. "So you did, Officer. So you did."

It took over an hour for Olivia to give her statement. Rawlings had put the fear of God in all his men, saying that each and every testimony, regardless of how brief or seemingly inaccurate, had to be recorded with the utmost precision. Olivia understood the chief's position. After all, the cases were now a matter of national significance. Rawlings undoubtedly wanted to show the world that the members of the Oyster Bay Police Department knew how to wrap up a case with professional efficiency.

Despite her appreciation of the circumstances, Olivia was thoroughly cross by the time Cook reviewed her statement for the third time. "Just let me read it and I'll tell you if it's accurate!" she snapped.

At that moment, an officer walked by the desk and Haviland caught the scent lingering on his pant leg. He barked excitedly, causing all of the policemen in the room to shoot dirty glances at Cook.

"He smells Greta, your K-9 unit," Olivia explained in defense of her dog's unwelcome clamor. "Quiet, Haviland!" she hissed at the poodle. "Your parts don't even function, so it would be a futile flirtation in any case!"

Haviland growled and stalked off after Greta's partner.

Olivia grabbed the printed statement from Cook's hands, signed her name with a flourish, and marched out in search of her mutinous poodle. Cook pushed back his chair with a jerk but was simply too tired to wrangle with the obstinate woman. Instead, he placed her statement in a file folder and turned toward the lobby in order to retrieve another witness.

Haviland had followed Greta's partner into the station's kitchen and was sitting in front of the refrigerator in a posture of angelic expectation.

"Manners," Olivia remonstrated, and together, they continued down the hall toward the exit. As they passed Rawlings' office, the door opened. Roy and Annie Kraus stepped out into the hallway. They wore the numb expressions of car-accident survivors. Annie's glazed eyes met Olivia's but then the other woman rapidly looked away. She took her husband's arm and hung on as though she couldn't stand of her own volition. Roy put his hand on Annie's lower back and Olivia noticed that every one of the cuticles on his free hand had been shredded. Several drops of blood beaded at the base of his index finger and Olivia wondered if Roy had been gnawing at his fingers throughout the entire interview with Rawlings.

"Ms. Limoges," Roy croaked, staring at some point beyond her head.

Part of Olivia wanted to move toward the couple, but she recalled all too well how she'd felt after her mother's death and her father's disappearance. She didn't want to speak a word or have anyone reach out to her. She only wanted to wander alone with her grief, her pain visible only to the anonymous ocean. Olivia was always deeply grateful to her grandmother for providing her with both safety and solitude. Jacqueline Limoges did not speak unless absolutely necessary and Olivia valued the long stretches of silence

"I'm sorry," Olivia said, knowing full well that the words were insufficient.

Mechanically, the couple nodded and shuffled toward the lobby. Olivia ducked into the chief's office and exclaimed, "You can't let them go out the front! The press will swarm all over them!"

Rawlings raced after the Krauses without comment. While he was redirecting the shell-shocked couple to the back door, Olivia and Haviland settled in his office to wait for his return.

"Coffee?" Rawlings placed a mug on the desk in front of Olivia. "Thank you for helping them avoid the media. They have enough to deal with without having microphones and cameras shoved into their faces."

As the chief sank into his chair, Olivia scrutinized him. With more than twenty years on Cook, Rawlings looked much the worse for wear than his junior officer. The skin on the chief's face was gray tinged, his salt-and-pepper hair was plastered to his scalp, and coffee stains were sprinkled across the front of his shirt.

"This is the miserable part of being a cop," he said as he cupped his hands around his mug. "Times like these. I will see the hidden emotions and the private and often unpleasant faces of the people in this community. They'll come in here over the course of the next twenty-four hours — drunk, cursing, elaborating, glory-seeking, and, like Roy and Annie back there, completely sucker-punched." He pressed his palms against his eyes. "At least you're a straight shooter, Olivia. Just having you sitting across from me allows me a moment to breathe."

Olivia was surprised to find the restlessness she'd felt in Cook's presence had passed now that she was with Rawlings.

I feel so at ease with this man, she thought once again and was looking forward to the time when he would join the writer's group, not as the chief of police, but as another writer. And as a friend.

Aloud, she quipped, "I suppose you had several volunteers willing to perform the lethal injection."

Rawlings looked pained. "Half the town would prefer to bypass the court system entirely. As a society, we're never as far away from lynch mobs as we'd like to think."

He took a sip of his coffee and then caught a drip from the side of the cup with the tip of his finger and licked it away with a flicker of his tongue.

"How did this whole mess begin . . . Sawyer?" Olivia tried out the chief's given name. "How did Atlas become so estranged from his daughter?"

Picking up a thick case file from the surface of his desk, Rawlings smoothed the cover and shook his head, his eyes sorrowful. "Mr. Kraus was always going to lose his wife. Jessie Kraus had wanted to leave Atlas early on in their marriage. He'd roughed her up a bit over the years — not enough to create a paper trail, but enough to force her to tread carefully when she finally decided to divorce him."

"And her maiden name was St. Claire?" Olivia surmised.

Rawlings nodded. "Well, she and Heidi moved out of their house one night while Atlas was at his favorite watering hole. The divorce papers were served early the next morning. Atlas tracked his wife and daughter from Iowa to Pasadena, California, where Jessie and Heidi had relocated to live with Jessie's new man."

"I can only imagine what happened when he found them," Olivia stated anxiously.

"Luckily, Heidi was at school when her father showed up. Jessie's fiancé was at work, but she was home. Her new guy was a structural engineer, so she didn't need to hold down a job anymore and she was happily folding laundry when her ex-husband arrived. By the time Atlas was done with her, she was so bruised and broken I couldn't recognize her in the photos. She had . . . imprints from the iron on her back and stomach."

Olivia shuddered. "Why wasn't he arrested?"

"He disappeared. Fled the state. He then picked up construction jobs, the kind involving hard labor. The kind where the bosses don't ask too many questions. Atlas told me he'd routinely return to Pasadena between jobs in order to see what kind of woman Heidi was becoming. He even watched a few of her school plays, hiding in the back row with a hat pulled down over his brow. He told me he knew after the first play that she'd take Hollywood by storm. Looks like he was right."

"Was it merely a coincidence that his brother-in-law lived in the same town where the Talbots owned a beach house?" Olivia asked in astonishment.

"Not quite. Roy never knew the specifics regarding Atlas's familial strife and while his younger brother kept in contact over the years, their conversations were brief and sporadic. When Roy was thinking about purchasing a B&B, it was Atlas who steered him to purchasing a house in Oyster Bay. Atlas believed Heidi might visit here eventually, being that she'd had a crush on Blake since she first saw photos of him in some celebrity magazine. Atlas knew that Heidi had pictures of the boy all over her room and taped onto the covers of her school-books."

Olivia imagined Atlas inside his daughter's bedroom, fingering her belongings, reading her diary, and inhaling her scent. The thought was repulsive. "Did he sneak into his ex-wife's house to spy on Heidi as she grew up?"

"Several times," Rawlings answered. "Even after Heidi was signed for that TV show, she admitted to members of the media that she couldn't wait to meet Blake now that they traveled in similar circles. Atlas was irrationally jealous of Blake before Blake and Heidi even met and started dating. He wanted his daughter's attention and resented how Heidi idolized and then, once they started dating, clearly loved Blake."

Olivia frowned. She'd tried to work out how Atlas Kraus had approached Max Warfield or Blake Talbot as the two men came from remarkably different worlds than the blue-collar construction worker. "So who hired him as a hit man? Max or Blake?"

Rawlings hesitated. "Well, Mr. Kraus claims Blake was the puppet master in regards to the first two killings. Mr. Warfield and young Mr. Talbot wanted to take over Talbot Properties, but in order to do so, they needed to get rid of Dean. The two men hired Atlas to kill the real estate titan, but Atlas had his own agenda. He murdered Camden in hopes that Blake would be suspected of the crime. However, Atlas wasn't aware of Blackwater's unscheduled Vegas tour stop, providing our Mr. Talbot with an airtight alibi." Rawlings paused. "Therefore, Atlas had to go along with the scheme to take Dean's life, drawing Blake to Oyster Bay in time to attend the meeting at the town hall."

"All of this to get his daughter to break up with an unsuitable boyfriend?" Olivia was astonished. She balled up her fists in anger. "Camden died because of a father's crazed possessiveness? And Max died because he might have prevented Atlas from murdering Blake? What about the poems?"

"I took down the confession myself, Olivia. Atlas swears that young Mr. Talbot wrote the poems and sent them, along with other instructions, as text messages on a disposable cell phone. The phones were mailed in unmarked padded envelopes along with a wad of cash." He placed the summer and autumn poems on the desk in front of her. "Of course these two were written by Atlas. He had grown accustomed to leaving them as a part of his tableau, so when he planned to kill Mr. Warfield and then Mr. Talbot, he wrote two poems in preparation for their deaths. The cycle of seasons would be complete and the threat of his daughter committing to an unsuitable young man would be over."

"Atlas has confessed to all of this, but what about Blake?" Olivia inquired sharply. "That conniving little brat needs to spend a long time in jail."

A disgruntled grumble emanated from Rawlings' throat. "We found no evidence incriminating Mr. Talbot inside Atlas's cottage at The Yellow Lady. It's going to take us some time to acquire Mr. Talbot's financial records and I can only hope that some serious amounts of money were withdrawn from his account close to the time of the murders."

Olivia felt chilled. "So you can't charge Blake with a crime?"

"I didn't say that," Rawlings chided. "And if Max Warfield was involved in the scheme, which, based on our listening in on his cell phone conversation at The Boot Top, I'd say he was, then he's already received his sentence. That man has been judged by a higher court."

The chief's words seemed to fill up the room. An unnatural death created such complexities for their town, heretofore known only for its beauty and tranquility.

Now, reporters would invade the streets and shops. Tourists looking for sensationalism would fill any house, condo, or spare room for let at exorbitant rates. The police would be up to their elbows in paperwork. The lawyers would be circling like greedy gulls. Roy and Annie Kraus would lay low for months, unable to look their neighbors in the eye. Wherever they went, the couple would feel crushed by the weight of the knowledge that they were responsible for offering hospitality to a murderer and for unintentionally allowing him to take advantage of the people and the peaceful hamlet they'd grown to love.

"Oyster Bay will recover." Rawlings spoke softly. He walked around his desk and took the chair next to Olivia's. He didn't take her hand, but placed his own on the arm of her chair. "And so will we. A good night's sleep followed by a big breakfast, a solitary walk on the beach, a beautifully written book . . ." He smiled at her. "Speaking of which, yours will be the next chapter we critique, will it not?"

Olivia's cheeks grew warm. "In two weeks' time, yes. We've decided to take this week off. Do you think you'll be able to join us when we meet again?"

Now Rawlings did touch the back of her hand, but only for a moment. "You can count on me."

Haviland woke from his nap and stretched his head toward the policeman, not wanting to miss the chance to be caressed. As the chief scratched the poodle under the chin, Olivia stood, slid her purse onto her shoulder, and returned Rawlings' smile. "No matter what is said after the news of what's happened here breaks, this town still counts on you, Chief." She paused in the doorway. "And that includes me."

CHAPTER 18

Silently, one by one, in the infinite mead-
ows of heaven, Blossomed the lovely
stars, the forget-me-nots of the angels.
— HENRY WADSWORTH LONGFELLOW

Two weeks later, Olivia prepared for a meeting of the Bayside Book Writers. It was July
fourth and there had been a parade in town
earlier that day. For the first time since she
was a child, Olivia and Haviland stood on
the sidewalk and watched the spectacle.

Standing shoulder to shoulder with Harris
and Millay, the three friends waved little
American flags and cheered as the Best
Decorated Stroller contestants kicked off
the parade. When Laurel strode past, her
jogging stroller transformed with the use of
Hefty bags and reconstructed wicker baskets
into Blackbeard's pirate ship, the three writers hooted and hollered in delight.

Dallas and Dermot carried plastic cutlasses and growled "arrgghs" at the onlookers. Olivia had to laugh as she took note of their skull and crossbones bandanas, mascara-drawn goatees, and clip-on hoop earrings. Dressed as a pirate captive, Laurel hurled candy coins into the crowd. The gold foil wrapping of the chocolates winked in the sunlight, and for a moment, it seemed as though Laurel was tossing lit sparklers to the eager children lining the sidewalk. Her face aglow with pride, Laurel was by far the loveliest mother in the parade.

The strollers were followed by tricycles and Big Wheels and Haviland howled in discomfort as toddlers rang shrill bike bells while their boisterous parents tooted air horns. Older children pedaled on the heels of this group, impatient with the slow pace. Their ten-speeds were covered with red, white, and blue streamers, flags, balloons, and quotations on liberty by America's forefathers. One boy was dressed in a full Uncle Sam uniform and was performing tricks on his mountain bike. When he pivoted in a circle using only one wheel, the crowd shouted in amazement.

"I'd say Sam is a shoo-in to win his category," Harris remarked, looking boyishly exuberant.

Millay glanced after the performing child.

"What do they get for a prize? Anything good?"

Harris nodded. "Something *I'd* be happy to take home. Every winner gets a gift certificate from Through the Wardrobe and a special hot chocolate mug with their name and the date printed on it in gold font."

Whistling, Millay stood on her tiptoes in order to spot their friend at the front of the procession. "Laurel would love that gift certificate, though her kids might need gold-emblazoned sippie cups."

"And low-sugar, organic, lukewarm chocolate," Olivia added lightly.

The friends laughed. As high school seniors drove by in decorated convertibles, jacked-up Wranglers, and pickups with oversized wheels, the majority of their passengers somewhat inebriated, Millay shot furtive glances at Harris.

"What's different about you?" she demanded, finally examining him outright.

Harris didn't appear to have heard her question. His focus, and the focus of every male spectator, had been captured by a blue convertible VW Beetle painted with silver stars being driven by a cute blonde wearing a red and white polka-dot bikini and a cowboy hat. The national anthem blared from her radio and her golden retriever, who was also dressed in a doggie cowboy hat, was perched on the passenger seat. He and Haviland exchanged friendly barks.

Millay put a hand on each of Harris's cheeks and swiveled his face away from the blonde. "She's jail bait, buddy."

Harris smiled at her and then, after the slightest hesitation, put his arm around her shoulders and squeezed. "Jealous, are you?"

Snorting, Millay turned her attention back to the parade while Harris and Olivia exchanged winks over her head. After three laser treatments, the skin on Harris's face had improved dramatically. Olivia already noticed a change in her friend's demeanor too. He stood a little taller and didn't look away so quickly during conversations. All of the women working at the spa in New Bern were smitten with him, but Olivia knew Harris had eyes for only Millay.

After a lunch of pulled pork sandwiches, corn on the cob, and watermelon, the four writers gathered on the lawn outside the courthouse to hear the winners announced. Laurel removed two blankets from her stroller, and after unfolding one decorated with racing cars for her sons, she introduced her friends to her husband and in-laws. Her husband, Steve, offered to watch the boys so that Laurel could enjoy a peaceful lunch alongside her fellow writers.

"Thanks, honey. But the boys have something to say to Ms. Limoges first." Laurel gave her sons a gentle prod in Olivia's direction.

"Thank you for our books!" they shouted in unison and then launched themselves into her arms.

Olivia, who hadn't expected the embrace, was nearly flattened, but suddenly, a strong hand pressed against her back, steadying her. She managed to give the twins a brief pat before releasing them, only to look down and see that her white cotton shirt was now covered with black mascara and that Flynn McNulty was silently laughing behind her.

"Are you truly planning to serve the youth of Oyster Bay homebrewed hot chocolate?" Olivia inquired saucily. "Do you also intend on keeping a spittoon nearby?"

Grinning, Flynn squatted next to her. The sun filtered through the magnolia trees and turned his gray eyes a soft pewter hue. He tried to keep a straight face as Olivia mopped at the black smudges on the front of her shirt with one of Laurel's wet wipes. "I think you're making it worse," he remarked. "Now it looks like you just finished changing the oil of your Range Rover. Would you care for some help?"

461

"No!" Olivia exclaimed before she realized he'd been teasing her.

Flynn glanced out over the crowd. His entire being radiated pleasure as though he were utterly content to simply be among the townsfolk.

Perhaps he's found a place to claim as his own and in turn, the place has claimed him, Olivia thought and followed his gaze. Two children ran by with a cheap kite, laughing as the plastic ladybug flopped to the ground alongside an older couple. Everywhere, people were talking and laughing. Oyster Bay was healing.

"And to answer your question," Flynn said after they'd sat in silence for a spell, "the hot chocolate will be store-bought. What exactly do you have against my coffee anyway?"

"It's weak," she answered honestly. "Your Wardrobe Blend calls to mind the miso soup one often receives as an appetizer at select Japanese hibachi restaurants."

"Ah, the infamous dishwater soup!" Flynn laughed. "Well, I can't be associated with the word 'weak.' Why don't you come into the shop and show me how to make coffee correctly."

Olivia grinned. "I think that's a fine idea. I'll even introduce you to my favorite brand of Kona bean."

"I look forward to it." Flynn straightened. "But now, it is time for the award ceremony. I must bestow gift certificates on Oyster Bay's impressionable youth."

Laurel watched him weave his way around the other picnickers toward the makeshift stage. "I think he's sweet on you," she teased and then clasped her hands over her chest. "Oh, a handsome bookstore owner. Now, *that* man is a catch. He could serve me weak coffee anytime!"

As it turned out, Laurel would have plenty of opportunities to sample the bookstore blend as she and the twins won first prize for the Best Decorated Stroller category. Laurel ran to the podium to claim her gift certificate while Dallas and Dermot shouted, "Go, Mommy!" over the applause. While Laurel accepted kisses of congratulations from her proud husband and beaming in-laws, Olivia and Haviland left the park. They had things to see to before the evening's meeting.

After stopping by The Boot Top to collect three bottles of dry champagne, a platter of strawberries dipped in white chocolate, and a few wedges of gourmet cheese, Olivia headed home. She'd finished revising the first chapter of her novel a week ago and had emailed a copy to the other writers. The edits had not only given her leave to think about something besides the murders, but the work had reaffirmed Olivia's belief that Kamila was a character worth developing.

That was a week ago, however. Now as she put the champagne and food in the cottage refrigerator, doubts wriggled their way into Olivia's mind, whispering that her chapter was far inferior to those presented by the rest of the group. Fearing that her Egyptian heroine was two-dimensional and uninteresting, Olivia flipped through her copy of chapter one and began to read a portion of the text out loud as Haviland stretched out on the floor for his afternoon nap.

"After the death of her parents, Kamila was taken from the only home she'd ever known to the stately house of her uncle. Her aunt Nebit, whose name meant 'leopard,' was displeased to be burdened with another mouth to feed. With four daughters of her own and none half as lovely as twelve-year-old Kamila, the sight of her dead brother's child turned her heart bitter.

"Kamila was given a small room off the kitchen in which to sleep. The room did not befit her station as the niece of a wealthy and influential man, and as the days and weeks went by, Kamila found herself performing tasks more suited to a slave than that of a beloved relative. Knowing the girl was powerless to protest, Aunt Nebit demanded that Kamila draw baths for her four daughters, comb, plait, and oil their wigs, and serve wine to the family's guests.

"On one such occasion, when her aunt and uncle were entertaining a most distinguished visitor, the Sandal Bearer of Ramses the Second, the Living God, Kamila was ordered to keep the esteemed member of the royal household's goblet full at all times.

"However, this tall, slim man with dark eyes and easy smile caught her by the wrist when she attempted to refill his glass for the third time.

" 'No more, child. I like to keep my wits about me, even when visiting friends.' He winked at her and she relaxed, withdrawing to stand behind his cushion should he require anything else from her.

"Kamila's aunt and uncle flattered and plied their guest with plate after plate of choice meats, sweet cakes, and honeyed figs, but he was content to merely sample each dish and clearly did not overindulge in the manner of his hosts.

" 'What I would like is to see this little beauty

dance,' the visitor said with a gentle smile in Kamila's direction.

"Nebit clapped her hands and two of her daughters appeared with lutes. 'My girls are skilled musicians. Nanu and Shebi, delight the ears of our honored guest while Kamila attempts to dance for him. Forgive us, she is not our daughter but our niece and we do not know if she possesses any skill as a dancer.'

"Kamila swallowed. At one time, she was considered a gifted dancer, but she had not practiced for many months and her body had become stiff and sore from all the labors her aunt had imposed upon her. Still, she feared that if she did not quickly obey, her chores would increase in severity.

"Closing her eyes, she allowed the slow and seductive music to wash over her. She swayed deliberately, unfurling her arms as though she were a blooming flower. She stretched her lithe body until it appeared as though she must break, pointing her toes as she twirled on one leg and then the other. Jealous of the enraptured look upon their visitor's face, Nanu and Shebi abruptly ended their song, leaving Kamila standing in a trancelike state in the middle of the floor. The sisters giggled wickedly behind their palms.

"When Kamila dared to glance over at her aunt and uncle, she saw that they were paying no attention to her. Her uncle and his guest were whispering back and forth while Aunt Nebit tried to control the look of avarice in her eyes. When the older woman gave Kamila a shrewd stare, the girl knew she was the topic of conversation.

"She was right, and by the end of the evening she became the property of the Sandal Bearer. He requested the use of her uncle's sedan chair and bearers in order to carry her to the palace. 'Your niece shall now serve wine to the Son of Light,' he declared and whisked Kamila into the night.

"On the short journey to the palace, the kind and gentle man told Kamila that he planned to present her as a gift to the Living God.

" 'You should rejoice,' he stated. 'This is a great honor. You are to become Pharaoh's concubine.' "

Olivia put down the pages and glanced at her sleeping dog. "That boring, eh?"

A few hours later, the Bayside Book Writers reconvened in the lighthouse keeper's cottage. Once the three regular members arrived, followed closely by a delighted Chief Rawlings, Olivia opened a bottle of chilled champagne and poured the contents into crystal flutes.

"To Camden," she said solemnly and raised her glass. After each of the writers touched rims, Olivia made a second toast. "And to Sawyer Rawlings, our newest member."

Rawlings dipped his head in acknowledgment. "I am honored to be counted among this fine group."

After helping themselves to chocolate-covered strawberries and a selection of crackers and gourmet cheeses, the writers settled on the sofa or in club chairs and laid out their marked copies of Olivia's work in progress.

Harris began the critique by praising the accurate feel of the setting. He then admitted that he felt there needed to be a more detailed physical description of each character.

Laurel said that she had a strong sense of the minor characters, but wasn't always clear as to what Kamila was feeling. "She's really just a young girl! And I know things were different back then — that kids matured much sooner than they do in the modern world. I know they married and bore children at Kamila's tender age, but she still seems too much of an old soul to me. Doesn't she long for her own family? Isn't she terribly lonely? Isn't she scared to have such an uncertain future?" Laurel's comments were filled with such passion that Olivia realized her heroine might indeed be lacking in emotion.

When it was Rawlings' turn to share his impression of the first chapter, he took a moment to review his notes. "Let me begin by saying that I feel invested in your character. I genuinely care what happens to Kamila and that means you've hooked me as a reader. I also thought you chose a strong line with which to end chapter one."

Harris lowered his voice in order to imitate the Royal Sandal Bearer. " *'You are to become Pharaoh's concubine.'* "

"More like Pharaoh's chattel," Millay said with disgust. "Maybe that's what your title should be."

Laurel tossed a pillow at Millay, nearly knocking the pages from her hands.

Rawlings cleared his throat and smiled at Laurel. "If you don't allow me to finish my critique I'll have to cuff you." She quickly sat on her hands and tried to look abashed. Olivia was amused by the effect a little champagne had on her friend. She turned her attention to Rawlings, slightly apprehensive over hearing the remainder of his commentary.

"I share Laurel's view regarding the

469

reader's inability to clearly sense Kamila's feelings. There is too much distance between her and us," he explained plainly. "Get us closer. If you do, we'll be on the edge of our seats from chapter to chapter. If you don't, we won't be as engaged, and no matter what happens to this fascinating young girl, we won't relate to her experience on any level. We can empathize over Kamila's fear of the future, her grief over losing her parents, or her anger over being treated like an Egyptian Cinderella by her aunt if you let us."

Olivia nodded. "I hear what you're saying. I'm not certain how to get those emotions across to the reader, but at least I know what needs to be improved. Thank you. This has been very valuable for me."

Laurel handed Harris an unopened bottle of champagne and signaled for him to do the honors. She squealed at the pop of the cork and then bustled about, topping off everyone's glasses. As she poured for Rawlings, she said, "Um, Sawyer? Can I ask you something about the case? I know you're off duty and all but since we're done with Olivia's chapter and we still have full glasses . . ."

Rawlings hesitated and Laurel took advantage of his silence. "There's something I haven't been able to figure out. How did Atlas Kraus make contact with Blake?"

"When Mr. Kraus discovered that his daughter was dating Blake Talbot, he found a way to get a job on a Talbot Fine Properties construction site in another state. Max Warfield spent a few days overseeing that project's progress and Atlas was able to offer his services as a hit man. Mr. Warfield had long been chafing at the bit and knew he could easily persuade Blake to finance the permanent removal of Dean Talbot. The two of them would then rule Talbot Fine Properties together." Rawlings took a sip of champagne, the flute looking too delicate in his bearlike hand.

Harris sat forward on the sofa, anxious to ask Rawlings a question of his own. "But if Dean was supposed to be the only victim, why did Atlas kill Camden?"

"Mr. Kraus wanted to frame young Mr. Talbot for the murder," Rawlings answered after a long moment of silence. "He lured Mr. Ford to that alley by offering an exchange of information for cash. For a few hundred dollars, he told Mr. Ford that he could prove that Dean Talbot's youngest son and right-hand man were plotting to overthrow him. Mr. Kraus made this call from the library pay phone and the number showed up on Mr. Ford's phone records."

"But why kill Camden?" Olivia interjected

471

heatedly.

"According to Mr. Kraus's confession, Blake wrote the winter haiku, but it was meant for his father, not Mr. Ford. Atlas made up some elaborate lie about the gossip writer having insider information about their wicked plot and that he needed to be silenced. He told Blake to mail him additional funds and another poem for Dean. He didn't have the chance to leave that haiku with the body because some teenagers arrived at the park to mess around in the gazebo. Atlas was at the top of the stairs and his victim at the bottom, so he had no choice but to flee."

The chief of police and the three writers fell mute; each of them picturing a broken body sprawled at the base of the deteriorating steps and a murderer racing into a copse of oak trees.

Finally, Millay shifted in her seat and made a noise of exasperation. "What's with the damned poems anyway? Was Blake going all Hamlet on his daddy or what? Why did he feel a burning desire to write a stupid haiku to leave on his father's murdered corpse?"

"I read a rather revealing interview about young Mr. Talbot," Rawlings said quietly. "He began writing poems as a small boy but hid them because his father ridiculed him for writing. He called him a fairy and a pansy and a loser. I believe Blake very much wanted to have the last word."

Rawlings and Olivia looked at each other. They could almost sense the scant lines of the four haiku lingering in the air around them. The poems had been brought to life for evil purposes and now they had gained a certain amount of power. Works of creativity transformed by the dark souls of their authors. The memory of the poems seemed a sharp contrast to the aspirations the Bayside Book Writers had for their own manuscripts.

"Blake got what he wanted after Dean's death, but Atlas's goals hadn't been satisfied," Olivia said as she cut slices of aged Gouda and Brie and laid the cheese alongside a fan of thin crackers. "In the end, he intended to murder Blake." She handed the plate to Rawlings.

He picked up a cracker and held the food suspended in the air. "Yes. Mr. Kraus deemed the young Mr. Talbot an unworthy suitor and also as someone who was sure to interfere with his plans to renew a relationship with his daughter. He wanted to take charge of Heidi's career. He feels she owes him for abandoning him and going to

California with her mother."

"Oh, that's rich! Why would she stay with an abusive lunatic? She would never have forgiven him. He beat her mother! He plotted to kill her boyfriend!" Millay scowled.

Rawlings ignored the outburst. "Mr. Kraus also had to get rid of Mr. Warfield, being that he and Blake were confederates. Mr. Kraus couldn't risk leaving Mr. Warfield alive. Mr. Warfield may have interfered with Mr. Kraus's attempts to go after Blake Talbot."

"Why do you call that scumbag 'Mr. Kraus'?" Millay was angry. "I can give you a few *choice* adjectives if you've run out."

The chief put his plate on the coffee table and clasped his hands together. "I do my best to treat everyone with respect. Mr. Kraus may be a criminal, a monster even, but it is not for me to judge him. I leave that weighty responsibility to others. He broke the law, so I arrested him. That's my job and I try to perform it with courtesy."

Olivia admired the chief's professionalism, but it was clear that Millay disagreed with his beliefs. Twirling a strand of hair around her index finger, she turned to Harris for support. "Don't you think *Atlas* deserves to fry like a piece of bacon?"

At the word, Haviland raised his head and

sniffed the air.

Harris didn't answer Millay. He seemed to be considering how to respond without giving offense. Laurel glanced at them and said, "Atlas has lost the only thing he ever cared about. His daughter." She reached across and touched Millay's hand. "Don't get me wrong. I *hate* Atlas Kraus. He extinguished such a bright light when he took Camden's life. He's sick and twisted. I mean, the way he so calmly planned these horrible things, and then to write those last two poems . . ." Her lips trembled and she sucked in a deep breath in order to steady her voice. "But I want to forget about him and focus on this instead." She waved her hand around the room. "Camden would be so pleased to see us together tonight."

"But what about justice?" Millay cried. "Is Blake going to walk? We all know he had something to do with at least one of the murders!"

Rawlings looked pained. "No one is going to escape justice, but gathering enough evidence *correctly* takes time. I can assure you that Mr. Talbot's freedom is temporary. We've held several meetings with the DA and as soon as we're through with our procedural requirements, this case will be wrapped up as tightly as a spring."

"Right now, Blake's a media darling. The boy who dodged death." Olivia felt she had to add weight to the chief's argument however much she understood Millay's indignation. "Talbot Fine Properties has a talented PR department. Have you noticed the expensive patio furniture at Bagels 'n' Beans or the new sign and awning hanging over Grumpy's? Dozens of local business owners received 'gifts of gratitude' from Blake Talbot, as a means of personally thanking them for their hospitality to his family and his fiancée. The locals have provided the newspapers with nothing but positive quotes in regards to the youngest Talbot but they'll turn on him like vultures the second one of Oyster Bay's finest finishes reading him his rights."

Laurel nodded in agreement. "It'll be easy to forget about him once he's been put away because he's an outsider. He was only a visitor here, so everyone can blame his crimes on his parents or his upbringing or his music, but then they'll put him out of their minds, like a guest that finally goes home after a long and miserable visit."

Millay shook her head in disgust and then barked out a dry, humorless laugh. "You know, this Atlas guy was actually really dumb. He should have just left Heidi and

Blake alone. They would have broken up eventually without his interference. Nobody stays together in Hollywood!" She threw her hands in the air, exasperated.

"He wasn't as smart as you," Harris whispered and Millay's hard look instantly softened. "Come on," he nudged her playfully. "Like Laurel said, it's time to move forward. Let's go watch the fireworks from the pier. We can pick up a six-pack and a pizza on the way."

"You read my mind." Millay gathered her belongings, downed the rest of her champagne, and then slowly extended her hand to Rawlings. "I'm glad you joined our group. You're not like other cops. In fact, you're kind of like Camden. A gentleman."

Rawlings took her hand, his face lit with pleasure. "I hope you're as forgiving with my chapter next week." He then gave Harris a hearty handshake and with feigned sternness said, "Make sure you don't get behind the wheel after you drink that six-pack."

The group dispersed. Laurel had promised to meet her family at the waterfront and Rawlings needed to swing by the station in order to ascertain whether the officers scheduled to assist the fire department with the fireworks display were prepared to carry out their duty.

Leaving Haviland inside to clean up a dropped hunk of cheese, Olivia walked the writers to their cars. She waved good-bye as they drove off into the lavender twilight.

After tidying up the cottage, she and Haviland took a leisurely stroll along the empty beach, a large, luminescent moon hovering over Olivia's right shoulder. They walked aimlessly for a mile and then turned around as the indigo sky reluctantly deepened into black. Suddenly, a deafening boom echoed across the water, followed by a burst of lights over the horizon, heralding the commencement of the fireworks display.

Kicking off her shoes, Olivia sat down on a soft dune in front of the lighthouse keeper's cottage and craned her neck upward. Many years ago, she had been in nearly the same position, but back then she had been flanked by the warm bodies of her mother and father. She remembered feeling so safe, as though every firework unfolding in the dark sky like a rare, night-blooming flower was a gift to her. She recalled her mother's excited laughter and how her father pointed at every fresh explosion, not wanting his only child to miss a single moment of beauty.

Olivia thought about Kamila and the group's critique. She knew that she could not expose the truth of a fictional woman's feelings until she was willing to bare more of her own. It wasn't necessary to reveal every secret or every memory to the world, but if she could share a little more of herself to a select group of people, that would be a start.

The cracks and reports increased in tempo as the fireworks finale began. Haviland barked in response, his eyes shining and his mouth curving into a toothy smile.

A rainbow of flickering lights dazzled the ocean, illuminated the shore, and bathed Olivia's uplifted face. Wave after whispering wave carried the starry reflections as close to the woman as they could, receding only after leaving her with an offering, a promise of things to come, bright and brilliant as the radiant sky.

ABOUT THE AUTHOR

Ellery Adams grew up on a beach near the Long Island Sound. Having spent her adult life in a series of landlocked towns, she cherishes her memories of open water, violent storms, and the smell of the sea. Ms. Adams has held many jobs, including caterer, retail clerk, car salesperson, teacher, tutor, and tech writer, all the while penning poems, children's books, and novels. She now writes full time from her home in Virginia. Please visit her at www.ellery adamsmysteries.com.

We hope you have enjoyed this Large Print book. Other Thorndike, Wheeler, Kennebec, and Chivers Press Large Print books are available at your library or directly from the publishers.

For information about current and upcoming titles, please call or write, without obligation, to:

Publisher
Thorndike Press
295 Kennedy Memorial Drive
Waterville, ME 04901
Tel. (800) 223-1244

or visit our Web site at:

http://gale.cengage.com/thorndike

OR

Chivers Large Print
published by AudioGO Ltd
St James House, The Square
Lower Bristol Road
Bath BA2 3SB
England
Tel. +44(0) 800 136919
www.audiogo.co.uk

All our Large Print titles are designed for easy reading, and all our books are made to last.